LET THE BELL RING

BY THE SAME AUTHOR

Season of the Long Grass
The Regis Connection
Nobeca

LET THE BELL RING

NORMA LLOYD-NESLING

Copyright © 2025 Norma Lloyd-Nesling

The moral right of the author has been asserted.

Apart from any fair dealing for the purposes of research or private study, or criticism or review, as permitted under the Copyright, Designs and Patents Act 1988, this publication may only be reproduced, stored or transmitted, in any form or by any means, with the prior permission in writing of the publishers, or in the case of reprographic reproduction in accordance with the terms of licences issued by the Copyright Licensing Agency. Enquiries concerning reproduction outside those terms should be sent to the publishers.

The manufacturer's authorised representative in the EU for product safety is Authorised Rep Compliance Ltd, 71 Lower Baggot Street, Dublin D02 P593 Ireland (www.arccompliance.com).

This is a work of fiction. Names, characters, businesses, places, events and incidents are either the products of the author's imagination or used in a fictitious manner. Any resemblance to actual persons, living or dead, or actual events is purely coincidental.

Troubador Publishing Ltd
Unit E2 Airfield Business Park,
Harrison Road, Market Harborough,
Leicestershire LE16 7UL
Tel: 0116 279 2299
Email: books@troubador.co.uk
Web: www.troubador.co.uk

ISBN 978-1-83628-187-0

British Library Cataloguing in Publication Data.
A catalogue record for this book is available from the British Library.

Printed and bound in Great Britain by 4edge Limited
Typeset in 12.5pt Minion Pro by Troubador Publishing Ltd, Leicester, UK

For Tracey and Johanna
Sisters at heart

The author has used the real names of structures with a few exceptions, For example, the term Shropshire Police Headquarters is purely historical. St Cadfael's does not exist and should not be confused with any other private school in or around Shrewsbury.

Let the Bell Ring is entirely a work of fiction. The characters, incidents and dialogue are a product of the author's imagination and should not be interpreted as real events. Names of actual persons, living or dead, actual names, actual places and events in the public domain, including the weather, are incidental to the plot of the novel and are not intended to alter the wholly fictitious character of the book.

1

HAMPSHIRE, 2003

Bloody Monday! She hated Mondays, especially checking the disgusting loos. Holding her breath, Emily marched inside. The air was heavy from illicit smokers even first thing in the morning. Immediately, the laughter and raucous conversation stopped. Girls sidled past her through the door while others studiously washed their hands and sniggered into the mirror. Clouds of smoke hovered above two of the locked cubicles. She kicked each door, folded her arms and waited. A bolt squeaked on the first door, then it partially opened. A tall girl with lank, dark hair shuffled out followed by an angelic little girl, her face a picture of pure innocence.

Emily pointed in the direction of the corridor, then concentrated on the other door. She was certain the miscreant inside the cubicle was Jessica Parker. There had been no sign of her in the stream of pupils going to registration.

Confrontations with Jessica were a daily event. Sixteen years old, she flouted school rules as a matter of principle, especially regarding uniform. Studying didn't interest her. Smoking, drinking and partying seemed to be her only pastimes. Emily had seen her one night on the Hoe with a gang of girls. Thick make-up and ample cleavage accentuated her low-cut, tight-fitting top.

Even in school she dressed provocatively. How many times had she told her about her ridiculously short skirt? When she ran up the stairs her panties were on show for all to see. Giggling boys waited at the bottom to get a good view. More worrying was her provocative attitude to some of the younger male staff.

Giving the door a last kick, Emily escaped into the corridor and headed for her classroom and the grind of the school day. She would catch up with her at morning break when the odious 'bog supervision' loomed again. Glancing at her watch, she cursed inwardly. Outside her room bleary-eyed pupils lolled against the corridor wall waiting to be let in. Most of them had probably been cavorting in the local disco the night before, or up half the night watching television instead of swotting for their mid-term assessment test.

She glared at a buxom sixteen-year-old girl whose skirt barely covered her bottom. Insolently, she stared back, eyes heavy with the previous night's mascara. After the usual fussing with pens and sorting of papers they settled down with a corporate grunt of resentment.

Emily was bursting for the loo, but hadn't had enough time between lessons to run all the way down the corridor and up to the next floor. There was no way she could leave thirty fifteen and sixteen-year-olds to relieve herself while they systematically trashed the classroom.

When the buzzer sounded she hurriedly dismissed the class, packed away textbooks and ran to the loo. Five minutes later she stationed herself in the corridor outside the girls' toilets sipping a coffee. Girls wandered in, giggling behind their hands. Some congregated in a corner casting baleful glances at the more timid individuals who darted in and out under Emily's watchful eye. Hearing a low curse, she barged through the door and tackled the locked cubicles in her usual way.

"Who's in there?" she said, turning to a group huddled in the corner.

"Dunno miss, she was in there before we came in."

"Come out, at once!" Emily shouted. She gave the door a hefty kick. "Do you hear me? Out! Now!" She turned to one of the girls. "Go and fetch Mrs Jackson. She's on duty outside the dining hall." If she was going to kick the door in she wanted a witness.

She waited for some sign of movement, the click of the bolt, but nothing happened. It was probably that bloody Jessica Parker again. She was always bunking off lessons and locking herself in the lavatory. She can't still be in there. Not even Jessica would stay in the loo that long.

"Jessica, I know it's you. If you're not out by the time I've counted to ten I'm coming in."

Still no response: Emily looked under the door. Two feet were planted either side of the lavatory pan. "I can see your feet. Come out and we'll say no more about it."

"What's up?" Mrs Jackson asked as she approached Emily.

"One of the girls is locked in the loo."

"Not Jessica again?"

"Probably. That's it. Jessica. I'm coming in!"

Emily gave the door a hefty kick and heard the flimsy bolt give way. The door crashed against the wall then swung back. In that brief moment she saw Jessica slumped on the lavatory, her eyes wide open.

"Oh my God! Jessica! Jessica!"

Lynn Jackson stood rooted to the spot, her hand stifling a scream.

Tentatively, Emily took Jessica's hand to feel for a pulse, then stepped back with a look of complete disbelief.

"I think she's dead," she whispered. "Get the girls away from here and fetch Mr Johnson. I'll ring 999."

"How did this happen?" Mr Johnson, the head teacher, asked in a stunned voice. He turned to Emily. "*You* were supposed to be on duty. God help us when the press get hold of it!"

"The paramedics and police are on their way," Emily said, her voice trembling.

Johnson was furious. "You should have waited for me before contacting the police."

Mrs Jackson shot him a scathing glance as she steered Emily to the door.

"We've both had a terrible shock. We'll be in the staff room until the police arrive."

"Very well," he said curtly. "I'm going to lock the

outer door. Make sure no pupils come anywhere near here."

*

Inspector Ben Wallace stood back from the cubicle. He hated this kind of death. It was so undignified for the victim, especially one so young. Light flashed as the police photographer recorded the body from every angle.

"What do you think?" he asked the white-suited pathologist at his side.

"She appears to have been strangled with her own school tie. There's some blood on her clothing and lower body, but no sign of any external wounds."

"Anything else?"

"I'd rather get the post mortem done before giving an opinion."

"Poor kid!" Wallace felt his guts churn.

"Once the CSIs have finished we'll move the body to the mortuary. How long has she been dead?"

"A few hours at most. I'll carry out the post mortem this evening. See you there."

Wallace didn't reply. Instead, he turned to Mr Johnson.

"I'd like to speak to the staff who found the body," he said tersely.

"They're in my office. Both of them are extremely shocked, as you can imagine."

"The parents will have to be informed. We'll send a

Family Liaison Officer round. She'll stay with them for support."

Johnson took a step backwards, his face ashen. He opened his mouth to say something, then changed his mind.

"Now, if you would like to join your colleagues, a police officer will be up to ask some questions very shortly. I would rather you didn't leave the building until our preliminary investigations are completed."

Wallace followed him outside, glad to get away from the stink of body odour and stale cigarette smoke. It seemed to cling to his clothing. He exited the building via the side doors and strode briskly towards his car. A group of scruffy boys eyed him brazenly as they kicked the tyres.

Wallace glared at them, daring them to do it again. Without a word he motioned to DS Linacre to get in the car. They screeched off across the tarmac to the sound of jeering. When he glanced in the driver's mirror they were giving him the finger. He slammed on the brakes and started to reverse. Suddenly, the boys ran off in different directions and disappeared inside the school. They were the least of his worries. His focus was the murdered girl, Jessica Parker. He drove towards Jessica's house without uttering a word.

Grey pebble-dashed houses with postage-stamp gardens ran the length of the street. Litter filled the gutters and stuck to the wire fences enclosing the houses. Ugly satellite dishes outnumbered the cars parked outside. Intermittently, a number of smarter dwellings stuck out incongruously from the others. They sported new front doors and well-tended gardens; a symbol for those who had bought their council houses.

Wallace and DS Linacre pulled up outside a shabby house. Grubby curtains hung limply at the windows. The front door was covered in scratches, presumably from the large dog sitting menacingly in the downstairs window. The glass panel was cracked and held together by brown parcel tape. The garden was more mud than grass, with liberal quantities of dog faeces scattered around.

"Obviously, not too fussy about hygiene, sir," Linacre said.

Wallace didn't respond. He was watching the group of hoodies lurking lower down the street. Satisfied they were just hanging around, he pushed open the rusty gate. Side-stepping dog mess, he took a deep breath and knocked the door. He could hear a baby wailing pitifully inside. Someone shuffled to the door and opened it a crack. A woman with dirty, blonde hair and red-rimmed eyes stared back at him.

"Mrs Parker?"

"If it's about the TV license you'll have to speak to Eddie," she said.

"It's not about the television, it's about your daughter Jessica. I'm Inspector Ben Wallace and this is Detective Sergeant Linacre."

"She's not here. She didn't come home last night."

"She was found in school."

"What do you mean *'found in school'*? What's she done this time?"

"I'm sorry, but we need to speak to you. Can we come in?"

Reluctantly, she opened the door. The shabby hallway stank of vomit and stale urine. He could feel the bile rising in his throat when she showed them into the tiny living room. Soiled napkins sat in a pile on the floor. A crying baby squirmed on the sofa, covered by a threadbare, filthy blanket. Another little girl sat on the floor nursing a grubby doll.

"Is your husband here, Mrs Parker?" Panic registered on her face at the mention of her husband.

"He's down the pub with his mates."

"Send someone to pick him up," he instructed Linacre.

"Jessie's not a bad girl," she wailed. "Don't tell Eddie what she's done. Please!"

"She hasn't done anything, Mrs Parker. I'm deeply sorry. I'm afraid she's dead… "

He didn't finish the sentence. Mrs Parker screamed, a long, drawn-out scream.

"Oh, my God! Oh, my God!" Sobbing convulsively, her whole body trembled like a sapling in the wind. "Please tell me she isn't dead," she whimpered. Wallace nodded. "No! No! Not my Jessica! It's not true! Tell me it's not true!"

"Where's your husband?"

"He's not my husband. Jessie's father was in the army. He was killed on manoeuvres in Germany when she was a toddler. She stayed out for a few nights last week. Eddie hit her… " A sob caught in her throat.

"Did this happen often?" Suddenly, the front door slammed and Eddie burst into the living room. "What's the little slag done now?" he snarled.

"Oh Eddie, she's dead, my Jessie's dead!"

Eddie's face was a complete blank, devoid of any emotion. He went straight to a bottle of whisky on the sideboard and took a long swig. Wiping his mouth with his sleeve, he finally sat down beside Mrs Parker.

"How long were you in the pub, Mr Parker?"

"Haines, Eddie Haines. Maybe an hour. I had a game of darts then went for a walk along the river bank."

"Did anybody see you?"

"It's been raining. There was nobody about. What are you saying? That I killed Jessie! I never touched her!"

"How do you know she was killed? The cause of death hasn't been established yet." Panic flashed in Eddie's eyes. "But you did hit her, didn't you? That's why she didn't come home, isn't it?" Wallace continued.

He turned to Mrs Parker. "Is there anybody we can contact to stay with you? A relative, neighbours?"

"No, we don't bother with the neighbours. Eddie doesn't like them nosing around. My parents and sister live in Church Stretton, in Shropshire, but we haven't been in contact for years, except for Christmas cards. I used to take Jessie to visit them, but Eddie didn't like it. In the end we stopped going."

"The Family Liaison Officer will stay with you, Mrs Parker. Mr Haines, we'd like you to come with us. We need to ask you some more questions."

"This is your fault!" he yelled at his wife. "Giving her big ideas!"

*

Wallace sat opposite Eddie in the interview room, alongside DS Linacre. Patiently, they waited until he stopped ranting. He was a little weasel of a man. Greasy hair hung in limp strands over his forehead. His thin lips parted in a snarl revealing missing teeth. He had the prematurely lined face of a heavy smoker. Eddie chewed nervously on his nicotine-stained fingernails.

"Okay, so I hit her. Superior little cow; always trying to lord it over me. That doesn't mean I killed her."

"What do you mean by '*superior*'?"

"Just like her mother and her bloody family! They think they're better than me!"

Not difficult, Wallace thought grimly.

"Is that why you stopped Jessie visiting them?"

"They were putting ideas into her head. Wanted her to go and live with them. Well, I wasn't having it. She was getting too big for her boots. I had to keep her in line. But I didn't kill her! I told you I was down the pub. Ask my mates."

"What do you mean '*too big for her boots*'?"

"Her mother encouraged her to be a little smart arse. Wanted her to go to university like she did. Jessica's father was an army officer. Didn't do him much good, did it?" He smirked revealing his rotten teeth.

Wallace visualised the scrawny, ill-kempt woman, the

filthy house and grubby children. It was hard to believe that this same browbeaten woman had been to university. How did she sink so low? He clenched his fists under the table, feeling the hot flush of anger suffusing his face. He wanted to punch Haines's lights out. DS Linacre looked at him warily. He knew that look. Finally, Wallace said, "You're free to go, Mr Haines, for now, but we'll want to question you again."

Haines pushed the table away and lurched to the door. "The little slag got what she deserved, but I didn't kill her!"

"Get him out of here, Linacre, before I do something I'll regret!"

*

Wallace took a huge breath and pushed back the plastic strips covering the door to the mortuary. The cloying smell of death hit his nostrils before he glimpsed the still form lying under the green sheet. His stomach rose up, its contents threatening to disgorge onto the cold, tiled floor. A technician was busy at a stainless steel sink set beneath glass storage cupboards full of preserved samples. The pathologist turned from the gleaming metal counter and threw him a surgical mask. Noting his pallor, he grinned underneath his own mask. He drew back the sheet. Jessica Parker looked like a beautiful wax doll, unreal, as though she had never breathed life. Wallace struggled to maintain his emotions. He would never get used to this part of his job.

"She wasn't strangled as I first thought. That was a ploy. She was only strangled post mortem. As I suspected, the bleeding was caused by a miscarriage although the foetus hadn't been aborted. There are some needle marks on her arms suggesting drugs were involved."

"She was an addict?"

"Can't tell until the blood tests come back from forensics. Though, I think it's safe to say she wouldn't have strangled herself," the pathologist declared facetiously.

Wallace sighed. Now he had a murder on his hands.

*

A temporary incident room had been set up in the school sports' hall, situated away from the main building. An area had been sectioned off for interviews at the far end. Those in Jessica's class would have to be interviewed along with teachers, staff, caretaker and cleaners.

A technician was busily setting up a computer and a whiteboard in another partitioned area. Wallace stepped over the cable leads and boxes littering the floor. Sighing audibly, he headed for a boxed-off room with his name on it. The press boys had got hold of the story already and were clamouring for information.

Rumours were rife amongst school staff. The kids looked frightened, their usual boisterousness replaced by furtive whispering. Neither Emily Lambert nor Mrs Jackson had given him much except for finding the body. A police officer stood near the door. Emily Lambert was sitting quietly with her hands folded, face pale and drawn. She appeared calm, but her hands trembled as she put them out of sight under the table.

"Miss Lambert, tell me how you found the body of Jessica Parker. Take your time."

"It's as I told you. Monday is my duty day. I have to supervise the girls' lavatories and that section of the corridor before school, before lessons start, at morning break and lunch time."

"You went inside to check on the girls?"

"To oust out the smokers. The cubicle door was locked. It was still locked at break time. None of the other girls had seen anyone going in or out. I suspected it was Jessica. She had a habit of locking herself in the loo to skip lessons. I sent for Mrs Jackson as a witness."

"A witness?"

"Teachers have to be extremely careful these days regarding false allegations. When she arrived I looked under the door to check and saw two feet. I threatened to kick open the door, but there was no reaction. I was getting very concerned so I kicked in the bolt. Jessica was sitting on the loo slumped to one side." Emily swallowed, a sob caught in her throat. "I thought she was just unconscious so I felt for a pulse. A few of us have had Red Cross training. We act as 'first aiders' for the school."

"So, you realised she was dead."

"Yes, but I still couldn't believe it. Lynn… Mrs Jackson… rang Mr Johnson and he came down straight away."

"How would you describe Jessica?"

"Rebellious, provocative, 'jail bait' for younger male members of staff, but underneath the bravado she was a good kid." Tears rolled down Emily's cheeks. Angrily, she brushed them away. "What a waste! She was so bright, a good all-rounder. Straight 'A' grades until she moved into lower sixth, then she started going off the rails. She was barely sixteen, almost a year younger than some of them. She was definitely Oxbridge material. Remarkable when you consider her background."

"What about her parents?"

"Mrs Parker always turned up for parents' evenings with the other two children in tow. I must admit I was very surprised. She was obviously educated and well-spoken, but the poor woman looked scared. When the kids came in for their exam results during the summer holidays she came with Jessica to discuss her 'A' level options. She was determined that Jessica would go to university, although I doubt she could have helped financially. It was a hot day and she was wearing a shabby old dress. When she lifted up the baby I saw bruises on the top of her arms. She kept looking over her shoulder as though she expected someone to be behind her."

Wallace sat back in his chair and folded his arms. Did her partner ever come with her?"

"No, I only met him once when Jessica was taken ill in school a few weeks ago. A nasty piece of work. Jessica cringed when he came near her. I questioned her when she came back to school about their relationship, but she clammed up."

Everything seemed to be pointing to Eddie Haines, but they had no proof other than he had hit her. They would need a lot more than that to arrest him for murder.

2

A chill wind ruffled the hair of mourners encircling the open grave. They huddled under umbrellas protecting them from a sudden downpour of lashing rain. Sarah Parker shivered in her thin dress and threadbare cardigan. The baby grizzled in her arms, gnawing at his fist. Her grief-stricken eyes riveted on the coffin lying in the grave. She couldn't cry. She had no tears left, only a numb feeling in her chest. Bewildered by the ritual, her little girl clung to her legs. At her side, her parents and a tall, grey-haired man, in army officer's uniform, gazed vacantly at the grave. Emily and Mr Johnson stood sombrely alongside the senior staff and the sixth form. Most of the girls were weeping uncontrollably. For some it was the first time they had been close to death. The boys awkwardly put their arms around them in a futile attempt to offer comfort.

The priest held out a box of earth to Mrs Parker. She stared at it and shook her head, not wanting to accept the finality of Jessica being laid to rest with her father. If only John had lived, her life would have been so different.

One by one, mourners took a handful of earth and threw it into the grave. The tall man put his arms around Sarah and hugged her to him. Her former father-in-law looked so much like John it brought on a fresh anguish. Gently, he drew her away from the grave and moved to the black limousine parked on the road below them.

Wallace followed at a discreet distance. When Mrs Parker was settled in the car he approached Brigadier Parker.

"I'm very sorry about your grand-daughter, sir. It must have been a terrible shock."

"She had everything to live for. First John and now... My wife couldn't bear to come today."

"I'd appreciate a chat with you regarding Eddie Haines, when you feel up to it."

"I'm flying back to Germany tomorrow. I'm stationed in Paderborn. We've organised some refreshments in Boringdon Park Golf Club. If you come back with us, we can talk."

"Sarah and the children are coming back to Shropshire with us." Wallace turned towards Mrs Parker's parents. "She should have left that pig years ago," her mother said. "We'll do everything in our power to stop her going back to him again."

Wallace sipped his orange juice and gazed over the course towards Plymouth Sound. He envied the golfers enjoying a game. He hadn't played a round for years. He never seemed to have the time.

"Wonderful view over Plymouth Sound, isn't it?"

Wallace turned to Brigadier Parker, simultaneously

taking in the entire room. Everything about the mourners screamed upper-middle-class respectability. It just didn't fit with the pathetic figure of Sarah Parker sitting huddled in a corner with her parents.

"You're wondering, aren't you? About Sarah, the way she is?" Wallace nodded. "She wasn't always like this, you know. Such a vivacious girl and bright, very bright."

"What happened?"

"Eddie Haines happened. When my son was killed she went to pieces. She and Jessica went to stay with her parents in Shropshire, but eventually she had to get back to her job. Believe it or not, she was a research chemist for a big pharmaceutical company. She had just completed her Ph.D. when she met John. Like me, he was a career soldier. It's hard to believe, seeing her now."

Parker's eyes momentarily flared with anger. "She started drinking and partying with people she met in the local pub. One day she turned up at work still a bit worse for wear. The first time she got away with a slap on the wrist, but when it happened again they dismissed her. She was a liability to their research programme."

"How did she meet Haines?"

"He was one of the pub crowd." Parker related how losing her job shocked her into stopping drinking. Her parents begged her to go back to Shropshire and make a new life for herself, but it was too late. She was already pregnant with Haines's child. Two miscarriages and another baby trapped her in the relationship.

"Sarah was determined that Jessica would have the chance to go to university. She tried to persuade her to go back to Shropshire, but Jessica wouldn't leave her with Haines. She was doing brilliantly at school. Suddenly, she started acting up, being rude to staff, not submitting assignments. I'm convinced something must have happened for her behaviour to change. It was completely out of character."

"You think Haines had something to do with it?"

Brigadier Parker's lips curled into a sardonic smile. "It wouldn't surprise me."

Wallace glanced over at Mrs Parker as he left the golf club. She was staring vacantly ahead, completely oblivious to her surroundings. He still found it hard to believe that this scrawny, unkempt woman was an academic. He wanted Eddie Haines; he wanted him badly.

*

Eddie Haines had been brought in for an informal interview. The smirk on his face disappeared when DS Linacre broached the subject of Sarah Parker's academic career. Wallace registered his reaction. What made him so antagonistic about it? Was it jealousy or vindictiveness? He hadn't worked for years, preferring to live on benefits. Claimed he had back problems. It didn't prevent him leaning over the pool table or slapping his wife about. No, there was something else; something to do with Jessica.

"You like to knock Sarah about, don't you, Haines?" Linacre said.

"She's always whinging about money, but I never hit her… maybe once or twice, that's all."

"Why does she whinge about money? Is it because you spend it down the pub?" Haines shifted in his seat and looked at the ceiling. "Was it for food?"

"What are you saying, that I don't provide food for my missus and kids?" Wallace raised his eyebrows. "She was always trying to get more out of me for that slag daughter of hers. Wanted to save it for her education." He guffawed. "A lot of good a fancy education did her. She was a drunken slut when I met her."

Wallace clenched his fists under the table until his knuckles turned white. Amber, Jessica's best friend, told them how he had beaten Jessica whenever he arrived home drunk.

"You hit Jessica when you were drunk, didn't you, Haines?"

"No, I told you I only hit her once."

"You made sexual advances towards her, didn't you?"

"That's a lie! I never touched her! She came at me with a bloody knife." He slumped in the chair, realising what he had just said. "You're trying to frame me for her murder."

Jessica had told Amber all about it. How she had grabbed a kitchen knife and threatened to kill him when he held her down on the sofa and tried to kiss her. She had refused to tell her mother in case she confronted Eddie and he laid into her."

"Where were you the night Jessica died?"

"I keep telling you, I was in the pub with my mates."

"We've asked your mates, Eddie. They said you left the pub just before it closed. They stayed drinking after hours, but you didn't come back."

"I went down to the Barbican to meet some friends, students."

"Students? I thought you didn't think much of education, Eddie."

Eddie's eyes darted around the interview room like a weasel looking for a way to escape. He rocked backwards and forwards in the chair, mustering a show of bravado. His dilated pupils shone like pools of black water. His skin was clammy and grey. He was on a high when they picked him up on Plymouth Hoe.

"What are you on Eddie? Cocaine, heroin?"

"A bit of skunk, that's all."

"Jessica knew you were dealing, didn't she? That's why you had to kill her."

"Okay, so I was dealing weed. I don't touch the hard stuff. She caught me once selling to some students, but I didn't kill her. Anyway, you haven't got any proof. The slag's dead."

Eddie shook his head vigorously. Wallace could smell his dirty hair and the foul stench of cigarette smoke mingled with bad breath. His clothes were stinking. Left to his own devices after Sarah and the children had gone back home to Shropshire, he looked like a filthy tramp.

Wallace bit his tongue. Haines was right. They had no real proof. They would have to catch him dealing. The most he could do was bang him into a cell for twenty-four hours and make him sweat. If they didn't come up with new evidence they would have to let him go.

3

The church hall smelled of a mixture of dusty old books, mildew and beer. It was a buzz of activity. A few men were sitting on the metal stacking chairs drinking from cans of lager. Others were busy carrying tables and other props onto the small stage. Some of the women were preening in front of a large Cheval mirror. They were rehearsing for 'An Inspector Calls.' Emily's eyes searched the room. For a moment she didn't recognise David Johnson with the fake sideburns and iron-grey, wavy wig. He looked so handsome and distinguished. Her heart thudded in her chest like a smitten schoolgirl. Her gaze wandered to his overbearing wife. As usual, she was bawling out instructions to the long-suffering cast. They all laughed at her behind her back and felt sorry for David, who meekly did as he was told.

He was a different man when he was in school. She visualised him at sixth form assembly. The consummate head teacher. Confident. In total control, blue eyes flashing with humour and intelligence. She couldn't take her eyes off him then or now.

"David, over here, quickly!" Mary Johnson bawled in her fishwife voice. "We haven't got all evening you know!"

Meeting Emily's eyes, he nodded and smiled. A look of pure lust passed between them before he scurried over to his wife. Emily walked over to the group of women trying on costumes. She laughed inwardly; if they only knew. Mary would leave early, because of her children and her pampered Pekingese. With floppy hair that almost concealed her eyes, she was beginning to resemble her dog.

Their affair had started when David invited her to join the drama group. He had come to her classroom dangling a script, a wide grin on his face. She found him charming and easy to talk to when he was away from his desk. It had happened quite casually, one evening after school, when he had arrived at her room to rehearse her lines.

"This looks very promising," he remarked, taking her hand. "You're a star. We've needed new blood in the group for a long time."

Emily felt the colour rise up her neck and suffuse her face in a hot blush. *It's ridiculous*, she thought. *I'm behaving like a silly schoolgirl. Besides, he's old enough to be my father.* Leaning over, he touched her cheek and grinned.

After parents' evening the following Thursday night he invited her for a drink, along with some of the other staff. They lingered behind when everyone started to leave. Politely, he offered to drive her home. There was nothing polite about the kiss he planted on her lips before she got out of the car. From that moment on she was lost. Her waking thoughts were of David and her last thought before she drifted to sleep was David's smiling face.

*

Emily walked steadily over the rough ground, dodging ant hills and rabbit holes. To her right, beyond the barbed wire fence, the sea broke into huge white-capped waves as they hit the rocks below the cliff. A warm, salty breeze ruffled her hair. She felt alive, stimulated by the anticipation of David. In the distance she spotted him walking towards her on the path between the dunes. She couldn't see his face clearly, but she knew it was him. The way he walked; how his head leaned to one side when he stopped and shaded his eyes against the mellow evening sun. He waved, then disappeared from sight.

A few minutes later she threw herself down beside him on the warm sand. Hidden by high, coarse grass he pulled her to him and kissed her. His lips were warm and salty. Lying back on the sand, she gazed at him. He was such a beautiful man. She admired his muscular arms and the way his muscles bulged. Dark good looks, tanned skin, chiselled jaw and the most perfect nose she had ever seen. So damned good looking. He could have had any one of a number of the female staff, but he had chosen her. She felt so grateful.

He swept a hand through his luxurious hair, She loved the way a lock of it fell onto his forehead, brushing her lips as he bent his head towards her. His hand traced the thin cotton of her skirt from her ankle to her thigh. A quiver of excitement and longing shuddered through her body. Suddenly, he was on top of her. There was an urgency to his kiss that was new and a little frightening. She pushed him away and sat up.

"What's the rush?" she asked, smoothing down her skirt.

"You drive me crazy," he said, reaching out for her again.

"Not here. It's broad daylight. What if we're seen? Can you imagine the aftermath?"

"I don't care. I love you."

"That's lust talking, not common sense."

"I thought you were ready. Don't you love me?"

"Yes, I do, but not here. It's too risky."

"Still Little Miss Goody Two Shoes," he sneered.

Emily struggled to her feet and playfully kicked sand at him. Laughing, he grasped her ankle as she turned to walk away. Unbalanced, she fell into his arms and lay there breathing in the sweetness of his aftershave.

"I hate you David Johnson," she sighed as his lips came down on hers. She couldn't live without him.

4

It had been a week since she had seen David. A whole week of self-doubt and loathing after their torrid lovemaking in the dunes. What was she thinking of, carrying on with a married man? She imagined her parents' shocked reaction if they ever found out. He had been ensconced in his office for days while she worried whether she had cheapened herself. That's it, she determined. It's not going to happen again. She knew she was fooling herself as soon as she saw him in the drama club.

It was the final dress rehearsal. David was standing slightly apart from the rest of the cast with a worried frown on his face. Emily eased between the players fidgeting with their costumes and sidled up to his shoulder. He gave her a cursory glance, nodded and walked towards his wife, leaving her standing alone in the middle of the room. Seething, she pushed past into the cramped room at the back of the hall to put on her costume.

"Where the hell have you been, Emily?" Mary shouted from the narrow doorway.

Emily cringed at the sound of the booming voice. She should have been a Sergeant Major in the bloody army!

"I was held up after school."

"Well, get a move on! We're all waiting!"

Emily swallowed a retort and hastily got dressed. By the time she appeared in the wings, David, who was playing Mr Birling, was surrounded by the cast. Ironically, she was taking the part as Sheila, Birling's daughter. He had reminded her so many times about the age gap between them. Not that she cared a hoot.

He was slightly greying at the temples, but he didn't look anywhere near his forty-one years. She liked older men. They knew how to treat a woman, not like the crass young men she usually dated. For a moment she thought of Paul, the architect from the village. Kind, attentive, good prospects, more her age. He was so obviously smitten with her, but she pushed him out of her mind.

"Opening scene. Everyone on stage," Mary yelled.

Sidling up to David, Emily whispered, "I'll be in the dunes waiting for you." He looked up briefly, then busied himself with his make-up. "Don't keep me waiting." The nights were drawing in. Soon they would have to find another meeting place.

She waited for him for over an hour. Finally, she saw his head bobbing above the reeds. When he saw her laying sprawled in the sand, he beamed and flung himself down beside her.

"You're late. I've been here ages." Looking contrite, he tried to kiss her, but she turned her face away.

"I'm so sorry, darling. Mary wanted me to help her

bathe the dog. What could I do? She loves the stupid mutt so much. Am I forgiven?" he pleaded, nuzzling her neck.

"If I thought you were just using me… "

She didn't finish the sentence. David's lips crushed down on hers as he pushed her back onto the sand.

During school hours they maintained a cool distance. Just a hint that she even liked him would set tongues wagging. We could lose our jobs, he told her, if parents get wind of it. So their affair had drifted on for over a year. Emily hated the deceit and subterfuge.

"We can't go on like this," she declared. "I'm fed up with sneaking around; making love on the back seat of cars. It's just too sleazy."

David sat without speaking, as though he knew what was coming.

"You have to make a choice," Emily said. "It's me or Mary. I want us to be together. We can both apply for posts outside the county; buy a house, have children. You're still young enough."

David didn't answer. Wind moaned through the trees setting them in motion. Rain lashed against the car, running in rivulets down the windscreen.

"I mean it, David. I can't go on like this."

Finally, he said, "You know I love you. I promise we'll be together soon, very soon, but it will take time. I can't leave straight away. She hasn't been well. I have to find the right moment to tell her about us. Besides, we've got the new play to think about. All the proceeds are going to charity. On top of all that, Jessica's murder investigation is still on-going."

"All right." Emily sighed. "We wait until the play is over at the end of term, then tell her."

"I promise, as soon as the term is over."

He gave her a wide grin when he dropped her off a couple of streets from her three-bed semi, away from prying eyes. Briskly, she walked down the road and turned into her street, conscious of every sound. The rustling of branches, a footstep, dark spaces; everything set her nerves on edge. Jessica Parker's murder had unsettled the whole school for months.

A tree had been planted in her memory on a patch of grass near reception. By September she would be forgotten, when the new intake came in and the older pupils left. Her heart contracted whenever she thought of Jessica and her bubbly personality.

She was almost at her front gate when a shadow caught her eye. A man stepped out from the lane at the side of the house.

"Paul!" she exclaimed. "You gave me such a fright!"

"I was passing and I thought it would be a good opportunity to call in."

Emily hesitated. She glanced at her watch. It was only nine-thirty, but she didn't really want to ask him in.

"I still have some marking to do," she said ruefully, "but I have time for a quick coffee."

Paul settled himself on the sofa while she went into the kitchen to make the drink. He was looking unusually serious, as though he had something on his mind. She regretted their on-off relationship. A pang of guilt caught in her chest. After all, she had never really told him she didn't want to see him again. Why couldn't she have fallen in love with solid, dependable Paul instead of David? Most women would be flattered to have the attentions of such a good-looking man. She pushed the thought out of her head and carried the coffees into the living room.

"Do you remember the competition to design that concert hall in Bristol?" Paul asked.

"Yes, you put in a design didn't you?"

"I heard officially this morning. They chose mine. The one I showed you, made entirely of glass like a giant crystal. It's a marvellous boost for everyone in the firm," Paul added modestly.

"That's fantastic!"

"That's why I called round, to ask you to come to our celebratory dinner the week after next. The play will be over by then, won't it?"

"Yes, but I'll be pretty exhausted after a whole week on the boards. I wouldn't want to be a party pooper," she said lamely. Taking a deep breath, she turned to him. Keeping her eyes lowered, she said, "The thing is, Paul, I've met someone; someone I really care about."

"I thought you cared about me?"

"I do, but not in the same way. I can't think about anything else except being with him all the time. I've never felt this way before."

"Who is it?" he asked harshly. "Do I know him?"

"No, he's from out of town," she lied. "I met him when I visited my aunt in Portsmouth a few months ago. We hit it off immediately."

Paul stared at her, his eyes betraying his calm exterior. For a few minutes he said nothing, then got up to leave.

"You've been seeing someone behind my back?"

"Paul, don't be upset. We can still be friends, can't we?"

"Friends? It isn't friendship I want. I love you. I want you for my wife, not my friend!" His eyes glittered with anger. "I just saw you getting out of a car. Was that him?"

Emily's heart thudded in her chest. Had he been watching her? How much had he seen?

"No," she lied. "That was David Johnson, the head teacher. He gave me a lift home after the dress rehearsal. His wife has been ill, so he dropped me off near the bus stop so he could get off home."

"Johnson – that rat!"

"What do you mean? Do you know him?"

"Oh yes, I know him. We go back a long way, a very long way. He was involved with my sister."

Emily suddenly felt weak, as though someone had sucked the life from her body with a straw. Trying to keep her voice from trembling, she put her hand on his arm. Paul shook it off. His eyes burned into hers, his face etched with disbelief. Without a backward glance he walked out, slamming the door behind him.

*

Rivulets of rain streamed down the glass patio doors, gathering in pools on the sill. A gunmetal grey sky hung low overhead. Wind lashed trees into frenzied motion above the sodden lawn. Paul gazed out onto the street where two lads were kicking water at each other from the swirling gutters. When they spotted him watching them they screeched with laughter and ran off down the street, mouthing obscenities.

Sighing, he flung himself down on the sofa in front of the television. He wished he had taken up the offer of a week in Cyprus with Jack from the office. What a fool he had been, thinking that Emily wanted a serious relationship. She was obviously smitten with this guy she had mentioned, but who was he? He had never seen her with anyone else.

Later that evening he set off for the wine bar in the Barbican, where Emily's friends gathered on weekends. Saturday night and the place was heaving. Music blasted from the speakers. He shouted to the barman.

"Pint of lager, please."

Sipping his drink, he surveyed the room. Usual crowd, mostly professionals unwinding over the weekend. Suddenly, he spotted Sarah Burke sitting in a corner booth with her usual cronies. When she caught his eye she waved him over. Pushing his way through the crowd he made his way to her table and squeezed in beside her.

"What are you doing here? This isn't your usual haunt. Golf club not good enough for you anymore?" she teased.

"I just fancied a quiet drink with some old friends," he yelled over the hullabaloo.

Looking for someone special more likely, Sarah thought. Such a hunk! Emily must be mad turning him down in favour of that odious creep she was hung up on.

"Emily not with you tonight?" Paul ventured.

"She's away for the weekend – Bournemouth I think."

"She's gone alone? I thought you always spent the Easter holidays together?"

"I think she's gone with an old school friend," Sarah shrugged.

"Would this old friend be a man?"

Sarah hesitated, wondering if she should say anything. Emily was her childhood friend. They had gone through school from nursery and then on to the same university. Now they taught in the same school. They were more like sisters than friends. This obsession with David Johnson worried her. During in-service training in Exeter she had heard a few rumours about him from a guy he had taught with before coming to Plymouth. She had put it down to jealousy, because one of them had failed to be shortlisted for David's current headship.

Emily had told her about her relationship with him and her hopes for the future. She had been sworn to secrecy. The last thing she wanted was to see her hurt. She hadn't realised the affair had become so serious that she wanted to spend the rest of her life with Johnson.

"Look, Paul, I shouldn't really be telling you this, but I'm really worried about her," Sarah said. "This guy she's seeing isn't right for her. That's all I can say."

"I asked her to marry me. She turned me down, because of him," Paul said bitterly.

Sarah stared into her glass of wine, her mind in a whirl. He knew more than she had supposed.

"It's always been Emily, from the first day we met.

I haven't slept a wink since she turned me down. Everything I've worked for over the past few years, my winning design, all of it is for her. Things were fine for a long time then she suddenly started making excuses every time I tried to arrange some time together. I was going to take her to meet my parents this weekend," Paul said ruefully.

He looked haggard, dark shadows under eyes filled with misery. How could Emily be so stupid? Handsome, intelligent, kind, a brilliant architect, recently made senior partner in his firm. On top of all that, he worshipped her. Most women would be over the moon to go out with him, let alone a proposal of marriage.

"Who is he? Is he local?" Sarah didn't respond. "You know more than you're telling me, don't you?"

"Emily is my best friend. I warned her not to get involved with him. David Johnson's got a reputation."

"Paul's face turned white. "Did you say David Johnson?"

"Paul, what is it?"

Disbelief, hatred, despair swept over his face, then total anger. Barely able to control his emotions, he pushed out of the booth muttering, "Johnson, Johnson."

"Paul, don't go like this. Stay until you've calmed down."

But he wasn't listening. In a red fug of anger he lurched out of the wine bar and headed for The Hoe.

Breathing deeply in the damp night air, he lumbered towards a bench that looked out to sea. Not for a moment had he thought she was having an affair with

Johnson. She had only mentioned him once when he had chastised her for leaving a class unattended. Then it hit him. She had been lying to him when he spotted her getting out of his car. All that time when she had been playing opposite him in the play she had been involved in a sordid affair with a married man. David Johnson filled him with loathing and disgust. *Doesn't she know what kind of man he is? Does she care?* he fumed inwardly.

His mind was whirling as he walked back towards the harbour. It was full of people ambling along looking at restaurant menus. Bloody tourists! He headed for the nearest pub. He was going to get drunk; very, very drunk!

He downed two double whiskies and banged the bar for another.

"Take it easy, you've had two doubles already and you've only been in here five minutes," the barman commented.

"Just get me another whisky, pal. No advice required, just whisky."

Paul glared at the ageing ex-sailor, a veteran of the merchant navy and no pushover in a fight. *Bring it on*, he thought. Anger boiled inside him like a raging river. He sat drinking for over an hour until the barman refused to serve him.

"That's it mate, you've had enough," he said when Paul started to argue. "I'll call a taxi to take you home." Paul eased himself off the chair and staggered a few feet. "Okay, let's be 'avin' you." The barman grinned and propelled him towards the door. "The taxi is outside."

Paul only vaguely remembered falling through his

front door. He couldn't make the stairs so he crashed out on the sofa.

*

Searing white light pierced his eyeballs accompanied by spasms of pain like jabbing, hot needles. He couldn't open his eyes. Wincing, he tried to force open his eyelids, but they seemed to be stuck with glue. His mouth was dry and tasted of booze and yesterday's food. For a few moments he lay prone, trying to gather his thoughts. Why had he got so drunk? It came rushing back to him like frames in a horror film. David Johnson!

Feeling slightly disorientated, he went into the kitchen, took a couple of aspirin and made a pot of very strong, black coffee. After the first cup he felt a little more human. He forced himself to eat a piece of dry toast then slumped back onto the sofa. His eyes wandered to the photograph on the mantelpiece. His parents looking carefree and happy at the seaside, holding the hands of their small children. Paul gulped, tears welling in his eyes. He and his sister Karen licking ice cream cones. They were twins, so alike they were often mistaken for identical twins, until Karen's hair grew longer. She was his closest confidante. They went everywhere together, even as teenagers. They even went to the same university.

That's where she first met David Johnson, in her final year. To think he actually introduced his sister to that vile man. They dated a few times and then went their separate ways when they left university. If only she hadn't not gone to London to work things might have been different. Paul sighed: no amount of wishful thinking would change what happened.

He remembered how excited Karen had been when she telephoned a few years after starting her first teaching post. She had bumped into Johnson in some educational conference. Within a couple of weeks they embarked on a serious relationship. Soon she was talking of marriage and children.

"Don't you think you're rushing things a bit?" Paul asked. "You haven't known him five minutes."

"Of course I have, silly. I went out with him a couple of times when I was in university. He's told me all about himself and his family."

"You're not even engaged yet!"

"He wants to get married so there's no need to get engaged, is there?"

"Mum and Dad won't like it," Paul said testily.

"They'll soon come round when they meet him. I'm bringing him down to Dorset next weekend. It's time they met their future son-in-law. I hope you'll be there for Sunday lunch. I need the moral support."

"Of course," Paul said as enthusiastically as possible. "I wouldn't miss it for the world."

For some unaccountable reason he had felt uneasy, not just because of the reaction of his parents. The whole relationship had been far too 'cloak and dagger' for his liking. He lapsed into a reverie filled with images of his sister and parents.

5

DORSET 1993

Paul dodged deep ruts in the icy lane leading to his parents' house. Their cottage was set in a rambling village with just a church, a pub that sold ice cream and a general stores that doubled as a post office. In summer it was a children's paradise. Lots of trees to climb, a stream to paddle in and horses pasturing in the fields. Beyond the garden the land fell away to the sea.

Even in winter the Dorset countryside was magical. Icicles on the trees overhanging the lane sparkled like diamonds in the pale, white light of a wintry sun. The fields all round were covered in a layer of thick first-fall snow. Ice-filled ruts in the road crackled under the weight of the car wheels, sending him sliding towards the ditches either side.

Expertly, he turned into the skid and righted the car. Ahead the road glistened like silver, threading like a ribbon up and over a slope. This was the part he loved the most, especially this time of year. As the car crested the hill, he had his first view of the village set in a shallow vale. The quintessential English village. At first glance it didn't look real; more like a Christmas card. Thatched cottages, roofs heavy with snow, dotted in a semi-circle around the village green. Its quaint pond was frozen solid. Quacking ducks ran from the snowy surrounds of the pond and slid to the other side, flapping their wings as though taking off from water.

His parents' cottage was set slightly apart on a spacious corner plot of around a third of an acre. As he pulled up outside the door flung open and his mother raced out to greet him. Dressed in dark-blue jeans and a red polo-necked sweater, she looked much younger than her sixty-five years. Suddenly, his father poked his head out of the door.

"Come on in and have a hot toddy before we all freeze! The others are already here."

His mother fussed over him, taking his coat and gloves, then pushed him towards the sitting room where David and Karen were sipping their drinks.

"Isn't this wonderful, Alan!" she exclaimed to her husband. "All of us here together for Christmas Eve."

"Don't start getting over excited Eileen, or you won't have anything left when Santa comes tomorrow."

"This is the start of something wonderful for us, isn't it darling" She smiled at Karen.

"They've just set the date for a spring wedding. It couldn't be more perfect!"

"That soon!" Paul exclaimed. The uneasy feeling he had resurfaced.

Christmas lunch passed in a blur of conversation and cracker popping. Looking round the table it looked like a typical family celebration. His father's face was flushed from too much brandy. His mother's from the anticipation of planning for a spring wedding. He was glad to escape to his room on the pretext of a much-needed nap.

Lying on the bed with his hands behind his head, he gazed out across the extensive garden. The stream that babbled throughout the summer months was frozen solid. In the distance a metallic grey sea, capped with white horses, crashed to the shore. It had started to snow again. Fat flakes drifted across the window, hurried along by a sudden wind. Everything should have been perfect, but he couldn't rid himself of a nagging presentiment about David Johnson.

*

It was an April wedding on the warmest spring day on record. Karen looked stunning in an off-the-shoulder, ivory satin gown. Paul had never seen her look so happy and radiant. Perhaps all his fears were unfounded. Spirits lifted, he threw himself into his best man's duties. He had thought it rather odd that David had asked him, the bride's brother, to be best man, rather than one of his own family or friends.

"My brother and his family are living in Australia,"

David had explained. "He went out there after my parents died. He's just set up a new business in Adelaide and is still in the process of hiring staff, so he can't come. There's no other family except a very elderly aunt in Cheshire and she's too frail to travel."

"What about your friends?"

"How do you choose between your life-long friends without causing offence? Besides, both of them are working overseas. They are so busy establishing themselves in their new jobs that they can't get away."

It was a small, intimate affair with just a few of David's recent acquaintances and their wives. They had to recruit the locals to fill up the pews on David's side. Paul was actually beginning to feel sorry for him. After all, everyone wanted their close family and friends at their wedding.

When it was time for them to leave on honeymoon, Karen threw her bouquet into the crowd of well-wishers. That's when he noticed the knowing look that passed between David and the tall blonde. It was a look that conveyed familiarity and intimacy. A look that chilled Paul's heart.

Karen was so happy when she first came to visit him after the honeymoon. She talked about David incessantly; how attentive and loving he was; how happy she felt. They seemed to live an idyllic life, wrapped up in each other to the exclusion of everyone else. Gradually, her visits became less and less frequent. Every time he or his parents suggested visiting her she put them off, saying she was too busy. If he telephoned, she was just on her way out and would ring back later, but she never replied. In two and a half years, she had only come down from London twice. Even when his mother rang to wish her a happy second anniversary, she barely stayed on the line for five minutes. Finally, she made a flying visit home just for the day, claiming that she was attending a conference in Bournemouth Conference Centre.

She looked drawn and tired. Her skin was sallow and her usually vivid, blue eyes darkened by black shadows.

"I'm worried about her, Alan," his mother said as they waved Karen off. "Did you see how much weight she's lost? She told me she's on a diet, but that's rubbish! It's more than dieting."

His father, who had been very quiet, ushered them indoors.

"I'm going up to London on Friday," he said. "There's something upsetting my girl and I intend to find out what it is."

"I'll go with you," his mother added.

"No, if we both go she'll be suspicious. I'll say that Aunt Jane is poorly and wants to discuss her Will. Karen knows I'm the executor so she won't think it strange. You know how many times Jane has changed her Will over the past few years. I'll make the excuse that as I'll be in Oxford I decided to pop into London. I don't need permission to visit my own daughter. She has to be around some time over the weekend."

"No, it's better if I go alone." Turning to Eileen, he caught her hand. "I'll ring you as soon as I get to her place. Don't worry, you'll be able to speak to her yourself."

Paul drove over to stay with his mother for the weekend. Anxiously, they waited for his father to ring, their apprehension mounting as the hours went by.

"It's nine o'clock," his mother said. "He must have been round there by now. I'll try him again."

"He's still not answering," she said, slamming down the receiver.

Suddenly, the telephone shrilled, making them both jump. Paul grabbed it before his mother had chance.

"Paul, is your mother with you?"

"Yes, she was very agitated when she rang me, so I drove down to keep her company. What's wrong?"

"Just listen carefully. I'm bringing Karen home with me. Tell your mother to get her room ready."

It was after four o'clock in the morning when they heard the sound of a car approaching. Eileen swung open the front door and rushed to the car. Karen was slumped in the back seat, eyes closed and face ashen.

"Help me get her inside and straight to bed," Alan said wearily.

He motioned to Paul to follow him downstairs while his mother fussed over Karen.

"You look as though you need a stiff drink," Paul said, handing his father a large brandy. Alan's lips trembled with emotion. "What happened, dad? Is she ill? Why have you brought her home?"

"When I arrived at her flat she wouldn't answer the door. I knew she was in there, because I heard her moving around. I thumped so hard the woman in the adjoining flat came out to see what was going on. Apparently, she had seen her coming home from work and asked if she was all right. Karen told her she was tired after attending two long parents' evenings that week so she was going to have an early night.

"I remembered I still had the key she copied for us when we went up to decorate the flat. I caught her red-handed taking a line of cocaine."

"What? I don't believe it! What are we going to do?"

"Let her sleep. In the morning we'll talk to her. What I'd like to know is where David has gone. Karen told her neighbour he was visiting his parents."

"His parents? He told us they were dead." They stared at each other in disbelief, their faces washed of colour in the weak morning light seeping through the parted curtains.

"Try not to worry, son. Go back to the office. We'll look after her now."

He had only just arrived at the outskirts of Plymouth when his mobile phone shrilled.

"Dad, is everything all right?"

"Paul, it's Karen. You need to come back."

When he arrived his father was on the sofa staring straight ahead, a look of total incomprehension on his face. Suddenly, the sound of his mother's anguished sobbing filtered downstairs.

"Alan! Alan! "

His father bolted upstairs. Paul followed, heart pounding in his chest, knowing the answer, but denying the thought.

"What's wrong? For God's sake, tell me what's wrong! Why is mum crying?" he cried from the landing.

"His mother's voice faltered. "My girl! Oh, my girl! She's taken an overdose."

Paul suddenly felt disconnected from his surroundings as though he had entered into a vacuum.

"How did she get hold of the stuff?"

"We don't know. She must have hidden it away before I brought her home. We called the paramedics, but it was too late."

"Too late… I don't understand."

"They couldn't save her. She's dead, Paul."

Outside the little church a small crowd of mourners lingered to pay their respects. Sombrely, David Johnson greeted each one with a hug, his eyes filled with tears. Hatred welled up in Paul as he watched the performance, because that's what it was: an Olivier-standard performance worthy of an Oscar. Johnson was enjoying every minute of the attention he was getting.

Putting his arm around his mother, Paul guided her to the black limousine. His father was standing slightly apart from the others with a lost expression on his face. Suddenly, he stepped forward and stood directly in front of David. He was shaking with anger.

"You killed her! You killed my girl!" David tried to grasp his arm, but Alan shook him off. "You killed her! You killed her!"

"Dad!" Paul cried, rushing towards him. "Come on, he's not worth it!"

Slowly the mourners dispersed to their cars, whispering and casting nervous glances over their shoulders.

Paul eased his father into the car alongside his mother and turned to David, his heart filled with loathing.

"My father is right. You're responsible for Karen's death. One day I'll make you pay for this Johnson."

David's eyes followed Paul as he marched back to the car, the sadness in his eyes replaced with a barely perceptible cruel smile.

6

LONDON

London was cold and wet, as it usually is in late March. Paul made his way to the taxi rank. He cursed under his breath when he saw the long line of waiting passengers, but they seemed to be moving fairly quickly.

"Royal Horseguards Hotel, Whitehall," he told the driver.

"Okay, guv."

The taxi rattled up the ramp and into the throng of traffic. The driver wound his way in and out of vehicles, occasionally cursing under his breath.

"Up on holidays, guv?"

"No, business," Paul replied, opening up his newspaper to discourage conversation.

Glancing at his wristwatch, he grimaced – eight fifteen. Lisa would probably be in school by now. He had tried to get her the evening before without success. Pulling out his mobile, he dialled.

"Hi Lisa, it's Paul."

Silence on the other end of the line.

"Paul Bryant, Karen's sister."

"Oh hi! I couldn't think of a Paul who would be ringing me this time in the morning. Long time no see."

"I'm in town for a few days and thought you might like to have dinner with me."

There was a distinct lapse before Lisa answered. Finally, she said, "I'm engaged now, Paul. In fact, I'm leaving at the end of the term, for Australia. My fiancé has a lecturing job in Sydney University. He's already out there, sorting out the house we've rented."

"Well, I'm at a loose end. What about joining me for a farewell dinner? We can catch up on old times before you fly off into the sun. I'll pick you up around seven thirty."

*

The maître d' hovered in the background, waiting for them to settle, then ushered a waiter in their direction. Lisa ordered bruschetta con pomodoro and pork tenderloin with figs, while Paul ordered carpaccio and veal with mushrooms.

"This is very expensive," Lisa murmured, sipping the Brunello di Montalcino wine.

"Don't worry, it isn't the most expensive vintage. Just enjoy."

Lisa gazed at Paul over the rim of her glass. They had gone out on a few dates, but they would only ever be good friends.

"I can't believe it's five years since Karen died. If only she had come to me for support instead of turning to drugs."

"You knew!" Paul said angrily. "Why didn't you tell us?"

"I only knew for certain a few days before your father took her home. She didn't look well and she was snappy and irritable. I asked her if there was anything wrong and she almost took my head off. When she didn't come into work for a few days I went round to her flat. I practically hammered on the door, but she wouldn't let me in. When I threatened to camp outside all night she finally opened the door. I was shocked when I saw her. I insisted on calling a doctor, but she wouldn't hear of it. Finally, she broke down and told me she had been using cocaine for ages."

"Where the hell was David when all this was going on?" Paul snarled.

"That's the point, he wasn't there most of the time. Karen told me he was away most weekends, supposedly on courses, but I didn't believe a word of it. I'm convinced he was up to something. I saw him in a restaurant in Soho when I was with my fiancée. He was with a girl and another couple. I suppose it could have been completely innocent, but it was just the way he looked at her; the body language, you know what I mean."

"You think he may have been having an affair?"

"I can't say for sure, but Karen just kept on going downhill. Apparently, the head teacher called her into his office. A number of parents had rung the school and complained about her teaching. The deputy head knew I was a close friend. He had noticed her erratic behaviour during a parents' evening. He's a good sort and asked me to have a word with her. I said she was a bit off-colour and needed a holiday, but I sensed she was being evasive. After I had been round to the flat she promised me she would see a doctor as soon as David returned from his course on the Sunday night. That's about as much as I know Paul, I swear."

"My father caught her red-handed when he went round there on the Friday night; the night he brought her home."

Paul's fingernails bit into the palms of his clenched fists. David must have known Karen was using cocaine. Why didn't he try to stop her? Why did he leave her alone instead of seeking help?

"The bastard! I could kill him!"

"Do you know any of David's colleagues, any of his cronies?"

"Not really. Hang on a minute! Harriet Bailey, our new head of maths, came from David's school. She might know something. I'll suss her out tomorrow and gave you a ring."

"Great! He's already shown he's a compulsive liar. I want to find out how many more lies he's told and where he's been going on his weekend jaunts. Now, let's enjoy the rest of the evening." He raised his glass. "Good luck in Australia."

Try as he might, he couldn't get the scumbag Johnson out of his mind.

7

LONDON

It was another foul day. Wet, miserable and windy. Paul didn't like London at the best of times, but he hated it in bad weather. His meeting finished just after lunch. After a hurried beer with some of his colleagues he scurried back to the hotel for an afternoon nap. Rivulets of rain blurred the buildings opposite. Over the noisy air conditioning the wind howled through the window vents, catching at the open curtains. Impatient vehicles honked and skidded their way along the street four floors below. Suddenly, his mobile jangled. Paul leapt off the bed and retrieved it from his jacket pocket. It was Lisa.

"Hi Lisa," he said apprehensively. "Any news?"

Lisa hesitated. "Yes, but… "

"Spit it out!"

"Okay, okay, keep your shirt on!"

"Sorry, but I've been really wound up since last night."

"It seems David has a bit of a reputation. Before he

took up his post as deputy head he was head of history. He had only been teaching for a few years, but he got the job over better qualified and more experienced candidates. The rumour is he had friends in the right places. According to Harriet it's not the first time he's wangled a job."

"That doesn't explain his frequent disappearances on weekends," Paul interjected.

"There's more," Lisa said. "He was nicknamed 'The Meteor' because of his rapid promotions. He had only been head of history for three years before landing a deputy head's job in a small school in Kent. The one he's in now is twice the size, with a much bigger salary; and get this, both schools have women head teachers."

"What are you saying?"

"It's rumoured that David had affairs with both of them and used the relationships to get what he wanted."

"But how could he do that?"

"Believe me, Paul, there are as many Machiavellian goings on in schools as there are in Westminster. Promotion is a cut-throat business. You might want to contact Maggie Clyne, the blonde woman who was in the wedding. She's still teaching in his old school. I'll give you her telephone number."

"Thanks, Lisa." Paul scribbled down the number. "You've been a great help. Good luck in Sydney."

Paul snapped his mobile shut and stood gazing out at the drenching rain. There was a lot more to this, he could feel it in his bones. Quickly, he dialled the number Lisa had given him. A gruff male voice answered.

"Derek Clyne."

"May I speak to Maggie please?"

"She hasn't come home yet. What do you want with my wife?" he asked suspiciously.

"My name is Paul Bryant. I'm ringing on behalf of my sister Karen. She's moving up north and didn't have time to contact all her friends. I just want to pass on her new address."

"You can leave that with me," he replied curtly.

Before Paul had time to respond, he heard a woman's voice in the background.

"I'm home. Where are you, Derek?"

"In the kitchen. There's some guy called Paul Bryant on the telephone."

"Maggie Clyne speaking."

"It's Paul, Karen Johnson's brother. A friend of mine told me you taught in the same school as her husband." Paul could almost feel the tension on the other end of the line. "I wondered if you could give me some information about him."

"I'm sorry, but I can't help you," she said coldly. "I hardly know him."

"But you were one of the guests in their wedding."

Silence. "What do you want?" she hissed. "He left the school some time ago for a bigger school in London."

"I know all that. What I want to know is how well you knew him. Obviously, well enough to attend his wedding."

"So what? We were colleagues. Four of us were invited altogether."

"Your husband wasn't with you."

"There was a problem in school after a break-in. He had to go in on the weekend for a meeting with the police."

So, her husband was teaching in the same school - very interesting. Had she been involved with David Johnson? He remembered his unease at the looks that had passed between her and David; intimate looks. He decided to take a direct approach.

"Were you involved with Johnson?"

"I don't know what you mean by '*involved*'."

"I'll spell it out for you. Were you having an affair with him?"

"How dare you?" Maggie spluttered.

"Just answer the question."

"I can't talk now. We'll have to meet somewhere. I'm coming up to London later today for an interview."

"I'm staying at the Royal Horse Guards Hotel. I'll meet you in the lounge bar at six."

Paul snapped his mobile shut, pulled on his jacket and headed downstairs to the hotel restaurant. Suddenly, he felt very hungry. A good meal and a few glasses of decent wine were what he needed. He needed to think on what had happened and how he was going to play it when he met up with Maggie. Anger surged through him when he thought about Karen. So devoted to that creep Johnson. *It's true*, he thought. *Love is blind. Why couldn't she see he wasn't worth her devotion.*

He gulped down the last dregs of his wine and headed for the bar, welcoming the buzz of conversation.

Finding a table in the corner, he buried himself behind a newspaper. He didn't want to talk. A thrill of anxiety coursed through him when Maggie came in ten minutes later and sat down beside him.

"I hope this won't take long?" Maggie said impatiently. "I've had a gruelling day."

"David Johnson. I noticed in the wedding how you looked at each other. It was pretty obvious there was something going on between you. What do you know about him?"

Maggie's shoulders slumped, her face registering fear and defeat. She took a long swig of her gin and tonic before answering.

"It was all over before he met Karen. He was much younger than me, charming and attentive. I was flattered. Derek isn't what you would call a considerate husband. All he's interested in is his bloody golf! It all kicked off when we took the sixth form on a field trip. After he had used me to get a promotion, he dumped me. Told me I was showing my age. Ironically, Derek liked him. They had the odd round of golf together. In retrospect, David turned manipulation into an art form. When the head of sixth form job came up, Derek used his influence as Chair of Governors to get him appointed."

Maggie raised her eyebrows cynically. "It's so sad about Karen. I know what kind of man David is; how persuasive he can be. I couldn't believe he had the gall to invite us to their wedding. I didn't want to go, but Derek insisted. That was the last time I saw him before he left to take up a deputy head post in Kent."

"He certainly rose through the ranks fast," Paul commented bitterly. "You had a lucky escape. He's up to his old tricks again."

Over the next few weeks David's attitude towards Emily changed. He made excuses about not being able to get out of the house now the play had finished. Eventually, she confronted him in his office.

"You've been avoiding me," she said accusingly. "Ever since I asked if you were going to leave Mary."

David's lip curled in a sardonic smile. "Leave," he said. "She's my wife. Do you think you were the first? You're just another little dalliance; a fling." Emily stared at him, speechless. "Besides, I've got my children to think about."

His words struck her like a physical blow. Struggling to control her emotions, she ran back to her classroom. The kids shuffled in and slumped into their seats. Ignoring them, Emily briefly closed her eyes against the harsh winter sun streaming through the windows. Years of tugging and pulling had rendered the Venetian blinds useless. She squinted through the mangled slats and tried to shut out the restless clicking of pens, noisy rustling of pages and shifting of bottoms on seats. She felt sick and her eyes burned with unshed tears. Hastily, she dabbed away a tear and glared at the boy sniggering at the back of the room.

A real smart mouth, always trying to get the last word. He tried to stare her down then gave up, more from lethargy than embarrassment. Glowering angrily, he picked up his pen and put the end into his mouth. She kept her eyes on him until he shuffled uncomfortably and hung his head. Only two more minutes until the bell. She willed it to ring as much as the kids perfunctorily scribbling away at their assignments. Suddenly, the shrill sound of the klaxon-like buzzer penetrated the air. *It's like a bloody football match*, she thought, as pupils hastily packed books into bags and pushed each other through the door.

It was all over. He had chosen. *How could I have been so naive?* she thought. *Paul was right. He was a rat.* She felt dirty, sullied. When she passed him in the corridor the following morning she ignored him. At the end of the Christmas term she avoided the ritual staff drinks at the local pub. All she wanted was to escape to the comfort of her childhood home and be with her parents who lived just outside Plymouth.

*

Christmas lunch was a nightmare. Her feelings fluctuated between self-pity, anger and loathing. The thought of seeing David again made her feel physically sick. She resolved to resign straight after Christmas. Her days were spent walking on the Hoe, bent against the wind and freezing cold. It gave her time to reflect and to escape from her parents' anxious probing. *I'll leave* my job, she decided; *start afresh, work abroad.*

It was just after New Year. Emily sat in her bedroom gazing out over the Solent. In the distance a ferry ploughed through the choppy waters on its way to Roscoff. She dreaded the thought of returning to school, but she had a mountain of end of term reports she had neglected. Suddenly, her mobile shrilled. Her heart leapt. Could it be David? It was Mrs Jackson. Why was she ringing her?

"Hello, Emily. I hope you've had a restful holiday?" She didn't have a chance to answer. "I'm ringing about David Johnson." Emily froze. She must have found out about their affair. Someone must have seen them together. "It's bad news I'm afraid. David and his family went to Phuket for Christmas. They were swept away in the Boxing Day Tsunami."

"David is dead?"

"Their bodies haven't been recovered. There are thousands still missing."

Emily clutched the phone. This wasn't happening. Not David.

"Emily, are you all right? It's been a terrible shock for all of us. We've called an emergency staff meeting tomorrow morning - nine o' clock. No doubt the sixth form will take it particularly hard. Jim Peters is taking over as acting head teacher and I'll be acting deputy head. You'll be taking my place as acting head of upper school for the time being."

"Yes, of course," she replied, struggling to conceal her emotions.

The shock numbed her for weeks. She walked around like a zombie, not seeing or feeling. When Paul bumped into her in March he couldn't believe his eyes. She was so thin. He kept doggedly at her side, cajoling her into eating.

As the months passed she realised she was slowly falling in love with him. In retrospect, she wondered what she had ever seen in David Johnson.

It was only after they married that Paul told her about David.

"He was married to my sister Karen. She died just after their second wedding anniversary."

"How awful for him."

"Don't waste your sympathy on Johnson. He was selfish and indifferent to the point of cruelty." Paul clenched his fists, his knuckles white. "After miscarrying with her first baby Karen became very depressed. As usual, he left her on her own most of the time. She overdosed on cocaine."

8

Wallace waited while the young girl sitting opposite took a sip of water. She dabbed at her eyes, red and swollen from crying. In the early hours of the morning her boyfriend had been found unconscious in the Barbican after taking ecstasy. He had been there all night. It was unlikely he would recover.

"I can't believe it," she said. "He's never taken drugs before. Neither have I," she quickly added.

"Can you tell us what happened, Laura?" Wallace asked.

"We had a few drinks, then I went back to the university library about eight. I had to research an assignment. We don't usually go out much together in the week."

"Do you know how Matthew got the drugs?"

"We all know where to get drugs. There's a guy… they call him Fausty, because he stinks. Everybody knows he deals. It used to be just weed, but lately he's been selling 'ecstasy' and 'skunk'."

"Can you describe this man?"

"Scruffy, bit of a beard, longish hair... looked as if he never washed it... a bit on the skinny side."

"Anything else?" Laura shook her head tearfully.

"Think carefully."

"He had a dog with him... a whippet, I think."

The girl had given a perfect description of Eddie Haines.

"Have you actually seen this man handing over drugs?" Fear sprang into the girl's eyes. "It's all right, you won't get into any trouble." Slowly, she nodded. "Can you swear to it?" She nodded again. At last they had something to use against Eddie Haines. He wouldn't squirm out of this one.

9

Wallace banged his fist on the door, then shouted through the letterbox. He knew Eddie Haines was inside. He'd heard him shuffling down the hallway.

"We know you're in there, Haines. Open the door!"

Haines sat on the floor behind the sofa in the living room, his knees drawn up to his chest. His hands trembled uncontrollably. He needed a fix and he was scared, very scared. He wasn't afraid of the police. They couldn't pin anything on him. He was scared of 'coming down'. Scared of how it made him feel. He had a stash hidden upstairs. No chance with the pigs outside.

Wallace motioned to a uniformed officer to go round to the back door. From his hiding place Haines heard the front door crash open. Two uniformed police officers with dogs charged in. The whippet raced into the hallway, barking in a frenzy of excitement. Haines sat on the floor, his hands covering his ears. He had to have a fix.

"Eddie Haines, we're arresting you for supplying a

controlled drug." He nodded to Linacre. "Get the cuffs on him."

Haines struggled to his feet. "You can't do this to me!" he screamed. "I haven't done anything! I don't deal! It's a lie! You can't prove it!"

Ignoring him, Wallace followed Linacre out to the squad car. Haines was still screaming abuse when the car pulled away, his face contorted with rage.

Wallace banged the desk with frustration. The dogs had sniffed out the drugs Haines had stashed away, but other than that they had nothing solid to charge him with Jessica's murder. At the last moment Laura had refused to give evidence. Haines was back on the streets the same day.

*

Haines hadn't been seen leaving the house for weeks. Neighbours reported that the dog was constantly howling, but it was never let out into the garden. The postman had peered through the letterbox when he tried to shove a large envelope through. A man lay sprawled on his back at the foot of the stairs, one leg sticking out at an unnatural angle.

When the police arrived and broke down the door the smell of vomit and human waste hit them like a physical blow. Haines was clutching a small packet of white powder in his right hand.

"Looks like an overdose," DS Linacre remarked. "He must have cracked his head open when he fell."

"Any thoughts?" he asked the white-suited pathologist examining the body.

"He's been dead at least a week."

"An overdose?"

The pathologist shrugged. "There are needle marks on his arm. What I *can* tell you is that he's been using a 'crack pipe'. Notice the blisters on the lips."

"What about the gash on the head?"

"Let's wait for the pathology report," he replied.

*

A mortuary attendant partially drew back the green sheet. Wallace felt his gorge rise, as he always did in these circumstances. Dawes, the pathologist, folded his arms and pointed at a cluster of pinpoint marks on the victim's right arm.

"I was correct in assuming that the victim had been smoking 'crack cocaine'. It appears he was also injecting."

"Appears? What do you mean?"

"He was pumped full of drugs, but I doubt he could have injected them himself."

"I'm not sure what you mean," Wallace said, looking puzzled.

"The victim was right-handed, so how could he inject into his right arm?"

"With his left hand," Wallace said scathingly.

"Look here," Dawes said, uncovering the left arm with a theatrical flourish. The victim doesn't have a thumb on the left hand. The upper part of the first and third fingers are also missing from the knuckle. Not impossible, but it would have been rather difficult for him to inject himself."

"You think he was murdered?"

Dawes shrugged. "It's likely that someone just helped him to inject, but why? He could have injected himself into his left arm." He pointed to the needle marks. "Look at the bruising. It doesn't add up, but murder… Dawes shook his head. "I can't be certain."

Nothing was found in Haines's house that pointed to him being murdered. Based on the pathologist's report and the lack of any concrete evidence, the coroner declared death was caused by an overdose of Class A drugs. Case closed.

Wallace left the inquest with a mix of emotions. The scumbag Eddie Haines had got what he deserved, but he had died as another hopeless addict instead of a convicted killer. In death he had evaded paying for the murder of Jessica Parker.

10

SHROPSHIRE, NINETEEN YEARS LATER
JULY 2022

Detective Chief Inspector Wallace bit into his stale, cheese sandwich and swigged a mouthful of lukewarm coffee. Chief Superintendent Charles Payne, nicknamed *'Crewcut Charlie'*, loomed in the doorway, all sharp edges and shiny shoes. Payne picked imaginary bits of lint off his peaked cap then parked himself in the chair opposite Wallace. *What a prat*, Wallace thought. *How the hell did he ever make Chief Super?*

"How is the burglary investigation coming on?"

"We're making some progress. The drugs-bust has taken priority over the past week."

"I want you to tie up the Giles Ponting burglary as soon as possible. He's a member of Parliament and a cabinet member. He's tipped for Home Secretary in the next reshuffle. It won't look good if we can't solve a simple burglary."

The telephone in the outer office shrilled. A few minutes later Phil Butler poked his head round the door.

"There's a body down by the river below Blackfriars. A couple of cyclists spotted it floating in the water."

"Sorry, sir," Wallace said, grabbing his jacket.

"Keep me informed about the burglary!" *'Crewcut Charlie'* shouted after him.

Wallace didn't reply. He was already running towards the squad car. News had travelled fast. A small crowd had gathered along the towpath. Wallace jumped out and barged his way through. Bystanders gawked at the constable putting up blue and white police tape.

"It's over there, sir." The constable pointed to something caught up against some debris near the bank. "The pathologist is on her way."

"Get those ghouls out of here." He pointed to the crowd. "I want this entire area cordoned off. Close the towpath and the hill leading down from Blackfriars. No pedestrians or cyclists until further notice."

Wallace turned at the sound of screeching tyres. A car skidded to a halt behind the police car. Looking slightly dishevelled Jo Barnett, the police pathologist, stepped out of the car. Blowing out her cheeks, she wriggled into a protective white suit and shoe covers and shuffled towards Wallace. The CSIs were already hovering around the body.

"Rough night?" Wallace asked with a hint of sarcasm.

"Med school reunion," she replied. "Not that it's any of your business." She knelt down beside the body, studying it with her usual intensity. "The body hasn't been in the water that long judging by its appearance. It could have been put in the water during the night. There are some injuries to the head, but that's not unusual. Bodies get buffeted around in rivers… could be post mortem injuries."

"Age?"

"Young, in her teens I would say."

She gestured to the young man behind her. "Okay, Tim. You can take your pictures now."

Tim moved around the body, taking photographs from every angle. He took a few close-ups of the face and head before standing aside for the CSIs to move in. Wallace gazed at the victim's clothes. Black skirt, white blouse under a dark jacket. The type of working clothes hundreds of girls wore in offices all over the country. Something nagged in the recesses of his mind, but he couldn't recall the memory.

"See you tomorrow," Jo Barnett said as a CSI zipped up the body bag. "I'll carry out the post mortem tomorrow afternoon. Try to get there on time."

Wallace glared after her, his face flushed with anger and embarrassment. What was it about this woman that drove him crazy? He was still smarting after their thwarted romantic dinner in their favourite restaurant on the river.

*

Three o'clock the following afternoon Wallace pushed through the strip plastic doors. The forensic pathologist was writing up notes on the gleaming stainless steel counter.

"Good afternoon, Chief Inspector," she said formally.

"What have you got for me, Dr Barnett?" he asked in an equally formal tone.

"Well, she didn't drown. She died of a massive overdose of drugs… heroin"

"What a waste," Wallace said. "Why do these kids get hung up on drugs?"

"There's no evidence to suggest she was taking drugs on a regular basis. It could be a single killer dose. I only found one needle mark." She turned over the victim's head. "Here, in the neck." She pointed to a small bruise surrounding a puncture mark. "Why inject that way when she could have injected into her arm? Injecting into the neck is much more difficult. She would need a mirror to see what she was doing. I'd guess it was administered by a third party. There are also pressure marks around her mouth. Someone must have had a hand over her mouth and stabbed into the vein in her neck at the same time. She was also nine weeks pregnant."

Like a long forgotten melody, something flitted to the forefront of Wallace's mind and slipped away again.

"And I found this." Jo held up a piece of striped material. "It was in her pocket. It's a tie, a school tie. It's not a local secondary school. I've never seen one like it in Shrewsbury. There are no name tags to identify her either."

"Jessica Parker!"

"I don't understand."

"Jessica Parker's murder was the last case I investigated when I was serving in Hampshire police. That was over nineteen years ago. The case was never solved. She was a sixth former. The killer had tightened her tie to make it look as if she had been strangled, but she had been injected with a massive dose of heroin. She was also pregnant. It's too much of a coincidence."

"There's no evidence of *recent* sexual activity."

"What do you mean by recent?"

"Within the past two weeks."

"DNA evidence will be difficult if the victim had been in school during the day. She would have come into contact with literally hundreds of pupils and staff. Apart from what she might have picked up going to and from school."

Jo sighed. "I'm sorry I can't give you any more, Chief Inspector," she said stiffly.

"Okay, cut the crap, Jo. I know I said the wrong thing over dinner the other night, but it wasn't intentional. I've got enough on my plate without you giving me the cold shoulder."

"Telling me women shouldn't be police pathologists wasn't intentional?"

"All I meant was that it can be pretty gruesome for a woman, that's all."

"I'm a Home Office pathologist. It's what I'm trained for; besides, you're not much of an example when it comes to strong stomachs."

Wallace held up his hands in defeat. "You're right and I apologise. Can we leave it at that? My place Friday night?"

"I suppose so," Jo replied grudgingly. "We'll know more when we get the forensic reports."

11

Wallace barged into the incident room. Detectives sat sprawled in front of computer screens or huddled over paperwork. Half empty coffee cups and sandwiches littered the desks.

"Get this place cleaned up," he barked. He glared at a detective with his feet on his desk talking into a mobile phone. "Baker, get round to the local schools and identify this." He handed him an evidence bag.

Baker took the bag and studied the contents. "No need, sir. It's part of a school uniform."

"I know that!" Wallace roared. "I want to know which one."

The buzz of conversation abruptly died until he disappeared into his office. Hurriedly, they cleared their desks of lunchtime debris and got to work. A tap on the glass door brought Wallace's head up from his desk. DS Butler stuck his head round the door.

"I've just come from the post mortem. It seems we have a murder investigation on our hands, Butler." Wallace outlined his discussion with Dr Barnett. "There was nothing on the body to identify the victim other than this."

Butler picked up the evidence bag and studied the black, red and cream striped tie. "I can't say I've seen this particular tie anywhere in Shrewsbury."

"I was going to say that I recognise it, sir," Baker interjected from the doorway. "I think it's from St Cadfael's. It's right out in the country, about ten miles from Shrewsbury."

"Never heard of it."

"It's a private school, sir. A mix of boarders and day pupils Very expensive. It opened about eight years ago."

Wallace nodded grudgingly. "Thank you, Baker. We'll get over there. In the meantime check out all the secondary schools in and around Shrewsbury, including the private ones. Sometimes sixth formers have different ties from the rest of the school."

The telephone jangled on his desk. "It's Payne," he mouthed at Butler. "Good afternoon, sir."

"What about the body found in the river near Blackfriars? Has it been identified?"

"Not yet," Wallace said through gritted teeth. "We're following up on the tie found in the victim's pocket."

"A tie! Is that all you have?"

"Not just any tie; a school tie. DC Baker thinks it's St Cadfael's. It's a private school. He's checking their website as we speak."

"Yes, I know the school. The victim was a schoolchild?"

"Not exactly, sir. Probably a sixth former, around

seventeen years old. If she's a local girl it shouldn't take long."

"Well, keep me up to speed, and Wallace, I'm still waiting for some progress on that robbery."

Pompous bastard, Wallace thought. One of these days he was going to punch '*Crewcut Charlie's*' lights out.

*

The wheels crunched on the gravel drive as Wallace swung round in an arc in front of the sand-coloured, stone building that housed St Cadfael's School. Pupils hurried between the main house and a modern annexe about a hundred yards away.

"Wasted journey," he said, watching a clutch of pupils walking towards the house dressed in red blazers, tartan skirts and tartan ties.

"That's the lower school," Butler said. "Sixth formers wear black blazers and greys for boys; black blazers for girls and black skirts. They usually have different ties."

Wallace gazed around the imposing reception hall. Wood-panelled walls were hung with tapestries, paintings of rural scenes and official school photographs. A single portrait, presumably of the original owner of the house, had pride of place. His heels clipped on the highly polished parquet floor as he approached a middle-aged woman staring into a computer screen.

"Detective Chief Inspector Wallace," he introduced himself, "and this is Detective Sergeant Butler. We'd like to speak with the head teacher."

"I'm afraid Dr Booth is busy at the moment in a governors' meeting, but he'll be free in about half an hour if you would like to wait."

"Please tell Dr Booth that I would like to see him *now*. It's a matter of urgency."

The receptionist glared balefully at Wallace, resentment sparking in her eyes. Reluctantly, she picked up the telephone and dialled an extension. *They're as bad as doctors' receptionists*, Wallace thought.

"I'm sorry to disturb you, Dr Booth, but there's a Chief Inspector Wallace here to see you. He says it's urgent." Wallace could hear the hesitation on the other end of the line.

"Very well, Mrs James."

"Please take a seat," Mrs James said. She gestured to a couple of leather armchairs set against the wall. "Dr Booth will be down shortly." A few minutes later a tall, elegant, silver-haired man with an Errol Flynn moustache came down the grand staircase.

"Dr Edward Booth. What can I do for you, Chief Inspector?" he asked, extending his hand.

Wallace gestured towards the evidence bag Butler was holding. "Do you recognise this tie?"

"It looks like one of ours; a sixth form tie. Where did you find it?"

"We're investigating the murder of a young girl. This tie was in her pocket."

"But I don't understand."

"We think she could be one of your pupils. Are any of them absent today?"

"It's possible one of the day pupils is off sick." He turned to the receptionist. "Mrs James?"

"There's a bug going around. Two of our girls are off sick with it, but their parents rang in this morning."

"I'd like their names and addresses, please."

"We don't usually give out that kind of information," Dr Booth replied. "It's confidential, but as you're the police I can make an exception."

Wallace's lips compressed into a tight smile, but he managed to keep his temper under control.

"Thank you. Now I'd like to see your list of pupils. Boarders and day pupils. How many do you have here?"

"We have two hundred and ten boarders and three hundred and thirty day pupils from the surrounding area."

"Where do the boarders come from?"

"They usually board if they live over fifteen miles away. We have a considerable number whose parents are overseas or living in another part of the country."

"I'd like you to check that they are all here."

"But that's ridiculous! Why wouldn't they be here?"

"Only two day pupils are absent so the victim could be one of your boarders."

The receptionist's hands flew up to her mouth, her eyes wide with shock. Quickly, she composed herself and tapped into her computer.

"All the girls were here for breakfast and first lesson, except Megan Pryce-Jones and Ella Chapman. They're in sick bay. I'll speak to Matron."

Quickly, she dialled an extension and listened

intently. "Megan is still there, but Ella Chapman left sick bay around three o' clock yesterday," she said, replacing the receiver.

"She should have double French now." Mrs James dialled again. After a hurried conversation, she looked at Dr Booth. A frightened look flashed across her face.

"She didn't turn up for French. Nobody has seen her since yesterday afternoon."

"Is she a day pupil?" Wallace asked.

"A boarder. Her parents are in Qatar. Her father has been working there for the past two years. Ella usually flies out there for the holidays."

"Do you have a recent photograph?"

"This is the most recent," Dr Booth said, pointing to a photograph hanging above the chairs. "It was taken at the start of term. That's Ella."

A pretty girl smiled shyly at the camera, surrounded by her peers. Wallace sighed. There was no doubt in his mind that Ella Chapman was the girl dragged out of the river.

"We'll contact her parents," Wallace said. "I'll need someone to identify the body." He turned to Dr Booth. "We have to be certain the victim is Ella before we contact them. We'll arrange it for this afternoon."

Booth visibly paled. "I'm sure that Matron would be the best person to ask. She's a qualified nurse."

"Under the circumstance we would like you to be present. Once the victim's identity has been confirmed we can contact her parents. We'll be in touch."

Later that afternoon, Nurse Fenwick and Dr Booth

formally identified Ella Chapman's body. Booth's face was devoid of emotion, like a wax mask. When the mortuary attendant pulled back the sheet they both nodded.

"It's her," Nurse Fenwick said in a shaky voice. "I was used to this when I worked in hospital, but Ella… poor child, so young."

Outside in the corridor, Wallace asked, "Did Ella have a boyfriend?"

"A boyfriend? I doubt it," Matron replied tearfully. "She was a rather quiet girl. She got on well with the others in her dormitory, but she spent a lot of time in the common room reading. Lower sixth had planned a party for her birthday at the end of the month. She would have been eighteen."

12

Wallace stormed into the temporary incident room in the annexe of St Cadfael's School. It resembled a trashed classroom. Half-opened boxes, stacks of files spilling over tables, more haphazardly piled on the floor. Booting-up computers whirred, monitors rapidly changing until the police logo filled the screens. Wires snaked along the floor, held down with black adhesive tape.

"I want everyone assembled for a briefing in ten minutes," he growled.

Wallace glared at the detectives lounging wearily in chairs, sitting on the edges of desks. He took a deep breath and held himself in check. They had been working flat out on the Ella Chapman case. Warily, they eyed his florid face and the bulging veins in his neck. He wasn't in a good mood after his session with Chief Superintendent Payne.

"Probably didn't get his leg over with Dr Barnett," Baker murmured. A smutty giggle rippled through the room. "He needs a good woman, that's his trouble."

"What was that, Baker?" Wallace asked, glaring in his direction.

"Trouble with my leg," he replied, rubbing his calf.

"Right, what have we got so far?"

"We've questioned all the staff," Butler stated. "They all said the same thing. She was bright, studious, top of her class... wanted to apply for Oxford to study English Literature."

"What about her teacher?"

"Richard Ellis; a pleasant chap, middle-aged married man with three children. He had great hopes for Ella... wanted her to apply to his old alma mater. She was also studying French and history. The other two, both women, said pretty much the same as Ellis. Miss Bunting is a real dish, not much older than the kids."

"What about Dr Booth?"

"A bit up himself; a cold fish. Still, I suppose he had had time to deal with it, especially as he identified the body."

Wallace put his hands together, linking his fingers in a praying position. He turned to the evidence board behind him and stared at the photographs of Ella Chapman. She looked so vulnerable, even in death. Blood rushed to his head as anger surged through him, sour bile filling his throat.

"She was pregnant, so either it was one of the sixth form boys or she met someone outside the school," Baker offered. "A lot of kids hang out in Shrewsbury town over the weekend. Maybe she wasn't as innocent as she looked. You should see some of the girls out of uniform... jailbait."

"There was no evidence of recent sexual intercourse so no DNA in that area. She was in school for God's sake, sitting next to kids in class, in the gym, sharing books, flicking their hair around. Trying to log everything would be a nightmare. We need something substantial to go on."

"We checked all the GP surgeries and clinics. She hadn't gone to any of them. The last time she saw a doctor was in Year Ten when she caught a bug. Apparently, it went through the school like a dose of salts," Butler stated. "She hadn't confided in the school matron, either."

"We're still waiting for the results of the forensic tests." Wallace continued. "Dr Barnett found something under the victim's right index finger, but couldn't say what it was with any certainty."

"Right, Butler, I want you to question all the sixth form kids. Take DC Hembrow with you." He nodded towards a tall, auburn-haired woman. "Boys respond better to a female."

"You can say that again," Baker snorted.

Wallace glared at him contemptuously. He didn't like Baker, but he was good at the grunt work. Baker crossed his arms and looked at his feet.

*

Edward Booth stared through the window of his plush office, taking in the immaculate grounds, the bustle of the Rugby XV clattering towards the pitch beyond the annexe. This was his dream; a school of his own.

He had spent almost nine years building its reputation and credibility. The walls of his study were lined with photographs of sporting successes and certificates, evidence of his diligence. He felt physically sick when he thought of how much he had done to achieve it. Now all that was at risk, because of Ella Chapman's murder.

A sharp rap on the door brought him back to reality. The governors were arriving looking for explanations. They would blame him.

"Good morning, Robert. Coffee?"

Squadron Leader Robert Pryce-Jones's face was stony. His daughter Megan had been a day pupil until the sixth form. When his wife had obtained a teaching post in Bangor, she had moved into married quarters on RAF Valley in Anglesey where he was stationed. Megan didn't want to leave her friends in Shrewsbury and had pleaded with them to let her board. A shiver ran down his spine when he thought about Ella.

The other governors turned up in quick succession. Canon Grayling; Janine Cook, a local hotelier; James Tillotson, property developer and benefactor; Anthony Brakeman, magistrate; Amanda Squires, a high-powered barrister based in Birmingham and Giles Ponting. Pompous Member of Parliament and ex-chairman of the Police and Crime Commission. The latter two were his main worry. There were four more to come, but they never questioned anything, just went with the flow.

"As you are aware, one of our boarders, Ella Chapman, was found dead… murdered," Booth began. "Obviously, this has been an enormous shock for everybody. I… "

Booth hesitated. "Matron and I identified her body. Since then her parents have flown over from Qatar. I need not tell you how devastated they are." The governors nodded. "The investigations will have a grave impact on the school. Already, three girls have been taken out of boarding."

"You could have a fourth, Booth… Megan," Squadron Leader Pryce-Jones declared. "What I want to know is why Ella was in Shrewsbury in the early hours of the morning? I thought they weren't allowed into town after six o'clock."

"That is correct, but obviously Ella flouted the rules." The telephone on Booth's desk shrilled. "Show them in. Ah, Chief Inspector Wallace," he said. "May I introduce you to the governors of St Cadfael's."

"What's the meaning of this, Booth?" Ponting snarled.

"I asked Dr Booth to assemble the governing body," Wallace said mildly. "We need to question everybody with any connection to the school. It won't take long."

"You can't think any of us were involved, surely?" Canon Grayling asked. "What will my parishioners think if it gets out we are suspects?"

"We're just eliminating people from our enquiries. It's normal police procedure."

"I'll have you know that I am a Member of Parliament," Giles Ponting declared. He stood up and glared at Wallace.

"I'm well aware of your position," Wallace said. "Please sit down, Mr Ponting."

"How dare you! I'll speak to the Chief Constable about this!"

"That's your prerogative," Wallace replied with a hint of sarcasm.

Ponting dropped into his chair, his face beetroot red. Amanda Squires opened her mouth to say something and changed her mind. Wallace had seen her a number of times in the crown court. She was an excellent barrister with a formidable reputation, justifiably deserved. He would have to handle her carefully.

"Oh, do be quiet, Giles," Squires said irritably. "You're not helping matters. Get on with it, Chief Inspector."

Half an hour later, Wallace and Butler slowly crunched down the drive through the elaborate wrought-iron gates and onto the main road.

"That was a waste of time, sir. What were you hoping to achieve?"

"Any one of them could be involved. Everybody is a suspect at the moment."

What he would give to drag that pompous ass Giles Ponting down to the station and give him a good grilling. No such luck. He had been in the House of Commons voting on a bill with a three line whip. After that he got legless in the Commons bar and had to stay with his chum, a fellow MP. He was too plastered to go back to his flat in Islington.

"I'm famished," Butler declared. "I need sustenance. What about a spot of lunch in the Boathouse?"

Settled under a sun umbrella over-looking the river, Wallace watched the swans and mallards scrabbling for bits of bread being thrown from the far bank. After Ella had been found people stayed away, but the river was busy today. Pleasure boats and rowers from the Boat Club were taking advantage of the warm weather. Wallace usually stayed away from town during the summer months. It was always crowded with tourists, especially during the Flower Show. Still, it was good for local business.

Butler grimaced as he sipped his non-alcoholic shandy. A pint of beer would have been great.

"This stuff is disgusting!" he complained.

"I don't think there's much mileage in the governing body," Wallace said. "We seem to have reached a dead end."

"We still have that lead from one of the residents of the flats overlooking Blackfriars," Butler said.

Both men leaned back, soaking up the sun. It was the only bit of sunbathing they were likely to get until the case was solved.

13

Wallace pressed the buzzer on the half-glass door and waited. A muffled voice asked, "Who is it?"

"Chief Inspector Wallace and DS Butler. I understand you may have some information for us?"

"Come up."

Wallace pushed the door open when he heard the click and gazed at the flights of stairs spiralling upwards.

"No lift," Butler groaned as he plodded up the stairs. "My legs are killing me."

"Too much booze and pies and not enough exercise," Wallace chuckled, taking the stairs two at a time.

They stopped outside a white-painted door. It opened before they could knock.

"Come in." A short woman in her late fifties held the door open for them and showed them into a large, airy living room. "Would you like some tea?"

"If it's no trouble," Butler said eagerly.

Wallace shook his head. "Mrs Archer, you called the police station regarding the Ella Chapman murder."

"Yes, poor girl, so young."

Wallace waited patiently for her to continue. She looked frightened. Her eyes continually flitted to the windows. She clenched and unclenched her hands as she spoke.

"It was the night before they found… the body. I was in bed, but I couldn't sleep. It was around two forty-five. A noise woke me up. Sound carries from the river, you know." Wallace nodded. "Anyway, I heard a scream. At first I thought it was an owl, then I heard it again, more muffled the second time. My bedroom overlooks Blackfriars, but the river is mostly hidden by the buildings down below. I'll show you."

She showed them into a chintzy bedroom. Wallace smiled inwardly when he saw the profusion of fluffy toys on her bed.

"My grandchildren," she said sheepishly. "They give them to me to keep me company. No pets here, you see."

Wallace could just make out the river through the trees beyond the buildings below.

"I watched for over five minutes, but I couldn't see anything. It was raining quite heavily that night and very dark on the river. It's not the first time I've heard screams. Kids larking about usually. This was different. I was so concerned I rang the police to report what I had heard."

"You rang the police? Did they send anyone out?" Butler asked.

"No, apparently they've had a lot of complaints about strange noises, especially before they built the flats down there. It used to be rough ground. Youngsters used to go there getting up to mischief. I don't think they believed me. They behaved as though I was a dotty old woman."

Wallace was seething with anger, his lips compressed into a straight line. Struggling to appear calm, he said, "Thank you, Mrs Archer. You've been most helpful. We may be in touch again."

Wallace stormed down the stairs, his face dangerously red. Butler struggled to keep up.

"When I get hold of the prat who took Mrs Archer's call I'll... I'll string him up!" Wallace spluttered.

*

Wallace barged into his office, slammed the door and threw himself into his chair. He had to calm down before he had a stroke. He thumped the desk in exasperation, took a deep breath and picked up the phone.

"I want to know who was on duty on the night of Ella Chapman's murder."

Butler retreated to the outer office to the safety of his desk. The other detectives looked enquiringly at him, but he shook his head. Somebody was going to get a rollicking before the day was out. He sighed. If only the call had been followed up, Ella Chapman would still be alive.

Suddenly, Wallace stormed into the incident room, eyes blazing with anger, and headed downstairs.

"Who was on duty the night of Ella Chapman's murder?" he growled.

"I was, sir," Sergeant Griffiths" replied. "I received a call from the operator."

"Why didn't you send an officer out to speak to her?"

"I didn't think it was necessary. Mrs Archer has reported noises before which led to nothing." Wallace nodded towards an interview room.

"In there! What the hell were you thinking of, Griffiths? Your action, or should I say lack of action, may have cost the victim her life."

"We were understaffed that night. Jenkins and Priestley were down with that stomach bug that was doing the rounds. I didn't feel too clever myself. I had to prioritise. I had a patrol car over in Meole Brace checking out the retail park, another in town. Besides, it was a rough night. It was bucketing down," the sergeant complained.

"So, you didn't send anyone out, because it was bloody raining!" Wallace roared.

"We get a lot of complaints about strange noises," Griffiths said lamely. "We haven't got the manpower to deal with all of them."

He knew the sergeant was right, but that was no excuse for him assuming that Mrs Archer was a serial complainer.

"I want the time the call came in." Griffiths shuffled to his feet and looked at the floor. Wallace followed the duty sergeant to the front desk and waited while he stared at his computer.

"Ah, here it is. Two fifty-nine – that's when the drunk was brought in and taken to the custody suite.

It fitted with the time Mrs Archer had given Wallace. At last he had something concrete to go on. Ella Chapman must have been alive when her killer took her to the river. She must have been murdered around two forty-five. Was it possible that she knew her killer and was meeting him on the towpath? The governing body and the staff had been ruled out. They had rock-solid alibis. He had the approximate time of Ella's death and a motive, her pregnancy, but nothing more to go on.

He climbed the stairs back to his office two at a time and motioned to Butler to come in.

"They found black fabric under the victim's nails. It could be from a coat or a suit; maybe a school blazer. But there was something else; a minute fragment of red silk."

"Every pupil in the sixth form wears a black jacket and red-striped tie," Butler remarked.

"Silk?"

"I suppose it could be silk. These kids' parents are not short of a few bob."

"We'll have to interview all the sixth form again, especially Megan Pryce-Jones."

Megan Pryce-Jones sat fidgeting next to her father. Squadron Leader Pryce-Jones and his wife glared at Wallace.

"Megan has already been interviewed. Why is she being subjected to this again? Do you realise how difficult it is to get time off in our jobs?"

Wallace ignored him and gave his full attention to Megan. He had some sympathy for them. They seemed decent enough people, but he also had a job to do.

"I appreciate that, Squadron Leader, but I have to find Ella's killer."

Pryce-Jones leaned back and folded his arms. His heart lurched. What if it had been Megan? He nodded. Wallace smiled reassuringly at Megan.

"Were you a friend of Ella's?"

"Yes, we were best friends. We did everything together."

"So you would know her other friends, where she hung out?"

"She didn't have any other friends, just me. We liked the same things, books, music."

"When did you last see Ella?" Wallace asked.

"She was in sick bay the day before… before… " Her voice faltered; tears sprang into her eyes. "She said she felt better and was going back to our room. We shared a room. I was in sick bay all night and most of the following day so I didn't know she was missing."

"Did she have a boyfriend?"

"Not really, but Mark Hilliard fancied her like anything. She met him in town a couple of times then she suddenly stopped seeing him. He was furious, said she had someone else. He sulked around for weeks; wouldn't even speak to her."

"And did she have a new boyfriend?"

"She may have. I'm not sure, but it wasn't a boy from school."

"Why do you say that?"

"It would be all over the school, that's why. Besides. I was her best friend. I knew she was up to something.

She became very secretive and started going off on her own into town. When I offered to go with her she made excuses. She usually told me everything, but she wouldn't admit she was seeing anybody."

"Thank you, Megan. We may want to talk to you again."

Wallace concluded the interview and showed them out.

"Let's bring Mark Hilliard in for an informal talk."

*

Wallace stared across the table at the thick-set lad. Captain of the school rugby team. For an eighteen year old, Mark Hilliard was powerfully built and very good-looking. Did jealousy, the old green-eyed monster, rear its ugly head? Did Mark Hilliard kill Ella, because she dumped him for someone else? According to his house master, he was in the common room all evening. As an upper sixth form prefect and head boy, he had his own room. He could easily have sneaked out after lights out. Most girls would be flattered to have his attention so why did Ella reject him?

Mark stared down at his hands in his lap, trying to keep his nerves under control. His mouth was so dry he could barely swallow. Tension, like a tight elastic band, over his eyes and temples, made him feel sick. Tears pricked his eyes. Roughly, he brushed them away and tried to focus on what the detective was asking him.

Wallace leaned back and watched the boy. Hardly a

boy he thought, a man physically strong enough to haul Ella into the river. Butler came into the room and sat beside him. Wallace switched on the tape and stated the time and date.

"You understand that this is an informal interview You are not a suspect at this time. I just want to ask you a few questions about your relationship with Ella Chapman. How well did you know her?"

"I started in St Cadfael's a year before her so it must be about six years."

"Were you friends?"

"Not straight away. We both belonged to the book club and drama group. We used to go into town, but Megan always came with us. We only had a few dates on our own, then she started seeing someone else."

"Were you jealous of Ella?"

"Yes... a little bit I suppose."

"Did you kill her, because she rejected you?" Wallace pushed a photograph of Ella across the table. Mark stared at it, his lips trembling with emotion. "If you couldn't have her yourself, you didn't want anyone else to have her. Isn't that right, Mark?"

"Yes, but I didn't kill her. How could I hurt her? I loved her. We were all right until this other guy turned up."

"Do you know who he is? Is he a sixth former?"

"I don't know. I tried to force it out of her, but she wouldn't say. She wouldn't tell Megan either. She was crazy about him."

"You tried to force it out of her? How?"

"It was the evening before… before they found her. I caught her sneaking out of school one night when I was going to the pub," he explained sheepishly. "I was pushing through the fence near the sports' hall. All the sixth formers do it when they want to sneak into the village after lights out for a quick pint. I'm eighteen! I wasn't breaking the law!"

"Go on."

"We walked as far as the pub together. I asked her where she was going, but she wouldn't say, so I grabbed her. She pushed me away and ran off towards the main road."

"What time was that?"

"About ten forty-five. The pub stays open until midnight."

"Did you follow her?"

"No, the guys from the local rugby team were waiting outside. Whoever she was meeting must have had a car. She wouldn't get a bus from there that time of night."

"What time did you get back to school?"

"It must have been around twelve-thirty. Gavin Merriweather and I walked back together. He has the room next to mine. Some of the other lads came to my room and we watched a video," he said guiltily. "It was Saturday night. They stayed there until gone four, just having a laugh. You won't tell Dr Booth, will you? He's very strict about that kind of thing."

Wallace smiled grimly. He wasn't interested in kids playing truant or watching dirty videos. He wanted to find out about Ella's mysterious boyfriend.

It had been scorching hot all day. Shrewsbury was jam-packed with locals and tourists taking advantage of the good weather. Wallace bounded up the steps of the Armoury, his eyes searching through the glass doors for Jo Barnett. A waitress showed him to his reserved table near the window. Both sides of the restaurant were already full, with people of all ages. Candles flickered on the tables giving the room a warm, cosy glow. One entire wall, from floor to ceiling, was covered in shelves full of books.

He gazed through the window at the gleaming river. It looked so calm and inviting. Late evening sun sparkled on the water. Swans glided with one leg tucked behind them, occasionally dipping their heads into the water for a titbit. Mallards paddled towards the reeds in convoy, leaving a trail of ruffled water in their wake. A pleasure cruiser glided past Victoria Quay packed with tourists enjoying a dinner cruise. Mark Hilliard's story had checked out. He felt rather sorry for the lad. His parents were divorced and living on separate continents. His mother in New York, his banker father in Hong Kong. What was it with these people? Mark may be built like a man, but he had the emotions of a teenager. Perhaps that was why he clung to Ella. Suddenly, he saw Jo's familiar figure walking past the window and felt a rush of pleasure.

Jo watched Wallace as he studied the wine list. The dark, brooding looks, startling green eyes, the way his hair curled around his ears. She blushed when Wallace caught her looking at him. Settled with a glass of cabernet sauvignon, Wallace arched his back to release the tension in his shoulders. He started to say something when Jo leaned over and put a finger to his lips.

"Not tonight, Ben. Forget about the case. Let's just enjoy ourselves. We both deserve an evening without talking about work."

Grinning broadly, he took her hand. "We could make a very long night of it. Perhaps a nice, gentle massage to de-stress the body?"

Jo smiled roguishly and patted his leg under the table. "Any more of that and we won't finish dinner!"

Wallace knew that he was becoming more than just fond of Jo. With a jolt he realised he had fallen in love, something he had vowed he would never do again.

14

Emily stretched her aching legs under the desk. She had been standing all day in front of a class of unruly kids. All she wanted was to go home and put up her feet. It was her last day today. She put her hand on her swollen stomach and felt the familiar movement. The baby was due in four weeks.

Breathing an enormous sigh of relief, she walked to the car where Paul was waiting for her. His face registered concern as she waddled towards him. They had argued constantly about her continuing work so late into the pregnancy, but she was determined. He jumped out of the driving seat and helped her into the car.

On the drive home he constantly glanced at her, concern written all over his face. How lucky she had been. Paul had helped her when her affair with David Johnson had ended so dramatically all those years ago. She had been a fool to think he would ever have left his wife. He had manipulated her infatuation. It was all about sex for him.

Settled with a cup of tea in front of the television,

Emily felt the strains of the day ease away. She was only half listening to the news reader. Conflict in the Middle East, warnings about the collapse of the Euro, a murder in Shropshire. Suddenly, she sat bolt upright, concentrating on the screen.

"Paul, come in here, there's something on the news!"

"What is it?"

"A schoolgirl has been murdered near Shrewsbury. They haven't found her killer yet."

"That's miles away. There's nothing to worry about," Paul said reassuringly.

Emily looked up at him. "She was only seventeen, strangled with her school tie. My God, it's just like Jessica Parker."

"That was years ago. Besides, it was in Plymouth, hundreds of miles away."

"They never found her killer, Paul. They suspected Eddie Haines, but it was never proved."

"It's probably a copycat, some weirdo who trawls the internet. People post comments about murders all the time and sickos pick up on them."

"I think we should contact the police."

"What would you tell them, except that you found Jessica's body?"

"What if Jessica's killer is still out there?"

"Fine, I'll ring the police if it will make you feel better."

The call from Paul Bryant was patched upstairs to the incident room. Initially, Wallace had irritably brushed it off; just another crank wasting police time. It was only when the name Jessica Parker was mentioned that he sat up and took notice. Why would anybody be contacting the police about a crime committed nineteen years ago?

*

Butler glanced at Hembrow as she crunched up the drive of a large, detached house set way back from the road in Acton Burnell. *Whoever owned it wasn't short of a few bob*, he thought, noting the elaborate frontage and gardens. Moments after he rang the bell a figure loomed behind the double glass doors. The tall, well-built man who opened the door ushered them in with a pleasant smile.

Everything about the interior registered good taste, from the solid oak staircase to the heavy drapes and baby grand piano. A heavily pregnant woman sat on the sofa, her hands folded on her stomach.

"Thank you for coming, Detective Sergeant. I'm due to have my baby any time now so I'm sticking close to home."

"I understand you have some information about the murdered girl."

"Not exactly, but I think it could be linked to another murder some years ago in Plymouth – a girl named Jessica Parker. I was the teacher who found her in the school toilets. My maiden name was Lambert. I confess I'm worried that it may be the same killer. It's too much of a coincidence."

"We have thought of that, but it could be a copycat murder. The killer may have got the idea from an internet website."

"That's just what I thought," Paul said. "I'm sure it's nothing for you to worry about."

"Your husband is right, Mrs Bryant. It's highly unlikely that it's the same person, but we'll keep an open mind about it. If you have any further concerns please contact us straight away."

"I've got an uneasy feeling about this," Butler said as they drove off. "What if she's right and we have a serial killer on our hands. Acton Burnell is only eight miles from Shrewsbury. We don't know whether Jessica Parker's killer knew Mrs Bryant. Assuming it's the same killer. If he's local he may recognise her if she comes into town to shop?"

"Why do you assume it's a man?"

"Ella was pregnant just like Jessica."

15

Mark Hilliard squatted on the towpath below Blackfriars staring into the glistening water. He hadn't been able to sleep or concentrate on his school work since Ella's death. He stared at the pink-covered diary he was holding. A shiver of fear ran through him. He had seen enough television police dramas to know he could be accused of perverting the course of justice if the police knew he had it. He had stolen it from Ella's room the day before she was murdered, thinking she may have written something about her new boyfriend in it. Until now he hadn't had the courage to read it.

He flicked through the pages. The usual stuff. A dental appointment, lunch in town with Megan, regular rehearsals of the school play. Little hearts doodled at the top of some pages under the date. *Perhaps that's when she was meeting her boyfriend?* he thought. The last two weeks in July and all of August were scored through for holidays in Qatar with her parents. There was nothing else apart from an optician's appointment in late September.

He studied the doodling closely and his heart contracted. A tiny 'P' next to the letter 'E'. He riffled through the pages again, noting the number of times the initial appeared. At least once a week and always on the same day. Ella had been seeing this other chap for months, since before Christmas. Angrily, he crushed the diary in his hands, tears surging down his face. All this time she was deceiving him. He hated her!

Clenching his fists, he vowed to find the boy Ella had been seeing. Was he someone he knew? One of the rugby club set or a boy from her class. Whoever it was, he wanted to smash his face in! Slipping the diary into the inside pocket of his blazer, he climbed the hill towards town and went into St Mary's Church. He needed to think, somewhere quiet where he wouldn't be disturbed.

Inside it was cool and dark, just a single tourist gazing up at the stained-glass windows. Sinking into a pew, he dropped his head in his hands and tried to pray, but the words wouldn't come. All he could think of was how much he loved Ella, how much he hated her. Not even tears would come, just a rage building inside him and a burning need for revenge.

On his way back to St Cadfael's he made a mental list of all the boys he knew whose names began with 'P'. Paul Lister, Patrick Naish and Pennar Rees-Morgan in upper sixth. Two others in the rugby club – Phillip Hunt and Pierce Middleton.

Megan must know something about the boy Ella was seeing. He glanced at his wristwatch. He arrived just in time to see her walking from the annexe. Roughly, he pulled her to one side and showed her the diary.

"No! No!" She pushed him away, a frightened look on her face.

"You're lying!"

"I told the police everything, now get lost!"

"I'll get lost when you tell me what you know!"

"Okay, I knew she was seeing someone she called 'P'. That's it! I don't know who he was."

"Why didn't you tell the police?"

"Because we made a pact we would always keep each other's secrets. We swore on the Bible."

"Was it Paul Lister or Pennar Rees-Morgan?"

"I don't think it was anybody from school."

"What about the rugby club?"

Megan screamed at him, "I don't know!"

Suddenly, a loud voice boomed from the path leading to the main building.

"What's going on here?" Dr Booth walked briskly towards them.

"Nothing, sir, just a bit of larking around, that's all," Mark answered. Megan nodded her head and grinned sheepishly.

"Get to your classes at once and please refrain from shouting in that unseemly manner."

Dr Booth strode away without a backward glance, his back ramrod straight. If there was one thing he despised, it was coarse behaviour, particularly in his pupils.

*

Wallace faced Mark Hilliard across the table in the makeshift interview room. The boy looked scared stiff, but at least he had had the balls to contact him about the diary.

"You stole Ella's diary. That's an offence in itself."

"I'm sorry. I know I shouldn't have done it. I just wanted to find out who Ella was seeing, that's all."

Wallace stared hard at the boy for a few seconds just to let him sweat. "It's just as well you brought it in, otherwise you *would* be in serious trouble for withholding important information. Taking into account you came in of your own volition, I'm inclined to ignore this. However, if I find you've withheld anything else I'll bang you up in the cells. Is that clear?"

"Yes, sir, very clear, sir."

"Now, get back to school and leave the investigation to the grown-ups."

"That's a bit of luck," Butler commented. "At least it gives us a bit more to go on."

Wallace tapped his lips thoughtfully. Everybody in St Cadfael's had strong alibis. Still, there was something about Mick Gilchrist, the school gardener, that bothered him. Mark had mentioned the way he looked at the girls, especially when they were in the swimming pool.

Gilchrist claimed that he and his partner had gone to see a film at the local Showcase Cinema. Afterwards they went back into town, had a few too many drinks then went straight home. She had verified his story. The neighbours had seen him half carrying her into the house, so drunk she could barely stand. Was it possible that he left the house to meet Ella when his girlfriend was in a drunken stupor? It certainly didn't tie up with the appointments mentioned in her diary. Butler followed him into the incident room.

"Baker, bring up anything you can on Michael Gilchrist, the gardener at St Cadfael's."

"We've already checked him out, sir."

"Check again," Wallace said impatiently.

Baker scrolled down the list on the screen and shook his head. "Nothing, sir, at least nothing that matches his age and profile." Wallace cursed under his breath. "Hang on, there are quite a few Gilchrist's with two names – Anthony Michael, David Michael, John Michael." He continued scrolling down. "Michael Derek, Peter Michael Gilchrist… he's the right age."

"See what you can dig up on him."

Baker pulled up the file. "Peter Michael Gilchrist accused of having sex with an underage girl in 2003. He was teaching in a comprehensive school in Devon. There's two 'drunk and disorderly', but nothing since 2007."

"Why the hell wasn't this found before?!" Wallace bellowed. "Didn't it occur to anyone that he could have more than one name? I want him thoroughly investigated."

"Do you think he's the 'P' in Ella's diary?" Butler asked, following him into his office.

"It's possible. I was the officer in charge of the Jessica Parker murder in Plymouth in 2003. Gilchrist worked miles away, but the similarities are worrying."

16

Gilchrist sat staring straight ahead, a slight smirk on his handsome, intelligent face. In his early forties, he had an air of arrogance about him. Wallace switched on the tape and leaned back in his chair.

"Mr Gilchrist, can you tell me where you were on the night Ella Chapman was murdered?"

"I told your officers where I was when they first questioned me."

"Well, perhaps you would like to tell me again."

"I went to the cinema with Jill, my partner, then had some drinks in town. After we got home I let the dog out in the garden for a bit then went to bed."

"Did you go back out during the night?"

"No, I went flat out… too much booze."

"When did you stop teaching?" Gilchrist's face flushed red, his eyes flashed with anger.

"We know you were accused of sexual assault when you were working in Devon."

"It was lies, all of it. She was a little slapper. How was

I to know she was only fifteen? " Suddenly, Gilchrist slumped forward, his face in his hands. "The way she dressed, the heavy make-up, she looked more like twenty-five."

"Tell me what happened."

"I was in a disco in Plymouth. She was there with some of her friends. None of them looked like schoolgirls. She was giving me the eye so I bought her a drink. We danced a few times then we took a walk along the Hoe. She couldn't keep her hands off me, so I did what any man would do when he's offered it on a plate. Afterwards I drove her home." Gilchrist swallowed hard. "The next morning the police arrived at my home and arrested me. Charged me with sexual assault. I was set up. She wasn't a pupil at my school, but she had friends there. One girl in particular I had kept behind for detention a few times. They were out to get me."

"Didn't this come out at the trial?"

"Her pals backed her up, lied about everything. I was cleared, but mud sticks. I didn't have a leg to stand on. She was sixteen the following week, but that didn't make any difference. Once parents got hold of it I was finished. My contract wasn't renewed. I lost my job, my reputation, everything."

"Why did you come to Shrewsbury, to St Cadfael's?"

"I came when my new partner moved here with her firm. I didn't work for a long time. I suppose I went off the rails a bit, getting drunk. Teaching was my life, but there was no hope of me ever getting another job in education. Eventually, I pulled myself together and took an Open College course, a diploma in horticulture and landscape gardening."

"Didn't the school run a check on you?"

"I had only been in my teaching post a few weeks before I was charged. I should have had another check, but Dr Booth accepted that as being recent enough and I got the job."

"Some of the girls complained about you leering at them."

"I was just being pleasant, that's all. They're great kids. It was that boy Hilliard. He was obsessed with Ella. He couldn't stand her even talking to another boy. His mates called him '*cow eyes*', because he was always watching her."

Wallace leaned back and rubbed his chin thoughtfully. A plausible story, but was Gilchrist a crass fool or a clever killer?

"All right, Mr Gilchrist, you're free to leave, but we may want to speak to you again."

"Are you going to tell Dr Booth about this?" Gilchrist asked.

"I think it would be better if you make a clean breast of it yourself."

It was unlikely that 'P' was one of the sixth form. They were all in the pub with Mark except Patrick Naish. He was playing in a table tennis match in the sports' hall all evening then went straight to bed. The lad who shared his room verified it. That left the two rugby players Mark Hilliard had mentioned.

LET THE BELL RING

*

Mick Gilchrist fidgeted with his woolly hat and looked down at his feet. Dr Booth glanced up briefly then returned to the pile of papers on his desk. His secretary waited patiently while he signed the last letter and discreetly withdrew. Booth stared at the gardener, a look of pure contempt on his face. He didn't like workmen coming into his room in muddy wellingtons.

"Well, what is it?" Gilchrist shuffled uncomfortably, a flush rising in his face. "Come on, man. I haven't got all day."

"I've been advised by DCI Wallace to inform you about something I didn't tell you when I took the job."

"What do you mean? Your references were in order, weren't they?"

"Yes, but an incident occurred just after my CRB check, as it was called at that time. You didn't think another one was necessary."

Booth shrugged and leaned back in his chair. "I wasn't aware of that."

"I was a teacher before I became a gardener." Booth's eyes shot up, a startled look on his face. "I lost my job, because I was accused of sexual assault. She was underage. It was lies. Trumped up, because I gave her friend detention. I was cleared of the charges, but my career was in shreds."

"My God!" Booth charged from behind his desk, his face contorted with fury. "How dare you? How dare you put me in this position. Get out, now! You're dismissed. I can't have someone like you working in my school."

With trembling hands, he pressed a button on the intercom. He had heard rumours about Gilchrist eyeing up the girls, but rumours like that were always rife in schools. What the hell was he going to tell the governors?

17

Bull-necked and florid-faced, Phillip Hunt sported a shaven head which made him look thuggish rather than fashionable. When he spoke, his accent was coarse and uneducated. In his late twenties, he didn't seem the type to be consorting with the likes of Mark Hilliard and his friends, but he was a good rugby player, an asset to the team. He glared at Wallace, his face contorted with anger.

"What are you trying to say? You can't pin anything on me."

"We just want to ask you some questions about your whereabouts on the night Ella Chapman was murdered."

"I was in the pub with some of the team and a few lads from St Cadfael's."

"What time did you leave the pub?"

Eyeing Wallace defiantly, Hunt clenched his fists on top of the table. "I've already told you, I was in the pub all night, until closing."

"Ella Chapman was murdered in the early hours of the morning. Where did you go after you left the pub?"

"Okay, I stayed in the pub all night. Jim, the landlord, was away playing darts so I stayed over with his missus."

"Why?"

"Why do you think?" Hunt sneered. "It's not the first time. She likes a bit of company when her old man goes off for days on end."

DS Butler had already interviewed the landlord's wife. Hunt's story checked out.

Middleton was a non-starter. He had called in for a drink on the way to meet his future in-laws in Ludlow and spent the night there.

Wallace had come up against a dead end again. Impatiently, he drummed his fingers on his desk going over the evidence they had accumulated. Nothing except the screams heard in the apartments above Blackfriars and the minute fragments of fabric found under the victim's fingernails. It had to be one of the sixth formers. Had Mark Hilliard managed to pull the wool over his eyes, he wondered? Was he clever enough to divert attention from himself by bringing in the diary? Wearily, he rubbed his eyes and wriggled his shoulders to ease his aching muscles. A tight band of tension enveloped his skull. He hadn't slept properly since the investigation started.

Donning a pair of rubber gloves, he picked up the evidence bag containing Ella's diary. Painstakingly, he turned the pages, poring over every entry. She had been nine weeks pregnant when she was murdered, so she must have conceived in early May. She had met 'P' every week since her diary began in January, but there were three meetings recorded for late June. Why? Was it to tell her lover that she was pregnant? On the entry for July the tenth, he noticed an abbreviation written under the entwined initials - *ab/wel/gym/12* - with an asterisk. He rubbed his chin thoughtfully. Was it some kind of gym session? Wallace stuck his head round the door.

"Butler!"

Butler came in slurping coffee from a plastic cup, a doughnut in the other hand. Slumping into a chair, he swallowed the last mouthful and gave a loud burp.

"Sorry, sir, but I was starving. It went down in a bit of a rush."

"Never mind about that, what do you make of this?" He pointed to the entry in the diary.

"Some kind of body-building class perhaps, or a slimming class?" Butler ventured.

"Check whether Ella Chapman belonged to any fitness groups."

Ella didn't belong to any fitness groups or any other kind of group. Occasionally, she and Megan Pryce-Jones went to the municipal swimming pool in the Quarry with some girls Ella had known before she started boarding at St Cadfael's. She was a bit of a loner and spent hours reading. If she was murdered down by the river, her killer must have driven her into town. As Mark Hilliard had pointed out, she couldn't get a bus at that time of night.

It was possible to walk the towpath right round the town. After murdering her, the killer could have run up the hill from Blackfriars towards St Mary's Place.

Alternatively, he could have walked towards English Bridge or crossed over to the Boathouse. There were a number of possibilities. In the early hours of the morning, there wouldn't have been many people about along the towpath. The killer could have parked his car in town and just driven away without creating any suspicion.

Wallace sent Baker and Hembrow along to the Quarry to find out if Ella had gone there recently. The young lifeguard knew her three girlfriends, because they swam there regularly. They all lived in Kingsland, an affluent part of the town."

It seemed that Ella hadn't been swimming for a couple of months before she died. She told them she was too busy getting things sorted out to go to Qatar, but promised to meet them before she left. They had only seen her once since then, at the railway station. She wouldn't say where she was going, but she definitely caught the train to Birmingham. Was she meeting her killer? Wallace strode briskly into the outer office.

"Did the girls say what time she left Shrewsbury?"

"About ten o'clock in the morning, sir."

"*Ab/wel/gym/12*," Wallace muttered, shaking his head. "I don't get it."

"What was that, sir?" Hembrow asked.

"It's something that was written in Ella's diary – *ab/wel/gym/12*."

"It sounds as though she was going to a gym at twelve o'clock. Hang on. Wellington is on the Birmingham line. She could have been going to a gym in Wellington!"

"Hembrow, I could kiss you!" Wallace exclaimed.

Hembrow blushed crimson, the colour clashing with her auburn hair. Heart racing, she hurried back to her computer, flopped into her chair, and took a deep breath. She wouldn't mind kissing him too, but it wouldn't be a cute thank you kiss. She thought about her dream the night before and felt the heat rising through her body. Wallace glanced over and smiled. Lowering her eyes, she pretended to be engrossed in her work, but her thoughts were elsewhere.

Wallace perched on the edge of a table in the incident room, arms folded across his chest. As usual, DS Baker lounged back in his chair, feet on his desk. Sighing, he lowered them to the floor when Wallace glared across at him. DC Hembrow sat upright and alert, hanging on Wallace's every word.

"CCTV footage revealed that Ella got off the train in Wellington. She went to the sports' centre, but not to the pool. Instead she went to the fitness centre. The instructor confirmed he had seen her talking to a woman, probably in her fifties, it was hard to tell. The older woman was wearing a baggy tracksuit and a floppy cloth hat. She appeared to be extremely angry. Ella started to walk away, but the older woman grabbed her arm. Ella started to cry, shook her off, and stormed out. The receptionist confirmed that she had run out of the building in tears."

"Why go all the way to Wellington to visit a sports' centre?" Baker mused.

"We checked with St Cadfael's. Dr Booth says she went back to school later that same day," Butler said. "The school was breaking up the following week. Ella was due to fly out to Qatar to join her parents a few days later. She told him she was going to finish her packing and have an early night."

"Sir," Hembrow intervened, "it all fits with the entry in her diary, *ab/wel/gym/12.*"

"We've already established that," Wallace replied impatiently.

"Yes, sir, but what about the *ab*?"

"She was going to a gym, – probably wanted to develop a six pack." Baker guffawed.

"It could be an abbreviation for abortion," Hembrow said hesitantly.

"That's stretching it a bit," Butler remarked.

"Is it?" Wallace looked thoughtful. "We were so wrapped up in sports' centres and gyms we couldn't see the obvious. It's possible Ella had a meeting with the woman in Wellington to arrange an abortion. That way she could join her parents in Qatar without them finding out. Well done, ! You'll make detective sergeant yet!"

Hembrow beamed. Baker glowered. *Cow,* he thought, *always sucking up to the guv.*

18

Dr Booth glared at his indolent wife. She had lapsed into one of her depressions again. When she wasn't watching rubbish on television, she was engrossed in a book. Still, it kept her quiet. She had recently chopped her hair into a jagged crop. That way she didn't have to worry about brushing it. Devoid of make-up, her skin looked pasty. Thank God they had bought the farm.

As usual, she was biting her fingernails and she was very overweight. She could hardly get off the sofa. He had loved her once, but all he felt now was revulsion. How could such a beautiful, vibrant woman turn into the dirty, foul-mouthed bitch she had become? Fortunately, his grace and favour house was almost a quarter of a mile away at the far end of the grounds, so he could keep her away from the school until parents arrived.

It would cost him a fortune to make Isobel look presentable before parents started bringing boarders back to school. At least he could rely on her to put on a show for the governors and parents. Still, she was his wife and it was his duty to care for her. Besides, being a married man was important to his career. The governors wouldn't contemplate a single man as head teacher. It wouldn't be good for the image of a boarding school. He hadn't slogged his guts out for years for it to be taken away now.

"Get off your backside and take a shower. I'll run you into Shrewsbury to get your hair done, if there's anything they can do. You can have a manicure at the same time."

He darted upstairs and opened her wardrobe. Her clothes hung in no particular order. Most of them were grubby or stained. He picked out a few expensive suits and a couple of cocktail dresses. He would drop them off at the dry cleaners when he drove her to town. Luckily, she hardly ever wore smart shoes, preferring to slop around in slippers or trainers. Her shoes and classy topcoats were the only pristine things in her closet. Tomorrow, he wanted to see some semblance of the old Isobel, even if he had to sew her into a corset.

Satisfied she was safely engaged for a couple of hours at the hairdressers, he headed for Marks & Spencer's. He picked out some of the support tights she wore, bought some face packs and hand cream in the Body Shop, then headed to the library. He settled in a quiet corner to catch up on the day's news while he waited for Isobel. He had an hour to kill before picking her up, then he would take her to the Red Lion for lunch. She needed a trial run to get her ready for greeting parents tomorrow. Casually, he flicked through the paper. For a moment his heart seemed to stop. Staring from the page was a smiling photograph of Ella Chapman. He felt the bile of anxiety rising in his throat as he read the headline.

Murdered Schoolgirl Affects Intake at St Cadfael's

Squadron Leader Pryce-Jones had told the press he was removing Megan from the school! He had to find somewhere he could speak to him without being overheard. Hurriedly, he made his way down Pride Hill and headed for the Quarry. There were a lot of locals sunbathing in the park and tourists ambling along the riverside. He sat on a bench pretending to feed the ducks until his call was answered.

"What the hell are you thinking of Pryce-Jones, taking Megan out of school without even telling me? You're a governor for God's sake. Do you know how disastrous this will be for St Cadfael's?"

"I'm well aware of that, but Megan's safety is paramount. Besides, she can't bear to return knowing that Ella won't be there. We've only just made the decision. I don't know how the papers got hold of it."

"You need to rethink your decision, Squadron Leader. You'll have to justify your decision to the Board of Governors. This is most unprofessional."

"Don't lecture me, Booth. Any questions the governors ask will be directed at you!" Pryce-Jones snarled, slamming down the receiver.

Damage limitation, Booth thought. He had to find a way to placate the governors otherwise his job would be at stake. They were gearing up for the new intake in September. Another boarder besides Megan Pryce-Jones would not be returning. He had kept that quiet from the governors. It would be forgotten by the time the next meeting took place, but this! This could prove to be disastrous for him. Quickly, he made his way to the Red Lion and waited for Isobel.

He glanced up when she entered the foyer. The untidy crop had been transformed into a sleek, fashionable style that framed her face. The new colour suited her; a rich mahogany brown. The flash of grey that ran from her forehead was lighter than the rest, giving her a more modern look. False fingernails, painted a subtle shade of pink, hid the ragged nails underneath. Booth sighed; at least she looked presentable.

He watched Isobel carefully as she delicately forked food into her mouth. The facial massage had smoothed the puffiness from under her eyes. The expert application of make-up made them look wider and more alert. For a moment he could see the woman he had married all those years ago.

"You look lovely, more like your old self," he said kindly.

Isobel didn't respond. She gazed into the near distance, wrapped in her own thoughts. She hated him. Hated his affectation, his pompous self-satisfied manner, his arrogance. Still, she loved him. She should have divorced him years ago instead of giving up her career for him. Now it was too late. She was trapped. On Monday she would simper to parents, smile at their pampered offspring, cosy up to the governors. But she would still hate him!

They drove back to St Cadfael's in complete silence, each of them wrapped in their own thoughts.

"What the hell is going on?" Booth cried as he turned into the drive.

A crowd of reporters rushed at the car, aiming their cameras. A young man in a scruffy anorak leaned over the bonnet to take a picture. Booth edged the car forward and shot up the drive, reporters running behind.

"Get out of the car, Isobel. Go up to my study and stay there until I fetch you."

Taking a deep breath to calm his nerves, he turned to the reporters and smiled.

"Can you tell us how many pupils have left the school besides Megan Pryce-Jones, Dr Booth?" asked a bearded journalist.

"According to the newspapers, you know that already," he replied calmly. "Apart from that one pupil I have absolutely nothing to add. Some boarders have already arrived. I don't want them upset or reminded about Ella Chapman's death. Now, I believe you are trespassing on private property. Kindly leave immediately or I will have to call the police."

Booth smiled like a Hollywood film star pandering to the cameras, then walked briskly inside.

"Not now, Mrs James," he said curtly, indicating the telephone receiver in her hand. "I'm taking my wife home. All the excitement has been too much for her."

He bounded up the stairs to his study. Isobel was staring through the open window, a sardonic smile on her lips. Roughly, he pulled her away and pushed her down onto the sofa.

"We'll go home as soon as they've gone. You are *not*

to speak to the press under *any* circumstances. Is that clear?"

Indifferently, Isobel kicked off her shoes and put her feet up. She took a bag of fudge out of her pocket and popped a piece into her mouth. With a look of pure loathing Booth grabbed the bag and threw it into the waste bin. Even with the new hairdo and fancy nails she was still a guzzling slob.

19

JULY

Isobel stroked the Staffordshire Bull Terriers nuzzled against her legs. They were her only comfort during the long evenings she spent alone in the converted farmhouse. As usual, Edward was working. A head teachers' conference in London. She sighed, anticipating the long hours stretching out in front of her. Mentally, she shook herself and went into the kitchen to prepare a snack. She never cooked herself proper meals when Edward was away.

She caught sight of herself in the hall mirror as she walked back into the living room with a large burger and chips. Her reflection never failed to disturb her. Double chins, wobbling backside. She glanced at the photograph on the piano. The slim, vivacious girl in her wedding gown smiled up at the handsome man gazing down at her. They had been happy then and so much in love. When had she become so miserable and ugly? Her thoughts wandered to their early years together.

She had been working as a naval architect in Scotland; a tough profession for a woman. Ambitious, energetic, with a host of admirers, her dream was to design ocean-going liners. She met Edward while she was on a walking holiday with her friend Diana. He was staying in the same hotel on Lake Windermere. He looked so lonely they invited him to join them on their walks. Three days into the holiday Diana fell, breaking her leg in two places. They decided to cut the vacation short and return to Aberdeen. When Isobel started packing to go home Diana suggested she stay on.

"Edward is still here. I've already mentioned it to him. He loves the idea."

"Oh great, now you're palming me off on a stranger."

"You know he's a teacher, that he's originally from Hereford and he's single. Please stay. If you don't I'll feel guilty about spoiling your holiday."

Reluctantly, she had agreed. For the next few days she spent most of her time with Edward. They had a lot in common besides walking. A love of good literature, fine dining, theatre and art. By the end of the first week they had become lovers. Isobel was head over heels in love with him by the time she returned home.

He telephoned her every day and flew up to Scotland at every opportunity. About a year later they returned to the hotel on Lake Windermere. Over dinner Isobel broached the subject of their future.

"I have a lot of things to sort out before I can think

of settling down," Edward said. "I don't want to stay a deputy head. There's a headship coming up in a few months and I'm tipped to get the job. You're up here in Scotland, hundreds of miles away."

"I can always move down south."

"But that would affect your career. As you said, there aren't many openings for women in naval architecture."

"What are you saying? You don't want me to move nearer to you?"

"No, I'm saying I don't want to ruin your prospects."

Isobel flounced off, leaving Edward at the mercy of stares from adjoining tables.

At breakfast the following morning she studiously ignored him and sat alone. Giggles rippled through the dining room from guests who had witnessed their little spat. What she needed was a long walk along the lake. She needed to think.

The water shimmered in the clear morning air. In the distance a steamer left a wake of white as it chugged up the lake. She decided to take one of the long walks from Windermere to Ambleside, starting out from Bowness Bay.

She walked north along the lake shore up to Orrest Head before dropping down again to cross Trout Beck. With any luck she could avoid Edward Booth for the rest of the week. Once she was back in Aberdeen she could bury herself in her work and forget about him.

Suddenly, the snap of twigs underfoot caught her attention. She whirled around to find Edward standing on the path about thirty feet away.

"Fancy seeing you here." He smiled sheepishly, like a small boy caught stealing conkers. "I missed you at breakfast."

"Well, I didn't miss *you*," she retorted angrily. "You can go to the farthest end of the planet for all I care."

"Come on, Isobel. We can work this out. I love you," he called as she shot off down the track. She stopped short and turned back again. He had never told her he loved her before. "I really mean it. I love you and I want us to be together."

Tentatively, he moved closer, took her in his arms and kissed her with such passion it left her breathless. It was no use. Hot waves of desire coursed through her until her body went limp in his arms. She knew she was lost. By the end of the summer she discovered she was pregnant.

They were married in a register office in Edinburgh during October half-term. Reluctantly, her parents flew up for the wedding. They didn't take to Edward, especially her father, who had dreamed of walking her down the aisle in their local church. After the children were born everything was forgotten. They tolerated Edward for the sake of their beautiful grandchildren. They had been happy then and so much in love. Now she was always miserable and lonely, but at least she had Edward.

Stifling a sob, she bolted down the beef burger. Edward's success was paramount. Nothing else mattered. When he took over St Cadfael's all his dreams were realised. Now he despised her as much as she despised him. Yet, she still loved him. She would always love him.

On speech day she would circulate amongst the governors, smile at parents, pat the heads of their pampered children. Edward would reign over his domain with a supercilious smile on his face. Isobel struggled off the sofa and waddled back into the kitchen to get a bar of chocolate and a large gin and tonic.

20

JULY

Hidden from sight, Mark Hilliard surveyed the school from beyond the poplar trees. He was supposed to be at his grandmother's home in Hereford for the holidays. If he was spotted here it would arouse suspicions, and that was the last thing he wanted. He fingered the small book in his pocket. The police might think he's a daft, lovesick kid, but he knew more than they did. He knew the identity of Ella's lover. He was going to expose her killer. Cautiously, he moved deeper into the shrubbery until he was at the side of the building. The caretaker and cleaners would be in there now, polishing, scrubbing floors and desks while pupils were away. He wanted to get inside and wait in the library. When her murderer came in, he would be ready for him.

He darted across the lawn into the main entrance. Holding his breath, he waited until he heard the cleaners singing a pop song somewhere upstairs. The women's voices mingled with the deep bass of the caretaker, Paddy, a good-looking Irishman who ogled the girls in their gym shorts. Some of the girls gave him the eye as he leaned on his brush, his eyes following them down the corridor. He had warned him about leering at Ella, the dirty old man! After ten minutes he heard footsteps outside. Suddenly, the door opened. Ella's killer was standing in front of him, smiling.

"What are you doing in here? The school is closed for cleaning."

"I've come after you, you bastard!"

"What the hell are you talking about?"

"You killed Ella, didn't you?"

"Don't be stupid! I didn't touch her."

"Oh, but you did touch her, didn't you, lots of times when you were having sex. She was having your baby, wasn't she?"

"I've had enough of this. You're mad! Go on, get out before I throw you out!"

Mark pulled out a sheaf of paper from his inside pocket and brandished it in the man's face.

"It's all here, all the times you met. All the times you had sex with her. You pig! You're old enough to be her father!"

"Give it to me!"

"This is a copy of pages from Ella's diary. Do you think I'd be stupid enough to let you get hold of it?"

Mark had found two diaries in Ella's room. The student diary he gave the detective and a small one bound in pink faux fur. He had seen her writing in it when he went to borrow a book. She had hastily stuffed it inside the hole in her broken guitar. He had thrown the police off the trail by giving them just enough information to interest them. The other one he had hidden in his locker at the gym.

He swallowed, remembering the disgusting things he had read. Things he didn't think Ella was capable of doing. Suddenly, he dived at the man with such force he fell backwards onto the parquet floor, toppling over a standard lamp. In a flash he was back on his feet. The first punch sent Mark reeling.

Snarling with rage, his attacker pushed him to the ground. Savagely, he kicked him in the groin. Protecting his head with his arms, Mark tried to crawl towards the door. Strong arms dragged him back. He grabbed at the man's legs, briefly sending him off balance. Eyes swollen, blood oozing from his lips, he staggered to his feet. Desperately, he lashed out, landing a blow to the man's ribs. He was about to charge at him again when he heard a woman's voice outside. A hand clamped over his mouth, stifling his cry for help. A violent shove sent him reeling forward. He never had a chance. The vicious blow to the back of his head killed him instantly.

His killer leaned against the wall, gasping for breath. He felt no remorse, only relief that the boy was no longer a threat to him. When he had composed himself, he calmly wiped away the blood and replaced the bronze statuette on the shelf. He had to get rid of the body before the women came in. The boy was heavier than he looked.

He dragged the body across the room, unlocked a store cupboard, and pushed it inside. Swiftly, he re-locked the door and pocketed the key. He would have to dispose of the body later after the cleaners had left.

Briefly, he surveyed the room, ensuring there were no signs of a struggle. Taking a deep breath, he stepped back into the corridor where one of the women was gathering up her bucket and mop.

"Oh, it's you," she said. "I thought I heard a noise in there."

"I accidentally knocked over a chair. I've finished here. If anyone wants me I'll be in the sports' hall."

Ambling casually to the main entrance, he breathed a sigh of relief. He walked over to the annexe whistling a jaunty tune. By the time anyone realised that Mark Hilliard was missing he would have moved the body.

21

Wallace gazed around the familiar living room. It was elegantly furnished, almost like a show home, but somehow it was still cosy and inviting. He felt comfortable sprawled out on the leather sofa. Late evening sun poured through the open French doors bathing the room in golden light.

There was a new painting on the wall of a snowy lakeside scene in Switzerland. Painted from one of the many photographs Jo had taken when they were in the Bernese Oberland. He could get used to this, then realised with a start that he already had. He would rather be here, with all its feminine touches, than in his own sparsely-furnished home. Except for his daughter, he hadn't felt so at ease with a woman for years.

The clattering of pots and pans came from the kitchen. Jo was singing along to a Lionel Ritchie song as she cooked dinner. He missed that too; the feeling of another heartbeat in the house. How much more comforting than the ping of the microwave signalling his pre-cooked dinner was ready.

"Pour me a glass of wine," Jo called. "I'll sip it while I'm cooking."

Wallace took the wine into the kitchen and placed it on the worktop. He put his arms around her and kissed the back of her neck. Closing her eyes, she squirmed deliciously, resting her head against his chest. Sauce bubbling on the stove brought her reluctantly back to her senses. She stirred it and lowered the heat.

"Now get out of here, Ben, before I ruin dinner!"

"I will when you answer my question." He pulled her round to face him. "Dr Barnett, will you marry me?"

Jo's mouth dropped open. The spoon fell into the sauce, splashing its contents over the rim of the saucepan. For a moment she thought she had misunderstood. Flustered, she smoothed her apron, picked up the glass of wine and took a huge swig.

"Steady on, you'll be tipsy, then you'll ruin dinner." Wallace laughed. His face clouded over when she didn't respond. "Well, do you want to marry me or not?"

"It's just so unexpected. It hadn't even occurred to me that you wanted to get married. Besides, I vowed I would never get too involved with a policeman again."

Jo felt confused and angry. Why had he thrown this at her now, when they were getting on so well? Her marriage to Jonathan, a detective superintendent in the Met, had been disastrous. Long hours working in the hospital, combined with him never being at home, had turned the marriage sour after just five years. She had built a life for herself alone. That's the way she liked it. But she knew she was lying to herself. She wanted more. She wanted a man to come home to; someone to share her evenings when she felt trapped by the darkness outside.

Both of them had failed marriages behind them. Could they make it work this time? Ben's luminous green eyes held hers and she was lost. Desire clenched the pit of her stomach. Standing on tiptoe, she kissed him with a passion that gave him the answer he wanted. He picked her up and carried her to the sofa, oblivious to dinner boiling over on the stove. *To hell with it*, Jo thought. *We'll eat out.*

It was raining heavily by the time they left the restaurant and drove back to Jo's house. As the car crunched up the gravel drive Wallace's mobile jangled.

"Sir, a body has been found on the railway track about eight miles from Shrewsbury."

Wallace turned off the engine to concentrate on the information.

"I'm on my way. That was Butler," he said, turning to Jo. "Apparently, a body has been found on the Birmingham line."

"Wait for it." Seconds later, Jo's phone rang. She listened intently and snapped it shut.

"We're going to the same place. I'll get my car."

Wallace was about to suggest that she travel with him. Jo read his thoughts and shook her head. "Let's keep it professional."

*

Wallace parked his car as close to the scene as possible. A train sat silently on the line about a hundred yards away. Harsh light from an arc lamp illuminated the area around the body. The CSIs had just arrived and were gearing up in protective clothing. A young constable sat holding his head in his hands on the slight gravel embankment.

"What's the matter with him?" Wallace growled.

"He was the first called to the scene sir; vomited his guts up. The body's over here. It's pretty gruesome," the uniformed sergeant replied.

The mangled lower half of the body lay sprawled on the track; the other half at the side of the line. It had been severed by the train's metal wheels. Wallace's stomach churned, but he managed to control the urge to retch. Jo, who had arrived shortly after him, handed him some protective shoe covers. Gingerly, he stepped closer to the corpse, Butler behind him. The face was turned slightly towards the track. Blood had congealed around the swollen eyes; eyes that registered terror even in death. A large diagonal gash stretched across the forehead, but there was no mistaking that face – Mark Hilliard!

"Dear God!" Butler said, moving to his side. "It's that young lad from St Cadfael's."

"I've seen a few suicides on railway lines in my time," the sergeant said. "Personally, I'd rather shoot myself."

The police photographer took shots of the lower torso on the track, the upper part of the body, close-ups of the face and the back of the head.

"The train must have hit him full on."

"Cover it up. It's quite likely it's suicide," Wallace barked, "but we won't know until a post mortem is carried out. Question the driver and the train manager. This part of the line will have to be closed and the train will have to remain where it is until the CSIs have done their job. British Transport Police will contact the rail authorities. They'll sort out transport for passengers. We'll have the commuter rush in a few hours. Passengers will have to be bussed along this section."

"You know who it is?" Jo asked.

"Yes, I interviewed him about the Ella Chapman murder."

Wallace shrugged. Mark had been in a pretty bad state emotionally. Suicide could have been the cause of death, but the boy didn't seem the type. He *was* upset, but he was also thinking rationally enough to steal Ella's diary and search it for evidence of her affair. His gut instinct told him that there was more to this than a lovesick boy killing himself.

"All right, you can remove the body now," Jo said. "I'll do the post mortem tomorrow morning. Eight-thirty sharp."

*

Wallace cringed as he pushed through the plastic doors into the mortuary. Even after all the murders he had investigated, he had never conquered his aversion to the smells and instruments. Just the sight of the stainless steel sinks and the drain in the floor was enough to unsettle him. He couldn't imagine how Jo had the stomach for it, or why she enjoyed her work so much.

A mortuary attendant busied himself disinfecting the tiled floor. His stomach lurched as dregs of swirling blood disappeared down the drain. Jo waved him over to the stainless steel worktop where she was writing up her notes. He skirted round the still form covered with a green sheet. In his mind's eye he could see Mark Hilliard's face contorted in death.

"Hi, how are you this morning?" Jo said. She pulled down her protective mask and smiled inwardly, knowing how the mortuary affected Wallace.

"What conclusions have you reached?" Wallace said, more sharply than he had intended.

"Well, it wasn't suicide, that's for certain. He was dead well before the train cut him in half. Somebody had given him a battering."

"So, you're saying someone put him there?"

"There's a large gash on the forehead and another on the back of the head consistent with a blow from a heavy object. Judging by the shape of the wound, it must have had sharp edges. The wounds indicate they were administered some hours previous to his encounter with the train."

"So, you think he may have been murdered?"

"Yes, unless he bashed his own head in. We'll have to wait for the toxicology reports. Other than that there's very little I can tell you. What is odd is that I found the same minute fragments of black stuff under his fingernails that we found on Ella Chapman. I can't be certain if it's fabric until forensics send the results. He was wearing his regulation black blazer when he was killed."

"Thanks Jo," Wallace said. "I'll let you know when we get the test results."

Driving back to the police station, he tried to control his impatience. Two murders and they didn't have a clue!

He stormed into the incident room, his face dark and brooding. A couple of detectives sniggering over a joke moved quickly aside. They had the ultimate respect for Wallace, but they didn't want to get in his way when he was in a mood. Hembrow smiled briefly and scuttled to her desk. Wallace motioned to Butler, who followed him into the office.

"I've just come back from the mortuary. Dr Barnett is certain that Mark Hilliard was dead before the train hit him."

"I would have put money on a suicide. He must have been thrown from the train."

"No, if the body had been thrown from the train it would have landed beside the track, not on it. Someone set it up to look like suicide. The killer must have dumped him on the rails knowing a train was due."

"Do you think there's a connection with Ella Chapman?"

"That's pretty obvious, I think," Wallace replied sarcastically. "There were also bits of black stuff under his nails similar to those found on Ella."

Wallace leaned back and rubbed his chin thoughtfully. Had they missed something when they interviewed the staff and pupils at St Cadfael's?

"Was the caretaker interviewed?"

"Yes, after locking up the labs and classrooms he

went back to his cottage. He and his wife went to play bingo in town, then met up with friends for a drink in the Armoury. Only the gym was left open, because the cleaners were still in there. The supervisor had a key to lock up when they finished. Apparently, they knocked off fairly early, because they were giving the school a spring clean while the kids are on holidays. The assistant caretaker had gone off on holiday to Majorca the week before. We checked that out."

Wallace sighed. It was almost two months since Ella Chapman's murder and they didn't have anything concrete to go on. Thoughtfully, he leaned back in his chair. Butler knew better than to interrupt his mood.

"There's a definite connection between the two victims. Mark was beside himself with jealousy. He admitted as much, but he didn't kill Ella."

"What if Mark confronted her killer with what he found in her diary? What if he worked out what *ab/wel/gym/12* meant?"

"It's possible. We'll have to wait and see if forensics come up with anything. They'll send it over straight away."

22

Wallace drove from Shrewsbury to Hereford with a heavy heart. Hembrow sat silently in the passenger seat. It was a part of her job that she hated. Wallace could have easily sent Butler to break the news to Mark's grandmother, but the nature of his death had affected him.

Wallace pulled up outside a neat, detached bungalow a few miles outside town. He didn't expect the frail, white-haired woman who answered the door. For some reason he expected her to be younger. His heart contracted. How could he tell her that her grandson had been murdered? He had no choice. Mark's parents were working abroad in different countries. His grandmother was his official guardian while they were out of the country.

"Mrs Rushton?"

"Yes," she smiled.

"I'm Chief Inspector Wallace and this is DC... ."

Fear leapt into her watery blue eyes. Her hand fluttered to her mouth. "What is it?"

"May we come in?"

"My God, it's Clare, isn't it? What's happened? Is she hurt? I only spoke to her yesterday."

"Please sit down Mrs Rushton. It's not your daughter… it's Mark, your grandson."

Relief flooded her face and quickly turned to anxiety. Wallace caught her under the arm as she stumbled to the sofa.

"What has he done?"

Wallace sat down heavily and swallowed hard. "He hasn't done anything, Mrs Rushton. I'm so sorry, but Mark has been in an accident; a fatal accident."

"Dead? He can't be. He telephoned me a few days ago to say he would be staying with a friend for a few days before he came home."

Wallace nodded at Hembrow. She disappeared towards the kitchen to make a pot of tea. Mrs Rushton was sitting perfectly still, tears running down her cheeks. Wallace handed her a tissue from the box on the coffee table.

"Is there anyone who can stay with you until your family arrive?"

"They know?"

Wallace nodded. "We know it's definitely Mark, but we'll need a formal identification. We can wait until your daughter and son-in-law get here. They're getting the first available flight."

"How did it happen? Was he in an accident?"

Wallace blew out his cheeks as he sought for the right words. "He was found on the railway line not far from Shrewsbury."

"How many times have I told him never to cross a railway line!" Mrs Rushton slumped back on the sofa, her face drained of colour. "Please, pass me my spray. It's on the coffee table." Wallace handed it to her and she sprayed some onto her tongue. "I have angina," she explained.

Wallace decided to spare her the grim details. Time enough for that when her daughter arrived.

"Could you ask my friend, Mrs Madeley, to come over. She lives in the bungalow at the end of the road – number eight."

Hembrow handed her a cup of tea and went to fetch her friend, thankful to get away for a few minutes.

"Can you give me your doctor's number? You've had a dreadful shock." Flipping open his mobile, he quickly dialled the number. "I'd like to speak to Dr Willis… "

"I'm afraid doctor is unable to take calls," the receptionist interrupted.

"I need him to make a home visit," Wallace said impatiently, "as quickly as possible."

"You'll have to ring back later."

"Just tell Dr Willis that Chief Inspector Wallace would like to speak to him," he said through gritted teeth.

"I'll see if he's available," the receptionist replied huffily.

"What can I do for you, Chief Inspector?"

"I'm with one of your patients; Mrs Edith Rushton. She's had a nasty turn and needs medical attention."

"I'm aware of Mrs Rushton's condition. It would be best if she is taken to A & E."

"Dr Willis, I've just informed Mrs Rushton that her grandson is dead. He was knocked down by a train. I can't give you all the details, except that it was a pretty horrific death. His body was cut in half. It may be a murder inquiry. I expect you to keep that to yourself. Is that clear?"

"Of course," Dr Willis answered in a shocked voice. "I knew the boy. He was my patient. I'll come over straight away."

23

JULY 2022

Relaxed in shorts and white linen shirt, Edward Booth looked younger without his usual pinstriped suit. He always took his annual leave in late July after the boarders had returned to their parents for the summer holidays. That was one of the perks of a private school. He wasn't restricted to the same holidays as the state sector.

Late evening, a blazing red sun hung low on the horizon, ready to set below the azure sea that glistened in the distance. That's what he loved about this time of year, being able to sit outside in the warmth until bedtime. He sipped his glass of chilled, white wine and closed his eyes.

Isobel's parents had left the villa between her and her sister Julia. He looked at Isobel, sprawled on a sun bed like a beached whale, and felt a rare moment of tenderness. The Mediterranean way of life suited her. She always looked better, more relaxed than she did at home. If only she would stop drinking, their lives would be so much better. So far he had managed to conceal from governors and parents that Isobel sometimes drank to excess.

He thought of the times he had packed her onto an aeroplane with Julia to dry out. Julia hated him. More than once she had tried to persuade Isobel to leave him and move abroad permanently. There was no way she would leave him, and *he* couldn't afford to be without a wife.

He sighed. Everything was working out perfectly. St Cadfael's had better numbers than he had expected. The few vacant places had filled quickly at the last minute. Isobel had performed with elegance and aplomb while greeting parents. She was the perfect hostess during afternoon tea and champagne reception. He had to hand it to her, her social skills were impeccable when she was cold sober. Even with all her faults, she was an asset to him at times.

Isobel eased off the sun bed and waddled to the pool. She jumped in with a loud splash, swam a few lengths and hauled herself back onto the patio. Relaxing at the side of the pool, she studied Edward behind her sunglasses. He was still a handsome man. She had seen the women in the village giving him the glad eye, but he didn't respond. He knew better than to upset her again. Over the years he had indulged in discreet liaisons, but if it happened again it would be the last. Next time she would ruin him once and for all.

Edward's mobile shrilled in his shirt pocket. It was his

deputy. Couldn't he manage for two weeks without him? Flicking the phone open, he listened intently. Suddenly, his face turned grey. Beads of sweat popped up on his forehead. Not again! Not again! He snapped the phone shut and leaned back squeezing his eyes together. This couldn't be happening!"

"What is it, Edward?" Isobel asked. "What's wrong?"

With an effort he murmured, "It's one of the pupils. Mark Hilliard, he's dead."

"How awful!"

"I have to go home. Chief Inspector Wallace wants to speak to me. They'll need me at the school."

"Poor boy - so young. How did he die?"

"I don't know. As soon as I find out anything I'll ring you. Julia will be back from Geneva early tomorrow morning, so you won't be alone."

Isobel settled back on the sun lounger, oblivious to the charms of her surroundings. Too drunk to go to bed, she slept on the lounger.

"Why do I do it?" she wailed at Julia the next morning. "I always feel so bloody awful afterwards. Edward was so distraught when he heard about the boy. He couldn't believe it was all happening again." She imagined him trying to charm the governors and laughed hysterically.

Julia stood in front of her, hands on hips, like an annoyed school mistress. She forced Isobel to swallow a few mouthfuls of toast and a cup of very strong coffee.

"You're going to end up on a slab if you don't stop drinking," she said angrily.

"Sorry, Jules, I just felt so... so bereft when Edward

left." She reached out and caught hold of her sister's hand. "I'm glad you're here. I don't know what I'd do without you."

"Why don't you leave the arrogant bastard? You should have done it years ago, the way he's treated you."

Isobel sighed. "I know you're right, but I love him. I always will. In his own way he loves me too."

"Love!" Julia scoffed. "Controls you more like. Can't you see that? Hasn't anything got through your thick skull? It's all about the money. It always was, wasn't it? It was part of the dream. He played his cards right until gramps died, knowing you would inherit a fortune."

Isobel winced. "Not now Jules. My head won't stand it."

She closed her eyes against the early morning glare. She could do with a hair of the dog, but she had no chance with Julia watching her every move. Edward was her life. That was something her sister would never understand.

*

Dr Booth sat upright in the chair opposite Wallace. Face ashen, dark shadows smudging his eyes. He looked as if he hadn't slept for days. *The boy's death has hit him hard*, Wallace though. Nevertheless, he was calm and composed.

"When did you last see Mark Hilliard, Dr Booth?"

"Not since he left the school to stay with his grandmother in Hereford."

"How did he seem to you?"

"Rather depressed and agitated. Ella's murder affected him deeply."

Wallace nodded. "He was run over by a train on the railway line a few miles from Shrewsbury."

"What on earth was he doing there? He was depressed, but suicide?"

"Why would you think that?"

"Why else would he be on a railway line? Obviously, he was still upset about Ella."

"He didn't kill himself. He was murdered."

Booth slumped back in the chair, his face drained of colour. If this got out he would be ruined; his career in shreds. A flicker of panic coursed through him. The governors would blame him just as they did over the Chapman girl.

"But you said he was run over by a train."

"He was, after he had been murdered. He was already dead when his killer threw his body onto the track. Just as well, he was sliced in half."

Booth blanched. Suddenly, he felt very sick and faint.

"Get Dr Booth a glass of water," he instructed the constable hovering near the door. Wallace glanced at the photographs on Booth's office wall. "Isn't that Mark?" He pointed to a group photograph of the Rugby XV.

"An exceptional player, schoolboy cap when he was fifteen."

"So, he was a strong lad, not a pushover for some bullying yob?"

Without waiting for a reply Wallace stood up to leave. Booth rose and put out his hand. Wallace took it reluctantly. He didn't like Booth. He was supercilious and arrogant, not the type of man one could warm to readily. But the school had excellent results academically and in sports. The staff and parents held him in high esteem. Only one or two of the governors had voiced criticisms during the Chapman murder, but in the end they had supported him in attacks from the press. Even Squadron Leader Pryce-Jones had relented and returned Megan to the school.

"Under the circumstances, it would be wiser if you didn't leave the country, Dr Booth. We may want to ask you some more questions about Mark."

"I'll always be needed here at the school. A ship is only as good as its captain." He smiled ingratiatingly as he opened the door for Wallace to leave.

Booth looked through the window, watching Wallace striding to his car. He was already rehearsing what he would say to the governors in the inevitable meeting. They would want answers and he would be ready for them.

24

AUGUST 2022

The baby was a month old when Emily and Paul went into town to buy some new clothes for her. She was already out-growing the little outfits bought by friends and family. They parked in St Mary's Place and walked through the side street past Watergate Mansions to Marks & Spencer. As they walked through the store she spotted a man at the entrance to the food hall. For a fleeting moment he turned, then quickly ran down the stairs. There was something vaguely familiar about him, but she couldn't quite put her finger on it. *I'm being paranoid again,* she chided herself. This business with the murdered girl had made her jittery.

The man had recognised Emily immediately. He strode down Pride Hill and cut across towards the square, his heart pounding. His brain whirled and for a brief second he felt disorientated. What the hell was she doing in Shrewsbury? Perhaps she was on holiday. That was it. So many people came to town from everywhere. He relaxed: she probably hadn't recognised him, but if she had something would have to be done about her.

He walked back onto Pride Hill and searched for Emily amongst the crowd of shoppers. There she was, coming out of Marks & Spencer with a man and baby in tow. Keeping at a discreet distance, he tracked their movements down Pride Hill to Nero's. When they went inside he breathed a sigh of relief and quickly disappeared into the throng of afternoon shoppers.

Emily couldn't get her mind off the man. She turned it over in her mind all the way back to Acton Burnell. They hadn't been living in Shropshire very long, certainly not long enough to make any acquaintances outside their own village. He probably reminded her of someone else. By the time they reached home she had resolved to push it out of her mind. It was another three weeks before they took another trip into Shrewsbury.

Taking advantage of the mid-August sunshine, she and Paul walked through the Quarry down to the river. Sun sparkled on the gently moving water. A family of ducks rushed to the shore, jostling for position when she threw bits of bread onto the surface. Some trees had already started to turn, lending splashes of gold and brown amongst the green. A couple of boys whizzed past on their bikes. Parents shouted after toddlers running ahead to be careful. On the green a young couple lay soaking up the sun. After a soggy few weeks they were having an unexpected Indian summer.

A man in a grey tracksuit jogged past them. He was

wearing sunglasses with a baseball cap pulled down over his eyes. He sloped up left towards the gate that led to the bottom of Pride Hill, where his car was parked in the council car park. He punched a fist into the palm of his hand. The bloody woman! She must be living locally or in a nearby village. He gambled on whether they would have parked near St Mary's again. Next time he was sure she would recognise him.

Quickly, he drove round the one-way system and into St Mary's Place. Fortunately, a few cars were leaving. He reversed into a space and waited. Just when he thought he had wasted his time, they appeared. They fussed for a few minutes, putting the pram in the boot and bags on the back seat.

"For God's sake, get in," he snarled under his breath.

Finally, the engine burst into life and they were heading for the exit. He followed them down Wyle Cop onto the main road to Bayston Hill. Where the hell were they going? He trailed them all the way to Acton Burnell. They turned into the driveway of a large house. Keeping his eyes straight ahead, he drove on. A thrill of panic surged through him. She was living in Shropshire. He could bump into her at any time. He had to do something before she recognised him.

25

LATE AUGUST 2022

Paul opened the front door and gently pushed Emily outside. Josie, one of the mothers from the mother and baby group, had invited her round for the evening. She didn't want to leave the baby, but she was running out of excuses. Reluctantly, she got in the car and rolled down the window.

"Are you sure you can manage? Call me if there's a problem."

"There won't be - now go and enjoy yourself. You need a break."

It was only two miles to Pitchford, but the drive took longer than anticipated. The windscreen wipers struggled to cope with the lashing rain, forcing her to crawl along at a snail's pace. Josie lived on the other side of the village down a remote country lane. Breathing a sigh of relief, Emily spotted the turn off and swung into the lane.

The four by four bounced over potholes as the lane narrowed into little more than a farm track. She peered through rivulets of water at a glimmer of yellow light ahead. That must be it. She pulled up outside large, wrought iron gates. Edging as close to the intercom as she could, she pressed the button. A man's disembodied voice answered. There was a slight buzz and the gates swung open.

"Hi, come on in," Josie called. "I was beginning to think you weren't coming; the weather is atrocious." Emily followed Josie into the spacious living room and sat down in front of an enormous log fire. Lulled by the warmth and ambience, she relaxed and started to enjoy herself. Time flew by and it was almost nine-thirty when she looked at her watch.

"It's time I went home," she said. "The weather seems to be getting worse."

Driving was even more hazardous on the way back. The four by four rocked slowly down the lane. With a sigh of relief Emily turned onto the main road. The rain had stopped, but a thick mist blocked her vision. She crawled along for half a mile. Suddenly, headlights loomed behind her. The vehicle crept closer and closer, tail-gating her for another quarter of a mile. Suddenly, it hit her bumper, sending her skewing towards the ditch. She couldn't apply the brakes, because it would crash into her with full force. It hung back when a car appeared, coming from the opposite direction.

Emily looked in her mirror. As the car passed, its headlights illuminated the vehicle behind her. She caught a brief glimpse of a figure in a woollen hat, face covered up. Seconds later the car shunted her again. She gripped the steering wheel, desperately trying to keep the four by four in a straight line. Suddenly, the mist cleared. She drove into Acton Burnell like a maniac and screeched into the drive. Heart racing, she tried to insert the door key, but her hands were trembling so much she had to ring the doorbell instead.

"What's wrong?" Paul asked when she pushed past him. "You look as if you've had a fright."

Emily swallowed hard. "Someone just tried to run me off the road. A car followed me from Pitchford. It shunted me half a dozen times. I'm lucky to be alive."

*

PC Jacobs searched Emily's face, trying to establish whether her anxiety was caused by nerves and a vivid imagination. She certainly didn't come across as someone who would scare easily.

"Are you absolutely sure the driver shunted you deliberately? It was a foggy night. Sometimes drivers get up too close and don't brake fast enough to prevent bumping into the car in front. That's how pile-ups happen."

"Of course I'm sure it was deliberate. I'm certain of it."

"Did you recognise him?"

"No, his face was covered up and he was wearing some kind of hat, like a beanie."

Jacobs wasn't convinced. She could have just freaked out when the car came too close to her. The driver could have misjudged the distance and bumped her accidentally. Emily cast him an angry glance.

"I didn't imagine it. He was so close I could see his eyes in my driving mirror when an on-coming vehicle passed. He deliberately tried to shunt me off the road. I'd like to speak to DCI Wallace about this."

"He doesn't deal with road traffic incidents, Mrs Bryant."

"I'm sure he'll be interested in what I have to say."

"Very well, I'll make sure he's aware of the situation."

*

Wallace rubbed his chin thoughtfully. He was vaguely disturbed by PC Jacobs's report of the incident involving Emily Bryant. What if there was a connection between Jessica Parker and Ella Chapman? The killer would want to get rid of anyone who could recognise him, assuming it was a man.

"I know what you're thinking," Emily said when he rang her, "and it scares me to death. I didn't get a clear look at the man I saw in Marks and Spencer, but I just had the feeling I've seen him before."

"Well, don't venture out of the house alone for now."

Wallace struggled to assimilate the information. The hat worried him. Gilchrist wore a woolly hat. Was the gardener playing with him? Trying to put him off the scent with his story? An uneasy feeling crept into the pit of his stomach. Was this going to be Jessica Parker all over again? Had he been wrong about Eddie Haines being her killer? He had been so convinced; now his convictions had evaporated.

"Butler, Gilchrist worries me. He could have been lying about being at home all night. The neighbours said his girlfriend was paralytic. Perhaps she was too drunk to know he'd left the house in the middle of the night."

"The house was searched thoroughly, boss. It was clean. Quite a bit of booze around, but definitely no drugs."

"I'm convinced he's holding something back. I want another search of the area and river below Blackfriars. We may have missed something."

26

AUGUST 2022

Gilchrist looked out over the river from the Boathouse pub. The riverboat, *Sabrina*, packed with tourists taking advantage of the good weather, sailed by, disturbing swans gliding gracefully on the water. Swallowing the last dregs of his beer, he made his way over the bridge and walked alongside the river. He was scared… very scared. The police had pulled him in again for questioning. He had bluffed his way through the interview, sticking to his original story. Without any evidence they couldn't hold him for long, but they suspected he was holding something back. The more he lied the deeper the pit he dug for himself. Dr Booth had sacked him on the spot when he found out about the sexual assault accusations. Worse than that, he had lied to DCI Wallace. A cold sweat beaded his forehead when he thought about it. It was only a matter of time before they picked him up again.

If I could only get my job back, he thought. It would show Wallace that Dr Booth had faith in him. He was a reasonable man who prided himself on being fair with pupils and staff. Booth knew how easy it was for kids to accuse teachers. It was worth a try. Snapping open his mobile, he dialled the number for St Cadfael's.

A couple of boarders who had returned from abroad early sniggered and raised their eyes when he mounted the steps into the reception area. They were used to seeing him in dungarees, a baseball cap or a beanie. Mrs James looked up, noting the dark suit, tie and highly polished shoes. Gilchrist looked the consummate professional that he had once been.

"I'm here to see Dr Booth," he explained.

"You can go up. He's waiting for you, but he only has a few minutes to spare this afternoon," she said sniffily.

The man who stood before Dr Booth was smart, clean-shaven and articulate. There was little semblance of the gardener who had bent his head, cap in hand, a few days ago.

"Well, what is it?" Booth looked at his watch impatiently. "I haven't got all day."

"I'd like my job back."

Dr Booth looked at him incredulously. "You must be completely unhinged if you think I would re-instate you."

"I've been a good worker and you had no right to sack me."

"No right! You lied to me about your credentials."

"I didn't lie. I just omitted some of my educational

qualifications, my degrees, teaching diploma. Hardly necessary for a school gardener. I was CRB checked and you accepted it. I admit I didn't tell you about the sexual assault allegations. I was exonerated, so there was nothing to tell, was there?"

"Exonerated or not, we can't have people like you working near girls. What would the governors think?"

"Exactly, they'll want to know why you supported my appointment without another CRB check."

"Are you trying to blackmail me into giving you your job back?" Booth spluttered.

"Let's just say I want you to exercise your sense of fair play and justice. After all, isn't that the image you convey?"

Booth tapped a pencil on the desk, trying to find an escape route. Gilchrist was right. The governors would start asking questions. He had enough on his plate with the ongoing police investigations without this. Another problem and he could be for the high jump.

"Yes, that is what I advocate, a high standard of behaviour and ethics. But you're still under a cloud, Gilchrist."

"We're all under a cloud Dr Booth. It would be in your own interests. You haven't yet sent me an official letter dismissing me. I've been a good worker and caused no trouble."

Booth pushed back his chair and walked to the window. For a few moments he stared out over the gardens, acutely aware of Gilchrist's eyes on him. He couldn't let him have the upper hand; otherwise he could try the same tricks again. He returned to his chair behind the desk and looked up at Gilchrist with a supercilious look.

"As you said, I'm a fair man. Against my better judgement I'll give you a three months trial. In the meantime I'll arrange another check on you. If you've told me the truth and you don't step out of line, I'll reinstate you permanently. One more thing... stay away from the girls. Is that clear?"

Gilchrist nodded, turned on his heel and strode out. His aura of confidence cracked when he got into his car. He badly needed a drink. Blowing out air from his lungs, he started the engine. Out on the open road he laughed out loud. He'd given that little shit Booth a taste of his own medicine. Now all he had to do was keep his cool with the police. He had admitted taking the dog for a walk. What he hadn't told them was that he had gone along the towpath the night of Ella Chapman's murder.

After stuffing his clothes into the washing machine he had had a very hot shower and slipped under the duvet next to his partner. She didn't even stir. As far as she was concerned, he had been lying next to her all night. He had slept fitfully, his head full of images of the girl. Every night it haunted his dreams.

The next morning he turned up for work as though nothing had happened. Dr Booth nodded on his way to the annexe in his usual peremptory manner. The kids scuttled out of his way as he strode haughtily ahead of them in a no-nonsense way. Gilchrist had to admit he cut a very imposing figure with his silver hair and

Errol Flynn moustache. It was rumoured a couple of the women teachers had the 'hots' for him, but he was oblivious to it. By all accounts he was a devoted husband. Still, it was odd how his wife only appeared for speech days and other important events, particularly as Booth had a grace and favour house in the school grounds. Most of the time she stayed out of sight in their isolated farmhouse, well away from St Cadfael's.

27

AUGUST 2022

Gilchrist drove aimlessly north of Shrewsbury, feeling more and more dejected. Spotting a farm gate, he pulled into the space and turned to his dog on the back seat.

"Okay, Barney, let's stretch our legs. Come on, boy!"

Walking was his way of escaping the trauma of the past few weeks. Deep in thought, Gilchrist trudged over the field, contemplating his future. He didn't want to be a gardener all his life. Much as he enjoyed the work, it offered no intellectual challenge. He missed teaching, but that was over.

No local authority would take him on if it was discovered he had been involved with a sexual assault charge involving a minor, even though he had been cleared of the charges. Perhaps a university or a college of further education. He had a 2:1 degree in biology and chemistry and a Master's. Surely, there was some way he could get back into education. His thoughts were interrupted by Barney, his Labrador. He was barking furiously at two dogs near the hedge separating the field from a nearby house.

"Barney, stop that! Heel, boy!"

The dog barked even louder and snuffled frantically at something on the ground. As Gilchrist drew closer he could see someone lying on the other side of the style. It was a woman, a big woman. Her leg was caught up in the strut holding up the step. A couple of dogs pawed at her and snarled at Barney. Startled, he realised it was Mrs Booth. That must be her house.

"Help me... my leg hurts. Don't worry about the dogs. They're just being protective," she said in a slightly slurred voice."

Bending over, he eased her leg out and examined it. "Can you stand up?" Leaning on him, she struggled to her feet. "Your ankle is a bit swollen."

"I'm all right now. Nothing broken, thank goodness."

Gilchrist could smell the drink on her breath. He had heard she was a bit of a lush, but eleven o' clock in the morning?"

"I'll help you back home."

"No need, I can manage." She took a few paces and grimaced. "I think I've sprained my ankle. Perhaps you could take me to the house."

When he had settled her on the sofa with her feet up, he went into the kitchen and soaked a towel in cold water. He eyed the bottle of gin sitting on the table. It was half empty. Another bottle jutted out of the bin. So it was true, she liked the booze.

"This will help a little," he said, going back into the sitting room, "but I think you should go to A & E and get it checked out, just in case. Shall I make you a cup of tea?"

"You're very kind. Haven't I seen you somewhere before?"

"I'm the gardener at St Cadfael's."

She stared at him, a look of utter panic on her face. "Dr Booth will be coming back soon. He'll take me to the hospital." Suddenly, her face crumpled. A huge, trembling sob shook her body. "He'll be furious, especially if he finds out I've been drinking this early in the morning."

"Why were you drinking?"

"I'm so lonely when Edward - Dr Booth - isn't here. You can't imagine what it's like being alone for hours and hours every day."

Gilchrist glanced at the photograph on the piano. Surely, this grossly overweight woman couldn't be the beauty in the picture.

"Are those your boys? I didn't realise you had children."

"Marcus and Phillip. They're grown up now."

Empty nest syndrome, Gilchrist thought. Kids left home, husband at work all day. It was fairly common. His own mother had felt the same when he left home for university.

"You must have some visitors, friends who call in from time to time?"

"Hardly ever and usually when Edward is at home."

"Would you like me to visit you now and again?"

Her eyes lit up, then darkened again. "Edward doesn't like me having visitors when he's not here. It worries him." She smiled shyly. "It would be nice to have someone to talk to though."

"Dr Booth doesn't need to know, does he? After all I work at the school, so I don't represent a risk, do I?" Isobel smiled and nodded. "I'll come over at least once a week when I know Dr Booth won't be here and we can have a good chat."

Poor cow, he thought as he trudged back over the fields. He genuinely felt sorry for her. She seemed to be a prisoner in her own home. He could just imagine Booth's reaction if he found out he had been in his home.

When Booth went off to a meeting in Birmingham the following week, Gilchrist trudged through the muddy field to the farmhouse. Isobel's face lit up when she opened the door. After she had made mugs of steaming tea they settled down to talk. Oddly, they hit it off. Both of them had problems and she was a good listener. He found himself telling her all about his life before he came to St Cadfael's, including the sexual assault accusation.

"I was young and stupid. The girls today, they look so mature, and I was flattered. It's hard to tell their ages. My career was finished. I went off the rails… drinking." He shrugged his shoulders. "Now I'm a gardener."

"Have you tried to get back into teaching?"

"Where would I get references? The head in my last school wouldn't give me one."

"What about private schools?"

"Not even private schools would employ me if they were made aware of it."

"Why don't you discuss it with Edward? I'm sure he would advise you."

Why hadn't he thought of that? The glimmer of an idea started to form in his mind. He might be the gardener, but he was well-qualified for a teaching post. Perhaps even a teaching job in StCadfael's. He smiled inwardly, imagining Booth's reaction when he put the idea to him.

*

Dr Booth sat rigidly behind his desk. He couldn't believe his ears. This man dared to ask for a teaching post in *his* school! He had given him his gardening job back. That was enough.

"You can't be serious, man. Do you really think I would let you near my pupils? It's out of the question. Now get back to your work."

Gilchrist held his ground. "I'm better qualified than a lot of your staff and I've got a post-graduate teaching diploma. Don't patronise me, Booth."

Startled, Booth sat up straight, his eyes hard and cold. "Dr Booth to you."

"Just think about it, Booth. Remember, my appointment was your mistake."

Gilchrist strode out and slammed the door behind him before Booth could respond.

Furiously, he paced his study. The man was getting too big for his boots. Why had he been so stupid? He couldn't employ a gardener in the classroom. All he was guilty of was appointing him without proper checks. Nothing to worry about except... the governors were after his hide. Two murders now this. Time... he needed time to think this out.

"Mrs James, I'm going home early today. My wife isn't too well."

His secretary smirked behind his back as he marched out. *One too many I expect*, she thought.

Isobel seemed unusually cheerful when he entered the sitting room. Her hair was neatly brushed and she was wearing a touch of make-up. She had even put on a smart, loose-fitting leisure suit that disguised the bulges.

"You're back early," she commented.

"I've got a lot on my mind." He sat down beside her and put his head on her shoulder. "I've got problems with the gardener."

Isobel's heart skipped a beat. She could feel the blood rising up her neck. Did he know about the visits to the farmhouse? She waited, heart in mouth, for him to continue."

"Poor dear, tell me all about it."

"He's blackmailing me."

"What?"

"Not for money. Believe it or not, he used to be a teacher in Devon. A fifteen-year-old girl accused him of sexual assault. The barrister tore her to pieces in the witness box. It was all a setup. He wasn't convicted, but he eventually had to leave his job. Too many parental complaints to the school."

"So, he's innocent?"

"There was a lot of mud-slinging. His teaching contract was almost up. It wasn't renewed. I didn't have him properly checked out. He admitted he had lied by omission, but I sacked him on the spot. The truth is, he threatened to inform the governors so I was forced to re-instate him, against my better judgement. Now the bloody man wants to teach in *my* school."

Isobel smiled to herself. Gilchrist had Edward where he wanted him and she had planted the idea in his head. She didn't want to harm Edward. She loved him, but he was such a supercilious, arrogant prat. It would do him good to have his ego dented.

"What am I going to do? If he goes to the governors I'm finished!"

"Why not let him teach a few gardening lessons?" That wouldn't look too strange. You could tell the governors you want to introduce some vocational courses. Something enjoyable for pupils after all the trauma of the murders. It wouldn't be the first time a teacher branched off into another career and decided to return to it."

"Isobel, what would I do without you? You always help me solve my problems. I'll let him sweat for a few days then I'll call him in."

He hugged her and gave her a fond kiss on the cheek. She had helped him save face again. Isobel sank back into the cushions. Her friendship with Gilchrist was paying off. Besides, she liked him. He didn't treat her as an appendage like Edward.

The following morning she waved to Gilchrist as he climbed over the style. Her dogs raced over, barking furiously at Barney until he played their games. Mick smiled and waved back. He liked Isobel and genuinely enjoyed her company. He hadn't heard a word form Booth about his proposal. It could all backfire and he could be out of a job altogether. Perhaps he had pushed him too far.

Isobel greeted him effusively, but didn't mention her conversation with Edward. She didn't want Gilchrist to know he had confided in her. If he slipped up and Edward became suspicious there would be trouble. He would put a stop to their little téte à tétes if he found out. They settled down on the sofa with a mug of tea and a wedge of Victoria sponge.

"I did what you suggested and approached Dr Booth for advice about re-entering teaching via the private sector," he told Isobel. He didn't tell her that he had issued him with an ultimatum. Nor did she mention her input. "He was very helpful and said he would let me know if anything is possible, but it wasn't very likely."

Isobel patted his arm reassuringly. "Don't worry. I'm sure he'll do all he can for you."

If he knows what's good for him, Gilchrist thought. *I'll give him one more day.*

The following morning Booth's secretary telephoned to inform him that his proposal was still under consideration. It was almost a week before she contacted him again with a summons from Dr Booth. He would spare him a few minutes between meetings. *He's a cool custome,* Gilchrist thought as she showed him into Booth's study. *Still trying to keep the upper hand, but not for long if I can help it.*

"You may sit," Booth said peremptorily. *Arrogant bastard,* Gilchrist thought. "I understand you qualified as a landscape gardener after you left education."

"That's correct." Where was this leading? Was he going to pull the plug on his gardening job?

"I've given it a lot of thought and decided that a vocational course in garden design would be useful for pupils. I don't want it interfering with their examination courses, but a few lessons after the normal school day would be acceptable."

"There are qualifications in garden design available."

"For now I'm restricting it to extra-curricular activities." Gilchrist opened his mouth to say something, but Booth raised a hand dismissively. "I've spoken to the governors. You can start the third week in September once pupils have settled into their academic studies. That will be all." Booth rose, walked to the door and held it open. "Don't try a stunt like this again. Next time I'll go to the governors myself." Giving Gilchrist a self-satisfied smile, he closed it after him and leaned against it until his heart stopped pounding.

Gilchrist raced into Shrewsbury, parked up near Watergate Mansions and headed into town. He needed a pint, but only one. If he played his cards right he could be teaching full-time again. It was his last chance and he didn't intend to mess things up. He couldn't wait to tell Isobel.

28

SEPTEMBER 2022

Gilchrist whistled cheerfully to Barney as he snuffled along the towpath. It was a glorious day. Crisp leaves crackled underfoot, heralding the beginning of Autumn. A bright azure sky brightened the day reflecting in the river. He felt more contented than he had for weeks. This afternoon was his first 'class' in garden design. Just mouthing the words filled him with exhilaration. Finally, he was on his way back. From now on everything he did would be to enhance his prospects for a permanent teaching post.

He was upstairs, wondering what to wear. A suit would be much too formal. The kids were used to seeing him in dungarees. What he wanted was a gradual transformation from school gardener to a teaching professional. He changed into a pair of corduroys and a sweater, then examined his appearance in the mirror. Perfect - just the right balance.

After the initial curiosity and sniggering, Mick's classes were a huge hit. The kids loved the relaxed atmosphere and he was good at his job. Even Booth complimented him on his success, promising a spot on the timetable in the new school year.

Booth was satisfied he had made the right decision. Squadron Leader Pryce-Jones had raised his eyebrows sceptically when he broached the subject of allowing the gardener to take classes.

"Apparently, he left teaching to pursue a career in landscape gardening. As you can see, he's transformed the school grounds. He now wants to combine his skills for the benefit of our pupils."

"Why didn't he tell us this when he applied for his job?" Pryce-Jones asked. "It all seems a bit bloody odd to me."

"As you know, we were left without a gardener and he fitted the bill. You gave me carte blanche to appoint him, because of the circumstances. It's quite common to switch careers. I once took a break myself - spent a year on an archaeological dig in Egypt."

"Pity he hadn't bloody stayed there, the smug sod," Pryce-Jones muttered under his breath. Canon Grayling shot him a disapproving look. Amanda Squires sniggered. Booth pretended not to have heard.

Dr Booth was about to get into his car when Wallace and Butler crunched up the drive to St Cadfael's. Booth sighed audibly when the DCI emerged from the police car. What did the tiresome man want now?

"We'd like to speak to your gardener, Mick Gilchrist."

"He's not here. He's gone for supplies to Percy Thrower's garden centre. What's this all about? If he's done anything wrong I need to know, especially now he's teaching classes."

"Teaching?"

"Just a few garden design lessons after normal school. He told me all about what happened in Plymouth. I decided to give him a chance to prove his worth in the classroom. He's not the first teacher to suffer from false allegations. He should have told me before he was appointed, but I'm a fair man."

Wallace winced at Booth's condescending tone. It made him want to punch him in the face.

"If he makes an appearance, please contact us immediately."

Booth got in his car and sat behind the wheel, contemplating his next move. Gilchrist had done something and he didn't want the good name of the school brought into it. He had enough on his plate convincing parents that their children were safe boarding.

29

NOVEMBER 2022

At 7:00 a.m. a loud knock on the door interrupted Mick's thoughts as he lay on the bed thinking about his future. He didn't want to push Booth too much, but he didn't want to back off either. *Lull him into a false sense of security, then I'll make my move,* he thought. His girlfriend shouted upstairs.

"Mick, there's a copper here to see you."

"What the hell do the police want now?" he muttered to himself. "Be right down," he yelled back. Shelley was beginning to irritate him. Not the right woman to enhance his prospects. Their relationship had been rocky for months. It was time to end it.

"We've got a few more questions to ask you," DS Butler said, "down at the station."

"I've told you everything. There's nothing more to say." "This is harassment! I know my rights!" *Steady*, he thought. *Don't panic, otherwise you'll play right into their hands.* Without another word, he marched out to the waiting police car.

Gilchrist shuffled in his seat; his eyes darted around the interview room like a trapped fox. Brazen it out, that was the only way. Any sign of hesitancy and he was in deep trouble. They haven't got a shred of evidence, he reminded himself.

"Interview with Michael Gilchrist, 7:55 a.m. Tell us again where you were on the night of Ella Chapman's death," Wallace said.

"Am I a suspect?" Gilchrist asked.

"We're questioning a number of people in relation to Ella's murder," Wallace replied.

"I keep telling you. I went to see a film with my girlfriend. The Showcase Cinema on the edge of town. After that we went straight home."

"Did you leave the house again?"

"No, only to let out the dog. I was too drunk to take him for his usual walk."

"What were you wearing at the time?"

Gilchrist shrugged. "The usual: jeans, sweatshirt and a hoodie."

"What about shoes?"

"I don't wear shoes very often… usually boots."

"What are you wearing now?"

"Trainers."

"Were you wearing trainers on the night Ella Chapman died?"

"I can't remember; probably." Why were they asking about trainers? He sat bolt upright, his lips pressed into a tight line. "I'm not saying another word until I have a solicitor present. I know my rights."

"That's your prerogative. You will stay here until your brief arrives. Interview suspended at 8:15 a.m."

Wallace waited until Butler joined him in the interview room. Mick sat opposite, next to his brief, sullenly staring into space.

"Ten forty-three a.m. Detective Inspector Ben Wallace and DS Butler interviewing Peter Michael Gilchrist in the presence of his solicitor, Graham Knowles."

"How many pairs of trainers do you have?"

Gilchrist shrugged indifferently. "Three."

"So why did we only find two pairs in your house? Where's the third pair?"

"They were old. I threw them out. You're trying to trap me... frame me for that girl's murder."

Butler produced a large, plastic evidence bag. Gilchrist froze, his face drained of colour.

"Are these your trainers?"

"No! I don't know. I put them in the re-cycling." He shook his head and whispered something to his brief.

"I'll ask you again. Are these your trainers?"

"No!" Wallace stared hard at him. "I told you, I threw them out. You often see homeless guys trawling through the bins."

"You threw them in the river, didn't you? After you murdered Ella Chapman."

"No! How many times do I have to say it? Anybody could have thrown them in."

"One of them snagged on the ledge above the water."

"I didn't kill her! I swear, you've got to believe me."

"That's not enough evidence to hold my client," Knowles said. "It's clear they could have been taken from the recycling bin."

"You were seen throwing them over English Bridge." Mick's heart hammered in his chest. Beads of sweat broke out on his forehead. He felt sick.

"I was nowhere near the bridge!"

"An old tramp sleeping by the wall close to the steps saw a man throwing something into the water. He matched your description."

"He's lying! Why didn't he come forward before?"

"We've moved him on from that spot a few times. We hauled him in for questioning when he was seen in the same spot by a couple out for a stroll."

"I tell you, I was nowhere near the bridge! It was dark! How could he know it was me? How do you know he didn't kill the girl?"

Wallace didn't answer. The frail tramp was barely conscious when they picked him up. He had been sleeping out in the freezing cold. That, coupled with cheap booze had taken its toll. He was in Shrewsbury Royal Infirmary in intensive care. The tramp had stuck to his story, but until he recovered, if he did recover, they had nothing else to go on.

Wallace stood up and walked to the door. "You're free to go Mr Gilchrist, for now."

Gilchrist breathed a huge sigh of relief when the cold air hit him outside. He hated confined spaces, especially like the interview room. Hot, stuffy and no windows. Inhaling deeply, he set out for Isobel's place.

Isobel ushered him into the kitchen and put on the kettle. He looked in need of a cup of hot, sweet tea.

"What's wrong?" she asked with concern. She fussed over him like a mother hen. "You look so pale. Are you ill?"

"I feel sick," he said. "The police took me in for questioning again about that girl's murder. I didn't have anything to do with it. I swear, Isobel."

Isobel put her arms around him and rocked him like a baby, stroking his hair and whispering endearments. She loved him like she loved Marcus and Phillip. She would protect him like she protected her boys.

"Edward is away from home for a few days. Why don't you stay here for tonight? You can sleep on the sofa. I'll cook dinner and we can share a bottle of wine. You can tell me all about your gardening classes."

Mick looked up at her. She was years older than him, overweight and drank far too much, but there was something about her. She had a beautiful soul that shone through the flabby flesh. He felt an acute sensation of tenderness towards her. She shouldn't be shut away in the wilds all day. No wonder she drank so much.

"I've got a better idea. Why don't we go out to dinner?"

"I couldn't. What would Edward think?"

"He'll never know. We'll go to the Mytton and Mermaid in Atcham."

*

Isobel gazed around the cosy dining room, drinking in the atmosphere. It was a rare treat for her to be taken out to dinner in the middle of the week. If only Edward would take her out more often.

Mick quietly studied Isobel. Her manners were impeccable, every inch the lady. Animated, intelligent; an educated woman. Every time he mentioned Booth she froze, an anxious look clouding her eyes. Mick couldn't fathom her lifestyle. What had turned her into this frightened, dysfunctional woman?

Over the ensuing weeks, he stayed overnight every time Booth went off to one of his conferences. Most of the time they chatted or sat in companionable silence. Mick's girlfriend had slammed out one night after a massive row. All he felt was relief that the relationship was finally over. Now he could concentrate on his future teaching career.

30

OCTOBER 2022

Isobel stretched out on the lounger beside the pool. It was wonderful to be abroad after the Coronavirus lockdown. After an anxious two years things seemed to be getting back to normal. Casually, she glanced at the sleeping figure beside her and sighed contentedly. Mick was such a good boy. He would never replace Marcus and Phillip in her affections, but she had grown to look upon him almost as a son. Edward would be livid if he knew about their friendship. Unlike Edward, Julia understood her need for companionship. She had suggested Mick coming out to the villa with them. They spent glorious days visiting San Gimignano, Lucca and Florence.

"What about a trip to Sienna tomorrow?" Julia suggested. She glanced at Mick. "Are you up for it?"

"I'd love it," Mick said.

Early the following morning the three of them drove to Sienna. After walking through the streets they emerged onto the Piazza del Campo. Mick was awestruck at the medieval architecture. They strolled along the square and ascended the steps to the grand Duomo.

"That's the Santa Maria della Scala Museum," Isobel said, pointing to a building opposite. "It's the oldest working 'hospital' in the world."

Later they re-entered the Piazza del Campo and ordered lunch. They sat outside drinking in the atmosphere. Crowds of tourists ambled around the square taking photographs. Three nuns in full wimples strolled past.

"It's like going back in time," Mick said, gazing around the square. He ordered some drinks and asked for a menu. "Lunch is on me, no arguments. Order me pasta arrabiata." He grabbed his camera and weaved between the tables. Turning at the edge of the square, he waved and pointed the camera at Isobel and Julia. Suddenly, a voice interrupted their conversation. A woman loomed in front of them.

"Mrs Booth, fancy seeing you here."

Startled, Isobel screwed up her eyes against the midday sun. It was Amanda Squires, one of the school governors. What the hell was she doing here?

"This is my sister, Julia," Isobel answered. "We're staying in our villa in Strove for a couple of weeks."

"And who is that young man I saw with you?"

Isobel shrugged and smiled innocently. "It's just the two of us. He was just asking about the menu. American, I think, judging by the accent."

Amanda turned and squinted into the square. There

was no sign of Mick, but she wasn't fooled. He was with the two women, of that she was certain. She hadn't seen his face clearly, but there was something vaguely familiar about him.

"Phew! That was a close call," Julia commented. "Who was she?"

"One of the governors at St Cadfael's."

Mick had recognised her immediately and scuttled off into the crowds. When he saw her leaving the square he re-joined the sisters.

"Don't worry," he said. "She didn't have a good look at me."

"We had better stay close to the villa for the rest of the holiday," Isobel said. "If Edward finds out… She swallowed the rest of the sentence.

Back at her hotel, Amanda Squires pondered on her encounter with Isobel. Why had she looked so frightened? Perhaps she was having an affair? She laughed out loud at the ridiculous notion. Isobel Booth? No! She was probably covering up for her sister. Perhaps he was her toy boy? After all, she had one. She smiled at the young Italian over her glass of Chianti.

31

Over the past few weeks, Isobel had been more lively than she had in years. Edward noticed that she had lost some weight, had her hair styled and wasn't tipsy every night when he got home. He put it down to her recent interest in computers. Most of her days were spent in the garden or surfing the internet. She had even asked him to buy a camera so she could Skype her old friends overseas. That's why she wanted to look her best. She didn't want them seeing what a slob she had become. It kept her happy and it suited his own agenda.

Surfing the internet was a rare past-time for Booth. He was looking for information on skiing holidays for the sixth form. For a change, he had nothing better to do. He had inadvertently left his iPad in his office at school. Isobel's laptop was in the study. He didn't think twice about accessing her laptop. Damn it! She must have changed the password. Why would she do that?

He tried various combinations: birthdays, family names. Nothing came up after trying her maiden name.

He rubbed his chin thoughtfully then tapped in the names of her dogs. Molly followed by Bertie. Both were incorrect passwords. He thought for a moment and keyed in MolBert. The 'Windows' desktop appeared.

Her inbox registered sixty-eight read emails. Who could be sending her so many? His curiosity got the better of him. Without a qualm, he opened them up. There were quite a few from friends she had contacted. Mary in Australia, Jackie in South Africa and Mae Ling. His heart lurched. Why was she in touch with her? He thought the friendship had fizzled out years ago. Who was Georgie? Another friend? She hadn't mentioned her.

He scowled and thumped the desk. She had no right to keep things from him! She had to understand how important it was for him to know everything she did. When she came back from Italy he would question her about this Georgie she was Skyping so regularly. Suddenly, he felt very alone. She was shutting him out of her life. For a brief moment he understood her loneliness. Snapping the laptop shut, he went into the sitting room and poured himself a large whisky.

At Heathrow, Isobel waved her sister off in a taxi while she and Mick made for the Heathrow Express to Paddington. They would have to separate before boarding the train for Birmingham. To all intents and purposes she would be travelling alone. Edward would pick her up in Shrewsbury.

She knew something was wrong before she got into the car. Edward sat stony-faced behind the wheel. He didn't speak a word to her all the way home. He didn't wait for her to take off her coat.

"What's the meaning of this?" he asked, pulling her into the study. He pointed to the open email.

"Just some emails from friends, that's all."

"And who is Georgie?"

Isobel's heart raced. She tried to keep the nervous tremble out of her voice.

"Why have you opened my laptop? You have no right!" she exclaimed angrily.

Edward ignored her. I'll ask you again. "Who is Georgie?"

"Oh, that's Georgia. We met her in Italy a few years ago. You must remember her husband. A rather pompous chap from Eton College. Bored us silly. She contacted me to say they were moving to New York. She Skype's me regularly, telling me about their house on Long Island.

Edward nodded. "Yes, I do remember her, but you must be careful, Isobel, not to get too involved."

He leaned over and kissed her on the cheek. "I'll make you a nice cup of tea."

Edward listened to the kettle boiling, his mind in turmoil. He didn't believe a word of Isobel's explanation nor did he remember anyone called Georgia. What was she up to? If she was meeting this woman he would soon find out. Mae Ling was another problem that would need resolving. She knew too much. He carried the tea tray into the sitting room, poured some for Isobel and went back into his study.

He opened one of Mae Ling's emails and forwarded

it to his mobile. The last one was sent over two months ago. Quickly, he tapped in a message of his own.

'Dear Mae Ling. I know this will come as a huge shock. It is with great sorrow that I have to tell you that Isobel died suddenly a few weeks ago following a short illness. I am going to Australia to visit relatives and intend to stay there permanently. My good wishes to your family.'

Smiling to himself, he tapped cc and added Mary and Jackie. That sorted that little problem. He rejoined Isobel in the sitting room. Now he had to find out what Isobel was up to with this Georgie.

When Edward left to go back to school, Isobel deleted everything in her inbox. She would tell Edward she had done it accidentally. She swallowed hard. If he knew that Mick was Georgie he would be furious. He had told her about his nickname as a child. The kids at school called him Georgie Porgie, because he was chubby. His old pals still called him Georgie even when he transformed into a tall, slim adult.

Every time they exchanged emails she would have to delete them immediately. She was afraid, but it didn't stop a thrill of excitement surging through her. This time she would outwit Edward. She had no intention of ending her friendship with Mick.

32

Edward devil-drummed on his desk. Isobel was getting out of hand. The stupid woman. After what happened last time. A knock on the door interrupted his thoughts. It was Mick Gilchrist.

"I've brought the design syllabus for you to see. I'm sure pupils will love the course and it awards a vocational certificate. It can be combined with computer studies; computer-aided design."

Booth scanned the page. He had to admit it looked promising. Gilchrist had added another dimension to his subject.

"How much time is involved?" he asked warily.

"I could incorporate it into a few computer lessons."

"Very well. I'll have a word with the head of computers and get back to you."

"If it takes off it could be extended the following year."

"Don't push your luck, Gilchrist, and remember you're still the gardener."

Booth leaned back in his chair when Gilchrist left. The governors would be pleased that he was so modern and forward-thinking. This could be another feather in his cap if he played his cards right. There was an open day during October half-term. He and Isobel would put on a show of confidence for prospective new parents.

*

Italy had been good for Isobel. Booth watched her chatting amiably to his head of English, Richard Ellis. Her hair had been cut into a fashionable layered style and her elegant suit was immaculate. She looked every inch the wife of a successful head of a prestigious school. She had changed, he realised with a sudden stab of concern. What had instigated the transformation? He still hadn't discovered the identity of her friend 'Georgie'. Could it be a man? No! Impossible! Isobel wasn't the type. Brushing the thought aside, he sauntered over and linked her arm with his.

October turned into a warm Indian Summer. Dr Booth had decided to hold the 'open day' outdoors.

"Come along, my dear. I want you to meet Sir Giles Ponting. He's a Member of Parliament; in the cabinet, you know."

Near the trees surrounding the expansive lawn Mick stabbed at the flower beds while watching Booth circulating amongst parents. Isobel had sent him a brief email warning him to stay away for a while. He had to speak to her and find out what had happened. In his shed he stripped off his overalls, put on a blazer and tie, changed his boots for smart shoes and wandered over to the mingling crowd. Booth was already standing on the steps, tapping a champagne glass for attention.

"Ladies and gentlemen, welcome to my school." Gilchrist noticed Booth's emphasis on '*my school*'. "I would like to introduce the excellent staff who have been teaching your children since September." Booth introduced each member of staff in turn, commenting on their examination successes. Finally, he turned to Gilchrist.

"I would now like to introduce you to our school gardener." Parents turned to Mick; looking rather perplexed. "You're probably wondering why. Mr Gilchrist is a qualified teacher. A few years ago he took a career break and trained as a landscape gardener. At the moment he's teaching some extra-curricular lessons that have been very successful. Based on that success, he will be enhancing his garden design lessons with CAD; computer-aided design." A murmur of approval rippled across the lawn. A few parents nodded enthusiastically. "This will in no way affect their normal academic subjects, but we must move with the times."

A number of parents approached Mick to ask questions about the course. Amanda Squires sidled up to him.

"Well done, Mr Gilchrist. It's time Booth introduced something innovative."

She took in Mick's blond hair and striking blue eyes. He certainly brushed up well. Quite a dish. For a moment something flickered in her memory, like a still in a slide show. Giving him a salacious grin, she wandered off for another glass of champagne.

Mick spotted Isobel sitting at one of the tables talking with two women. When they got up and walked off to join another group, Mick wandered over casually and sat down. Amanda Squires followed Mick's progress, admiring his lithe physique.

"You can't sit here," Isobel said. "What will Edward think?"

"What's wrong, Isobel?" Mick said, noting her frightened expression. "What's he done?"

"Nothing, just go away. I'll contact you soon."

Mick rose and leaned over to Isobel. "All right, but if you don't contact me I'm coming over."

It may have been the angle of his silhouetted head or the familiar way he was bending over Isobel. In that moment Amanda remembered the Piazza del Campo in Siena.

"My God, she was with the gardener!"

She laughed out loud. So she had a toy boy. Who would have thought it? Glancing over at Isobel, she caught her eye and winked. Swallowing a thrill of fear, Isobel walked over to Amanda.

"Something wrong?" she asked.

"You dark horse! I didn't think you had it in you."

Isobel feigned ignorance, but she knew that Amanda had sussed out that Mick was with her in Siena.

"Piazza del Campo, darling?"

"It's not what you think, Amanda. Mr Gilchrist was on a camping holiday. It was pure chance that he spotted us having lunch in the Piazza."

"So why did you lie about knowing him?"

"I didn't. I don't know him. He spotted us and came over, that's all."

Amanda smiled knowingly. She knew a lie when she heard one. "Don't worry, I won't tell Booth." Isobel was still protesting when Amanda strolled off in the direction of Mick Gilchrist.

33

NOVEMBER 2022

Isobel peered disconsolately through the sitting room window. It was bucketing down. Swords of glistening rain slashed down on the Range Rover parked in the drive, filling old potholes. Mick wouldn't walk over the fields in this weather. Days of rain had transformed the adjoining meadow into something akin to a bog. She was about to turn away when she spotted a movement near the trees at the far end of the field. It was Mick. Seeing him trudging over the sodden ground, her heart contracted. How she had grown to love him; not as Amanda Squires thought, but as a son. Her life was so different now and she was determined that Edward would not spoil it.

She waved at the approaching figure, then dashed into the kitchen to make a hot drink. Her boy would need it after braving the wind and rain.

"Come in," she said. "I didn't think you would come over on such an awful day."

"I couldn't miss our little chats, Isobel," Mick said, planting a kiss on her cheek. He had grown very fond of her. A stab of nostalgia hit him. She was the nearest thing he had to a mother since his own had passed away.

When they had settled comfortably, nursing their hot chocolate, Isobel told him about Amanda Squires.

"She knows it was you in Siena. Something must have jogged her memory. She promised she wouldn't tell Edward, but what if she does? He'll go ballistic."

"Why, because I'm a man or because I'm the gardener?"

"Both. He went into my laptop and found the last few emails I sent. Now he wants to know Georgie's identity. I think it would be better if you stayed away for a few weeks until he's calmed down. If he suspects you he'll pull the plug on your classes."

"You're right, but more importantly, I don't want him harassing you. I won't come to the farm, but we could meet up for lunch when he's away for the day."

Satisfied that their plans would work, Mick set out across the fields, head down against the howling wind and torrential rain. He tied the hood of his anorak securely and pulled the flap up over the lower part of his face. As he swung his leg over the style a figure disappeared round the bend in the opposite direction. Mick took off his coat and dropped gratefully into the driver's seat. He was soaked, but he didn't care a jot. Everything was coming together for him and he had no intention of lousing it up.

Edward sat in the car, fury building in his chest, the

binoculars he always kept in the car dangling from his neck. From the build he was sure that the person he saw coming from the farm was a man. He couldn't make out his face, because it was covered up and he was bent over against the wind. His back was turned to him when Isobel waved him off through the window. She couldn't be having an affair. It was impossible! Who would be interested in her? She may have smartened up, but she was still an overweight, matronly woman. His thoughts raced. If she was involved with anyone it could be disastrous for them both, particularly his career. From now on he would have to keep stricter tabs on her. Perhaps he could return home unexpectedly and catch them at it. His guts churned. He couldn't bear the thought of Isobel with another man. How could she when she has me? He shuddered involuntarily... unthinkable!

He had to stay away for the rest of the day, otherwise Isobel would question why he had returned home early. Tomorrow was Saturday. It would give him an opportunity to corner her about the man he had seen leaving the farm. Revving the engine, he shot off in the direction of St Cadfael's. Mick was already in the computer room, instructing Year Ten on translating their ideas on how to design a garden pond onto the screen.

He walked to the window at the sound of an approaching vehicle. Booth was racing up the drive, sending gravel shooting in all directions. He got out of the car and slammed the door. His face was like thunder as he stormed up the steps. Mick grinned. Something had ruffled the feathers of the arrogant sod.

Ignoring Mrs James, his secretary, Booth mounted the stairs to his office and slumped down into his chair. For a fleeting moment he felt a surge of panic. What if Isobel was having an affair? What if she left him for this other man? He had to put a stop to it now before it got out of hand. He got up and paced the room. Calm down… you're making assumptions. It could have been anybody. A rambler perhaps. No, it was too wet and windy for rambling.

He had seen a car parked near the style. Perhaps, whoever it was had broken down. The driver must have crossed the field to use the telephone. There were a number of black spots in the area where it was impossible to get a mobile phone signal. That must be it! How could he have doubted Isobel?

Back at the farm Isobel trawled through her emails and deleted everything from her inbox. From now on she would be very careful to get rid of emails as soon as she read them. Mick had saved her from a life of loneliness and torment. She couldn't bear the thought of not seeing him again. She gazed over at the photograph of her boys on the piano. If only they could be with her at the farm.

The rain stopped during the night and the wind had blown away the dark clouds. Overhead a dazzling sun kissed the clouds in an azure sky. Across the meadow threads of steam rose from the grass as it dried out. The dogs bolted through the door as soon as Isobel opened it and raced towards the field. It was a glorious day. The brilliance of the day made her feel young and vibrant; a feeling she hadn't experienced for years. Edward watched her through the window as she ran after the dogs. His first instincts had returned. She was different. Why hadn't he noticed it before?

When she returned thirty minutes later he was sitting in the conservatory reading the newspaper. He glanced up with a half smile on his face and patted the seat beside him.

"Would you like some coffee?" He poured some into a mug and handed it to her. "Sit down, Isobel. I want to talk to you."

Isobel dropped heavily onto the wicker chair. She knew what was coming. She had to play it cool and relaxed. The slightest falter and Edward would interrogate her as though she had committed a crime.

"Now dear," he said gently, "What's all this nonsense about Georgie?"

"I don't understand what you mean by nonsense. I told you we met her in Italy a few years ago. You can ask Julia, she was with us. I haven't actually seen her since, but we exchanged email addresses. I can't say I liked her much. She usually contacts me when she has something to boast about. Don't you remember, she sent a round robin at Christmas."

He didn't remember, because it never happened. Isobel was lying through her teeth. She was being clever, he'd give her that, but she wasn't going to outwit him. No doubt Julia would back her to the hilt.

"Who was the man I saw leaving the house yesterday?"

Isobel froze. How could he have seen Mick leaving? She sipped her coffee, her mind racing for a plausible explanation. She looked directly into Edward's eyes and smiled warmly.

"Oh, him; he was lost. His satnav had taken him all over the place. When he spotted the house from the road he decided to walk over and get his bearings. He couldn't see the driveway further on down the road. It was such a filthy day I asked him into the hall." She patted his knee and rose to adjust the blinds. "Really, Edward, it's happened to us more than once. How did you know he was here? Are you spying on me?"

"Don't be ridiculous! I had to go into Shrewsbury on school business and decided to avoid the traffic."

She sat back down, grabbed the Saturday insert and nonchalantly studied the television programmes, her heart thudding so hard she thought she would pass out. Edward watched her covertly. He still wasn't convinced. His trip into town was the truth. It was pure coincidence he slowed down after he passed the car parked in front of the gate. He resolved to do just what she thought he had been doing.

From then on he watched the farmhouse at odd intervals during the day. Occasionally, he spotted Isobel moving about the house or opening the door for the dogs. Once he pretended to go to Birmingham and spent hours sitting under cover of the trees, watching for any sign of another person in the house. After four weeks he hadn't seen a soul except the postman's red van. Perhaps she had been telling the truth after all.

Isobel suspected he was spying on her; it wouldn't be the first time. He was probably out there right now, watching her every movement. Mick hadn't been to the house for weeks, but they kept in touch via email, making sure that each one was deleted immediately. On one occasion they met in a little country pub for a quick lunch after Isobel visited her hairdresser. Thankfully, Edward was tied up in a governors' meeting.

Next Thursday he was attending an independent head teachers' conference in London and wouldn't be back until late Saturday night. Dutifully, she waved from her bedroom window as he drove off from the farm. She was going to spend a whole day with Mick. He was taking her on a picnic into the Carding Mill Valley and Shropshire Hills. She shared his love of walking, but Edward hated the outdoors.

34

Bright sunlight pierced her eyelids as she lay dozing between sleep and wakefulness. Suddenly, Isobel shot up in the bed and flung back the duvet. Saturday had dawned bright and clear. The only sound was the chirping of birds in the nearby trees and the faint scuffling of the dogs pawing the back door.

Quickly, she let them out and they raced into the meadow, cocking their legs here and there until she called them for food. Half an hour later she bundled the dogs into the muddy Range Rover and put the picnic hamper, stuffed with goodies, onto the front passenger seat. With a broad smile of anticipation, she drove to Church Stretton where she had agreed to meet Mick.

It was pure chance Edward spotted her leaving the farm. Deciding not to stay in London until Saturday, he had travelled back with a colleague as far as Birmingham on Friday evening. They had a late dinner and far too much to drink, so he had stayed over in the De Vere Hotel. Early Saturday morning he caught a train to Shrewsbury, where he had left his car in the station car park.

He watched Isobel leave the farm and drive in the direction of Shrewsbury. She had promised never to leave the farm when he was away from home. Where was she going? Perhaps she was going to stock up on booze. Would she never learn? To think he trusted her and she had betrayed that trust. He couldn't understand why she was going in the direction of Church Stretton. She didn't know anyone there and she could have bought drink in town.

Isobel didn't notice the dark blue BMW that followed her three cars behind. Edward watched her getting into a Honda hatchback. He couldn't make out the driver, but he recognised the car and the number plate. Gilchrist! What the hell was she doing with him? He slowed down when a couple of cars overtook and squeezed into the line of traffic ahead. The traffic lights turned red just after the Honda went over the roundabout at Meole Brace. By the time he reached Bayston Hill they were nowhere to be seen. Seething with anger, he drove home to wait.

It was almost five o'clock when Isobel crunched up the drive. Edward watched her from the sitting room window. She looked happy and had a glow to her skin he hadn't noticed before. When Isobel saw him at the window she stopped, half in and half out of the Range Rover. The blood drained from her face. Why was Edward back so early? Was he still spying on her? Mind in a whirl, she shooed the dogs out of the car into the field and dragged towards the house, desperately trying to think of an explanation.

"Where the hell have you been?" Edward gave her a

challenging look. "You know you shouldn't go out alone when I'm not here. Have you been drinking?"

"No, I wouldn't drink and drive. I'm not that stupid!"

"Well, where *have* you been?"

"The hairdresser."

"Since ten o'oclock this morning? I saw you leave, Isobel."

"I made an appointment for eleven o'clock. They had a wedding on so everything was pushed back after the bride had a wobbly with the stylist. By the time they finished it was gone twelve. When I left, around one thirty, I decided to stay in town for a spot of lunch and have a mooch about the shops. I don't have to ask you every time I go out," she retorted.

Taken aback by her vehemence, Edward took a step back. She was lying. This wasn't like Isobel at all.

"Where were you going with Mick Gilchrist?"

Shocked, Isobel slumped onto the sofa, her lips trembling with anxiety. She knew she was beaten. Edward wouldn't leave her alone until he found out the truth.

"We went on a picnic in the Carding Valley. You know I love walking and he offered to take me."

"Why would he do that? How long has this been going on? Are you having an affair?"

"What! Are you mad? I'm old enough to be his mother!" Isobel said in a shocked tone. "There's nothing going on, not what you suggested. I fell off the style and twisted my ankle… you remember. Mick was walking his dog in the field. I was shivering with cold. He helped me back to the house and made me a hot drink." Edward looked at her sceptically, an angry glint in his eyes. "He came back again to see if I was all right. Ever since he's been coming to visit at least once a week. I promise that's all there is to it." Isobel sat down beside him and took his hand in hers. "You know I love you. It's always been you, Edward."

"Mick Gilchrist, the school gardener! That's why you were so eager for me to help him have another crack at teaching."

"He's been very kind to me, almost like a son. I've been so lonely, Edward. I look forward to seeing him. We talk about art and books and travel. I haven't been drinking so much since he's been coming round."

Edward scowled, but he knew Isobel was right. It must be lonely, stuck miles from anywhere for days on end. Gilchrist must have arranged his visits on his day off when he knew Edward was tied up in school.

"Please don't stop him coming, Edward. I need the company. If I'm on my own all day I'll be tempted to start drinking again."

Edward weighed up the position. At least Isobel kept herself more presentable and sober these days. Perhaps Gilchrist was a blessing in disguise. It kept her from brooding and it gave him a hold over Gilchrist.

"One more thing, Isobel. There was no Georgie in Italy, was there?"

"It was Mick's nickname when he was in school. They called him Georgie Porgie, because he was a bit on the chubby side."

"So that I didn't catch on."

Isobel lowered her eyes. "I know you're angry, but can't you understand just a little?"

Edward was silent for a few moments. Isobel searched his face, anxiously waiting for an explosion of anger. It didn't come.

"Very well, Isobel, he can come round to the farm, but I don't want you going out with him again. What would people think if they spotted you together?"

"I promise I'll restrict his visits to the farm."

"Just make sure he doesn't come around unannounced while I'm here. One other thing. You're not to tell him that I know he comes here. I don't want him thinking I condone your behaviour. I can't risk anyone finding out that my wife is having the school gardener round for little chitchats. Is that clear? "

35

Booth followed Mick's progress as he moved around the grounds. He had the man's measure all right. He was a liability. Something would have to be done before he ruined the reputation of St Cadfael's. Mick glanced up and spotted Booth at the window. He raised a hand in acknowledgement. Booth pretended not to have noticed and quickly moved aside.

First of all, he had to plant a seed of doubt with the governors. Gilchrist was a huge success with pupils and parents. He would have to tread very carefully, but he was determined to get him out of the school. Moving back to the window again, he watched girls gossiping as they walked to the sports' annexe. Mick looked up and smiled when they chanted together, "*Good morning, Mr Gilchrist.*" Giggling, they sashayed off, casting admiring looks over their shoulders. Booth felt his blood rising. Gilchrist was at it again.

Blood boiling, he ran downstairs and marched across the lawn to where Mick was weeding the flower beds. In his haste he tripped over a spade handle, almost losing his balance. Mick couldn't conceal the grin on his face. Booth towered over him, his face a mask of fury.

"Gilchrist, what have I told you about ogling the girls?"

"Come off it, Booth, I wasn't ogling. They were just passing the time of day. What's wrong with that?"

"Dr Booth to you. Don't be so bloody insolent. This is the last time I'm warning you, Gilchrist. Keep your eyes off the girls or you're out."

Turning on his heel, he marched off. At the foot of the steps he turned. Mick was staring after him, a smirk on his lips. Booth stopped at Mrs James's desk before he went up to his office. He was sure she would have seen him talking to Gilchrist from the window.

"Mrs James, I've just had a few words with the gardener. I'm not happy about the way he interacts with pupils, especially the girls. If you see him talking to pupils I want to know about it."

"Of course, Dr Booth. I'll keep my eyes peeled."

Taking a deep breath, she watched her idol mount the stairs with a feeling of intense satisfaction. She never did understand why he let that man into a classroom. Pulling out a notepad, she wrote down the date and details.

From her vantage point she diligently watched Mick's every encounter with pupils over the next few days. Twice she saw him touch a girl as they talked. To Mrs James the action was akin to molestation. Booth summoned Mick to his office. He was ready for him this time.

"It was a reassuring pat on the arm, that's all," Mick

explained. "She was asking me about the design course. Ask her yourself."

"You are essentially the gardener, Gilchrist. If a pupil has a problem it can be discussed with a member of the teaching staff or Matron. It's not your place to counsel them. I'm afraid I'll have to report this at the governors' meeting this afternoon."

"What happens when they find out you took me on without a CRB check?"

"I'll just have to admit my lack of thoroughness. I won't be blackmailed, Gilchrist."

He may have fooled Isobel, but he won't fool me, Booth thought as Mick walked out and slammed the door. Gilchrist had to go before Isobel took him deeper into her confidence.

Mick packed away his tools in the potting shed and slipped out of his overalls. Instead of going home, he went into Shrewsbury. He was fed up of eating on his own every night. He needed some company. After downing a couple of pints in Cromwell's he headed across to Pride Hill.

As usual on a Friday night there were a lot of people out and about. Tourists sussing out restaurants, groups of rowdy youngsters showing off. Outside Morgan's, at the bottom of Pride Hill, a few people sat outside quietly smoking. Inside it was buzzing. There was no way he was going to get a table for one, so he walked across to the Armoury.

It was just as crowded, but he waited at the bar, hoping they could squeeze him in. When he glanced to the back of the restaurant a hand waved at him from near the fireplace. A few lads he often chatted with in the Boathouse were with their wives and girlfriends. Mick edged his way through the tables.

"Come and join us. Budge up, everybody."

"I don't want to intrude."

"Sit here next to Hannah. She's just landed a promotion. Any excuse to eat and drink."

Mick commandeered a spare chair from the adjoining table and squeezed in next to the attractive blonde. She was bright, bubbly and single. When it was time to leave he asked her out on a date the following night. He had seen her in the Boathouse a few times and knew she was a lecturer in Birmingham. She lived with her parents in one of the big houses in Kingsland.

His ex didn't have much intelligent conversation. Their relationship had been more earthy. When the sexual attraction wore off there was nothing left. It was different with Hannah. She was everything he had ever wanted. Over the next few weeks they went out regularly. They always met in town and she took a taxi home. After each date he couldn't wait to see her again. He planned to take her someone special for her birthday.

The following Friday he dressed carefully. *Not bad*, he thought, gazing into the mirror. His smart grey trousers, blue shirt and navy blazer looked good on him. Suddenly, uncertainty gripped him. *It's a bit conventional,* he thought. Perhaps he should have worn jeans and a short-sleeved shirt like the youngsters he saw about town. No, best to be himself.

Hannah had gone into town to browse the shops before meeting him. She was approaching the Buttery just as he parked opposite St Mary's Church.

"You look beautiful," he said. "Happy birthday."

Hannah blushed and pecked him on the cheek.

"Thank you, sir."

Mick grinned. His heart beat a little faster as they went inside. Everything was perfect, just as he had hoped. While they were waiting for pudding Mick ordered a bottle of champagne.

"I'm quite happy with wine, Mick. Champagne is so expensive in restaurants."

"It's a special occasion," he said. He pulled out a box from his pocket and handed it to Hannah. "I hope you like it."

"Oh, Mick, it's beautiful. You shouldn't have, but I love it," she said, taking the bangle out of the box.

"It's Clogau gold." Mick said slipping it onto her wrist. "It suits you."

Hannah leaned over to kiss him. "It's been a wonderful evening, Mick. I just want to text my father to tell him I'm ready to be picked up."

"There's no need. I'll drive you home."

"You live in the opposite direction."

"I insist."

"No, there's no need, he's in the Red Lion with some friends."

Reluctantly, Mick walked her to the Red Lion and watched her go inside, wondering if her parents would be happy that her boyfriend was a school gardener. He would have to be patient and wait for an opportune moment before he made his next move. He felt a stirring in his groin when he thought about the last kiss they had shared. He wanted her desperately.

*

On Wednesday afternoon of the following week Dr Booth summoned him to his office. He sat behind his desk with his hands under his chin in a praying position.

"Close the door, Gilchrist. I won't beat about the bush. Your contract has been terminated by the governors."

"Why? I've done nothing wrong! You can't sack me just like that. I know my rights."

"It was a decision made by the governors this morning. I've had occasion to warn you more than once about talking to the girls. When you start touching them it becomes a matter of concern for me and the governors."

"I don't know what you're talking about! You're trying to set me up to get rid of me to cover up for your own failings."

"Not at all," Booth replied calmly. "I've informed the governors of my… shall we say… folly in appointing you on trust. They weren't best pleased, but understood that I was taken in by you. We were all taken in by you."

"You can't do this!"

"You'll be paid up until the end of the month, but you must leave by the end of the week." Booth rose, walked to the door and held it open. "Thank you, Gilchrist. That will be all."

Stunned, Mick stumbled downstairs in a daze. Mrs James was sitting at her desk gazing out of the window. Suddenly, it hit him. The conniving little bitch!

"It was you, wasn't it?" he shouted accusingly. "You've been spying on me for Booth! It's all lies! You'd say anything to keep in his good books. The whole school knows you've got the hots for him."

"How dare you!" Face aflame with embarrassment, she tried to quell the pounding in her chest. "Get out, you odious little man, or I'll call Dr Booth."

Mick stormed out. He had to see Isobel and find out why Booth had turned turtle.

Seething with anger he sat on Isobel's sofa nursing a glass of Irish whiskey. She stared at him, a shocked look on her face.

"I don't understand. Everything's been going so well the last few weeks. Why has he sacked you?"

"He said I've been coming on to the girls. I promise you, Isobel, I've been friendly and that's all. I may have patted a couple of them on the arm, but it was just to reassure them about their work. I would never touch a pupil inappropriately. I had already told him about the incident in Plymouth. I wasn't convicted of anything, Isobel, I swear."

Suddenly, a flash of realisation came into her eyes. Edward wanted to get rid of Mick just like he got rid of all her friends. She wouldn't let him; not this time.

"Edward knows you're coming over here," Isobel said quietly.

"What? I don't understand."

"He found out the day we went to Carding Mill. He followed us and recognised your number plate. When I arrived home he was furious. After he had calmed down he agreed that you could visit, but we were not to go out anywhere in case we were seen together."

"Afraid his wife would be seen with the school gardener," Mick said sarcastically. Isobel didn't answer. "That's why he sacked me, isn't it?" She nodded. "Well, he won't get rid of me that easily."

*

It was fortuitous that the track-suited man in a beanie hat had seen Hannah crossing the road outside Vinegar Hill after he had been to the gym near Market Hall. He waited to see if anyone came out behind her. She crossed the road towards him, carrying a Waitrose bag, and jumped into a little red Fiat parked outside St Mary's. Nosing his vehicle into the street, he followed her on to Wyle Cop. When she reached the T-junction she turned right into the one-way system and headed for Welsh Bridge and Kingsland.

As Hannah pulled up outside her house the front door opened letting out a stream of yellow light. A man silhouetted in the light ushered her inside and closed the door. He sat low in his car, pondering his next move. It was Saturday. Perhaps she would be going into town later on. If she did he would follow her.

He would have a long wait, but he was a patient man. His patience paid off. Around eight she left the house with a grey-haired man and got into a silver Jaguar parked outside. He dropped her near Victoria Quay. She waved to a group of people and they all went into the Armoury together. Walking past the window ten minutes later he noticed the group were sitting together on a table near the far wall. A waiter was taking orders for food. They didn't tumble out until after eleven, shouting goodnights and going their separate ways. Hannah ambled to the end of the road with another woman.

"Bye, Hannah," she called as she went off in the direction of Pride Hill. "Don't hang around on your own too long."

"Don't worry. My dad is on his way. I can see his car up by the traffic lights."

Suddenly, an arm went round her throat and a hand clamped over her mouth. Struggling to free herself, she tried to kick out, but her assailant was too strong for her. He dragged her into the shadows at the side of the restaurant and pushed her to the ground. Suddenly, he was on top of her, his hands clawing at her clothing.

In the split second he released his hand from her mouth she screamed. A middle-aged couple coming out of the Armoury stopped in their tracks. The man raced in the direction of the screaming, shouting to his companion to ring 999. When he reached Hannah she was lying on the ground, crying hysterically.

36

From far away he heard pounding and a voice calling through the letter box. Glancing at the clock on the bedside table, Mick groaned. It was eleven o' clock. He must have overslept. His head was thumping after a belly full of booze the night before. Swinging his legs over the side of the bed, he grabbed his dressing gown and stumbled downstairs, head banging with a hundred hammers. What the hell was so urgent on a Sunday morning? He winced and screwed up his eyes against the light as he opened the door.

"DS Butler and DC Baker, West Mercia CID."

"I know who you are. What do you want this time?"

"We'd like a few words, Mr Gilchrist. May we come in?" Mick shrugged and walked into the living room. *He looks as though he's had a night on the tiles*, Butler thought.

"We'd like you to accompany us to the police station to answer a few questions."

"No way, I'm not going anywhere. I've told you all I know about Ella Chapman."

"If you would prefer, we can come back with a warrant."

"Okay, okay, I just need to get dressed, if that's all right with you," he retorted angrily, "and I want a brief there."

*

The interview room smelled of body odour. A faint, sickly smell of disinfectant permeated the fetid air. Wallace turned on the tape.

"Chief Inspector Ben Wallace and Detective Sergeant Phillip Butler interviewing Peter Michael Gilchrist, eleven fifty-five a.m."

Mick stared straight ahead, his face unreadable. He knew their tricks, how they try to trap suspects. This time he was ready for them.

"Where were you last night, Mr Gilchrist?"

"In town having a few drinks. Why?"

"Where did you go drinking?"

"I had a couple of drinks in Cromwell's then walked over to the Boathouse."

"What time did you get to the Boathouse?"

"Around eight. I met some of the guys."

"What time did you leave?

"About ten-thirty. We decided to call it a night. We'd all had a bit too much to drink. The guys were getting a bit too rowdy and knocked over a few glasses on the next table. A couple of them went across to Morgan's, but I decided not to bother. I got a pizza in town and went straight home. Why?"

"Were you near the Armoury last night around eleven fifteen?"

Mick didn't answer immediately. His mind whirled. What was this all about?

He shook his head. "I walked over the bridge near Victoria Quay, but I went straight into town."

"Do you know a young woman named Hannah Jarvis?"

"Yes, we've been dating. What has Hannah got to do with it?"

"She was attacked last night after leaving the Armoury, around eleven fifteen."

"Attacked! Is she all right?"

Wallace sat back in his chair, arms folded across his chest, and stared over the top of Gilchrist's head.

"Someone tried to rape her."

"You think it was me? I'd never harm Hannah. I love her."

"Love or lust, Mr Gilchrist?"

Mick shot up out of his chair, his fists clenched. He leaned over the table, his face flushed and angry.

"Sit down, Gilchrist. We haven't finished yet. What time did you get home?"

"Around midnight."

"It took you an hour and a half to walk home to Belmont?"

"I went into town to get a pizza. You're trying to trap me like you did with Ella Chapman. After that I went home. I went out like a light until you started banging on my door this morning."

Mick slumped down. It was happening all over again. His solicitor leaned in and whispered something in his ear. Taking a deep breath, he said, "I love Hannah. She's the best thing that ever happened to me. There's no way I would harm her."

Suddenly, Wallace rose, nodding to Butler to follow him.

DCI Wallace wanted Gilchrist to sweat a bit. There had been dozens of people walking near the Armoury. Unless someone identified him, they had nothing to go on. Taking a deep breath, he went back into the interview room.

"You're free to go, Mr Gilchrist."

*

Mick sat in front of the television nursing a brandy. Fiona Bruce smiled out from the screen with a crowd of onlookers behind her. He was looking, but not registering anything about the '*Antiques Road Show*'. Perhaps he should go over to Kingsland, just ring the doorbell and ask about her. Suddenly, his mobile vibrated in his pocket. It was a text message from Hannah.

"I'm going to stay with my sister in Staffordshire for a few weeks. I've sent back the bangle. Please don't contact me."

What had the police said to her? Why was she behaving like this? He had to find out. Grabbing his keys, he jumped into his car and drove over to Kingsland. He spotted a Jaguar parked outside an imposing detached house. Seconds after he rang the bell a tall, grey-haired man opened the door.

"I'm Mick Gilchrist, a friend of Hannah's. May I speak to her?"

"I'm afraid you can't. She's not here. Hannah has gone to stay with her sister in Staffordshire. I would advise you not to try to contact her," Hannah's father said, firmly closing the door.

As Mick crossed the road he glanced up and saw a curtain move across the window, but not before he glimpsed Hannah staring out at him. For a brief moment he thought of knocking again and demanding to see her, but he knew it was useless. Their brief relationship was over.

37

Mrs James looked over the top of her spectacles at Wallace and Butler. Ignoring them, she returned her gaze to the computer screen for a few moments, then looked up.

"Mrs James, please inform Dr Booth that we want to see him." Teeth clenched, Wallace glared at her. Such a haughty cow. What was it about receptionists that they always wanted to talk down to people. "*Now,* Mrs James. I'm a very busy man."

Mrs James opened her mouth to say something, thought better of it and pressed a button on the telephone instead. An echoing, irritable voice emanated from the machine.

"What is it?"

"Chief Inspector Wallace to see you, Dr Booth."

Wallace and Butler started up the stairs, not waiting for a response from Booth. He was waiting for them with the door open, the usual supercilious smile on his lips.

"What can I do for you, Chief Inspector?" He waved him to a chair and sat down behind his desk. Butler stood near the window, glancing out at pupils moving about the grounds.

"I'd like to ask you a few questions about Michael Gilchrist. Have you noticed anything different about his behaviour over the last few days?"

"Mr Gilchrist is no longer employed at St Cadfael's. Unfortunately, I had to report him to the governing body. We decided it was in the best interests of the school to terminate his employment."

"I don't understand."

"Mr Gilchrist had an unfortunate habit of touching the girls."

"Touching them… how?"

"On the arms and shoulders, as far as I know," he added. "He claimed he was just reassuring them about their work. As you are aware, I gave him the chance of getting back into the classroom. However, considering what happened to Ella Chapman we felt he was being far too familiar with the girls. If parents found out they could very well withdraw their children from the school. Is he under investigation again?"

Wallace rose to leave without acknowledging the question. "Thank you Dr Booth. You've been most helpful."

Booth picked up the newspaper he had been reading as soon as he had shown Wallace and Butler out. On the front page the headline screamed out at him.

Attempted Rape of Young Woman Near Victoria Quay

Wallace must be investigating the case and Gilchrist

was in the frame again. It couldn't have worked out better for him. Perhaps the police should know that Gilchrist was pestering Isobel. He could be at the farm now.

"I have to go home for a while," he told Mrs James as he passed her desk. "I've left behind some important papers I need for the meeting this afternoon."

When he arrived at the farm, he parked outside on the road where he couldn't be seen from the house. Perhaps he could catch him red-handed. Quietly, he let himself in through the back door. He could hear voices coming from the living room. Gilchrist was sitting on the sofa next to Isobel, who had her arm around his shoulder.

"What's the meaning of this? What the hell are you doing in my home, Gilchrist?"

"But Edward, you said it was all right for him to visit!" Isobel cried.

"I said nothing of the sort! You must have misunderstood me. Do you think I'd let a possible rapist into my home with my wife?"

Mick got up from the sofa, his face scarlet with rage. He took a step towards Booth in a menacing manner.

"Get out now before I call the police! DCI Wallace has already been to the school asking questions about you. I'm afraid I had to tell him why you were sacked."

"You bastard! You know I didn't touch any of the girls. It was that cow Delia James. She would lie through her teeth to keep in your good books. She would be quite happy if you touched her up. Thinks the sun shines out of your backside."

"How dare you? Get out!"

"Edward, why are you doing this? The boy hasn't done anything wrong," Isobel whimpered.

"Don't worry, Isobel! He can stop me coming to the house, but he can't stop us meeting in town."

Mick drew himself up to his full height. "You'll pay for this, Booth. Come on, Barney." He lunged out of the house and across the field, the dog yapping at his heels. Turning to look back at the house, he saw Booth standing in the window. Isobel was nowhere to be seen. He shook his fist and yelled, "You'll pay, Booth! I promise."

Isobel ran up to her room and locked the door. She didn't want to be anywhere near Edward. *I won't listen to* him, she vowed. *Not this time.* When she heard a soft knock on the door she covered her ears with her hands.

"Isobel, please come out. I'm sorry. I didn't mean to upset you. I was just trying to protect you. The police came to see me this morning about Gilchrist. I was so scared he may have harmed you I had to come home to make sure you were safe." Isobel put a pillow over her head and pressed it against her ears. She had no intention of answering him. "Please, Isobel."

Booth gave up and went downstairs. He had to think how he was going to tell the police about this. He would make Isobel a nice cup of tea. Once she realised the kind of man Mick Gilchrist was she would come round. He picked up the telephone and rang West Mercia CID.

"I'd like to speak to Detective Chief Inspector Wallace. I have some information he may be interested in."

What does that smug sod want? Wallace thought as

he picked up the receiver. "DCI Wallace speaking. What can I do for you Dr Booth?"

"I had occasion to return home this morning to pick up some papers. Mick Gilchrist was in the house with my wife. She knows him, of course. He often walks his dog across the fields. He was berating her, because I sacked him."

"Did he threaten her physically?"

"No, but he was verbally abusive. He climbed over the style when he saw her in the garden. She was absolutely terrified. My wife isn't a well woman, Chief Inspector. She suffers from depression." *Booze, more likely*, Wallace thought. "I would appreciate it if you would caution him about staying away from my home."

"Do you want to lodge a formal complaint?"

"No, just warn him to stay away from my wife."

This couldn't have worked out better. Booth went back to St Cadfael's certain that he had solved the problem of Gilchrist once and for all. Now all he had to do was get Isobel to see sense.

Isobel got off the bed and watched Booth walk to his car parked at the end of the drive. So, he had been spying on her. All this time he had been waiting for the opportunity to ruin her life again. She loved him, but she despised him too. Why couldn't he let her have a little happiness in her life? She went into the kitchen and retrieved the bottle of vodka she had stowed away behind the tins on the top shelf. For a few moments she stared at it, then quickly poured it down the sink. She had to stay sober.

Mick had told her all about his girlfriend Hannah and how he had been hauled in for questioning. She believed him when he said he was innocent. He would never do anything so cruel. The newspaper on the worktop screamed out at her. Poor girl. Some men were pigs. Snapping open her mobile phone, she called Mick and arranged to meet him in the Corn House for lunch. Edward could go to hell.

Mick was already sitting at a table in the window when Isobel walked into the restaurant.

"I'm glad you came," she said. "I was so worried about you." She leaned over and patted his hand. "We have to talk. There's something I want to tell you. Not here, you must come over to the farm."

"I can't. What if Edward finds out? Knowing him, he's already told the police about my last visit."

"It's my house, not his. I've let him rule me too long."

"I don't understand."

"We, that is Julia and I, inherited a substantial amount of money from our grandparents and parents. A fortune even by today's standards. Do you really think a headmaster could afford a luxury BMW and a farm covering fifty acres? They also left us the villa in Tuscany, a house in Provence and a cottage in Wales. He can rule every other part of my life, but he can't touch my inheritance."

"Then why do you let him control you?"

"I love him. I still do. Can you understand that?"

"I suppose so, but I can't stand the way he treats you."

"We'll talk about this tomorrow at the farm. Let's eat."

*

Isobel waited impatiently for Mick to arrive. When she saw him coming across the field, Barney racing along at his side, she beamed with pleasure. He kicked off his trainers and followed her nervously into the big, bright kitchen. He settled himself in an easy chair while Isobel fussed with sandwiches and cakes; enough to feed a small army. When they were both settled, she said, "There are a few things you should know about Edward and his teaching career."

"I can't believe it!" Mick exclaimed when she told him. "And he had the cheek to chastise me about my professional behaviour."

"I've only told you, because it gives you a bit of leverage to get your job back."

Mick grinned broadly. "I can't wait to see his face when I tackle him about this."

Isobel smiled, her eyes misty with emotion. If he only knew the whole story.

38

Booth slumped into his chair, his face grey. Bile rose in his throat, threatening to engulf him. He poured a glass of water from the carafe on his desk and gulped it down. For a few moments he stared unseeing through the window. Summoning all his guile, he sat up straight and stared at Mick Gilchrist. He had to knock this on the head *now* before it got out of hand. Attack was the best defence.

"How dare you come in here and question my integrity. *You* of all people! I don't know where you heard this ridiculous rumour, but I can assure you that's all it is, a rumour. Now get out of my office."

"I had it straight from the horse's mouth, so to speak. Isobel told me."

Booth swallowed hard. He was too shocked to speak. Isobel had betrayed him to this, *this gardener*. How could she? For a moment he couldn't quite grasp the implications of her betrayal.

"You're a liar and a cheat, Edward," Mick stated, deliberately being familiar. "You accused me of unprofessional behaviour, but you're worse. You lied about your doctorate to get this job."

"That's not true. I read for an M.Phil/Ph.D."

"Yes, but you dropped out."

"I completed all the research. Research that had significant importance in the field of education."

"Cut the crap, Edward. I want my job back. I don't care how you do it, but I want it back. Perhaps you should sack your secretary instead. Don't try contacting DCI Wallace. Falsifying educational qualifications to secure a post is considered to be fraud. You could land in jail."

"I didn't falsify my credentials. I'm a qualified teacher and I have a degree in history!" Booth spluttered.

"I'm not questioning your intelligence, Edward, just your integrity and honesty. You've got until the weekend. I intend to be here bright and early on Monday morning whatever the consequences, otherwise the governors will hear about this."

Booth was too shocked to retaliate. This wasn't happening, not now when his career was on the up. What else had Isobel told Gilchrist? Mick stormed out of his office, slamming the door behind him.

Isobel watched Edward get out of his BMW and stride towards the house, his face a mask of fury, but she didn't care. He would have to let her see Mick as often as she liked and he couldn't do a thing about it.

"Isobel! Isobel!" Booth shouted up the stairs. "Get down here at once. Do you hear me?"

"What is it, dear?" she asked calmly when she came down. "Is something wrong?"

"You know damn well what's wrong! Why did you tell that little shit Gilchrist about my doctorate?"

"Surely you mean lack of a doctorate, Edward?"

Stunned, Booth dropped onto the sofa, clenching his hands over and over again. Why was she acting like this? She loved him and he loved her.

"Oh, just one other thing, Edward. Remember that the farm is *mine*, and everything else for that matter. You have nothing; you never did. From now on I'll do exactly as I please."

Edward jumped up, barely able to control his anger, and pushed her onto the sofa. He stood over her, clenching his fists until the knuckles turned white. She had no right. Hadn't he protected her all these years? She should be grateful, not trying to ruin him.

"Now listen to me, Isobel. The property may be in your name, but I have rights. I'm your husband so legally I'm entitled to half of everything."

Edward was a control freak. He had dictated her life since the day they were married; stripped her of her independence. Controlled her through fear and uncertainty while he sailed through one success after another. Now it was her turn to control him.

"You have no rights. Actually, the property belongs jointly to me and Julia. The only way you can get your hands on it is if we divorce. You wouldn't want that, would you Edward? All that dirty linen in public. All sorts of things could come out, couldn't they," she said with a knowing smile.

"Let's sit down and talk things over," Booth said,

changing his tone. "I'll pour you a gin and tonic." A few strong shots would loosen her up. "Perhaps I have been a bit pig-headed about Gilchrist."

"No thanks, there's none in the house, but you can make me a nice cup of tea."

Booth slunk into the kitchen totally fazed by Isobel's behaviour. He searched her hiding places for bottles of booze. It was all gone. She had stopped drinking, but not for him; for Gilchrist. He would be a laughing stock with parents and pupils if they found out about his Ph.D.

The image of his humiliation haunted him all over the weekend. He had asked the clerk to the governors to call an extra-ordinary meeting to discuss Gilchrist. The irritation showed on their faces. They had better things to do on a Monday morning, like a round of golf.

"What's this all about Booth?" Amanda Squires asked. "You're lucky I have a conference this afternoon and I'm not in court."

Sounds of muttering emanated round the room. A few governors shuffled irritably, others stared sullenly into space, willing Booth to get on with it.

"It seems we have a problem. Michael Gilchrist has threatened to take action against the school for unfair dismissal if he's not reinstated immediately... an industrial tribunal."

"According to you, he was being over-familiar with the girls," Giles Ponting said. He looked round at the others. "We couldn't have that, could we?"

"I did think we were being a bit harsh at the time.

After all, nothing was really proved," Canon Grayling added. "Most of the pupils seem to like him."

"Have pupils themselves complained, or any parents?" Amanda Squires asked. "I wasn't in the last meeting, neither was Pryce-Jones."

"We had a quorum, so the decision was taken to dismiss him," Booth said defensively. "After Ella Chapman I didn't think we could take the risk."

"A very narrow vote in my opinion," Canon Grayling interjected. "Certainly, there was some room for doubt. I voted against his dismissal."

"He was dismissed based on your assessment of his behaviour, Booth," Ponting added. I would prefer not to be involved with this kind of dispute at the moment. The Party wouldn't like it. I suggest we get him in here and hear his side of the story."

"Very well. He's downstairs. I'll ask him to come up."

"Please sit down," Booth said, when Mick came into the room.

"I prefer to stand." Mick was familiar with the psychology in meetings, particularly with governors. He wanted to be in command of the interview, not give them a chance to talk down to him. "I won't prevaricate. I want my job back, otherwise I intend to take this matter further. You had absolutely no reason to dismiss me other than inaccurate information provided to you by Dr Booth."

Amanda Squires studied Mick. There was no sign of nervous tension; more veiled anger and resentment at his situation. With his good looks, dark pin-striped suit and university tie he looked the epitome of a successful professional. On the other hand, his persona could conceal a man who prowled on children. Whatever decision was taken it had to be based on factual evidence, and they didn't have a great deal.

"Dr Booth's secretary spied on me from the window in her office. She saw me pat the girls on the arm and shoulder a few times. There was absolutely nothing in it. I explained to Dr Booth that they were concerned about their garden designs. They needed some reassurance, that's all. He construed it as touching them inappropriately. If you question the girls concerned I'm sure they will support what I've said."

"Thank you, Mr Gilchrist. Is there anything more you wish to add? If not we'll get back to you in due course," Ponting said.

"Today," Mick said firmly. Turning on his heel he marched towards the door and spun round. "I want it resolved *today*."

"The best way to tackle this is to speak to the girls informally," Ponting said. "We don't want parents getting suspicious. Perhaps you could help us out here, Amanda. A stroll around the grounds at lunchtime. Booth can point out the girls. Have a bit of a girly chat."

Amanda glared at him. It was typical of that pompous ass. He always ran scared whenever he thought his position in the Party would be at risk. Finally, she nodded. She had the expertise to question them without them realising what she was after.

Directly after lunch the governors resumed their

meeting. Anxiety registered on every face except Grayling's. He sat smiling benignly with his eyes closed.

"Well, what did you find out?" Ponting asked Amanda Squires.

"Nothing. I spoke to the girls concerned and quite a few others, including some boys. None of them had a bad word to say about Gilchrist. Quite the reverse in fact. He's obviously well-liked, not just for his amiable manner, but because they think he's a good teacher. They love his garden design course and were devastated when he left, although they don't know why.

"In my opinion, he should be reinstated. There's absolutely no evidence to suggest he touched anyone inappropriately. We wouldn't have a leg to stand on if it went to an industrial tribunal. If that leaves egg on your face, Booth, it's too bad. You'll have to think up something between you and Gilchrist about his absence."

Booth's face flushed with anger. He was furious at being outwitted by Gilchrist and it was all Isobel's fault. She had always been so compliant, knowing that he had her interests at heart. His stomach lurched at the possibilities. His income didn't come anyway near his expenditure. Without her money he couldn't maintain his lifestyle. He fingered the lapel of his bespoke suit as he glanced at his Rolex. Now he had to humiliate himself even further and give Gilchrist his job back. Well, he wouldn't be the one to tell him. The governors could do their own dirty work.

Mick was at Isobel's when the call came from the

chair of governors. Giles Ponting gave him the news in clipped tones.

"You've been reinstated, Gilchrist, but I have to say that your familiar behaviour with the girls has been noted. You must understand that we had to act to protect pupils and the good name of St Cadfael's."

"I repeat what I told you this morning. I didn't touch the girls inappropriately."

"We've agreed that Dr Booth will tell pupils that you were taken ill with a viral infection and needed some time off. Don't push your luck, Gilchrist. If anything like this happens again you will be dismissed immediately. Is that clear?"

Mick winced when Ponting slammed down the receiver. Pompous sod! He had won this time, but he had to be extremely careful in future. Booth was out for his blood. One foot out of line and he would use it against him. If it hadn't been for Isobel he would be ruined. He owed her so much. Mick had seen the other side of Booth. A calculating, selfish bully who had controlled her for years. Now it was his turn to be controlled.

*

Booth braked hard, sending gravel shooting out in all directions. The dogs romping towards him yelped as bits of stone hit them. Clenching his fists, he took deep breaths, trying to calm the thudding in his chest. Rivulets of sweat coursed down his back, dampening his shirt. He had to appear calm, composed. Grabbing his briefcase, he crunched over the drive. Isobel was staring through the window, her face unreadable. She turned away abruptly without even acknowledging him.

"Isobel, I'm home!" he called as though nothing had happened. She was in the kitchen preparing dinner. "Good news, darling. Gilchrist has been reinstated."

"For how long this time, Edward? Until you find another excuse to get rid of him?"

Edward put his arms around her, but she pulled away. This was going to be harder than he supposed. Isobel ignored him, busying herself laying places at the big oak table. She would prepare his meals, do his washing, look after the home, but she wouldn't pander to him. Her life would be different now. She felt confident, valued. Mick had done that for her. Her days of burying herself away on the farm were ended.

39

NOVEMBER 2022

Seemingly engrossed with his mobile phone, the man parked a hundred yards along the road from the large, detached house. He stared covertly into his driving mirror. A woman was standing in the open doorway waving, as the Volvo estate swung out of the driveway and headed in the opposite direction. The light was already failing and it would soon be dark; dark enough for him to approach the house without being seen. Fifteen minutes later he started the car and drove towards a group of semis where a number of vehicles were parked outside. He reversed into a shadowy space between two cars, well away from any street light.

He pulled his hood up over his baseball cap and zipped his jacket high enough to conceal most of his face. Carrying a long box, he swiftly walked back to the house. The curtains were drawn in the living room and the hall light was off. Like a cat, he moved stealthily around the back of the house to the kitchen. Through the slat blinds he could see the woman pouring milk into a cup and adding a spoonful of coffee. He waited until she had taken the drink into another room and switched off the light. Slowly, he tried the door handle. It was locked. He would have to try the front.

Taking a deep breath, he rang the doorbell and waited. The outline of a woman appeared behind the glass door. Quickly, he pulled down his hood, keeping in the shadows. The door opened partially. It was on a safety chain.

"I'm sorry to bother you, but I'm looking for 'The Orchard'. My satnav seems to have brought me to the wrong place. It's supposed to be along here somewhere. I'm a courier. If I don't deliver these flowers soon they'll be half dead."

"There's no property here by that name. Wait a minute. It may be that new house about half a mile away. You'll have to get back on to the Shrewsbury road. There's a lane about fifty yards away. You can just see it. It's a short cut."

Suddenly, the man lunged against the door. It crashed open, leaving the safety chain dangling. He slammed it shut. Before she had a chance to scream, he clasped his hand over her mouth and shoved her into the living room. In the seconds before he brought the heavy glass paperweight crashing down on Emily Bryant's head, her eyes registered recognition. She fell to the floor, unconscious. He had to finish her off this time, make the bitch pay.

Suddenly, a child's cry came from upstairs. He froze, the paperweight still in his hand. He waited momentarily, but it was all quiet. He had to make it look like a sexual attack. In a frenzy he tore at her clothes, ripping off her underwear. Suddenly, he heard a vehicle coming up the drive and footsteps walking towards the house. He had to get out. Frantically, he ran into the kitchen and fumbled with the Yale lock. The door wouldn't budge. There were two bolts, one at the bottom and another at the top of the door. It was like Fort Knox. Suddenly, a voice called from the front door.

"Emily, what have I told you about leaving the door unlocked? Oh my God, what's happened?" The baby started to cry again. Paul dialled 999 then bolted upstairs to fetch her, his heart in his mouth. Grabbing her out of her cot, he raced back to Emily. "The ambulance will be here soon, darling."

Frantically, the intruder slid the locks, lunged through the back door and disappeared into the night.

*

Emily was lucky the intruder had only hit her once. She suffered a serious concussion and was kept in hospital for a couple of days for observation. DCI Wallace stood at the end of the bed looking at her still form. He hadn't really believed her when she had told him someone was out to get her.

"Do you think it could have been the same man who tried to run you off the road?"

"I can't remember anything about what happened," Emily said. "I remember answering the door and giving directions, but he was standing in the shadows. I knew it was a man, but it was too dark to see him properly. After that it's a complete blank. His voice was muffled by the coat pulled up in front of his face."

"Sometimes patients will have amnesia after an experience of this nature," the doctor said. "Often it's temporary, but there's no way of knowing if she will ever remember what happened. It's a way of blocking out traumatic incidents."

"If there's anything at all you remember, please let us know," Wallace said. Emily smiled feebly. "Don't worry, we'll find him."

"The CSIs have scoured the house for any evidence," Wallace said as Butler drove back to the police station. "Zilch! No fingerprints on the paperweight or anything else. They couldn't even find a hair; not that it would do much good. If the attacker doesn't have DNA on record we're stuffed."

"Do you think it's the same man who attacked Hannah Jarvis outside the Armoury?"

"Possibly, he was wearing a baseball cap like Emily's attacker, but that's not enough to lead anywhere. Thousands of men wear baseball caps, although there are some similarities," Wallace mused. "A random attack. The victim's clothing was torn, but there was no evidence of sexual assault."

Butler shrugged his shoulders. "It's a bit strange, but both men were frightened off before they could do anything."

"I'm convinced Mrs Bryant's attacker was the same man who tried to run her off the road; the same man she saw in Marks & Spencer. He wants her out of the way before she recognises him. He may try again."

*

Emily stirred in the bed and opened her eyes briefly before dropping back into sleep. The nurse shook Paul's shoulder gently.

"Mr Bryant. Mr Bryant. Why don't you go home, get some rest and come back in the morning. Your wife is fine, but she'll be a bit groggy for a while. By tomorrow morning she'll probably be much brighter." She smiled and walked off to the nursing station at the end of the corridor.

Reluctantly, Paul walked to the door and looked back at Emily. She looked so small and vulnerable. His heart clenched. His eyes were red with fatigue and worry. A good night's sleep would do him good.

A doctor in green hospital scrubs, stethoscope thrown casually around his neck, stepped out as he got into the lift, coughing into a handkerchief. He made his way down the corridor towards the nursing station and went into a side ward. An elderly man lay snoring gently, the remote control for the television still in his hand. The doctor waited a few seconds and looked out. Two nurses were sitting at their station with their backs to him, gazing at a computer screen. Another flicked through a batch of patient records. She picked them up, walked into the inner office and closed the door.

The doctor pulled up his surgical mask, walked quietly past and looked into the bays. His heart quickened when he saw Emily. This time he had to do the job properly. She was in a deep sleep. Taking a pillow from the chair, he approached the bed, leaned over her and pressed the pillow down on her face. Suddenly, her eyes shot open. She kicked out and flailed her arms, knocking over the jug of water on the bedside cabinet. Startled, he loosened his grip. Emily screamed when she saw his eyes above the mask.

Running footsteps came down the corridor. Two nurses burst through the open door and rushed to the bed. The 'doctor' pushed them aside and bolted through the door.

"He tried to kill me," Emily sobbed. "The doctor, he tried to smother me."

"Call security!" the sister said to the young nurse. "Quickly! Tell them a man wearing scrubs is impersonating a doctor."

The 'doctor' walked through the main entrance of the hospital just as security received the call. *Don't panic!* he thought. *Walk normally or you'll look suspicious. Get in the car and drive slowly.*

A mile from the hospital he stopped the car and peeled off the scrubs. He couldn't risk being seen in them and he couldn't throw them away. They would have to be burned. Forty-five minutes later he dumped them in an industrial bin behind a derelict warehouse. He set them alight and waited until they turned to ashes. He had failed again. Both times she had looked into his eyes, she registered a fleeting recognition. It was only a matter of time before she remembered him.

40

Things had worked out better than he expected. Mick had his teaching job back and he could see Isobel whenever he liked. He was in control now. Edward Booth had met his match and Mick was going to exploit it as much as possible. He wouldn't allow him to get the upper hand again. In fact, he had plans to extend his role in the school and Booth wouldn't dare to object. Whistling softly to himself, he trudged over the field, Barney bounding ahead.

From the bedroom window Booth stared down at Gilchrist. This was too much. Hadn't Isobel humiliated him enough? Didn't she understand that everything he did was for her benefit? All he wanted to do was protect her from herself, and this is how she repaid him. He moved away from the window and lay on the bed, thinking. Anger flared as he listened to the laughter and conversation coming from the kitchen. They were laughing at him; laughing at his helplessness. Somehow or other he had to get Gilchrist off his back; discredit him in Isobel's eyes.

"You should have seen his face when I mentioned his doctorate," Mick laughed. "I thought he would have an apoplectic fit."

"Edward is my husband and I love him, never forget that Mick," Isobel retorted with a hint of anger. "What I told you was to help you get back on your feet, not to hold it over Edward's head." "I'm sorry. I thought…

"I value our friendship, but don't overstep the mark. I know how to handle Edward. He's upstairs. He won't come down while you're here. Perhaps it would be better if you only come over when Edward isn't here."

"You're right. He's bound to feel embarrassed. I promise I'll stay out of his way as much as possible in school."

That evening Isobel cooked Edward a large steak and opened a bottle of Rioja; his favourite. She couldn't bear to see the stricken look on his face and the way he hung his head every time she looked at him. He was such a little boy at times. When he finally came into the kitchen she kissed him on the cheek. He looked up at her, tears in his eyes. She had forgiven him, but he hadn't forgiven her. She had stabbed him in the heart as surely as if she had wielded a knife. She loved Gilchrist more than she loved him. He couldn't allow that. There was only room for one man in Isobel's life.

The following morning Booth watched Mick striding down the path towards the annexe carrying a pile of exercise books. He had to admit that his classes had progressed well. Pupils were developing a real interest in garden design, which Gilchrist was combining with technical and computer studies. He might have to sacrifice their interests for his own. Every time they passed each other on the way to classes they studiously ignored each other, neither wanting a face-to-face confrontation. To be fair Gilchrist had been the epitome of discretion, but he still knew something he shouldn't ever have been told. He hated him for knowing.

"Mrs James, ask Gilchrist to come to my office at the end of his class."

He was going to play him at his own game. *I'm Dr Edward Booth and nobody outwits me.*

Mick ran up the stairs to Booth's office, taking them two at a time. He felt full of energy and optimism. Perhaps Booth was ready to give him more teaching work.

"Sit down, Gilchrist. I have a proposition for you."

Mick regarded him quizzically, a cocky smile hovering on his lips. Booth felt his craw rising, but managed to control it.

"Regarding our little conversation the other day. As I told you at the time, I carried out all the research for my Ph.D. when I took over St Cadfael's, but I didn't have time to write it up. I've contacted the university and they've agreed to allow me to continue. My previous tutor has taken up an appointment in Toronto. It means going up to London for meetings with my new tutor. Once he's satisfied, my viva voce will be arranged."

"You still lied to the governors. You're a fraud, Booth."

"I'm going to be fair with you, Gilchrist. You keep quiet about this and I'll ensure that in due course you'll get a full-time teaching job here at St Cadfael's."

Mick stared at him, not sure whether to believe his luck. A permanent job. It's what he had been dreaming of for years.

"What's the catch, Booth?"

"Within the next year or so I should have a valid doctorate. It's a foregone conclusion. I've discussed it with my original tutor on Skype. If I have to, I'll inform the governors that I hadn't quite completed my Ph.D., because it was referred for adjustments. I haven't had the time to work on it since I took over as head teacher. It's partially true, of course. The research was ongoing. My appointment wasn't dependent on it."

"If you think I'll let you get away with that you can think again, Booth." Mick grinned. He wasn't about to let Booth off the hook just yet

"That's another thing. From now on you call me Dr Booth and nothing else. Is that clear, Gilchrist? Take it or leave it!"

Mick stood and walked to the door. "Okay, Dr Booth. It's Hobson's Choice for both of us. I can live with that, but don't try any of your tricks. We both have a lot to lose in this partnership."

Booth sat down, smiling to himself. If that little shit thought he could ever outwit him he was sadly mistaken. He would have to grit his teeth, knowing that Gilchrist would be spending time with Isobel in his absence. If he was patient it would pan out as he had planned.

He felt quite light-hearted on the drive home through country lanes. The farm came into view as he rounded a bend. They had bought the meadow and adjacent fields for the dogs to run around. In the outer fields sheep grazed peacefully. The lowing of a cow broke the stillness in the air. He could see the herd of Hereford's gathered around a small copse.

Unfortunately, an occasional rambler trespassed on his land; people like Gilchrist walking their dogs. He would have to put up another sign warning them off. He couldn't wait to tell Isobel about his latest idea.

"Isobel!" he called. "Isobel, where are you?"

She came running downstairs, concerned at the urgency in his voice. He smiled broadly and held out his arms to her.

"Let's have a sherry," he said, "and sit in the conservatory for a bit. It's such a glorious day. I've got something to tell you."

Isobel frowned. What was he up to now?

"I thought we'd settled all this business with Mick."

"It's not about Gilchrist." Edward handed a glass of sherry to Isobel and motioned her to sit down beside him. "Firstly, I've decided to complete my Ph.D. It's about time. Secondly, I'm going to buy you a horse."

"A horse! Edward that's wonderful. You know how much I love riding." Her face fell. "It won't be much fun on my own."

"I'll ride with you, like we used to years ago. We can build a stable in the field. It will give you something to do when I'm at work. We can take the dogs for a run at the same time. I can see us now, mucking out the stables and grooming the horses. We'll pop to the auctions in Hereford next week."

They sat in the conservatory, watching the sun go down and making plans. Isobel was like a child, even planning their riding outfits. She couldn't wait to tell Mick. Dear Edward, to think of something like this. Perhaps this was a turning point in their relationship. Standing up to him had been good for both of them.

Edward lay in bed next to Isobel. She had fallen asleep almost as soon as her head touched the pillow. Feeling a sudden surge of tenderness, he leaned over and kissed her gently on the cheek. He was going to be the perfect husband from now on.

41

The wizened man in the hospital bed opened his eyes. A lifetime of booze and sleeping rough had made him old before his time. It was hard to believe he had only just turned sixty. Three meals a day and a warm bed at night had transformed him. A hint of colour touched his cheeks and his hands had stopped shaking. His lined face had started to fill out and his eyes were bright and intelligent.

"How are you, Mr Jaynes?"

"Much better. The food here is great." Wallace smiled inwardly. It wasn't often patients enthused about hospital food. "The doctor tells me you'll be leaving hospital soon."

"Tomorrow… social services have found me a place to stay in a hostel for the homeless. If I stay off the booze they may get me into an old people's home. I'm getting too old to be on the streets. I expect you're here about the bloke I saw on the bridge."

"Do you think you would recognise him from a photograph?"

"He was standing right under the light near the bridge. When he turned his head towards me I could see his face clearly."

"I'll send a car to bring you to the police station in a few days, once you've had chance to settle in the hostel."

If the man he saw was Gilchrist it would be a massive breakthrough. He was convinced he was as guilty as hell. The sooner he was banged up the better.

Three days later Mick sat in the outer room, his mind whirling. Why had he been picked up to take part in an identity parade? Surely, they would have done it before now? According to Wallace, an old tramp had seen a man on the towpath. They were clutching at straws to get a result for the Ella Chapman murder.

Wallace directed Sammy Jaynes to a chair by his desk. He was still excited about arriving at the police station in a squad car.

"I want you to look through these photographs. Tell me if you recognise the man you saw that night near the bridge."

Jaynes slowly picked up each photograph and studied it carefully. He shook his head.

"Mr Jaynes, are you sure you don't recognise any of these men?" he asked.

"No, sorry."

Wallace placed another one on the table. "Okay, let's have a look at this one."

"Him, that's him!" he exclaimed.

"Are you sure that's the man you saw throw his trainers into the river?"

"Absolutely positive. I could have done with a good pair of trainers myself."

"And you would swear to this in a court of law?"

"Definitely."

"Thank you, Mr Jaynes. Butler, tell Baker to arrange transport for him back to the hostel. Give him a coffee while he's waiting."

Gilchrist sat slouched over the table in the interview room, his eyes closed. They snapped open when Wallace came in.

"Gilchrist, we want to question you further about the murder of Ella Chapman."

"I didn't kill her! I swear it!"

"Sit down, Gilchrist. No more lies. You were seen throwing your trainers over English Bridge on the night of Ella Chapman's murder."

"So what? I'd had a few drinks, stepped in some dog muck. It was all over my trainers. They were old, not worth cleaning up, so I threw them into the river."

He kept his hands under the table to conceal the trembling. One false move and he was finished.

"Forensics didn't find any trace of dog faeces."

"The river was flowing fast. It must have washed off."

"You're lying, Gilchrist. You killed Ella Chapman. Dr Booth told us how you like to chat up the girls. You tried it on with Ella and she rejected you, so you murdered her."

"That's not true! I didn't touch her! She was already dead!"

Mick stopped, his head hanging on his chest. His

shirt was soaking with sweat. He had just landed himself right in it.

"Okay, okay! I'll make a statement."

"For the benefit of the tape, Peter Michael Gilchrist, in the presence of his solicitor, has agreed to make a statement in connection with the murder of Ella Chapman."

"After taking my girlfriend home that night, I went back out. I descended the steps at English Bridge and walked along the towpath intending to climb the hill at Blackfriars and back into town. The pubs were still open. I still had time for a couple of drinks."

Mick paused. His throat was as dry as cardboard. He gulped some water from the glass on the table.

"I felt a bit whoozy and needed some fresh air. As I walked below Blackfriars I heard a kind of scuffling and a faint cry. I thought it was some animal foraging around. When I was about thirty yards away I spotted the shadowy outline of a couple. They were locked in an embrace close to the water. I couldn't see them clearly, but I guessed they were at it… you know what I mean. It goes on all the time down by the river."

Gilchrist took a deep breath. "I coughed loudly so they would know I was heading towards them. I was close enough by now to make out that it was a man and a woman. You never know these days."

"Are you absolutely certain?"

"Yes, it was definitely a man and a woman. Suddenly, the woman dropped to the ground, her upper body hanging over the river. When I shouted out the man turned and bolted up the hill towards Traitor's Gate. The woman was still lying on the ground. I thought she was drunk so I walked past her. I didn't want to get involved with a drunken woman. She might have accused me of something. Once bitten. I didn't want a repeat of what happened in Plymouth. Damn it! She was too close to the water. If she tried to get up she could have gone in head first. I doubled back and shouted at her. 'You silly cow! Get up before you fall in.' She didn't budge, so I nudged her with the toe of my trainer, but she didn't respond."

"You assumed she was drunk?"

"At first, but when she didn't move I pushed her over with my foot. Her eyes were wide open, vacant. Horrified, I stepped back, almost falling sideways into the river. The woman wasn't drunk, she was dead. She was just a kid and I knew her. It was Ella Chapman."

"Why didn't you call the police?"

"I panicked. What if I was accused of killing her? I forced myself to calm down; to control my panic. I looked down the path in both directions. There wasn't a soul on the towpath. The body was half in the water. All I had to do was push it in with my foot. I didn't even have to touch it. It slid into the river with barely a splash."

Wallace looked at Butler and back to Gilchrist. "So you threw your trainers into the river in case, because they had been in contact with the body."

"Yes, I wasn't thinking straight. I raced back towards English Bridge, up the steps onto the pavement. I kicked off my trainers and dropped them over the balustrade into the water below and headed home. There was nothing to connect me with the girl's death. After a couple of whiskies I felt calmer. Nobody had seen me and I hadn't touched the body. My girlfriend was in bed snoring like a pig when I crawled in beside her. She wouldn't even know I'd left the house."

"The truth is, you killed Ella and pushed her body into the river."

"No! I slept badly that night. The girl's face swam in and out of my dreams. Wide, terrified eyes accusing me. In the middle of the night I woke up bathed in sweat, my heart pounding like a sledgehammer. Remembering the girl who accused me of sexual assault in Plymouth. It was happening all over again."

"I'll ask you again. Why didn't you just call the police?"

"It was too late. How could I have been so stupid? There was no way I could tell the police anything. I would have been arrested like before."

The thought of prison brought him out in a fresh sweat. He knew what happened to men in prison who assaulted kids.

Wallace played with his bottom lip... a habit that infuriated Butler. It usually meant that his boss was undecided about something. Suddenly, he stood up and faced Mick.

"Interview terminated." He headed for the door, Butler close behind him. A uniformed officer stood silently against the wall.

"I didn't do it! You have to believe me!" Gilchrist shouted.

"Get hold of the CPS to ascertain if we can charge him with Ella Chapman's murder,"

Wallace said, as they walked down the corridor.

Gilchrist hadn't confessed, but everything pointed to him being Ella's killer. But why would Gilchrist have made up such a convoluted story? Why would he make it up at all? All they had was a pair of water-damaged trainers and a seemingly plausible story related by a very frightened suspect. Jaynes would testify in court, but would the jury believe him? He was a well-known vagrant, fond of the booze. He had been picked up by the police on a number of occasions. Unless they could come up with some solid evidence they could come unstuck.

After a week in the water the trainers were unlikely to produce viable DNA. Apart from the eye witness and the trainers, they had no other evidence. All Jaynes could testify to was that he saw Gilchrist throwing his trainers over English Bridge. It was quite common for drunks to throw things in the river; pizza boxes, bottles, even shoes for a lark.

Gilchrist had admitted to seeing a couple struggling and pushing the body into the river with his trainers. They could only hold him for so long.

Gilchrist left the police station with his solicitor, still protesting his innocence. Wallace watched him leaving from his office window.

"I have a nasty feeling about this case, Phil," he said. "Everything points to Gilchrist, but my gut feeling tells me he may be speaking the truth. His account of events hasn't altered even after extensive questioning. He's very definite about what he saw."

"We've had killers like that before. He's a clever man."

"Clever people make mistakes, usually through arrogance. They like to think they can outsmart the system. The Super would never agree to twenty-four hour surveillance, so we'll have to manage as best we can."

Baker was bored stiff. From his vantage point he could see Gilchrist's front door. Gilchrist hadn't left the house for two days except to open the door for his dog to run out into the small patch of garden. He could see the back door in a side alley that didn't lead anywhere except to the pine end of another house. The only way out was at the front. He took a sip from the congealed coffee in a plastic cup and grimaced. It was stone cold.

Suddenly, the front door opened and the dog came out, followed by Gilchrist. He walked to a Honda parked at the curb and opened the door for the dog to get in. Gilchrist drove out of town into the countryside. About fifteen miles outside Shrewsbury he pulled into a lay by and let the dog out. He climbed over a style and set off purposefully over the field towards a large farmhouse.

Taking out a pair of binoculars, Baker followed his progress. As Gilchrist approached the house a woman came out followed by a pair of yapping dogs. She embraced him and they went into the house. Baker yanked out his mobile phone.

"Sir, I followed Gilchrist for about fifteen miles outside Shrewsbury. He walked his dog over the fields and went into a house. A woman seemed to be waiting for him."

"That's Dr Booth's home. Gilchrist is friendly with his wife. Stay with it, Baker, and make sure he goes home."

Baker parked up in front of a farm track gateway in a bend in the road from where he could easily survey the area. He settled back to wait.

Inside the farmhouse Mick sat close to Isobel on the sofa, his head in his hands.

"They dragged me in for questioning again, Isobel. Apparently, an old vagrant saw me dropping my trainers into the river."

"Why? Why did you throw them away?"

"It's a long story, but I swear I didn't kill the girl."

"I want to know everything about that night, Mick, and your part in it."

Mick took a deep breath and took Isobel's hand. He kept it there until he had finished relating the story. Sighing, he got up and walked to the window.

"They won't leave me alone until they get a conviction, Isobel. I don't know what to do anymore. It's a nightmare. You do believe me, don't you?" he said turning towards her.

Isobel grabbed his arms and looked deep into his eyes, trying to fathom his actions. "You've been very stupid, but I don't think you're a killer. It's not in you." She led him back to the sofa and sat down beside him. "We have to find a way of proving your innocence."

"How?"

"We could start by hiring a private detective to verify your movements on the night in question."

"The police have already done that; they've scoured Shrewsbury."

"If a drunken old tramp saw you, perhaps you were seen about town by others the police haven't questioned. Anything is worth a try."

"There's no point, Isobel! They've already issued a description asking for people to come forward with information." His shoulders slumped. There seemed to be no way out.

Baker had waited almost two hours before Gilchrist came out of the house. He watched him bend to kiss Isobel and start back over the fields. They must have had a hell of a lot to say to each other for it to take so long.

Mick drove home, feeling better after speaking with Isobel. She always gave him such strength; helped him to see things more clearly. He didn't think hiring a private detective would help, but at least it gave him something positive to think about.

42

Wallace slapped his hands on Butler's desk. His frustration with the Chapman case was getting to him twenty-four seven. They had nothing on Gilchrist. Nobody other than Jaynes, the old vagrant, had seen him on the night of Ella Chapman's murder.

"Where do we go from here, Phil? Any ideas? If we could only find out the identity of 'P' it might help."

"Maybe is on the right track," Butler replied. "Perhaps she *was* going to Wellington for an abortion."

"They've already been questioned. Why a gym? That's what puzzles me. Okay, let's try the sports' centre again. Send and Williams up there."

*

Williams flashed his ID card at the young receptionist. "Has this man visited the centre during the last six months?" He put an identikit picture of Mick Gilchrist on the counter.

She shook her head. "I don't think so. We have hundreds of members. I can't remember them all." She examined the picture again. "No, I think I'd remember a guy *that* good-looking." She giggled. "I only work days. Perhaps the evening staff would recognise him."

"Thank you." Williams started to walk away, then doubled back. "How many staff work on reception?"

"About eight altogether, mostly part-time."

He pulled out a photograph and held it up. "Perhaps you've seen this girl?"

"Oh, yeah, she came here a few times with a woman. She wasn't a member, but they used to go into the café. The last time I saw her she was crying when she came out."

Williams' heart jumped. A decent lead at last.

"Can you describe the woman she was with in the café? Was she young or an older woman?" asked.

"She was quite old, maybe in her fifties or sixties. Hard to tell really."

"How was she dressed?"

"She wasn't wearing a miniskirt, that's for sure!" The teenager tittered. "Trousers and an anorak, I think. That's all I can remember. Oh, and a big hat with a brim, like a man's hat."

"Thank you," said. "If you remember anything else you can contact us on this number." She pushed a card under the glass screen.

"What an airhead!" Williams exclaimed. "Still, at least we know Ella met somebody here on more than one occasion."

"The girl's description matches the previous information we already have," told Wallace when they got back to the station.

"We've *got* to find out the identity of that woman," Wallace said. "Until we find her we've got zilch!"

They had been watching Gilchrist for seventy-two hours. He had only left home once, to see Isobel. They had no concrete evidence to pursue a conviction. Nobody referred to him as Peter. They had checked with his university, his old school friends and on the landscape gardening course he had taken. Unless it was for official documents, he never used the name Peter. He definitely wasn't the 'P' in Ella's diary. The CPS had already informed him that there was insufficient evidence to charge Gilchrist with Ella Chapman's murder. Deep down he was convinced that Gilchrist was innocent. Now they had to find 'P'.

*

Dr Booth came down the stairs, followed by the school Matron. She looked warily at Wallace and Butler. Her eyes darted nervously from Wallace to Booth.

"Mrs Jarvis, were you aware that Ella Chapman was nine weeks pregnant?"

"No! She was such a quiet girl. Very polite and respectful. On the day she died she came to me complaining about a migraine. She looked very pale and unwell. I thought a day or two resting in bed would do her good."

"You're absolutely sure?"

"I am a State Registered Nurse, you know," Matron retorted huffily. "If she had come to me feeling ill from pregnancy I would have recognised the symptoms."

"I'm sure you would."

"All boarders are registered with a GP in Shrewsbury, if that's of any help. Dr Booth's secretary has all the details."

"Thank you, Mrs Jarvis."

Wallace turned to Booth. "Do you know if Ella had any women friends? Someone more mature that she may have turned to for help?"

"Why would she? All the help she needed was right here at the school. Well, if that's all, Chief Inspector, I have a great deal of paperwork to get through."

"It's possible that Ella went to see her GP, because she didn't want Booth to find out," Butler remarked on their way out. "You know what it's like these days. A doctor won't inform the parents even if a girl is underage. If they had, she might still be alive today."

Ella's GP had no knowledge of her pregnancy. In fact, she had never attended the surgery to see him or any of the partners.

43

Wallace took a sip of his coffee while he turned the pages of Ella's diary. Butler looked at him enquiringly.

"Nothing!" he exclaimed. "Absolutely bugger all!"

"That's that then," Butler said wearily. "I suppose we could have another shot at Megan Pryce-Jones. She may be holding something back."

"Hang on," Wallace said. "We could have been on the wrong track all this time. Why didn't I think of it before? What if 'P' is a woman? We've only been looking for a man, because Ella was pregnant. What if the woman she was with in Wellington is 'P'? We need to question the airhead again."

"Okay, let's go," Butler said, motioning to .

The teenager behind the glass counter sighed. "I told you everything last time. The girl only came here a few times. She always seemed upset."

"What about the woman she was with?"

"She seemed to be comforting her, patting her on the arm and shushing her when she was crying."

"Anything else?"

"No, but she did have a funny name, more like a sort of nickname. When the woman went up to fetch a drink I heard her call out to her not to get coffee, because she had gone off it. I can't quite remember it."

Wallace devil-drummed impatiently on the counter. "Think harder!"

"P... P... Pish, Prish, that was it, definitely Prish."

"Thank you," Butler said, barely able to control his exhilaration.

On the drive back to Shrewsbury, Butler's exhilaration soon dissipated. He sighed audibly. They were moving one step forward and one back. They knew the woman Ella had been meeting was 'P', but they were no further ahead in knowing her identity.

"We know she was a mature woman, but why would she be helping Ella to get an abortion? It doesn't make any sense. All she had to do was see her own doctor."

"Perhaps she was afraid someone from the school would see her at the surgery." replied. "If it got back to Booth or Matron they would probably have contacted her parents if she refused to tell them why she needed to see a doctor. This Prish obviously knew her well enough to offer her help."

"It's all supposition," Wallace argued, when they arrived back at the police station. "We don't really know she was actually giving her advice on abortion."

"We could put out an artist's impression of the woman."

"Without a description of her face?" Wallace snapped.

He tapped his lips with his index finger. "Okay, let's concentrate on her clothes, especially the hat. The receptionist described it as a man's hat with a big brim."

"Lot's of women wear hats," Butler retorted.

"True, but how many wear hats with big brims during the day unless it's a sun hat? She must have been trying to disguise herself. Old-fashioned clothes, anorak, big man's hat in summertime. It could give us something to work on."

They put out the artist's impression in Wellington and surrounding areas. A couple of people came forward, claiming they had seen her in the sports' centre. Other than that she seemed to have disappeared into the ether.

Wallace's desk phone shrilled. He groaned as Butler handed him the telephone. Butler had fielded calls from the Chief Super for days. He couldn't avoid him any longer.

"What the hell is going on with the Chapman case, Wallace?" Chief Superintendent Payne growled.

"We've made some progress, sir. Frankly, it's very difficult with so little to go on. We've established that the woman Ella Chapman was with in the sports' centre was called Prish. A couple of people saw them together, but were unable to identify her except by the clothes she was wearing."

"Never mind about what she was wearing. I want to know who she is. The Chief Constable has been on my back. I want to see some progress and sharpish. *Is that clear?*"

Wallace gritted his teeth. "Yes, sir." He carefully replaced the receiver in its cradle, resisting the urge to slam it down hard. "One of these days I'll punch his lights out!"

Butler grinned. "Let me know when and I'll come and watch," he said, heading for the door.

Wallace swung from side to side, contemplating his next move. Suddenly, the phone rang, the harsh sound interrupting his thoughts.

"Sir, I've got a bloke on the blower who says he's seen the woman in the Chapman case."

Wallace sat bolt upright. "Another crank?"

"He seems pretty sensible to me, sir. The name's Boswell, Gerald Boswell."

"Okay, take him to the interview room. I'll be down in five minutes."

Wallace made a quick study of the man when he entered the interview room. Middle-aged, well-spoken, well-dressed, possibly a professional man.

"Thank you for taking the trouble to come into the station Mr Boswell. Now tell me where you saw the woman in question."

Boswell shifted nervously in his seat, eyeing the recording equipment.

"Don't worry, this isn't being recorded. It's just an informal interview."

Boswell visibly relaxed and settled back in his chair. He had thought twice about getting involved, but his sense of duty always got the better of him.

"She was walking down Pride Hill. I was behind her. When she reached Theatre Flats she went straight up the hill then down towards the Quarry. She looked very preoccupied. A young girl in school uniform was sitting on a bench by the side of the river. The woman sat beside her on the bench. It was obvious they knew each other, because they were sitting so close and whispering to each other."

"Why do you think it's the woman we want to see?"

"The clothes she was wearing. It was a hot day and she seemed to be bundled up for winter. She was wearing a hat like the Barbour waxed hats."

"Why were you in the Quarry?"

"I'm a Chartered Accountant. Boswell and Willard. We've been practising in the area for over twenty-five years. My job involves sitting down in front of a screen most of the day. I like to get out into the fresh air and eat my lunch down by the river."

"Do you go there every day?"

"Not every day, around two or three times a week unless the weather is really bad." Wallace nodded. "I'm also an amateur photographer. I like to take candid pictures of everyday scenes. I took a picture of the two of them sitting together on the bench with the swans and ducks in the background."

Boswell took a photograph out of his pocket and handed it to Wallace.

"It's only the back of them, I'm afraid."

It could have been a photograph of mother and daughter. Even from the back it suggested intimacy and a sense of protectiveness.

"It just looked like a good shot. Two people enjoying the river and wildlife."

"Was it just one shot?"

"This is the only other one, but it's blurred. The woman looked up the road as I was about to take the first picture."

Wallace examined the photograph. He couldn't make out the woman's features from the side view, but he was convinced she was middle-aged as opposed to elderly.

"I hope I haven't done anything wrong, Chief Inspector? I would never take a photograph showing their faces," Boswell said anxiously.

"Thank you for coming forward, Mr Boswell. You've been most helpful. Please let us know if you see the woman again."

44

Emma occasionally had flashes of that terrifying night when she had been attacked in her own home by a masked man. The same man who tried to smother her in the hospital. That's all it was... fleeting memories that dissipated like smoke into the ether. When she tried to piece elements together, her brain felt like a knitted sweater being unravelled.

She no longer felt secure at home, or anywhere else for that matter. Their resources were stretched to the limit. Paul was working from home to help with the baby, but she didn't feel safe. She would never feel safe until her attacker was caught and put away.

It was the eyes. She couldn't get rid of the feeling she knew those eyes. Emily shuddered. *What if the police couldn't find him?* she thought. She stifled a sob.

"What is it, Emily? Paul asked as he came into the sitting room with a cup of tea.

"I just wish I could remember more about the night I was attacked."

"It's as the doctor explained. You've blocked it out,

because your mind can't cope with the trauma. It's temporary amnesia. It could take months or even a year to recall what happened. Is there anything at all you can remember?"

"I told you, Paul, I can't remember anything about the man except the eyes. They were piercing, so frightening."

"I know." Paul took her in his arms and rocked her to and fro. *What would I do without him?* she thought. "I think you need to get out of the house for a bit. Have a change of scenery. It will do you good."

"What if he's out there, lurking around?"

"You have to go out sooner or later. It's not good for you to be cooped up indoors. Whoever he is, he knows the police are looking for him. He wouldn't risk coming anywhere near here. We'll take the baby for a short walk this afternoon. It will do us all good." Little Ava gurgled and smiled up at them as they pushed the pram together down the pavement. It felt good to be outside.

"You're right, Paul. I feel so much better having some fresh air," Emily said, as they strolled down the pavement. "Let's go as far as the village and have coffee and cakes."

A car passed them going in the opposite direction. The driver stared straight ahead. *She might as well make the most of it*, he thought. *The little bitch won't be around much longer.* He smiled inwardly. Next time he wouldn't mess up. Third time lucky. Once he had rid his life of Emily Bryant he was free and clear.

He wasn't sure if she had recognised him. The local rag had mentioned some kind of temporary amnesia. He had to find out for himself. It was risky, very risky, but he had to be certain.

He pulled into a parking area, negotiated a three point turn, and waited until he knew they had had enough time to be way ahead of him. *They must be going to the village,* he thought. He eased out of the lay-by and drove slowly passing them just as they got to the outskirts. He watched until he saw them enter the tea room.

For a moment he lost his nerve. She was bound to recognise him. No, it was far too risky! He sat in the car for ten minutes, weighing up the possibilities. There was no point in a disguise. That was the whole point. She had to see him as himself, no mask. Wearing jeans and sunglasses he casually walked in and sat at a table near the door. He might have to make a quick exit. Emily's back was to him. Now what?

Glancing towards the rear of the tea room. he spotted a sign for the loos. Taking a deep breath, he rose and walked towards the door. It was locked. He turned and walked back to his table. Emily was nursing the baby. She gave him a cursory glance as he walked past, but there wasn't a flicker of recognition. The risk had paid off in spades. A thrill of relief coursed through him. *Don't be rash, give it time,* he thought. *Lull her into a false sense of security.* Now he could concentrate on getting rid of her for good.

Over the next two weeks Emily's confidence improved. She looked forward to going into the village with Paul and Ava, but when he suggested going into Shrewsbury, she balked.

"I'm not ready, Paul. That man is out there walking the streets."

"He knows the police in Shrewsbury will be on the lookout for him. He's probably long gone."

"I don't know," Emily replied tentatively. "Let's give it another week."

"Okay, another week. Ava will enjoy the hustle and bustle of town. We can get her some new clothes from Marks and Spencer."

"That sounds good," Emily said, sounding more enthusiastic. It was time Ava had some new clothes.

45

Deep in thought, Wallace slumped in his chair and stared vacantly at the opposite wall. Slowly, he tapped his lips with his index finger. They had no leads except for the photograph taken by Gerald Boswell.

Who was the woman with Ella Chapman? Judging by her clothes, it was the same woman she had been meeting in Wellington. It had to be someone she knew. Was it the mother of one of her friends? Could it have been Megan Pryce-Jones's mother? Had Megan asked her to help Ella? Unlikely, but it was worth a try. He pressed a button on the intercom.

"Butler, come in here for a minute."

"What's, sir?"

"I think we ought to pay Mrs Pryce-Jones a visit."

"Mrs Pryce-Jones! Why?"

"Only her husband has been interviewed. Probably a waste of time, but we have to do something. By the way, any sightings of the man in the grey tracksuit and hoodie?

"Fat chance with that, sir. It's usually a look

associated with youngsters... teens and twenties. There are lots of them wandering around Shrewsbury with their 'builder's bottom' on show and no socks." Butler laughed. "Apparently, it's the fashion to show your underpants these days. The girls seem to like it. There's no accounting for taste."

"You might have something there. We've been looking for a man, but it could have been a teenager." Butler nodded. "Emily Bryant only saw his eyes. She gave no indication of his age, did she?"

"It's a thought, sir. It's more likely that Ella was meeting up with a young guy, someone nearer her own age."

"The only one interviewed who fits that age group was that lad helping out the caretaker on a casual basis." Wallace filtered through his notes. "Twenty years old, tall, mature build. Studying for Level Three Diploma in Public Services at Shrewsbury College. Apparently, he applied for the Police Service when he was eighteen. He was considered too immature, but advised to re-apply when he was a bit older. He's pretty determined to get in. That's why he's taking the course, to help him when he re-applies."

"We checked him out, guv. He's living with a girl in Belleview. Cast iron alibi. He was a bit worse for wear after a stag do and landed up in A & E after falling down the steps and hitting his head on the way out of the pub. His partner picked him up from the hospital, absolutely furious. A decent young couple expecting their first baby. I don't think there's much mileage there."

"Well, let's get up to Oswestry and interview Mrs Pryce-Jones."

"I thought Pryce-Jones was stationed in Anglesey."

"He is, but they have their own house near Oswestry."

*

The house wasn't at all what Wallace had expected. The RAF didn't provide such luxurious accommodation for its officers; certainly not for a Squadron Leader. Butler drove through massive wrought iron gates, following the tarmac drive. Manicured lawns on either side, mature trees and flower beds in full bloom. A folly stood on the hill behind the house.

The house was an enormous sandstone structure with steps leading up to a wide double-front door behind a stucco portico. Typical Georgian architecture. Long, high windows and attic rooms. It was magnificent.

"Wow!" Butler exclaimed. That must have cost a pretty penny."

"Pryce-Jones hasn't bought that on a Squadron Leader's salary," Wallace observed.

They mounted the steps and rang the doorbell. A petite, dark-haired woman answered the door. Wallace noted her clothes and the smart, expensive shoes.

"We would like to speak to Mrs Pryce-Jones," he said.

"I'm Mrs Pryce-Jones," she replied warily.

"Detective Chief Inspector Ben Wallace, Shrewsbury CID. I'd like to ask you a few questions about Ella Chapman. May we come in?"

"I have an important meeting in an hour."

She motioned them inside and directed them into a large, sumptuously furnished sitting room.

"How well did you know Ella?"

"I didn't really know her *that* well, but she and Megan were very close. She stayed here for a few weekends. Once for Megan's birthday. Well mannered. Very quiet and thoughtful. She was missing her parents dreadfully. I got the impression she needed a mother figure. That's why I was so shocked when I heard she was pregnant."

"Did you notice any changes in her?"

"No, I didn't see her often enough. Megan told me that Ella had become very secretive and often went off on her own. She knew she had a boyfriend."

"Did she mention anything at all about the boyfriend. His age, where he lived?"

"Nothing. It was a bit suspicious, because they usually told each other everything. We asked Megan about it a number of times, but she denied knowing anything about him."

"Thank you, Mrs Pryce-Jones. You've been most helpful."

"You have a beautiful home," Wallace observed as he and Butler walked out.

"It was left to me by my parents." Wallace raised an eyebrow. "It's been in the family since the eighteenth century. The family accumulated a massive fortune from metal products. It all started off with a little workshop in a back street in Birmingham. Originally they made shoe buckles. Eventually, they owned a couple of factories and started producing guns. All of this is the result of hard graft," she said proudly.

"It certainly is a gorgeous house," Butler remarked as they crunched over the gravel to the car."

"It explains a lot," Wallace replied. "Pryce-Jones married into money."

He couldn't help a sneaky feeling of admiration for the wife. Compared to the Squadron Leader's overbearing, uppity attitude, she was a breath of fresh air.

"Chief Inspector!" Mrs Pryce-Jones called, coming down the steps. "I don't know if it's relevant, but Ella and Amanda Squires seemed to be in deep conversation on parents' day. I can't imagine why? She isn't the most approachable woman."

"Why would she be having a long conversation with Squires, I wonder?" Wallace remarked as they drove back to Shrewsbury.

"Confidential legal advice perhaps," Butler replied.

"Hmm," Wallace mused. "It's possible, I suppose, but unlikely. Let's get some lunch."

*

Wallace leaned back and stretched his long legs as he gazed out over the water from the Boathouse. The river was like a mirror, reflecting the trees and greenery. A pair of swans glided past like sailboats on the serene, sun-dappled water.

For a few moments, he allowed himself to imagine a

peaceful, summer afternoon with Jo, lying on the banks of the Severn, sipping champagne. Butler interrupted his daydream.

"We could interview Amanda Squires again," Butler suggested.

"On what grounds? She would be at us like a bulldog, gnashers bared. "Wallace deliberated on her reaction. "Okay, we'll tell her we're interviewing those who attended parents' day."

Amanda Squires was conducting a trial in Birmingham Crown Court. Wallace and Butler arrived just as the judge was about to adjourn the case until the following morning. They sat in the public gallery until the court rose and the jury filed out.

Squires was gathering up her files when he tapped her on the shoulder.

"We'd like a few words with you about Ella Chapman." She glared at him over the top of her half-glasses. "We're interviewing some of the women who attended parents' day at St Cadfael's."

"And?"

"Apparently, you were seen having a long conversation with Ella."

"So? I'm not aware that's a crime," she replied sarcastically. "I was talking to Ella about my son."

"Your son!"

"Yes, Julian *was* a pupil at St Cadfael's. He's reading PPE at Oxford. I have another son, Miles, in Year Seven."

"Why didn't you tell us this before?" Wallace said, trying to control his anger.

"It wasn't relevant. Julian left over a year ago. Miles is a bit young to have fathered a child, don't you think?"

"So, why were you discussing your son?"

"Just general conversation. How he was getting on. Was he enjoying Oxford? He and Ella were in the book club; both avid readers. When he went up to Oxford he gave her some of his old books."

"When was your son last home?"

"Julian has only been home once, at Christmas, since he left for university. Too busy working and enjoying himself. What are you implying?" Squires asked testily.

"Did they meet up at Christmas?"

"Not possible. Ella went to her parents in Qatar. Julian had returned to Oxford by the time she got back." She glowered at Wallace. "I have nothing more to say," she said dismissively.

"She's a piece of work," Butler remarked as they walked towards the car.

"She certainly is," Wallace replied. "She's also a first-class barrister. If I was facing a murder charge I'd want her as my brief."

Wallace glanced at his watch. "Neither Squires nor Mrs Pryce-Jones fit the bill. Go home, Phil. Play with the kids for a change. I've got plans of my own tonight."

Butler smirked. Everybody in the station knew the guv had the hots for Jo Barnett.

46

NOVEMBER 2022

Winter had taken hold by early November. Already the roadside was littered with brown and gold detritus. Dead leaves floated down from gently swaying trees, filling the gutters. A light rain was already turning them into a slushy mess.

How depressing, Wallace thought as he drove to the station. He hated Autumn. Everything reminded him of decay and death. The colours were vibrant, beautiful, but they would soon be gone, replaced by bare branches and mud. In winter it would be crisp and cold. Glistening white frost gave the countryside a fresh, clean smell. Snow transformed everything into a fairytale scenario: and there was Christmas. Christmas with Jo. He smiled inwardly as he pulled up outside the station.

Wallace and the team had been investigating Ella Chapman's murder for over five months. Months of leads going nowhere. Frustration with the case was affecting the whole team. They still hadn't established the identity of the woman with Ella in the photograph. The only clue they had to go on was the way she was dressed.

Wallace marched into the incident room. Immediately, the chatter stopped. The team looked at him expectantly.

"Briefing in thirty minutes," he barked. "Eight thirty on the dot." He went into his office and closed the door.

"If you want coffee you had better get one now," Butler said, and be sharpish about it."

A wave of grumbling voices swept around the incident room.

Wallace emerged from his office and stood near the incident board. Photographs of Ella Chapman and Mark Hilliard were stuck to the board with magnetic studs. Underneath were pictures of Mick Gilchrist, the old tramp, Sammy Jaynes, and a blow-up of the woman seen with Ella by the river.

"This is all we've got," Wallace said. "Jaynes can be discounted and we have no solid evidence against Gilchrist. This," he said, tapping the blow-up, "is our only real lead."

"There's been no trace of her sir," Hembrow commented. "She was obviously disguising her appearance."

"That's very observant of you, Hembrow," Wallace interjected sarcastically. Hembrow blushed bright red and hung her head.

"I *know* that, sir," she said defensively, a hint of anger creeping into her voice. "What I was about to say was *why*? Why did she *need* to disguise herself at all, by the river or in the sports' centre in Wellington? Why didn't she want to be recognised? Because she was with Ella? She must have been someone Ella already knew. Not the abortionist, but someone who was arranging it for her."

"A good point, Hembrow. Presumably, because she could be easily recognised, so she must be fairly local. We've assumed that Ella was meeting with an abortionist, a stranger. If she knew her it puts a whole new angle to it."

"Perhaps it's someone associated with St Cadfael's, sir," Baker ventured. "We've questioned everybody, including some of the mothers who attended parents' day."

"What about the matron?" Baker continued. "She would be well-placed to give Ella advice on abortion."

"We've already questioned her: she identified the body."

"What about that battle-axe, the school secretary? She seemed to know everything," Butler chimed in.

"Hmm," Wallace mused. "its a possibility. Okay, let's get down to the school. We'll question them both again."

Pupils were changing classes when Wallace and Butler pulled up outside the school. Such a contrast to their previous visits. Lower school pupils looking smart and colourful in their tartan kilts, giggling and whispering with their friends. Boys swinging their bags and pushing each other in rough-and-tumble fashion.

A sixth form prefect shouted imperiously. "Keep those bags on your shoulders and stop pushing each other around!"

"May I help you, sir?" he asked Wallace.

"Thank you, but we know our way around," Wallace replied, ascending the wide steps.

Mrs James, the school secretary, looked disapprovingly over the top of her half glasses.

"Chief Inspector, how may I help you?" she asked brusquely. "Dr Booth isn't available, I'm afraid. He's gone to Birmingham for a conference."

"Snooty cow," Butler whispered.

"It's you we've come to see. We would like to ask you a few questions about Ella Chapman."

"I've already told you everything I know."

"When did you become aware that she was pregnant?"

"Not until after her murder."

"Did you notice anything unusual about her behaviour? Did she ever ask you for advice? Did you ever make any phone calls for her?"

"She had a mobile phone like all the children here. If they are worried about anything they can ring their parents, even overseas. Most of them have these expensive Apple iPhones."

"Did you see her talking to anyone in particular on parents' day?"

"No. I was in here dealing with correspondence for Dr Booth."

"Thank you, Mrs James. You've been very helpful." *More helpful than she knew*, Wallace thought.

A crimson flush rose above his shirt collar when he and Butler returned to the car.

"Shit, why the hell didn't we think of a mobile phone?"

Butler shrugged his shoulders. "The specialist search team scoured Ella's room. There was no mention of a mobile phone."

"So, where is it? Did she hide it somewhere in her room, like the diary? We'll have to do another search."

"There's probably another kid using her room by now."

"We won't *know* if it's there unless we search again!" Wallace retorted angrily. "Remember how she concealed her diary in her guitar."

He was fuming. It took all his self-control to be charming when they went upstairs to the matron's room.

It had the same antiseptic smell associated with all medical rooms. Disinfectant, a slight odour of vomit and starch. The matron looked at them warily as they entered.

"Good afternoon, Matron. I'm hoping you can help us further with our investigations into Ella Chapman's murder."

"I don't see how. I've told you everything."

"Did you notice any change in Ella's behaviour in the weeks before she died? Did she come to see you about any medical problems?"

Matron shook her head. "Not really. I noticed that she looked rather pale, but I put that down to exam nerves. She was a worrier. Girls, in particular, get very homesick for their parents, especially those overseas. Sometimes they just need a mother figure; someone they can turn to for advice and comfort."

"Why did she come to see you?"

"I asked her to come up for a chat, but she seemed rather reluctant. She told me she had been having period pains and felt a bit under the weather."

"Anything else?"

"One thing that did strike me was that she didn't seem very excited about going to Qatar during the school holidays. There's always a buzz of excitement in the air towards the end of term. She wanted to stay here at the school. That was very odd, especially as her best friend Megan Pryce-Jones would be going home. I thought perhaps she was going to spend some time at her place."

"Why didn't you mention any of this before?" Wallace asked peremptorily.

Matron shrugged her shoulders. "Girls can be very moody during their time of the month."

Wallace nodded. "Apparently, she had a mobile phone?"

"All the children have them, even in primary school. It's not unusual. Older pupils tend to have very expensive models. Apple iPhones and the like." She smiled ruefully. "I certainly couldn't afford one."

"I assume another pupil is using her room?"

"Not yet, but it's been cleared out in readiness. A new boarder will eventually be allocated the room. It's still a very sensitive subject."

"We would like to take another look at it, please. If you would kindly escort us."

They made their way downstairs to the sixth form girls' rooms. When he opened the door the starkness of the room took him aback. It was completely empty: even the carpets had been removed. They searched the fitted cupboards and built-in wardrobe. Nothing!

"There's nothing here, boss," Butler remarked. "Hang on, what about Mark Hilliard's room?"

"He was sharing with another lad," Wallace said. "We questioned him. They've probably emptied that room too. Come on, we'll soon find out."

The sixth form boys' quarters were on the other side of the house. Wallace pushed open the door.

"Hey, who are you?" A young man jumped up off the bed, looking flustered.

"I'm Detective Chief Inspector Wallace and this is DS Butler. What's your name?"

"Josh, Josh Clements. What do you want?" he asked in a surly tone. I haven't done anything!"

Matron started to leave. "Please stay here while we speak to Josh. We're not here to see you, Josh. We're investigating the murders of Ella Chapman and Mark Hilliard. This was Mark's room.

"Well, it's mine now," he said defensively. "This is all my stuff. I only came to the school last March. My parents had to go out to Dubai. The school didn't have a room for me, but Mark was willing to share, because he was leaving at the end of the summer term."

"Was there anything left in the room; anything belonging to Mark?"

"I don't know. I had to move out until the police had finished their investigation," Josh replied. "Eventually, his parents came and took everything away. They gave me a few textbooks though." He was looking frightened now. His face was flushed. "Except…" His eyes darted from Wallace to Butler.

"Except what?" Wallace barked. Josh took a step backwards. Butler shot Wallace a warning look. "Come on, lad," he said more gently. "You're not in any trouble."

"Well… I found a mobile phone inside a plastic sandwich box stuck at the back of that drawer." He pointed to the small desk, littered with textbooks and magazines. "It was wrapped up in a paper napkin. I didn't steal it!" he whined. "I swear!"

Wallace's heart raced. "Where is it now?"

Guiltily, the boy rummaged through piles of paper in his desk drawer. He produced a cardboard box filled with various objects. A Swiss army knife, an old plug, some loose coins, a couple of condoms, a dirty magazine and a package covered in bubble wrap. He handed the package to Wallace.

Wallace ignored the items that were bringing a hot flush to the boy's face and unwrapped the phone.

"It's definitely not yours?"

"No, sir."

"And you haven't used it?"

"I was afraid to. I hid it until I thought the heat was off."

Butler smirked at the phraseology.

"Please don't tell Dr Booth about this. I'll be expelled." His shoulders sagged. "My parents will be furious. I've never done anything like this before. You must believe me, sir! It's just that I've always wanted that model."

"Don't worry lad, We won't be reporting you to Dr

Booth, but you could have been in serious trouble for withholding important evidence."

"I didn't know that, sir," the boy replied, looking very relieved.

"Take my advice, son. Don't do anything like this again. Believe me, there could be serious consequences."

They left the boy standing in the middle of the room, looking shaken and bewildered.

"What a stroke of luck! Let's get back to the station and see what's on it."

Wallace was elated. This was a real find that could possibly move the case forward.

47

An unseasonable warmth had settled over Shropshire after a very cold, wintry start. It was set to continue at least a week. TV channels glumly focused on climate change as the reason for the warm weather.

Emily lounged on a sun bed just inside the summer house while she rocked Ava to sleep. A bright, white sun hung overhead in a clear blue sky. An orb of pure silver shining relentlessly down on her. She moved further inside and wheeled the baby away from the open doors. Paul had gone to the village without her to pick up some fresh vegetables and ice cream. She looked at her wristwatch. He won't be long now. Lazily, she watched a robin perched on a nearby branch. Such a pretty little thing. She picked up a magazine and tried to focus on the words, but the warmth lulled her into a sense of delicious torpor. Her eyelids felt so heavy she could hardly keep them open. In seconds she was fast asleep.

The man parked higher up the road estimated how much time he had before Paul returned. Time to get into the house and do what he intended. Best to go round the back and slip into the kitchen. Cautiously, he crept along the path to the back of the house. He pulled up short when he saw Emily through the open doors of the summer house. She was fast asleep. *Now, he thought, the interfering bitch will get what's coming to her.*

As he moved towards her, the baby woke up and started to cry. Emily jumped up and bent over her, but not before she saw the man in the balaclava. She froze, a silent scream caught in her throat. Ava! She lunged at the man. Caught off guard, he stumbled and lost his balance. Suddenly, a voice called, "Yoo hoo! I'm back!"

The intruder turned and found himself face to face with Paul Bryant. Paul lunged at him and grabbed at his balaclava.

"Show your face, you bastard!" he screamed.

He swung a missed punch. Temporarily unbalanced, the intruder clamped his hand over the balaclava, pushed Paul into the evergreen shrubbery and bolted. By the time Paul crawled out of the foliage the man had run round to the front of the house.

Paul ran up and down the road, but he had disappeared into thin air.

"He must have had a vehicle parked nearby," he told Emily breathlessly. She was trembling uncontrollably. "Sit down. I'll call the police. I've got Chief Inspector Wallace's direct number."

When Butler and Williams arrived, Emily was sipping a cup of sweet tea. She raised frightened eyes at them.

"He was going to kill me," she said. "If Ava hadn't woken up…

"He's obviously been watching the house," Paul interjected. "If only I hadn't gone to the village." He slammed his fist into the palm of his other hand. "You've got to provide police protection for Emily."

Butler turned to Emily. "We're doing all we can to apprehend your attacker, Mrs Bryant."

"What *are* you doing? Five months and you're nowhere nearer to finding Ella Chapman's murderer." The frustration was evident in Paul's voice. "Sooner or later I have to get back to work if my business isn't to fall apart," he said angrily.

"I think it would be better if you went to stay with a relative or friend for a while. "

"You must, Emily, for all our sakes," Paul agreed. He shuddered. "What if he had harmed the baby? Your mother has been asking you for months to visit with Ava. She'll be over the moon."

"She doesn't know anything about this, "Emily interjected. "I didn't want to worry her."

"Where does she live?" Butler intervened.

"My parents moved to Llandeilo after Dad retired. It's where they were born. What if he follows me there?" Emily said, a hint of panic in her voice.

"That's unlikely, but we'll inform the local police of the situation. We'll give you a personal alarm and get a panic alarm installed in your mother's house."

"You and the baby will be safe there, Emily. It will be a load off my mind *and* I can go back to work."

"You're right, Paul. I'll ring Mum straight away."

"I think it would be wise to let your mother know what's been going on. She needs to be wary of anything unusual. We'll keep in touch."

Williams and Butler walked up and down the road outside the house, looking for a place where Emily's attacker could have waited, concealed from view. There were only a couple of detached houses with driveways.

"Let's go," Butler said. "There's nothing obvious along here. I'll drive."

They drove down the straight stretch of road for about three hundred yards. "Slow down," Williams said. "Reverse back a bit. There! Let's take a look."

Butler pulled onto the grass verge opposite and cut the engine. He sprinted across the road, followed by Williams. It was a small opening, barely visible from the road. It was almost completely concealed by low, overhanging branches. Pushing aside branches, devoid of foliage, they ventured into what appeared to be a disused area for bins. Rubbish spilled out of a container. The ground was covered with filth and debris.

"Hmm," Butler mused, "just enough space to drive in a small car. Some of these branches are broken. Probably pulled off the trees to conceal the entrance."

He stepped back out and looked up and down the road. In the distance he could clearly see the Bryant's house. Emily's attacker could park up and watch the property through the trees.

"This could be it, Williams. This is probably where the scumbag has been lurking, waiting his chance. Push those broken branches back into place. We don't want him to know we've sussed out his lair. We need the CSIs down here asap."

Butler snapped open his mobile as he walked back to the car. With any luck they would find traces of the attacker's DNA. *He must have got out of the car to move the branches*, he thought. He took a deep breath and mouthed a silent prayer.

48

Wallace picked up Mark Hilliard's mobile phone. The tech nerds in forensics had opened it and download its contents. Fortunately, the boy had not used facial recognition. He scrolled down the list of contacts. Nothing unusual. His parents, grandmother in Hereford, St Cadfael's, names of a couple of sixth formers he recognised from the investigation. Ella Chapman and Megan Pryce-Jones jumped out at him.

"Obviously, he would have kept Ella's number," Butler commented. "She and Megan were in the book club. Look at phone calls. That may give us a clue."

"He had made a lot of calls to Megan, probably checking up on Ella's whereabouts."

"Let's have a look, boss." Butler flicked the settings and pulled up the 'gallery'. "Lots of photos in here. Bloody hell! Take a look at this."

Wallace grabbed the phone and stared at a picture of Ella sitting outside the Bear Hotel with a woman. Ella seemed happy and animated.

"It's dated March ninth, well before Ella had even

become pregnant. This isn't the abortionist, Phil. This is someone she had known for a long time."

The woman was wearing the same kind of wide-brimmed hat as the one in Boswell's photograph.

"She certainly looks more affluent than the later picture. The hat looks like a Barbour," Butler observed. "Very popular with country people." He peered more closely at the picture. "The coat seems to be a Barbour as well. They're quite expensive. Looks fairly new."

"How would you know?" Wallace asked.

"Barbour's last for years, but they can fade after a time and need re-waxing. They often have a yellowy tinge on them. This one is dark green so it's either fairly new or it has been re-waxed. Barbour offer a re-waxing service online."

"Do you think the woman may be a relative?" Wallace queried.

"Unlikely. Apparently, the family were originally from Kent. Ella's father moved here for his work."

"It's obvious she was coming into Shrewsbury to meet Ella without anyone knowing. Why would she do that? Why couldn't Ella go to *her* home? Why would she go to all those lengths not to be recognised?"

Butler shrugged his shoulders. "Beats me, boss."

"I'm certain this woman is 'Prish'. Let's get the phone down to forensics and see if they can come up with anything else."

"She could have bought the hat and coat online or from a shop in Shrewsbury."

"Right. Get Baker on it. Any outlets within a six-to-twelve miles radius. If she did buy it or had it re-waxed, someone should have a record of it. Tell him to take Hembrow with him."

"Why Hembrow?

Wallace raised his eyes to the ceiling. "She's a woman, Butler, in case you haven't noticed. She'll have a better idea of where women like to shop."

"Outdoor and Country Clothing in the square is the best place to purchase a Barbour coat. It's where I bought mine," Hembrow declared as she and Baker drove towards Shrewsbury centre.

"Didn't know you hob-knobbed with the country set, Hembrow."

"I was brought up in the country in North Wales. Hundreds of country folk wear Barbour coats."

Five minutes later they were back on the street. None of the sales assistants could tell them anything, except to try one of their other stores in Hereford or Worcester.

"I know from experience there's no point in trying the smaller shops. This is the main hub for country clothes."

Baker sighed audibly. "Okay, we'll have a spot of lunch in town and drive down to Hereford this afternoon."

*

It was a dank, Autumn day. A low mist clung to the tops of the trees shrouding the backdrop of fields on all sides. Butler was relieved when the spire of the cathedral came into sight through the mist. It looked slightly ethereal standing stark against the sky.

Outdoor and Country Clothing was based in the Maylord Shopping Centre.

"Sod it!" Baker said between gritted teeth. The car park was jam-packed.

He pulled up outside the entrance to the shopping centre and got out of the car.

"It's not too far to walk. A bit of exercise will do you good, get your beer belly off," Hembrow chortled.

Baker grimaced and set off towards the shops. He hated going to shops and his feet hurt.

"Here it is," Hembrow said, pushing open the door. "They should have a good stock of Barbour stuff here."

Baker approached an assistant and asked if they stocked many Barbour coats. She raised her eyebrows and pointed at the racks of coats and jackets.

"Yes, sir. Are you looking for anything in particular? We have a wide range of items for men."

"Has this woman ever been into your store to buy a Barbour coat?"

Baker flashed his ID.

"I've only been working here since April. I'll call the manager. Perhaps he'll be able to help you."

Baker repeated the question to the manager. "Have you ever seen this woman in your store?" He showed him the photograph.

"It's hard to tell with the hat partially obscuring her face." He looked closer. "She's definitely wearing a Barbour coat."

"Are you sure?"

"Absolutely! It's a Barbour Vonn Wax jacket. Expensive… top of the range."

"Look here." He pointed at the photograph. "The hood has a faux fur lining and a draw-string for warmth. You can see the elastic pulls. The model closest to this has a tartan-lined hood. What clinches it is the black and yellow logo badge on the left sleeve. That means it's a Barbour International original."

"That's very interesting," Baker said. "You are absolutely sure you don't recognise the woman?"

The manager shook his head. "All I can say is that we sell fewer of these than the others. The only one I personally sold was last year, just before Christmas. Quite a smart young woman, well-spoken, probably in her twenties." He shrugged his shoulders. "That's about it."

"Well, at least we know what she was wearing, even if it was the wrong woman," Hembrow said, as they walked back to the car. "It's the type of coat someone would wear in Autumn or winter."

"There was no response to the press release, except the usual cranks claiming a long-lost relative, so it's all we have," Baker replied gloomily.

49

An air of despondency fell over Wallace as he entered the incident room. His team looked exactly as he felt. One or two were gloomily sipping coffee from polystyrene cups. Baker lounged back from his computer screen, waiting for the usual barked orders. Hembrow looked thoughtful and preoccupied, while Butler was pacing up and down like an expectant father.

"A meeting in five minutes," Wallace growled. "Now's the time to freshen your coffee cups. This could be a long session."

A corporate moan swept across the room. The boss wasn't in a good mood.

"What have we got?" Wallace asked, pointing at the whiteboard. "Ella Chapman... murdered- no witnesses. Mark Hilliard... murdered-no witnesses. Michael Gilchrist... suspect with insufficient evidence to charge him. These three are linked, because they are all linked to St Cadfael's."

"The next strand is Emma Bryant. There have been

a number of attempts on her life. Trying to run her off the road. The initial blow on the head. The attempt to suffocate her in her hospital bed. The foiled break-in at her home and a few days ago another attempt in her garden. Fortunately, her husband returned in time to stop the perpetrator."

Wallace inhaled deeply. "The killer is afraid she'll recognise him. The question, again, is *why*?"

"He's safe at the moment while she's still suffering from amnesia," Baker interjected, "but he can't risk her recovering her memory."

"Precisely," Wallace said. "Mrs Bryant insists she recognised the eyes through the balaclava, but she can't remember the man. She described them as being like cold, hard steel."

"So, we still haven't moved much on the investigation," DC Williams chimed in.

"We have one new clue," Wallace interjected. "We found a mobile phone in Mark Hilliard's room in St Cadfael's. The lad who was sharing with him had hidden it. He didn't find it until after the CSIs had searched the room, so he kept it hidden away. It was a very expensive Apple iPhone."

"That was a piece of luck, guv," Baker said.

"Don't call me guv," Wallace said in a threatening manner. "What I'd like to know was why it wasn't discovered earlier. Didn't anyone think of looking for a phone?"

Wallace coughed guiltily. He hadn't thought of it either, but he wasn't going to admit it.

"There was nothing on it except for a photograph of Ella and the mystery woman enjoying a coffee outside the Bear Hotel in Shrewsbury. Over to you, Butler."

A wave of mumbling swept the incident room as Butler stood up and addressed his colleagues.

"Most people would recognise the type of coat the woman was wearing, especially in this area."

"I know where to purchase a Barbour in Shrewsbury. Outdoor and Country Clothing in the square," a pixie-haired DC said.

"No luck there," Baker intervened, "but we went to one of their stores in Hereford. Same story. They had only sold one of that particular model to a young woman just before Christmas. "

"This could be a long job," Hembrow intervened. "Hundreds of people wear Barbour's, not just country folk who wear them for practical reasons. For some they are a status symbol. The upside is that the coat had the original black and yellow logo on the left sleeve. It makes it more identifiable."

"Stands to reason that the mystery woman probably bought it in one of the nearby towns," Williams suggested.

"Let's hope so, "Baker rejoined. "We're going to Worcester tomorrow."

"I want to target Shrewsbury centre this afternoon with as many officers as possible," Wallace instructed. "You'll have copies of this photograph. Show it in all the shops, the library, etc. In addition, check with walkers in the Quarry and over in the Boathouse." He sighed audibly.

"We've also got Chief Superintendent Payne 'in the arse' on our backs to produce results on the case."

"A corporate snigger went round the incident room at the play on words. It was rare that Wallace made derogatory remarks about senior officers. He must be really peed off with *'Crew cut Charlie'*.

50

Most of the trees had turned to brown, gold and red. Carpets of coloured leaves sprinkled the grass around the feet of the trees. Mounds piled up on the verges in a slushy mess. The ancient Shrewsbury Castle, first mentioned by Oderic Vitalis in 950 A.D., glowed russet pink in the morning sun as locals and visitors scuttled up the hill from the railway station. The town looked fresh and bright after a fall of rain during the night.

DS Morris and DC Williams walked over Welsh Bridge and headed for the riverside. It was crowded with people taking advantage of the late Autumn weather. Inside the Quarry swimming pool, Baker and Hembrow were showing the photograph of Ella Chapman and the mystery woman to the receptionist.

"Yes, the girl used to come here with her friends a couple of times a week. It's scary to think she was murdered."

"Why didn't you come forward when the photograph was released in the press?"

The girl shrugged her shoulders. "I was too scared. I didn't want to get involved."

"If you remember anything else make sure you inform us." Baker growled and handed her a card.

Williams and Morris walked past the swing bridge down towards the Quarry. Suddenly, Morris came to a stop and pointed.

"Up there! Going towards the gate that leads into town." Williams squinted against the glare of the sun. "It's her! I'm sure of it!"

They caught a final glimpse as the woman slipped through the gate. "Come on, before she disappears altogether!"

They raced up the green through the gate, across the road and down onto the bottom of Pride Hill.

"There was no sign of the woman. Where the hell did she go?" Morris asked breathlessly.

"She must have gone into one of the shops," Williams replied, "or into the car park round the corner. Probably long gone."

"You take the right side and I'll scour the stores on the left. If you don't have any luck, take Riverside Arcade while I take Pride Hill Shopping Centre. I'll get on to Baker and. If she's in town, we'll find her," Harper declared.

It took the whole morning to cover the centre and they still didn't know where the mystery woman had gone.

"Between all of us we've covered the entire town," Williams said in a tired voice. "I suppose she could have gone down towards English Bridge. Let's get down there."

They walked towards Wyle Cop, down past the Lion Hotel.

"I could murder a pint," Williams said. Morris ignored him and led the way inside.

He flashed his identity card at a young waiter wiping down a table in the bar area. "Have you seen either of the individuals in this photograph?"

He shook his head. "No, sorry."

"What about you?" Morris asked the middle-aged man behind the bar. "Has she ever been in here?" The barman studied the photograph and shook his head.

DS Harper turned on his heel and started to walk towards the door.

"Hang on a minute. Let's have another look," the barman said. "Hmm, I can't say she's ever been in here, but she looks very much like a woman I saw earlier on this morning."

"What time?" Morris asked brusquely.

"About an hour and a half to two hours ago. I was standing in the lane at the side of the hotel having a sneaky fag when she passed by. I'm not a hundred percent certain. I only gave her a fleeting glance, but I think she was wearing a Barbour."

"Where did she go?"

"Not a clue. She just walked down the hill and crossed over about half way down."

"Thank you. If there's anything else you remember, contact us straight away." He handed the barman a card. "This is my direct line."

Retracing the woman's steps, they walked halfway down Wyle Cop and crossed the road.

"Shall we try the hairdresser's first?" Williams asked.

None of the assistants nor the manager recognised her or the clothes she was wearing. At the bottom of the hill they crossed over to the Corn House. No luck there either. They walked up as far as the chocolate store. A gorgeous smell hit their nostrils as they went in.

"May I help you?" the assistant asked.

"We're trying to trace this woman." Morris showed the photograph. "It's vitally important that we find her as soon as possible."

"Oh yes, she came in last week."

Williams' heart jumped. "So, you recognise her?"

"I'm afraid not. I recognise the coat and hat. She bought some rum truffles and a few individual chocolates. She had a scarf covering the lower part of her face. Her voice was rather muffled. She apologised and said she had been having trouble with her teeth."

"Has she been in since?"

"No, I'm afraid not."

"You can contact me on this number," Morris said, handing the assistant a card. "If you remember anything, however trivial you think it is, please contact me immediately."

He inclined his head towards Williams and they both exited the shop. As soon as they stepped onto the pavement Morris darted back into the shop. He emerged a few minutes later with a large box of chocolates.

"Chocolates and a good film, eh?" Williams chuckled. Morris ignored him. He had only just remembered the wife's birthday.

"We've covered everything except Tanner's Winery just before the bridge."

"It's a bit of a long shot," Williams commented as they entered the winery. He pushed open the door and gazed around the shelves.

"They have excellent wines," Morris rejoined.

An assistant approached them and asked, "May I help you, sir? Are you looking for anything in particular? We have a very wide selection of wines."

"Detective Sergeant Morris. This is DC Williams. They flashed their identity cards. "We wonder if you can help us identify this woman."

The assistant shook his head. "It's difficult to tell with her face shaded, but she does look familiar. Middle-aged, I guess. I think she may have been in here recently, but I can't be certain."

"What about her clothes? They look quite expensive," Morris interjected.

The assistant grinned. "It's not uncommon for clients wearing Barbour to come in here, mostly the country set. They come in on a regular basis to place an order. We also have local shoppers and out-of-town visitors who come in to browse and taste. Would you like to sample some of our wines, sir?"

Williams opened his mouth and closed it quickly again when Morris glared at him.

"No thank you, we're on duty. Do you keep records of your customers?"

"Email addresses, but only those who signed up to

our newsletter. Most people pay by Visa or credit card. Very few pay cash."

"I assume you keep receipts?" Wallace asked.

"We have to for tax purposes, but they wouldn't show a customer's name and address."

"But it would show the items purchased?"

"Yes, and the price, of course. Some people buy a couple of bottles. Others buy in bulk, either in the store or online. The bulk buyers are usually regular customers."

"Well, that wasn't much help," Williams said.

Morris didn't answer. He wished he had bought a couple of bottles of wine to go with the chocolates for his wife's birthday.

51

The incident room looked like a trashed teenager's bedroom. Coats flung over chairs. Desks littered with packets of half-eaten stale sandwiches and polystyrene cups. A sickly smell of body odour permeated the air.

"Right, open a window, get this mess sorted out, and get yourselves smartened up. Sloppy dress creates a sloppy attitude," Wallace growled. He had a lot of sympathy for his team, but they had lost impetus in the case. Months of thwarted investigation and hard grunt work had produced very little. He had to give them something to work on. Besides, this wasn't the only murder they had to investigate. There was also Mark Hilliard.

Hembrow and Jewson, his two female DCs, made a dive for the women's restroom. The men pushed up their ties and tucked in their shirts. Some went off for a coffee refill.

In the restroom Hembrow and Jewson splashed water on their faces, studiously applied fresh make-up, then grabbed a coffee before returning to the incident room.

"Ooh, look at you two," Baker mocked as they walked past his desk. "Tarted up for the guv?"

"One of these days… Hembrow was interrupted by Wallace emerging from his office.

"Between us we've covered the whole town," Wallace said. "Any luck?" he asked, gazing around the room.

Hembrow shook her head. Baker blew out his cheeks and spread his hands palms upwards.

"Zilch, boss."

"We have got one lead," Wallace stated. "One of the assistants in Tanner's Winery thought she looked familiar. She He was fairly certain that the woman had been in choosing wine, but couldn't formally identify her, because her face is partially covered in the photograph."

"Where to now, guv?" Baker asked. Wallace gave him a withering look.

"Any suggestions, Baker?"

"I don't think she lives in Shrewsbury or even nearby, otherwise she would have been more familiar to locals even with the poor photograph. She's from way out of town."

"You could be right," Wallace replied grudgingly.

"She was seen in Wellington Sports' Centre with Ella Chapman. She could be from around that area," Baker continued.

Wallace rubbed his chin thoughtfully. Baker was a cocky little sod, but his instincts were usually reliable.

"Okay, we'll broaden our search up to twenty miles around Shrewsbury."

Their search proved fruitless. Nobody recognised the woman in the blurred photograph.

"Lots of the farming fraternity wear those kind of clothes," a ruddy-faced farmer explained. "Farmers, the county set. It's tantamount to a uniform. If I could see her face I might be able to help but… "

Hembrow sighed. This was a waste of time. "Thank you. If you think of anything, ring the number on this card."

52

DECEMBER 2022

Wallace felt unsure about his visit to Emily Bryant. The last time he had spoken to her she had absolutely no memory of her attacker. She had recently returned from her mother's, worried that she and Ava had been away from Paul for so long.

It was probably another time waster to add to his workload. Still, he had nowhere else to go on the case. Wallace gazed around as the car sped towards Acton Burnell. The trees were white from frost that had settled overnight. It sparkled on branches and shone on the grass verges. Two weeks to Christmas and six months since Ella Chapman's murder.

They still had nothing to move the case forward. The odd crackpot still came into the police station claiming to be Ella's killer, usually druggies or those with mental health problems. What the hell was going to happen to his plans for a family Christmas with Olivia and Jo? This year of all years he was looking forward to having his two favourite girls around the Christmas dinner table. Fat chance!

Butler turned into the drive of Emily's house and scrunched to a stop. A curtain twitched in the hall window. The front door opened and Paul Bryant came out to greet them.

"Chief Inspector Wallace. Have you got news for us?"

"I'm afraid not. Is Mrs Bryant at home?"

"She's in the sitting room with Ava. Please, come in."

Emily was sitting with Ava on her lap, reading from a colourful book.

"Don't get up," Wallace said. "Goodness me, how she's grown since I last saw her."

"Would you like a cup of coffee or tea?"

"Actually, I'd love a cup."

"Thanks," Butler added. "Just what I need. It's parky out there."

Paul went off to the kitchen to make the drinks. Emily settled the baby for a nap and turned to Wallace.

"Have there been any developments?"

"No, that's why we're here. Have you remembered anything, anything at all about the man who attacked you in the hospital? We are assuming that each of the attacks was perpetrated by the same man."

Emily shook her head. "Nothing except the eyes, as I said previously. His eyes frightened me. Cold, blue eyes. The odd thing is they seemed vaguely familiar, but I don't know why."

"Cast your mind back to when you were teaching

in Plymouth. Was there anyone on the staff who would want to harm you?"

Emily shook her head. "Not around the time Jessica was murdered." She thought quietly for a few seconds. "I did have a run in with one of the male teachers about Jessica, but he left the school a long time before she was killed."

"Go on," Wallace urged. "Anything at all you remember may help."

"Tony Haskins. He taught art and crafts. He was a bit hands-on with the girls, if you know what I mean. Putting his arm around them when he explained things; a pat on the bottom. That sort of thing."

"Was anything done about it?"

"He said he was just being friendly. Some of the sixth form girls treated it like a bit of fun. Others resented it, especially Jessica. She often came to me if she was worried about anything. She told me that she didn't like Tony touching her, but she was afraid to tell her mother."

"Understandable, from what I saw of the family during my investigations. What did this Tony Haskins look like?"

"He was quite good-looking, a bit like Frank Sinatra. The staff used to call him 'Old Blue Eyes'. Always wanted to sing a Sinatra song on our Christmas outing."

"Blue eyes, you say. The same as your attacker."

"No, definitely not! I couldn't stand Tony, but he had rather twinkling eyes, mischievous even."

"So, he got away with his behaviour?"

"No. A number of staff had hinted to the head teacher

about his behaviour, but I went to see him and put in a formal complaint. He had no option but to follow it up. Subsequently, Tony was dismissed, but that was about eighteen months before Jessica died. She was only in Year Eleven when she came to see me about it. Somehow or other it got out that I was the one who reported him. He was furious. His last words to me were, 'I'll get you for this'."

Wallace pulled at his top lip. This could be another lead. The most promising so far.

"Has he ever contacted you, threatened you?"

"No. The last I heard he was working in a bar in Spain. Somewhere on the Costa del Sol."

"We'll check it out. Find out what he's been up to over the years."

"Do you really think Tony tried to kill me?"

"Anything is possible. You cost him his career. Definitely a strong motive."

Wallace rose. "Thank you, Mrs Bryant. You've been a great help."

Wallace and Butler drove back to Shrewsbury in silence, both engrossed in their desire to solve the mystery of Emma Bryant's attacker.

The temperature had dropped considerably, bringing a sharp chill to the air. Snow had been forecast for the weekend. The last thing Wallace needed to hold up the investigation. Dispiritedly, he parked up outside the police station. There was an atmosphere of quiet diligence in the incident room, everybody intent on whatever was on their computer screens. Quickly, he took off his overcoat and slung it on the back of the chair in his office.

"Okay, listen up everybody. Our visit to Emily Bryant threw up some interesting information. It seems she was instrumental in having a member of staff sacked." He turned to the whiteboard. "Tony Haskins, art teacher, too fond of the girls. A bit too touchy-feely by all accounts."

"What's that got to do with Ella Chapman's murder?" Williams asked.

"That's what I aim to find out. Apparently, he threatened to pay Mrs Bryant back. In short, he left the school under a cloud and wasn't able to find another job in teaching."

"You think he may be Emily Bryant's attacker?" Hembrow asked.

"He certainly has a motive."

"But why now, after all these years? Does he have a link to Ella's murder?"

"It's possible he may have killed Jessica Parker, but unlikely. He had left the school about eighteen months earlier. Still, I want him checked out. The last Mrs Bryant heard of him he was working in a bar on the Spanish Costa del Sol. Right. Get to it. I want this guy found asap."

An hour later Baker knocked on his door. "I think I've found him, boss. There was an Anthony John Haskins living in Bristol until about six months ago. He was working as a freelance artist." Wallace looked up from the papers he was reading. "Listen to this. He moved to Worcester about six months ago and opened an art gallery." Baker had all of Wallace's attention now.

"Good work, Baker. This could be our 'Tony'. Have you got an address?'"

"Yup, he lives just outside Worcester. Apparently, he has a gallery in the Crown Shopping Centre."

"Butler! In here! I think Baker's found our man on the electoral roll. At least we know where he lives. Morris, take Baker and pay him a visit."

"There was no sign of Haskins at his home. A neighbour shouted over the garden hedge and said he often went away," Baker said. "He hadn't seen him for a couple of weeks. Perhaps he's holed up in his gallery, sir."

"There's only one way to find out."

*

At six-thirty sharp Butler picked up Wallace and they headed for Worcester via the A458. The skies were black. Rain lashed down against the windscreen, creating hazardous driving conditions. It was a foul morning. The surrounding countryside lay under a canopy of grey mist. It would be close on another hour or so before sunrise.

"We should get there around eight-thirty, providing we don't hit too much heavy traffic," Butler said. "Couldn't be a worse time. There'll be Christmas shoppers everywhere."

They fell into a companionable silence for the rest of the journey. At last the spire of Worcester Cathedral rose up from the mist like a dagger piercing the murky sky. The city looked bleak and uninviting until they turned towards the Crowngate Shopping Centre. Dozens of cars were already in the large car park. People poured out of the warmth of two coaches into the cold and drizzle. Umbrellas of various hues bloomed as they huddled together, creating a gigantic flower shape. Mainly Japanese tourists out for a good time, chattering and gesticulating despite the miserable weather.

"We'll park up here, Phil, and walk in," Wallace said. "The art gallery is in Chapel Walk."

It was just eight-thirty, but the centre was buzzing with activity and Christmas shoppers. They eventually found the gallery squeezed between a large store and a small craft shop. It was closed.

"Damn it!" Wallace exclaimed. "Perhaps he doesn't open until nine o' clock."

"We've got time for a coffee, boss," Butler said, eyeing the coffee shop opposite. "We can watch the gallery from there."

For half an hour they sat drinking steaming cups of coffee while observing the gallery. Just before nine a man stopped, tried the door and walked into the craft shop next door. They waited another fifteen minutes. There was no sign of Haskins.

"Right, let's get over there," Wallace said.

He marched over to the gallery and tried the door. It was firmly locked. He banged on the glass panel and peered through the window. There was no sign of any activity within the shop.

"Sod it! You'd think the place would be open on a Friday, especially at this time of year. Let's try next door."

"Any idea when the gallery will be open today?" he asked casually. He didn't want to reveal he was a policeman at this stage.

"It's closed for the weekend. Tony won't be back until Monday."

"Odd sort of time to close, isn't it?"

"He's gone to Paris on one of his trips, buying paintings. Goes regularly, but usually just overnight. Are you looking for anything in particular?"

"Just general interest. You say he'll definitely be here on Monday, Mr… "

"Glover, John Glover. We have an arrangement. I keep an eye on his gallery, provide information, etcetera, and he does the same for me if I have to close the shop for any reason. I'll tell him you called."

Glover followed them with his eyes as they walked away. *Something fishy about those two*, he thought. *I'd better keep a close eye on the gallery this weekend.*

"Of all the sodding luck!" Wallace fumed as they drove back to Shrewsbury. "Well, there's nothing for it. We'll have to drive down again on Monday."

When they arrived back at the incident room it was a flurry of activity. DS Williams nobbled him on the way in.

"Sir, our mystery woman was seen again in Shrewsbury town centre. A guy rang into the front desk claiming he recognised her from the press release."

"So, she's not bothered about being seen in town. Why would she walk around the centre if she was afraid of being picked up?" Butler interjected. "She must be living way outside Shrewsbury. Maybe she knows we're looking for her, but the photo is so indistinct she's not worried."

"It's a possibility. All we can do is follow up every sighting. We'll catch up with her sooner or later. We need a police patrol in town, otherwise she'll slip through our fingers every time."

"Right, boss, I'll get on it," DS Morris said.

"In the meantime contact Border Control. I want to be certain Tony Haskins actually left the country. If so, when he re-entered the United Kingdom. He may have done a runner."

53

Wallace and Butler sat in the same coffee shop and waited. Just after 8.30 a.m. a tall, wiry man with greying dark hair, dressed in jeans and a parka, unlocked the door of the art gallery. Quickly, they walked across and tried the door. It was locked. They could see Haskins inside, taking off his coat and scarf. Startled, he looked up and mouthed, "The gallery isn't open until nine." Wallace held up his ID card.

"What do you want?" he asked in a surly tone.

"Are you Tony Haskins?"

"Yes, so what"

"Open up. We need to speak to you with regard to a police investigation. I think it would be better if we come inside."

"What's all this about? I haven't done anything wrong. If it's about that parking ticket last month, I've paid it!"

"We want to speak to you about Emily Bryant."

Haskins looked puzzled. "I don't know any Emily Bryant."

"You would have known her as Emily Lambert, an ex-colleagues of yours in Plymouth."

"That cow!"

"We understand you threatened her before you left the school under a cloud."

"What if I did? She cost me my career. It was all lies."

"Why have you come to live in Worcester after all these years?"

"I had a chance to rent the gallery."

"Have you been anywhere near Emily Bryant?"

"No, why would I? Don't even know where she lives."

"She lives in Shrewsbury. Numerous attempts have been made on her life in the past six months."

"Now look here. You can't pin anything on me."

"What about Jessica Parker?"

"Jessica Parker! That was nothing to do with me! I'd left the school and gone to Spain months before!"

"You were over-familiar with the girls at your school. Jessica complained to Emily Bryant about your behaviour."

"All lies!"

"Where were you over the weekend?"

"In Paris buying some paintings for the gallery. There are lots of aspiring artists who display their work on the pavements on the banks of the Seine. I buy what I can as cheaply as possible. That's where a lot of famous artists start displaying their work."

"I'm sure that's the case, but you didn't go to Paris, did you Mr Haskins? You didn't leave the country. I'll ask you again. Where were you over the weekend?"

Haskins blew out a huge breath. His shoulders slumped. His eyes darted from Wallace to Butler like a caged animal.

"Okay, so I didn't go to Paris. If you must know, I went to see my girlfriend, Carole, in Bristol. She can vouch for me. I went down on Friday and came back last night. I visit her regularly, but I usually only stay one night."

"What was so different this time?"

"My wife went to see her parents in Wrexham with the kids."

"Your wife!" Butler exclaimed. "Does she know about this woman?"

"What do you think? Look, I've got three kids that I love to bits. If my wife finds out I have a bit on the side she'll pack her bags and take the kids with her. She doesn't have to know, does she?" Haskins whined.

"We can't make any promises, Mr Haskins. I'd like your girlfriend's full name and address."

"Carole Vernon. She's a primary school teacher. She doesn't know I'm married with kids," Haskins said sheepishly.

"Thank you, Mr Haskins. Don't try disappearing again. We'll be in touch."

"Slimy sod!" Butler exclaimed. "Can you imagine him around schoolgirls?"

"Let's get back to Shrewsbury. I think it's better to contact this Carole Vernon outside of school hours." He flipped open his mobile phone and rang the incident room. "Williams, any activity at the Bryant's?"

"Very quiet, sir. Not a sign of anything all over the weekend."

As soon as they were settled back in the incident room, Wallace glanced at his wristwatch. A quarter to one. Carole would probably be on her lunch break now. He dialled her mobile number. It went to voicemail. Just as he was about to leave a message a young woman's voice said, "Hello, Carole Vernon speaking."

"Good afternoon, Miss Vernon. My name is Chief Inspector Ben Wallace. I'd like to ask you a few questions about Tony Haskins." There was a slight pause before she replied.

"Is there anything wrong? Has Tony been in an accident? My God, tell me he's not dead!"

"No, he's alive and well. When did you last see him?" Wallace could hear her panic receding.

"Why, has he done anything wrong?" Wallace ignored the question.

"What time did he arrive at your home?"

"Let me think. He got to Bristol early on Friday. He took me for a quick bite to eat during my lunch break."

"What time was that?"

"About twelve fifteen. We grabbed a pizza and a coffee. I had to get back by one o'clock for afternoon lessons."

"Do you know where he went after that?"

"Some of the older boys were playing in a Rugby match on the field. He went out to watch them. He picked me up again at four thirty and we went home. We were together all over the weekend. As usual, he had to rush home Sunday afternoon to his family."

"Oh!" Wallace remarked in a surprised tone. "You know he's married with children then?"

"Married! No I did *not* know! He has children?"

"Three, I believe."

Wallace waited patiently during the deathly silence that ensued. He felt sorry for Carole. She had obviously been misled by Haskins, a serial philanderer by the sound of it.

"I can't believe it! He told me he had moved in with his parents to help look after his father who is suffering from dementia. How could he!" She started to sob, then stopped. "That doesn't explain why you want to know about his whereabouts."

"There have been a number of attacks on a former teaching colleague in Plymouth. This was about nineteen years ago. He threatened her, because she reported him regarding an incident in the school."

"Has he attacked her?"

"We don't know it's Mr Haskins, but we have to investigate every avenue."

"Well, he won't be coming here again!" she exclaimed with a catch in her voice. "I don't go around with married men and I don't break up families. I hate him. I never want to see him again!"

Wallace switched off the speaker phone and sat back with a satisfied look on his face. Butler was grinning like a Cheshire cat.

"He won't be getting his oats in that quarter again. I don't think he's involved with the attacks on Emily Bryant, but let's let the little skunk sweat a bit longer."

54

Wallace felt a quick flutter of anticipation when he closed the door of his office. Mick Gilchrist had been asked to attend for an interview again on a voluntary basis. He had been sitting in the interview room for ten minutes, but Wallace wanted him to sweat a bit more. There was something decidedly odd about his relationship with the Booths. Why had they all suddenly become big pals? Surely, there was no question of a *ménage à trois*. He believed Isobel Booth when she said Gilchrist was like a son to her, but Dr Booth was a different matter. His attitude to Gilchrist had been toxic during the early investigations into Ella Chapman's murder. Why a complete change of mindset?

He motioned to Butler to follow him as he walked through the incident room and downstairs. They paused for a few minutes to observe Gilchrist through the one-way screen. He was devil-drumming on the tabletop, his left knee jiggling up and down.

"Okay, let's hear what our man has to say." Gilchrist

looked up when they walked in. "Good morning, Mr Gilchrist… "

"Why have I been brought in for questioning again?" Gilchrist interrupted. "You've got nothing on me and you know it!"

"We would like to know a little more about your relationship with Isobel Booth."

"What are you trying to imply? It's true we have affection for each other, but not in the way you think! Isobel is like a mother to me. She helped me get back on my feet when I was at my lowest."

"We understand that, but how was she able to help so much when Dr Booth was so disapproving of your behaviour with the girls in St Cadfael's?"

"No comment."

"You must realise this may impact on your credibility with regards to your original statement."

"No comment."

Gilchrist's solicitor leaned over and spoke quietly in his ear.

"Okay! Okay! I told you the truth when I gave my statement. Things changed afterwards. I visited Isobel regularly after helping her when she suffered a fall near her home. She had sprained her ankle. I took her back to her house and put a cold compress on it. It was obvious she was lonely and I… well I was grateful for her interest in me. Booth didn't know I was going to the farm for a couple of months. When he found out he was furious. He kept watch on the farm, coming home at odd times to catch us out. He even followed us when we went on a little drive. He thought we were having an affair."

"Were you? It wouldn't be the first time a young man became entangled with an older woman, especially, if there was something in it for him."

"You dirty-minded… !" Gilchrist stopped short and clasped his hands together.

"Did you force the relationship?"

"Absolutely not! We became very close friends. I could tell her anything. All my worries about the murder investigation, my problems with Booth… everything."

"How did she react?"

"She believed me when I told her I had nothing to do with Ella's murder. It was like a weight off my shoulders. I started blubbering and she comforted me. Like I said, she's like a mother to me."

"What about Booth?"

"He warned me to stay away from Isobel, or I'd lose my job. What made it worse was that Isobel had stopped drinking. She had a drink problem for years. Anyway, she had smartened herself up and lost a lot of weight. He was so jealous!"

"Did you stay away?"

"Yes, I did. About two weeks later she rang and asked me to go and see her. She was in a very lively mood. She had warned Booth that if he tried to keep me away she would let slip that he didn't really have a Ph.D. Apparently, he had included it on his application form. He had started it, but didn't complete it."

"Is that how you got a job on the teaching staff?"

"Initially. I am a well-qualified school teacher. My academic credentials are over and above what I need to teach in St Cadfael's. Landscape gardening came later. As it turned out, the course was a huge success with pupils and parents. The exam results were excellent, which pleased the governors. It gave me a bit of leverage to negotiate more teaching time."

"Did Booth comply?"

"He had the gall to lecture me, the supercilious sod, but I was ready for him. I suppose you could say I held him to ransom, but it worked. He was apoplectic with rage. Eventually, he agreed, but not without warning me of the perils of crossing him."

"So, things have been going well since?"

"Yes, but I suspect that Isobel has been getting flak from him, although she doesn't seem to care anymore. She seems to be in complete control. If I ask her about it, she just laughs it off and tells me not to worry."

"You said he was very jealous. Do you think he may have threatened her physically in any way?"

"I doubt it. He's afraid of something. I don't know what, but she exerts control over him now. When I first met her she was a shrinking violet. Very cowed down. I think her stance is new to him and he doesn't know how to manipulate her anymore. What I can be certain of is she absolutely adores him."

"Do they have any children?"

"Two sons living abroad, in South America. Both civil engineers. One in Brazil and the other in Argentina.

I've seen a photo of them when they were children. Both dead ringers for Booth."

Are they in regular touch with their parents?"

"Apparently, Booth cut all contact with them after an argument. Isobel became very tearful and wouldn't say any more. The boys moved around so much they eventually lost all contact with them. I think that's why she clings to me. I was the catalyst for her to escape Booth's control."

"Has your teaching post been threatened since?"

"That's the odd thing. He tried, but Isobel wasn't having any of it. Booth backed down straight away."

"Did she tell you why?"

"No. He hates my guts. If it wasn't for Isobel he would have kicked me out long ago. He would have found something to discredit me with the governors."

Wallace sat back and tapped his bottom lip. Very strange. Why would a woman who had been controlled for years suddenly turn turtle? She obviously valued her friendship with Gilchrist, but there had to be more to it.

"Okay, Mr Gilchrist, you're free to go."

Gilchrist breathed a huge sigh of relief and flopped back into the chair.

Wallace and Butler went back to the incident room to brief the team. Unusually, it was very quiet. They were all hunched over their computers.

"Gilchrist is no longer in the picture. There is no further evidence against him."

"Why did you bring him in, boss?" Baker asked.

"Gilchrist and Dr Booth have gone from being bitter

enemies to being buddies. At least on the surface. It seems his wife has turned on him and taken Gilchrist's side. She's got something on her husband - enough to keep him in check. I want to find out what it is. I think another visit to St Cadfael's is in order."

55

Wallace had to admit that St Cadfael's was situated in a magnificent setting. Even at this time of year it looked imposing. In the dim winter light it possessed a certain grandeur, with its portico and steps rising to the enormous double-fronted door. A place for the kids of well-to-do parents who wanted the best for their children. Every window was a blaze of light. Chattering youngsters thronged outside, making their way to various classrooms and annexes.

He pushed open the heavy, mahogany door and walked into a Christmas grotto. A huge Christmas tree dominated the foyer, rising from floor to ceiling. Baubles shone in the glow of numerous fairy lights. The walls were tastefully decorated with Victorian Christmas scenes. Each window sill held a figurine. Santa Claus and his reindeer, carol singers, elves, etc. In the corner nearest the reception desk a beautiful crib and Nativity scene. Everything looked spectacular. He couldn't imagine any child not loving it. His heart clenched with the memory of his own Christmas's as a boy. Like his mother, he had always loved the festive season.

"Wow!" Butler exclaimed, looking around appreciatively. "Booth certainly hasn't spared the pennies on this little lot."

He followed Wallace to the reception desk. It was manned by an attractive, dark-haired girl with a name tag declaring her to be *Sandra Bellamy*. There was no sign of the draconian Mrs James.

Wallace held up his identity card. Sandra screwed up her nose and peered at the card.

"Detective Chief Inspector Wallace," he said. "I'd like to speak to Dr Booth."

Suddenly, the door behind Sandra opened and Mrs James appeared. She glowered at Wallace, her lips set in a straight line.

"I'm afraid Dr Booth is unavailable. He's very busy in a senior staff meeting," she declared. "May I help you?"

"No, I need to speak with Dr Booth, now."

"I told you he's extremely busy."

"As am I," Wallace replied. "I'm following up on our investigation into Ella Chapman's murder."

"Poor girl," Mrs James said. "Such a sad business. Very well, I'll inform Dr Booth. but I can't promise he'll see you straight away."

She flounced off into her office to contact her idol, throwing a withering backward glance at Wallace.

"Silly cow," Butler murmured. "She's obviously still besotted with Booth."

A few minutes later a voice greeted them from the landing above.

"Ah, Detective Chief Inspector Wallace."

Dr Booth came down the stairs, immaculate in a navy, pin-striped suit. Like a slightly ageing old Hollywood film star making a grand entrance at an awards' ceremony.

"I bet he's had Botox," Butler whispered. "No wonder the old dragon has the hots for him."

"So nice to see you again."

"We would like to ask you a few more questions regarding Ella Chapman."

"Certainly, if you would like to come up to my study we can talk in private. Please hold all my calls, Mrs James."

Mrs James looked at him with an upturned face. For a moment Butler thought she was actually fluttering her eyelids.

"Please sit. Now, how can I help you?"

He swung to and fro in his plush, leather armchair, his fingers cradled beneath his chin. A supercilious smile hovering on his lips.

"Early on in the investigation you were concerned about Gilchrist's behaviour with the girls. It seems he's now on the teaching staff. What changed things?"

"He came to me to request the possibility of teaching some garden design. It seems he was a very well-qualified teacher, but there were problems. He had left his former school under a cloud after being accused of sexually assaulting a girl."

"We are aware of that fact."

"The girl had some beef against him, because she had been given detention. It's a case of *'There but for the grace of God go I'.*"

Wallace raised an eyebrow. "What do you mean?"

"It's very easy for a pupil to wreck a teacher's career, because of false allegations. It occurs in schools, churches, youth clubs. Sometimes an allegation is based on resentment after a misdemeanour or being given detention after school. A way of hitting back at a teacher."

"What changed your mind?"

"He's still the gardener," Booth said curtly. "He approached me to offer a few sessions with pupils on computer-assisted design and landscape gardening. Until then I was unaware that he was a teacher, because he hadn't declared it on his application. That in itself made me very wary. I assumed he had something to hide and I was right. However, his teaching career, voluntary youth work and the accusations made against him were put before the governors."

"Did you have any particular reason for deciding to employ him as a teacher, Dr Booth?"

Wallace emphasised the word 'Doctor' but Booth's face was a mask of indifference.

"Initially, I opposed him having any input whatsoever, but the governors over-ruled me."

"They weren't concerned at all?"

"Squadron Leader Pryce-Jones and Giles Ponting objected."

"So what changed?"

"We decided to let Amanda Squires discreetly

question the girls. All the pupils liked him and were enthusiastic about his lessons. The governors felt he should be given a chance to prove himself, although I was not entirely comfortable with the proposal. To cut a long story short, it was a huge success with pupils. More importantly, parents were very impressed. Their children were getting design and computer experience that would stand them in good stead."

"So, your opinion of Gilchrist changed?"

"As far as his teaching was concerned. After a couple of short introductory courses it was agreed to make him a permanent member of staff; to allow him to coach pupils for more formal exams next year. They will be studying graphic and computer-assisted design with a bias towards engineering. It could point them into various careers, such as car design, industrial machinery and naval architecture."

"So, you are now satisfied with his appointment? Wallace asked. "Well," he continued, you'll be glad to know he is off our list of suspects. "

"That's very good news, Chief Inspector. It supports the faith the governors have in him." He was careful to leave himself out of it.

"Thank you, Dr Booth. Now, I'd like a word with Matron."

"I'll ask her to come down."

"No need, we'll go up to the sick room," Wallace said.

"Before you go, we have our annual Christmas celebration here on December the fifteenth. We break up a few days later. Parents, staff, governors and the sixth form will be providing musical entertainment. I would be delighted if you would consider attending. There will quite a few notable people in the area you may like to meet. The Chief Constable will be here."

Wallace was about to refuse the invitation, then backtracked. *Perhaps it would be a good idea*, he thought. People had loose tongues when drinking champagne.

"That's very kind of you, Dr Booth. We would both be delighted to attend, wouldn't we?" he said.

Butler gritted his teeth. The last thing he needed was an evening with the smarmy Dr Booth and his social climbers.

"Did you have to include me?" Butler complained. "If I'm to have a night off I'd rather put my feet up with the wife in front of the telly."

"It won't be a night off, Phil. We'll still be on the case. We may be able to gather more information."

"If you say so, boss."

Mrs Jarvis, the school matron, was waiting for them. "How may I help you?" she asked stiffly. "I told you everything the last time I was questioned."

"On the day Ella should have been in sick bay, she went off without telling you. Would you say that was normal behaviour for her?"

"No, not at all. She was a very studious, considerate girl. Spent most of her spare time reading."

"You had no indication that anything was troubling her?"

"Well, now you mention it, she had been more subdued than usual. She looked tired and pale. I didn't think too much of it. Lots of girls look like that, especially when they have a period."

"It didn't occur to you she might be pregnant?"

"No, Ella didn't have a boyfriend. She was very friendly with Mark Hilliard, poor boy, but that's about it. Why didn't she come to me? I could have helped her," Mrs Jarvis cried, wringing her hands.

"I'm sure you would have, Mrs Jarvis. There's no need to blame yourself."

"I can't forget how she looked when Dr Booth and I identified her in the mortuary. So still, so vulnerable. What kind of monster would take an innocent child's life? I believe she was an innocent even if she was pregnant. She wasn't very worldly wise."

They left Mrs Jarvis slumped in a chair, still wringing her hands and crying bitterly.

"Poor cow," Butler said. "I hope I won't have to wear a penguin suit to this school shindig. "

"A suit and a *tie*," Wallace emphasised. "We don't want to show ourselves up in front of the Chief Constable now, do we?"

Wallace grinned as they walked to the car. The evening could prove to be very enjoyable and informative all round.

56

Wallace looked around the incident room. His team looked exhausted, but they hadn't flagged for a minute. They had to have a break in the case soon or it would break them. They looked up expectantly when he walked in. He noted the black circles under Hembrow's eyes and the worn expression of most of his detectives. They were operating on caffeine and hope. Only Baker looked alert, but then he always did. He seemed to thrive on stress. He was a good detective, but lacked discipline. Always the smart mouth.

If only he had something to give them, something to bolster them up, but he had nothing. Parking on the edge of a desk, he pointed to the whiteboard. A row of photographs set out with names attached.

"So, what have we got so far?

"One - Ella Chapman, victim, aged seventeen, strangled with her own school tie. Quiet, studious girl. Pregnant. No evident boyfriend.

Two - Mark Hilliard, aged eighteen, cut in half by the Birmingham express. Initially, suspected suicide, but that was ruled out. Another murder victim. Nuts about Ella and very jealous.

Three - Michael Gilchrist, former teacher in Plymouth around the time Jessica Parker was murdered. Gardener in St Cadfael's, now on the teaching staff.

Four - Jessica Parker, victim, strangled with her own school tie. Troubled teenager, nasty, vicious stepfather. Pregnant. Mother cowed down with beatings and living in squalor. University educated. Introduced to drugs by her mother's partner Eddie Haines.

Five - Tony Haskins, a touchy-feely teacher from Jessica's school. Jessica had complained about him to Emily Bryant. Sacked as a consequence.

Six - Mystery woman, lives in or around Shrewsbury. From the hazy photograph she appears to be middle-aged and friendly with Ella," Wallace suggested.

"We can rule out Mark Hilliard," Williams said.

"Not so fast," Hembrow interjected. He had found out that Ella had a boyfriend. Maybe he killed her out of jealousy."

"It's a thought, but Mark was also murdered."

"Perhaps the father of Ella's baby killed him after discovering Mark had murdered Ella."

"Nah, can't see it," Baker butted in. "Whoever murdered Ella had to kill Mark, because he had found out too much. Same killer."

"Gilchrist is out of the picture," Butler said. "There's no real evidence against him other than the trainers. Forensics couldn't find any traces of blood."

"That leaves us with Tony Haskins," Wallace said. "He

worked in Jessica Parker's school. He had been accused of sexually inappropriate behaviour with Jessica and other girls. A slimy piece of crud. He's been out of the country for years, until recently. Still, we can rule him out as far as Jessica's murder is concerned. He had been in Spain for at least eighteen months before she was murdered."

"Perhaps Ella's murder was a copycat killing," Hembrow ventured.

"That's a possibility. Jessica's killer was never found. Haskins definitely had a motive for the attacks on Emily Bryant, but that line of investigation has proved fruitless. We've accounted for all his movements since he moved back to Britain. The only thing he's guilty of is 'playing away' with a Carole Vernon in Bristol."

"Where do we go from here, guv?" Baker asked.

Wallace shot him a scathing glance. He hated being called guv and Baker knew it.

"We're back where we started. The mystery woman is our only tangible lead. We've been back to St Cadfael's and questioned the school matron. She's beating herself up that Ella was pregnant and didn't go to her for help."

Wallace tapped his bottom lip thoughtfully, a sure sign he was frustrated.

"We also spoke to Dr Booth about Mick Gilchrist. He confirmed everything Gilchrist told us, except that he failed to mention some important details."

"Such as," Baker interjected.

"Booth made it look as though he was being benevolent, giving Gilchrist a second chance. That's not the story Gilchrist gave us yesterday morning. According to him Booth had a change of heart after a confrontation with his wife, Isobel. She and Gilchrist have been close friends for some time. Apparently, Booth doesn't have a Ph.D., so he shouldn't be using the title 'doctor'. Isobel threatened to tell the governors if he didn't give Gilchrist some teaching duties."

"Lying little prick!" Baker exclaimed.

Wallace nodded. He wondered what else Mrs Booth had on her charming husband. He was beginning to look forward to the Christmas celebration evening in St Cadfael's.

57

St Cadfael's was aglow with Christmas lights as they drove through the massive, ornate iron gates. The trees either side of the drive were lit with trailing, bright-white lights that looked like falling snow. The grounds were covered with a hard frost that gleamed in the car's headlights. Illuminated reindeer with three fawns stood under a tree. On the other side of the drive a ruddy-cheeked Santa and his sleigh welcomed guests.

They continued down the drive for a quarter of a mile until the house came into view. It looked magnificent. Towering Christmas trees stood either side of the front entrance. Light blazed from every window. The double-fronted doors were partially open, spilling golden puddles onto the tarmac.

The caretaker offered to park the car for them, but Wallace declined. A sixth form boy, dressed as an elf, directed them to a parking space close to the house.

They thanked him and walked up the steps into the foyer. The same tree and decorations they had seen on their previous visit were in place, but more lights adorned the walls. More sixth formers, wearing Santa hats, circulated bearing trays of champagne and canapés. Guests huddled in groups talking and laughing. The strains of *'We Wish You a Merry Christmas'* drifted from somewhere above the stairs. Suddenly, a hand clasped his shoulder.

"Chief Inspector! How are you?" Giles Ponting grinned broadly. "Glad you could come. It's always a splendid evening." A tall, elegant woman, expensively dressed, approached them. "Oh, hello, Isobel. Lovely to see you," he said planting a *'moi'* kiss on both cheeks. Chief Inspector Ben Wallace, Isobel Booth."

Wallace was a little taken aback. After Mick Gilchrist's description of her, he expected a nondescript, mousy creature, not this attractive, confident woman who had obviously been quite a stunner in her time.

"I hope you enjoy the festivities, Chief Inspector. Please excuse me. I must circulate amongst the parents and guests."

Isobel crossed the foyer to join a group standing near the Christmas tree. She put her hand on a man's arm. He turned and smiled. Mick Gilchrist! *I suppose I shouldn't be surprised*, he thought. He is on the staff. Wallace motioned to Butler, who had been standing back waiting to grab another glass of champagne.

"Start circulating, Phil. Remember you're here to get information, not just to stuff your face."

Butler was obviously beginning to enjoy himself. "Okay, boss. We are staying for dinner, I hope," he mumbled through a mouthful of canapés. "I can't believe I'm eating caviar and drinking champagne in a school."

"See that group by the tree. Go over and try to join in the conversation. See if you can pick up any useful snippets."

Butler wended his way through the throng and lingered on the edge of an animated exchange between Amanda Squires and Squadron Leader Pryce-Jones.

"I'm not entirely happy about this appointment. We need to keep an eye on Gilchrist."

"He's been thoroughly vetted. I have my contacts in the police." She looked across the room. The Chief Constable smiled and acknowledged her with a slight wave of the hand. Suddenly, he spotted Wallace and headed his way.

"Chief Inspector! What are you doing here? Are you on duty? Is Payne here too?"

"I don't think so. Butler and I were invited by Dr Booth personally. I thought it would give us a chance to speak to parents and staff on an informal basis."

"Humph! I am not happy with this state of affairs. You can make your apologies and get the hell out of here! Now!"

Wallace turned to the Chief Constable. "We're not on duty, sir. Dr Booth invited us." The ‚Chief Constable glared at him. Before he could say anything, Booth came alongside.

"We'll be going into dinner in a couple of minutes. Come along, Chief Inspector and you," he said, as Butler appeared at his elbow. He hadn't really wanted to invite

Butler. Too low down the ranks, but he had wanted to appear gracious.

The Chief Constable glowered and marched off towards the stairs. Wallace almost choked with laughter.

"Wait until *'Crewcut Charlie'* hears about this!"

"Well, did you pick up on any conversations?"

"Nothing we didn't already know about, but there was a lot of whispering going on about Mick Gilchrist and Mrs Booth. Apparently, rumours have been circulating about their friendship. Amanda Squires soon squashed that bit of gossip. Having said that, most parents were pleased he was on the staff full time."

Dr Booth was about to announce dinner being served when Giles Ponting sidled up to him.

"Edward, a quiet word in your ear. You know the Member of Parliament for Witherington has popped his clogs. There'll be a by-election. I want you to stand in the seat."

"Me? But I've never been involved with politics."

"You would be perfect. You have all the qualities we need. Headmaster, good background, unblemished reputation, well-respected in the area *and…* " he emphasised, "a very supportive wife with all the right connections."

Booth shook his head. "I don't know. I'm not even a member of the Conservative Party."

"Don't you worry about that… you can join straight away. Lots of people will help you canvass. It's a strong Conservative seat, a definite shoe-in."

"What about my position here in St Cadfael's?

Assuming I'd be elected, I could be voted out in four years. It's too much of a risk."

"All that can be arranged. The governors can appoint a temporary head teacher on a short-term contract. Most schools operate that way nowadays, even state schools. Your post would be kept open."

"What if the governors don't agree?"

"They will. Leave it to me. You could become an education minister or eventually join the cabinet as Secretary for Education. You could even be knighted, or become rime minister," Ponting cajoled, recognising the gleam of ambition in Booth's eyes.

"I'll have to discuss it with Isobel."

"Well, don't leave it too long old boy, or you'll miss the boat. Ah, Chief Inspector. Our new Conservative candidate for Witherington," he said clapping Booth on the back."

"Damn the man!" Booth cursed under his breath. He resolved to speak to Isobel as soon as they arrived home after the dinner.

When they arrived home Booth ushered Isobel inside. She could see he was anxious and excited about something. He poured himself a generous portion of whisky. His hands shook slightly as he handed Isobel a gin and tonic. Isobel's stomach churned with nervous anticipation. Was he going to leave her, because of Mick Gilchrist?

She couldn't let that happen. She adored Mick, but she loved Edward more. Even with all his faults she couldn't imagine life without him. He *was* her life. She shouldn't have been so harsh with him over her friendship with Mick.

"Isobel, I have something I want to discuss with you."

"Edward, darling, you're upset." Isobel felt sick. "Tell me what's wrong."

"There's nothing wrong my dear, but I have a big decision to make." Isobel held her breath. "Giles Ponting has asked me to stand as the Conservative candidate for Witherington."

"What!" Isobel laughed out loud.

"I didn't think you would find it *that* funny, Isobel. You obviously think I'm not suitable!"

"Oh, but you are, you're eminently suitable. I assume you're going to accept? I'm so proud of you Edward… so proud."

"Just think, I could be knighted in due course. You would like that, wouldn't you, darling?" He raised his glass. "A toast to Sir Edward and Lady Booth. Of course, you'll have to buy a whole new wardrobe. There'll be lots of functions and events to attend." Isobel felt a warm glow course through her veins as Edward took her in his arms. This could be a whole new lease of life for them both.

58

Ben had ignored Jo's protests and bought her an engagement ring. They had arranged to meet in their favourite restaurant near the river. He couldn't wait to see her face when he showed her the ring. He felt flushed and excited, like a teenager on his first date. He breathed in deeply through his nostrils and slowly released it through parted lips. A deep breathing exercise he used to lower his blood pressure and calm down in an emergency.

The grounds were covered with a thin layer of snow. He crunched up the drive over the frosty gravel feeling elated, but not without a few butterflies swirling in his stomach.

Trees either side of the drive were illuminated with bright, white lights. Feathery hoar frost hung from the branches, turning the woods into a magical, fairytale place. Nature's winter wonderland. It was breathtakingly beautiful.

The restaurant was lavishly decorated for Christmas. Guests seated in window seats were animatedly talking and laughing. A couple were toasting each other with glasses of champagne. Even from outside he could see the atmosphere was festive and convivial. Suddenly, his anxiety lifted. He felt light-hearted. *It's going to be a great night,* he thought. *A night to remember.*

Golden light shone from the entrance and spilled onto the path, creating a pool of light as he opened the door. A warmth surrounded him as he entered. The smell of coffee and roasting meat assaulted his nostrils, reminding him he hadn't eaten properly all day.

The dining room looked magnificent. Large red, silver and gold baubles hung from the ceiling. The walls were tastefully decorated with snowy Christmas scenes. A tall Christmas tree filled one corner of the room. It was perfect. Jo was already seated in a secluded window seat, sipping a glass of sherry. He noticed she had ordered a glass for him. She looked up and smiled when she saw him. His heart lurched. He loved the woman with every fibre of his being.

"To us," he said. Jo raised her glass and looked at him over the rim. She felt a warmth in the in the pit of her stomach and it wasn't from the sherry."

Full and contented after a delicious dinner of venison followed by chocolat au crumble de fraise. Ben ordered a bottle of pink champagne. After the waiter had poured the sparkling wine, Ben pulled out a box and flipped it open.

"Oh Ben, it's beautiful!" Turning it to catch the light, Jo admired the sparkling sapphire and diamond ring. "It must have been horrendously expensive. I love it, but I thought we agreed that it was a bit pointless at our age."

"Okay, I'll take it back tomorrow if you don't want it," he teased. Taking her hand, he slipped the ring onto her finger. It fitted perfectly. "Now, I want a kiss from the future Mrs Johanna Wallace."

"I'll still keep my own name." Wallace's face darkened. "Relax, Barnett is my maiden name. I've always used it for professional purposes, even when I was married to Jonathan."

"We'll make a go of it, Jo. You'll see when we celebrate our golden wedding."

"You may be a good detective, but you're lousy at maths," Jo grinned. "Unless you plan on becoming a centenarian."

Wallace sat back and sipped his Rioja. It had been a perfect evening.

"How about a February wedding? Valentine's Day. What do you say, Jo?"

"Whoa! What's the rush? That's only about eight weeks away."

"Well, you said you wanted a quiet wedding, not too much fuss. Registry Office."

"Actually, I would rather like to marry in church. My first wedding was a civil ceremony. It was brief and forgettable. Olivia could be bridesmaid, and my sister's two little girls would make pretty flower girls." Ben grinned. "How could I refuse? My two favourite girls dressed up to the nines. I love it. What about Butler for best man?"

Jo giggled. "Couldn't think of a better choice."

Ben reached over and put his hand over Jo's. Suddenly,

his mobile reverberated in his pocket. He pulled a face and whispered. "Talk of the devil. It's Butler. I'll take this out in the foyer."

"What's up?" he asked curtly. "It's my night off. I'm having dinner with Jo."

"Sorry boss, but this won't wait. Megan Pryce-Jones has been attacked."

"What! Where?"

"Near her home in Oswestry. She went for a sleepover with a friend, Katie Bennett, straight from school on Friday night. When she hadn't arrived by nine o clock Mrs Bennett telephoned Megan's mother. They went out looking for her, but she was nowhere to be seen. Squadron Leader Pryce-Jones called the local police, but they said it was too soon for her be classified as a missing person.

"Her parents were still driving around searching at midnight when a call came through on her father's mobile. It was Megan. She was hysterical and incoherent. She kept babbling over and over again about a man in a black mask… and listen to this, boss. He tried to strangle her with her school tie."

"Dear God, not another murder! "

"No, she's alive, but badly bruised and shaken up. Apparently, some teenagers were walking down the lane, laughing and horsing around. She managed to push off her attacker and screamed for help. One of the boys recognised her and called the police. They took her to the Royal Shrewsbury Hospital. I'm going over there now."

"I've been drinking. Can you come and pick me up? I'll call a taxi for Jo." Wallace sighed. *I wanted a night to remember*, he mused, *but not quite like this.*

59

The smell of disinfectant and wet mops hit Wallace as soon as he stepped out of the lift. The corridors looked clean, but nothing masked the familiar hospital odours. He wrinkled his nose as he passed a ward. The smell of urine and bedpans turned his stomach as an auxiliary nurse passed him with the contents of a patient's stomach. Not a job he could perform.

Megan was in a room of her own, just lying there. Her face was white like a porcelain doll. Her father stood over her bed, fists clenched, while her mother held her hand and stroked her hair.

"I'll kill the bastard if I ever get my hands on him!" Pryce-Jones snarled. "What kind of man does this to an innocent girl? She's barely more than a child."

Megan opened her eyes. She reached up and grasped her father's hand. Tears sprang into Pryce-Jones's eyes. He turned his head away and furiously wiped his eyes before turning back to Wallace.

"We need to question Megan, Squadron Leader." A

doctor came in carrying a millboard. "Is she well enough to answer some questions, Doctor?"

"Yes, but we've given her a sedative so she'll be a bit sleepy. You can always come back in the morning."

"Megan, can you tell me who attacked you? What did he look like?"

"I couldn't see his face. He was wearing a black mask, a sort of balaclava. He pushed me into the bushes and I fell backwards."

"Did he hurt you in any other way… sexually?"

Pryce-Jones groaned. "If he did, I'll kill him," he vowed for the second time.

"No, he didn't touch me in that way. He tried to kill me. I was still wearing my school uniform. He pulled my tie and twisted it until I could hardly breathe. He was going to strangle me with it. "

"Could you see his eyes? The colour?"

"It was too dark, but a car passed when he pushed me into the hedgerow. The headlights just caught his face for a moment. I think they were light eyes, blue, maybe grey. I'm not sure."

"Thank you, Megan. We'll come back tomorrow." There was no response. She had already fallen into a deep sleep.

"Are you thinking what I'm thinking, boss," Butler asked.

"It's the same man who killed Ella and attacked Emily Bryant. It doesn't make sense. Why would he want to murder Megan?"

"She was Ella's best friend. Maybe she found out

something about Ella that could reveal her killer's identity. Something that she didn't know before."

"Could be, but how would the attacker have found out what she knew? Her parents will probably stay in the hospital, but I want a policeman on duty outside Megan's room twenty-four seven."

"I'm on it, boss. By the way, I'm sorry I ruined your evening with Dr Barnett."

"Well, we enjoyed most of it, Phil. Jo and I got engaged tonight."

"Wow! About time too. It's the best thing that could happen to you. Someone to go home to every night." He thought about his long-suffering wife, putting up with his lengthy, unsocial hours.

"By the way, Phil, how do you fancy being my best man… Valentine's Day next February."

"I'm honoured, boss," and he meant it. "I'll tell the wife to splurge on a new outfit for the wedding."

Valentine's Day. It's a Sunday. Couldn't be better Wallace thought as Butler dropped him off at home. He let himself in, threw his overcoat on the back of a chair and settled down with a double whisky. A broad grin spread over his face. *Now all I have to do is persuade Jo to stick to next February.*

The whisky had the desired effect. Within minutes he was fast asleep.

60

Wallace awoke with a start. His head thumped with a hundred hammers and his body ached unbearably after a night on the sofa. *Why didn't I have the sense to go to bed?* He groaned and stretched one long leg after the other. *I shouldn't have had that whisky.* He stumbled into the kitchen and made a cup of very strong coffee.

After a quick shower and shave he felt almost human. It was eight o' clock and he needed to get to the hospital pronto. He grabbed a breakfast bar and took a large bite. He imagined Jo chastising him for not having a proper breakfast, not that he had one very often. His mobile shrilled as he slid into the driver's seat of his new BMW. Butler's name illuminated the screen. "Where are you?" Butler asked.

"I'm on my way to the hospital."

"Turn around and go back to the station. There's no point in turning up this early. Everybody will be busy with breakfast and sorting out patients. I'll see you there."

Shrewsbury was heaving with early-bird Christmas

shoppers by the time he drove through town. It would be even worse later on. Twenty minutes later he pulled up outside the police station. He took the stairs two at a time and marched into the incident room. It was deathly quiet. Suddenly, Baker started clapping, then all the team joined in. *What the hell?!*

"Congratulations, boss," Hembrow said quietly.

Baker smirked and leaned over to her. "You've been beaten to the post, Hembrow."

"Oh, shut your cakehole, Baker!"

"Yeah, shut it," Williams said.

Wallace glared at Butler, who was looking distinctly sheepish. "You didn't say it was a secret, boss. Everybody is pleased for you and Dr Barnett."

"Invitations all round then? " Baker asked.

Wallace ignored the question and motioned Butler to follow him into his office.

"Before you give me a rollicking, boss… "

Wallace brushed the comment aside. "Forget it. They had to know some time." He rubbed his chin thoughtfully. "Did our masked attacker really intend to kill Megan, or just frighten her off? She's only a slip of a thing. Let's get over to the hospital."

Ambulances were queued up in front of A & E. Butler parked behind the last one. A voice said, "You can't park here, sir." Wallace flashed his warrant card. "Is your visit an emergency? If not, you'll have to go to the visitor's car park." He pointed across to where a long tail of cars were waiting for spaces.

"Not exactly an emergency. We are here to question

a young girl who was attacked last night. " The security man looked uncertain before directing him to a space with diagonal yellow lines.

"Thank you," Wallace said politely. There was no point in ruffling the guard's feathers. He pitied the poor devils stuck in the ambulances for hours on end.

Ignoring the 'no smoking' signs, a few patients were outside puffing away. One in a wheelchair was attached to an oxygen bottle. She coughed from deep in her chest as they passed.

They avoided the lift and walked up the stairs to the wards. When they reached Megan's room they were surprised to see her sitting in a chair, fully dressed.

"How are you feeling?" Wallace asked.

"The doctor said I can go home. I'm waiting for my parents to pick me up."

"Can you tell us any more about the attack last night?"

"No, I've told you everything I can remember. It happened so quickly. He just appeared out of nowhere."

"You're sure it was a man?"

"Yes. He didn't speak, but when he fell on top of me he grunted. It was definitely a man. He was going to strangle me with my school tie, just like Ella!"

"What's going on here?" Pryce-Jones stood in the doorway with a face like thunder. His wife nudged past him and put her arms around Megan.

"We have to ask these questions, sir. The nature of the attack was similar to that of Ella Chapman."

"Oh my God!" Mrs Pryce-Jones cried. "Why would he want to kill Megan?"

"That's what we're trying to establish," Wallace said gently. He turned to Megan. "I want you to think hard about anything connected to Ella that may impact on you." Megan shook her head. She looked as if she were about to cry. "Please don't let Megan go out unaccompanied," he told Squadron Leader Pryce-Jones, "not even to visit friends. Her attacker could be watching the house and monitoring her movements."

"That's a given," he replied. "I'm sorry, Chief Inspector. Please accept my apologies. I know you're just doing your job. This has been such a shock for both of us. He squeezed his wife's hand. Just the thought of what could have happened if those lads hadn't come along… he choked.

"If you see anything suspicious, contact us straight away." He handed Pryce-Jones his card. "We'll be in touch shortly."

Wallace took a great gulp of air as he and Butler walked out of the concourse. The hospital smell always seemed to linger in his nostrils for days.

"There's something odd going on with Megan. I can feel it in my gut. She's being evasive. I'm sure she knows something she hasn't told us yet."

"She must have been very frightened," Butler said. "She's just a kid."

"Even so, I think she's holding something back. I want to know what it is." He pulled out his mobile and dialled a number. "Jo, I'm going to send someone to pick up Megan Pryce-Jones's clothes. She was wearing them when the paramedics took her in to A & E. I'll keep you up to speed later today."

"Back to the station, boss?"

"No, St Cadfael's."

"St Cadfael's! Why?"

"I want to have another look around Megan's room."

"The school will have broken up for the Christmas holidays."

"Pupils with parents abroad sometimes remain in the school. There'll be a skeleton staff there to look after them."

The school looked deserted when they pulled up outside the main door. There wasn't a pupil in sight. Mrs James glared at them as they entered the foyer. Young Sandra was nowhere to be seen.

"Chief Inspector, what can I do for you?" Mrs James asked. A simmering anger lay just beneath the surface. She sighed impatiently. "I've told you everything I know."

"We'd like to take another look at Megan Pryce-Jones's room."

"She's gone home for the holidays. I can't possibly let you rummage through her personal possessions. Dr Booth is on holiday at the moment and won't be back until January. I'm sure he wouldn't be best pleased. May I ask why you need to search her room?"

"Megan was attacked last night on her way to a friend's house. A man tried to strangle her with her school tie."

The colour drained from Mrs James's face. Covering her face with her hand, she dropped heavily into a chair. "My God! Just like poor Ella. Is Megan all right?"

"No, she isn't dead, but she's badly shaken up. She didn't suffer any serious injuries, just some cuts and bruises. Fortunately, her attacker ran off when a group of lads appeared. They rang for an ambulance. She was kept in for observation overnight and discharged this morning."

"I don't understand. Why would anyone attack Megan?"

"That's what we want to find out. What can you tell us about her friendship with Ella Chapman?"

Mrs James shrugged her shoulders. "Typical teenagers, although they were more studious than most. Both played tennis and hockey and joined in the usual activities of their '*house*'. They belonged to the book club and spent a lot of time with Mark Hilliard. A sob caught in her throat. "Poor Mark, such a nice boy." She stood up and squared her shoulders. "I'll show you to Megan's room," she said querulously, "then I must contact Dr Booth."

"We'll need to speak to him as soon as he returns," Wallace said.

Wallace and Butler closed the door and surveyed Megan's room. It was typical of a seventeen-year-old girl. A well-worn teddy bear and a few fluffy toys on the bed. Some cosmetics on the dressing table. One wall was covered with posters of Ed Sheeran, Bruno Mars and Harry Styles. Another with snowy scenes of the Swiss Alps, the Spanish steps in Rome and a Caribbean atoll. A blown-up poster of Megan and Ella with a group of teenagers carrying rucksacks adorned the wall facing her bed. Mount Snowdon loomed in the background.

"Lots of books, boss," Butler said, pulling out a few

paperbacks. She obviously read a great deal. Classics, Jane Austen, the Bronte's, chick lit and some non-fiction. '*Fifty Shades of Grey*'! A bit juicy for a seventeen year old. Wouldn't let my Sophie read it."

"Wait until she's a teenager, Phil. Believe me, you would be horrified if you knew what they get up to at that age. Innocence disguised as pseudo sophistication."

"Well, that kind of filth isn't coming over my front door!"

Wallace grinned. He had a lot to learn about teenage girls.

Butler pulled out a folded piece of paper from a hardcover version of Philippa Gregory's '*The White Queen*'. It was a charcoal sketch of a young man wearing jeans, a tee-shirt and a baseball cap. He was leaning against a sports car.

"Nothing much here, boss." He handed the sketch to Wallace.

"It could have been drawn from a photograph. Maybe a boyfriend or a relative," Wallace said. "Stick it in an evidence bag."

Butler pulled out a sketch pad and flipped it open. "There must be a dozen sketches here of the same bloke." He handed it to Wallace. "Perhaps she has a crush on the guy."

Wallace examined the drawings. Megan definitely had talent. They looked fresh, as though they had been recently drawn. He traced a finger across one of them. It left a smudge on his fingertip. It was the same young man in various poses. He flicked through the rest of the drawings. Megan had drawn a large heart around a head and shoulders sketch of the boy. Of course, one of her subjects was art. She was also taking Mick Gilchrist's computer-assisted landscape design courses.

"Take a closer look,. Phil. Does he remind you of anyone?"

"He shook his head. Nope, haven't got a clue."

Wallace stroked his chin thoughtfully. "Hmm, there's something vaguely familiar about the face. I can't quite put my finger on it. There's only one way to find out. We'll have to ask Megan Pryce-Jones."

On the way out Wallace showed the drawing to Mrs James. "We found this drawing in Megan's room. Do you recognise this boy?" She studied the picture for a few moments then shook her head. "Is there anything about him that looks familiar?"

"No." Her lips quivered and she hung her head. When she looked up her eyes were filled with tears.

"Thank you, Mrs James. If you recall anything, please let us know."

"Not such an old dragon after all," Butler commented as he got behind the wheel of the car. "Almost felt sorry for her."

Wallace was deep in thought as they drove back to the station.

*

Hembrow still looked as though she had the weight of the world on her shoulders. What on earth was wrong with her?

"Listen up! You'll know by now that Megan Pryce-Jones was attacked last night. Same scenario as Ella Chapman. He tried to strangle her with her school tie."

A corporate gasp echoed around the room. "What the hell is going on, boss?" Williams asked. "Have we got a serial killer on our hands?"

"It looks like it, but I don't think so. Serial killers usually murder their victims for pleasure. I think our killer is frightened." He turned to the evidence board and pointed to a photograph. "Ella Chapman... I believe she was murdered, because she was pregnant by her killer. Mark Hilliard, because he discovered the identity of the murderer. Now we've got Megan, a close friend of Ella's, almost strangled by the trade-mark school tie. We know there's a connection between the three."

"What about Emily Bryant?" Baker asked.

"I'm convinced that Emily Bryant's attacker and Jessica Parker's murderer are the same man. Don't forget, Jessica was also pregnant. The similarities are too much of a coincidence."

"That doesn't mean he killed Ella or Mark, though," Baker interjected.

"They could be copycat murders to put us off the scent," Williams said.

Wallace shrugged. "That's a possibility, of course, but the time frame is wrong. Why wait fifteen years to carry out a copycat killing? It doesn't make any sense. Apart from the geographical distance between them."

"I think Emily Bryant is the link," Butler said, "not

because of Tony Haskins. He's a real slug, but he's been ruled out. A cast iron alibi."

"Any ideas?" Wallace asked the team. They shook their heads. "Okay. DC Hembrow, I'd like you to question Megan Pryce-Jones. Take Jenny Bartlett, the family liaison officer, with you. A softly, softly approach. Megan may open up a bit more to you."

"Baker and Williams, contact the boys who helped Megan. They may remember something in retrospect. Any detail, however small, I want to hear about it immediately. The rest of you, I want you out scouring the town for our mystery woman. Revisit the shops, especially the hairdresser's and cafés."

"What about Wellington, where she was first spotted?" Sam Jukes asked. He was a young, skinny DC with the remains of acne pimpling his face. Enthusiastic, ambitious and impatient for an opportunity to shine.

"Not much point," Butler replied. "There hasn't been a sighting there since she was spotted with Ella right at the start of the investigation."

"Unless something vital turns up, I'll see you here tomorrow morning, seven thirty sharp. sharp. That's all."

Hembrow shot him a mournful glance. "What the hell is up with her?" Wallace asked.

Butler grinned. "Don't tell me you haven't noticed, boss. She's had the 'hots' for you since she first came here. Your engagement has hit her for six."

"Never get involved with colleagues, Butler. First rule of the job." Butler raised his eyebrows. "Dr Barnett is *not* in the Police Service. I have no jurisdiction over her," Wallace said tartly. "She is employed by the Home Office. I'm going to see the Super."

Superintendent Charles Payne looked up from the file he was reading when his secretary showed Wallace in.

"I hope you're here to tell me something positive, Wallace. What's the state of play with the Chapman murder?" He was devoid of emotion.

"We've investigated every lead, but we're no further ahead. The attack on Megan Pryce-Jones mimics the attack on Ella."

Payne glared at Wallace. "I'm aware of that!" he spluttered. "The Chief Constable has been on my back about it this morning. He wants all the stops pulled out on this one. Two pupils murdered from one school and a serious attempt on Megan Pryce-Jones's life. Are you aware he has grandchildren in the school?"

"No, sir." Wallace could feel his hackles rising. "*All the pupils are important, sir, every single one*," he stated icily.

"Quite so, Wallace," *Crewcut Charlie* said in a milder voice, realising the significance of what he had said. "What about the boy? Mark Hilliard."

"We believe whoever killed Ella murdered Mark Hilliard."

"You're running side-by-side investigations?"

"Yes, but we're short on manpower, sir. We need a few more officers out on the streets to do the grunt work. Our mystery woman has to be found. Without extra manpower that's going to be difficult." Wallace kept his voice steady. "I still think that the murder of Jessica Parker nineteen years ago is pertinent to the Chapman case. I want to go to Plymouth to talk to some of Emily Bryant's friends."

"Hmm," Payne mused. He swayed back and forth in his chair, his fingers devil-drumming on the desk. "Very well, you've got three days."

"I think Butler should come with me to help cover the area. DS Morris can cover for him."

"Very well, but don't push it, Wallace. I'll speak to the Chief Constable about it. He'll need to okay it."

61

Wallace and Butler set off for Plymouth at 5:00 a.m. It was cold, dark and wet. Visibility was restricted to a few yards. Shadowy trees stood sentinel at the sides of the road, their branches swaying low in the wind. Ditches overflowed with muddy water as natural drainage struggled to cope with the excess. It was a pig of a day. Only the overhead motorway lights relieved the pitch blackness all around them. The headlights of cars coming towards them on the adjacent carriageway were framed with orbs of light like Christmas decorations blinking in the torrential rain.

It was almost three hours before they drove over the Prince of Wales Bridge and headed for Bristol. Pale fingers of light crept over the horizon, probing the darkness. Wallace looked at his wristwatch. Eight o' clock. It would be light in about ten minutes. They merged with the M5 and a straight run to Plymouth. Butler pulled onto the hard shoulder for Wallace to take over the wheel from Butler, whose bleary eyes had been riveted on the road ahead. They should arrive before eleven o'clock. Butler settled back and dozed for the remainder of the journey.

"Wakey! Wakey! Phil, we're almost there." Wallace nudged Butler. He sat up, rubbing his eyes.

"I need a pee. Pull in."

"You'll have to hold it in for a bit longer until it's safe."

A mile further on they climbed over the steel barrier and relieved themselves.

A gunmetal grey sky shot with streaks of black loomed overhead. Wallace cursed when they hit heavy traffic. They had to negotiate the outskirts of Plymouth before reaching the Barbican. Paul Bryant had told them that Emily went there frequently with her friends when she lived locally.

The smell of frying bacon hit their nostrils as they parked up and started walking down the hill towards the little harbour, glad to be stretching their legs after such a long drive.

"I think a fry-up is in order, Phil. I'm famished."

A large restaurant set on the cliff above the Barbican on Plymouth Hoe looked inviting. They wandered across and found it was quite lively, even at that time of the morning. More tantalising smells assaulted their noses as they walked in. Butler gazed longingly at a huge breakfast being devoured by a workman.

"That's definitely got my name on it. "

After consuming a full English and two mugs of tea, they took stock.

"I want to question Lynn Jackson, head of Year Eleven at the time of Jessica's murder. She was a close friend of Emily Bryant. I have a list of names of those interviewed at the time, but I want 'intel' on particular friends of Emily. She's deputy head now, still working in St Catherine's Comprehensive."

They arrived just as the kids were surging out for the lunchtime break. A mobile chippy stood waiting, well away from the school gates.

"We're here to see Mrs Jackson, the deputy head."

"Do you have an appointment?" the receptionist asked in a familiar supercilious tone.

Wallace showed his warrant card and smiled inwardly at the change of attitude.

"I'll show you to her office. She's just gone in to supervise lunch. I'll inform her you've arrived."

Hoards of youngsters were pushing and yelling as they filed through the doors.

A diminutive, middle-aged woman, a head shorter than some of the older kids, came out and barred their way.

"*That's enough!* Line up or you'll go without dinner."

Silence fell over the queue as they shuffled forward.

"I wish my kids listened to me like that," Butler said with a hint of admiration.

A few minutes afterwards the tiny woman came into the office.

"The kids are playing up more than usual today. It's the weather!" She laughed. "How can I help you, Chief Inspector?"

"I was the senior investigating officer on the Jessica Parker murder nineteen years ago. A seventeen-year-old girl was murdered recently in Shrewsbury. The circumstances were identical to those of Jessica. We believe there may be a link between them and Emily Bryant."

"Emily Bryant! I don't understand. How could it be Emily? She left the school years ago. We're still close friends, albeit at a distance. She's been happily married to Paul for years."

"Several attempts have been made on her life over the past six months or so. She was seriously injured and lost her memory. She has regained some recall, but her recollection of the attacker is very sketchy."

"Tony... Wallace held up his hand.

"Tony Haskins is no longer part of the investigation. Is there anyone at all you think may want to harm Emily She shook her head. "No, she was well-liked by staff and pupils."

"Any serious confrontations with parents?"

"No more than anybody else. It's part and parcel of the job. Teaching isn't what it was thirty years ago, I'm afraid. Now it's all about *rights*. It isn't unusual for parents and pupils to rant on about their social worker or psychologist."

"Did she have any romantic relationships"

"She had the odd date with Geoff Berryman from the maths department. A lovely chap. He was really sweet on her. She hesitated. "I don't know if I should be telling you this."

"Go on," Wallace urged.

"She was obsessed with David Johnson, the head

teacher. He was a lot older than her; a married man with kids. I tried to warn her, but she wouldn't listen. The relationship was doomed from the start."

"What happened?"

"He went on holiday with his wife and children to Thailand. They were all swept away in the Boxing Day Tsunami. Poor things. Emily was spending Christmas with her parents just outside Plymouth when I rang to tell her. She was hysterical… eventually she had a complete nervous breakdown. It took her a long time to recover. She took an overdose of sleeping tablets. Without Paul's support, I doubt she would have survived."

"Do you have any names we could follow up?"

She shook her head. "Paul Bryant is probably the person to speak to on that front."

As soon as they went back to the car Wallace rang Paul Bryant.

"Mr Bryant… Chief Inspector Wallace. I'm in Plymouth. I've spoken to the deputy head in St Catherine's. Zilch information. However, she said you could provide some names regarding David Johnson, head teacher at the time of Jessica Parker's murder."

There was complete silence on the other end of the phone.

"Mrs Jackson told me about her relationship with him." Still no response.

Paul let out a huge sigh. "That was all dead and buried a long time ago."

"I understand how you feel, but we must follow up

anything that may be pertinent to the attacks made on your wife. Names that may be useful."

"David Johnson was a bastard," Paul said vehemently. "He was responsible for my twin sister's death. Got her on drugs, played away a lot of the time. He had a string of women on the go. I'm glad he's dead!"

"I'm very sorry," Wallace said.

"I can give you a few names. Lisa Jenkins, Lisa was Karen's best friend when she lived in London. She was living in Australia, but moved back to the UK when her husband changed jobs. Harriet Bailey and Joanne Evans. I'll give you their telephone numbers. They may have moved on by now. Talk to Lisa first. She's probably still in touch with Harriet."

"Anything else?"

Paul shook his head. "Their numbers should still be in my contacts' list. I'll text them to you as soon as possible. As far as I know they have no connection to Emily other than David Johnson, and he's been dead for years."

"Thank you," Wallace said. "If you think of anything that may be pertinent regarding the Jessica Parker murder and Mrs Bryant, please inform me as soon as possible."

Butler turned to Wallace. "What now, boss?"

A text message appeared on Wallace's phone. The telephone numbers from Paul Bryant.

"We'll follow up these leads."

*

Harriet Bailey was the first to ring. Wallace had left his name and rank on her voicemail. She sounded fraught, her voice high-pitched and urgent.

"What is this about, Chief Inspector. Has there been an accident? "

"No, no," Wallace said quickly. "We're just following up some leads regarding an historical murder investigation. A schoolgirl, Jessica Parker, was murdered about nineteen years ago in Plymouth. David Johnson was the head teacher at the time."

"David Johnson!" she said, contempt in her voice. "I heard about the poor girl. It was in all the newspapers. I was still teaching in London at the time. What's it got to do with him? He's been dead for years."

"Yes, but we're trying to establish any connections between him and an Emily Bryant."

"Sorry, I don't know anybody of that name."

"Her maiden name was Emily Lambert. Paul Bryant told us you worked with David Johnson before he became head teacher in Plymouth?"

Harriet let out a huge sigh. "He was an opportunist, a liar and a cheat. He cultivated friendships with people who could help him enhance his career, especially women; older women."

"Can you elaborate?"

"He was a charmer. I know of at least two head teachers, both women, who fell under his spell. He used them to get promotion. Eventually, he obtained a deputy headship, but he didn't stay in post more than a couple of years. He moved from school to school. Every move meant a bigger school and salary."

"Sounds as though he was a man on a mission," Butler interjected.

"Did you know Maggie Clyne?"

"Not really, but I heard on the grapevine that she had an affair with David. Once he had the promotion he was after, he dumped her. There was a terrible stink."

"Where is she teaching now?"

"She left her school under a cloud. Rumours were circulating around parents. Her position was completely untenable, especially as she was married and head of a church school. She had no option but to take very early retirement with a substantial loss of pension."

"What about her husband?"

"Apparently, he threatened to kill David. It wasn't long before Johnson moved on again. The last I heard of him he had been killed in the Boxing Day Tsunami."

"Have you got an address for Mrs Clyne?"

"I'm afraid I haven't. Her husband's name is Derek. That's all I know about her."

"Thank you, Mrs Bailey. You've been very helpful."

"Paul Bryant was David Johnson's brother-in-law. A friend of his asked me for information about him after Paul's sister died of a drugs' overdose. A bad business."

"Can't see any mileage with the Clyne woman, boss," Butler said as Wallace rang off. "A jealous husband, but no connection with Emily Bryant. Another dead end."

"I still want to speak to Maggie Clyne. Get on to the team. We need to find out her whereabouts."

"Let's get over to the hotel and book in," Butler said. "It's within walking distance of the Hoe."

After booking in they sat near a window, gratefully sipping a lager. Below them, Christmas lights glittered and twinkled along the famous Hoe where Francis Drake played bowls as the Spanish Armada approached.

"I'm starving and completely bloody knackered. I could murder another pint," Butler declared.

They finished their drinks and wandered down towards the Barbican. It was packed with winter tourists and youngsters having a good time. Wallace remembered it was always frequented by students. He scowled remembering Eddie Haines and his drug dealing.

They managed to get into a small Italian restaurant. Wallace ordered bruschetta, lasagne and salad. Butler settled for spaghetti and meatballs with a side of garlic bread.

"Forget the pint, Butler. Let's have a bottle of red wine. I think a little relaxation is in order."

62

Wallace awoke with a rotten headache. Too much red wine the night before. His mouth felt like he had been sucking carpet all night.

"Come on," Butler said, "or we'll miss breakfast. I'll see you in the dining room."

"Order me some strong coffee, Phil. I need a shot of energy."

It never failed to amaze him how Butler relished his food after a night on the booze. After a hot shower, a clean shirt and underwear, he felt ready to face the day. Last night had been a rare occasion. Usually, he kept off the drink when he was on a case. He checked his emails on the way downstairs. Williams had sent him Maggie Clyne's address.

"Maggie Clyne lives in Salcombe. It's roughly about twenty-five miles away."

"I know it," Butler commented. "I used to spend my holidays there when I was a kid."

"We'll pay her a visit straight after breakfast," Wallace said.

Butler didn't answer. His mouth was full of egg and sausage. For a brief moment Wallace felt his gorge rising. He took a huge gulp of coffee and nibbled on his toast. An hour later they were on their way.

It took them approximately forty-five minutes to drive to Salcombe via Shadycombe Road.

"It's certainly changed since I came here as a kid. It was fairly quiet in those days. Wow! Did you see the price on that house?" Butler said, craning his neck towards a modest cottage. He tapped into his mobile and gasped at the cost of holiday accommodation. "Even the B&Bs are charging over a hundred pounds a night during high season."

Overhead, the sky loomed dark and menacing. Light snowflakes hovered in the air before settling on the roadway. In seconds they had disappeared. A heavy, gunmetal grey sea surged towards the shore, breaking white on the beach. Everything looked miserable and drab in the cold winter light.

They pulled up in front of a spacious house. Even the greyness of the weather couldn't detract from the stunning sea views.

"This must have cost them a pretty penny," Wallace remarked as he rang the doorbell. "I wonder how they managed it on teachers' salaries?"

An elderly man with a shock of white hair opened the door. He looked very frail.

"Good morning, sir. I'm Chief Inspector Ben Wallace and this is my colleague, DS Butler."

Derek Clyne looked at them suspiciously.

"What do you want?" he asked unceremoniously. "I haven't got any unpaid parking tickets." A slight sneer entered his voice.

"We'd like to speak to your wife."

"Why?"

"As I said, we would like to speak to your wife."

Clyne shuffled down the passage and shouted. "Maggie, there's some cops here wanting to speak to you."

A tall woman with dyed blonde hair appeared and pushed past Clyne.

"Mrs Clyne? Mrs Maggie Clyne?"

"What is it?" she asked with a tremor in her voice. "Is it my parents?"

"No, I just want to ask you a few questions about someone you knew years ago… David Johnson." Maggie's hand flew to her mouth. She looked terrified. For a few moments she stood rooted to the spot.

"Please, not in front of my husband. He has early onset dementia. I don't want anything to upset him. He can become very aggressive at times."

"I'm sorry, but it's very important."

"I'll meet you in about thirty minutes in town. There's a restaurant near the beach. *The Albatross*. One of the few that stays open all year. We can talk there."

Wallace looked at Butler and shrugged. "We're pushed for time, Mrs Clyne. It's imperative we get back to Plymouth as soon as possible."

Twenty-five minutes later Mrs Clyne sat down at their table. She wrung her hands continually and looked around her like a frightened bird.

"We're investigating the murder of a young girl in Shrewsbury. There are striking similarities between that and a schoolgirl, Jessica Parker, who was killed in a similar fashion in Plymouth nineteen years ago."

"What's that got to do with me? I was living in Kent at the time."

"I understand you were very friendly with a David Johnson," Wallace ventured. Panic swam into Maggie's eyes. Suddenly, she clasped her chest.

"I can't breathe," she said. "Any stress sets off my asthma."

"There's nothing for you to worry about," Wallace said gently.

"Just the mention of that pig's name sets me off!"

"I understand, but I have to ask you some questions. Did Johnson show any inclination towards young girls?"

"What do you mean?"

"Jessica Parker's murderer was never found. It's still an open case. We're trying to establish a link between her and Ella Chapman, a seventeen year old in Shropshire. She was strangled with her school tie and she was pregnant, just like Jessica."

"No, Johnson was a pig, but he never touched any of the girls in my school, or anybody else's as far as I know. He liked women; women who could advance his career." A sob caught in her throat.

Wallace held up his hand." We know all about the reasons why you left your old school. Were you jealous of Johnson and other women?"

"Of course I was, until I discovered his true nature. I was a complete idiot. Why do you ask?"

"Did you follow his progress when he left Kent? Did you want to pay him back for humiliating you?"

"I was devastated. It almost broke up my marriage. Derek was very difficult to live with when he found out about David. I just wanted to forget all about him. I despised him."

"Why did you move to Devon? Were you hoping to see Johnson?"

"No! My parents live just outside Salcombe. I was brought up here. We only moved to the area about six years ago. Our house belonged to my parents. They moved into a small cottage and signed the house over to me. That pleased Derek. It was the reason he agreed to come to Salcombe. He's been persuading me to sign it over to him ever since, but my parents put the kibosh on that, legally, before giving it to me."

"I see. Thank you, Mrs Clyne. You've been a great help. We won't need to speak to you again."

"She's one scared lady," Butler said as they walked to the car. "That husband of hers is a nasty piece of work. Well, boss, that's put the kibosh on that line of inquiry."

They drove back to Plymouth in silence. In the distance lightning streaked the sky, followed by a loud boom of thunder. Bare trees stood stark against the horizon like brooding scarecrows. Suddenly, huge drops of rain hammered the windscreen, running in rivulets that defied the wipers. Visibility was restricted to just a few yards. Potholes and ditches quickly filled with dirty brown water and overflowed onto the road, making driving difficult.

By the time they reached their modest hotel the rain was still bucketing down. "I think we had better eat here," Wallace said, shaking his sodden coat. "I don't fancy walking down to the Barbican in this weather and it's too far into the centre."

"Suits me, boss," Butler agreed. "A nice thick steak and chunky chips will do me nicely."

Suddenly, Wallace's mobile shrilled. "Hello, is that you, Chief Inspector?" a woman's voice shouted down the phone. "It's Mrs Jackson."

"What can I do for you?" Wallace asked.

"I have some information you may or may not find useful. I didn't think of it when I spoke to you. You may want to speak to the chairman of the local drama society. He may be able to help you. Johnson was a member for years. So was Emily."

Wallace's heart skipped a beat. This could be very useful indeed. "Do you have a name or an address?"

"I'm afraid not."

"Thank you, Mrs Jackson."

Butler looked at him expectantly. "What's up, boss?"

"We need to locate any theatrical societies in and around Plymouth. David Johnson was involved with amateur dramatics."

"I don't understand why we're pursuing this Johnson bloke if he's dead."

"We may find out a bit more about his relationship with Emily Bryant. There could be another guy involved. Someone with an axe to grind. Unrequited love or the little green-eyed monster. This will involve a lot of grunt work, Phil."

A quick search on the internet revealed that there were at least eight societies, most of them attached to outlying villages.

"We've got names and contact numbers for all of them," Wallace said. "I'll take the first half of the list. You do the rest."

An hour later they met in the bar and settled into a secluded corner where nobody could eavesdrop on their conversation.

"Three of the groups have closed down through lack of support since the Covid lockdowns. The other one is fairly new. None of them had a member named Johnson. A complete dead end," Butler groaned.

"Mine have all started back up, but no members named Johnson." Wallace spread his hands. "One of the chairpersons did mention a church group, but it disbanded about seven years ago. I saw a list of churches in the hotel information book. There's one not far from the Hoe. We'll go there first."

The vicar was a jolly-looking fellow, slightly overweight, with overlong snow-white hair and old-fashioned mutton-chop side whiskers. In his black cassock and white surplice he looked like a character from a Jane Austen novel. Only his shrewd, piercing blue eyes belied the dithery manner.

"How may I help you, Chief Inspector?" he asked after examining Wallace's warrant card. "Can't be too careful you know. Duty of care to parishioners and all that."

"I understand that you run a theatrical group here in the church hall," Wallace said.

"A very successful group indeed, but I'm sure you haven't come to join," he said with a twinkle in his eye.

Wallace laughed. "No, we're trying to track down anyone who knew this man." He showed the vicar a photograph of David Johnson.

The priest shook his head. "I don't recognise him. I've only been here about five years. You could have a word with the church warden, Ken Roberts. He may be able to help."

"Yes, he is vaguely familiar," Roberts said, but I can't put my finger on it."

"He was the deputy head of St Catherine's School about nineteen years ago."

"Of course! Didn't he die in the Boxing Day Tsunami in 2004? His face was all over the papers. The whole family drowned. Terrible business."

"Was he a member of your dramatic group?"

Ken shook his head. "I really don't know. I only joined about nine years ago. Maybe old Harry Bessemer, the verger, could help you. He's been a member forever. That's him going into the vestry."

"David Johnson? Yes, he and his wife were members here for quite a few years," Harry said.

"What can you tell us about him?"

"Nothing really." Harry shuffled away complaining about the flower arrangement near the font.

"He's very forgetful. Dementia, I'm afraid," Ken said. "Still, he's pretty good for ninety-one."

"I'll show you my photos," Harry called and disappeared into the vestry again.

Wallace followed him. "Did you say photos?"

"Aye, they're in my loft somewhere"

"If you want to see them you'll have to help me get them down from the attic."

Butler grimaced as they walked back to the car. "He's a bit doolally if you ask me."

"Doolally or not, we have to see those pictures. I've arranged to go to his house early tomorrow morning before we go back to Shrewsbury. He lives outside Eggbuckland."

*

It was still dark when Wallace and Butler left the hotel and drove to Harry's house. A glimmer of silvery light on the horizon heralded the onset of dawn. It was a filthy morning. Heavy rain made driving conditions hazardous. It had been chucking it down for most of their stay in Plymouth, with no sign of it letting up. Dawn broke, revealing heavy, black clouds being swept across the sky by an icy wind. Trees trembled and swayed in a wet, frenzied dance.

Harry lived in a quaint cottage set in a neat garden that had been prepared for the winter. Ken Roberts had told Wallace that the old boy lived alone since his wife had died five years earlier. He looked at his watch. Five to nine. The curtains were pulled back. Harry was sitting in front of the television drinking a cup of tea.

Wallace rang the bell and waited with Butler while Harry shuffled to the door. He looked taken aback when he saw them and kept the door on the safety chain.

"Good morning, Mr Bessemer. Chief Inspector Ben Wallace. This is DS Butler. I spoke to you yesterday about David Johnson. You said you had some photographs we might like to see."

Harry hesitated, struggling with his failing memory. "Yes, of course, I remember you now. Please come in. They're up there," he said, pointing towards the ceiling. "There's an entry panel in the spare bedroom. I put everything on the edge just inside. That's the only way I can reach anything. I'll get some steps."

He placed a set of steps firmly on the carpet and started to climb. "Whoa! Whoa!" Wallace exclaimed. "I'll do that. Go on, Butler. See what you can find."

Butler shone a Maglite inside the space. There was quite a lot of stuff there, mostly packed in cardboard boxes.

"What's this? There's a couple of albums here and a few boxes of loose photographs."

He handed them down to Wallace. Harry grabbed the albums and disappeared into the living room. When they followed a few minutes later, he was turning the pages with a wistful look on his face. "These are all personal photos. You might find something in one of the boxes."

Wallace and Butler each took a box. There were a lot of photos of the cast on stage from various plays. 'Hobson's Choice', 'An Inspector Calls', 'The Importance of Being Earnest'.* There was a picture of some of the cast celebrating after the show, still in costume, holding glasses of champagne.

"Do you recognise any of these people, Mr Bessemer?"

Harry examined the photo for a few moments. "Ah, yes, it's the cast of *'An Inspector Calls'*. That's young Jonno Smith," he said, "and the tall thin chap in the trilby is Graham Phillips. He was playing Inspector Goole."

"Who is the burly, grey-haired man in the front?"

Harry peered at the photograph. "Oh, that's David Johnson. He was all padded out for the part. He was wearing a wig too. I remember, because he kept complaining it was too big." Harry laughed. "It almost fell off at one point. He was a bumptious little bugger!"

Wallace looked beyond the group. In the background, a shadowy figure in a large hat stared out at the camera. Wallace's heart was hammering in his chest. *It couldn't be*, he thought. *It couldn't be!*"

He handed the photograph to Butler. "Take a look at this."

"What am I looking for, sir?"

"The woman in the background in the big hat."

"Bloody hell! She looks a bit like our mystery woman. It's a bit difficult to be certain."

"Mr Bessemer, do you know this woman?" he asked, pointing at the figure.

Harry squinted at the photo. "I think she was our stage manager." He shook his head in exasperation. "Was she Johnson's wife?" he asked himself. "I think so, but I'm not absolutely certain."

Wallace and Butler looked at each other.

"When was this picture taken?"

"I'm not sure, it was years ago."

"Did you see much of David Johnson when the play closed?"

"No, he stopped coming to rehearsals after that poor girl was murdered in the school."

"What about his wife?"

Harry shook his head. "Never saw her again. There were often rumours about Johnson… a bit of a womaniser by all accounts."

"May I keep these photographs?" Wallace asked.

"Aye, they're no use to me. I've got what I want," he said, fingering the albums.

"Thank you, Mr Bessemer. You've been extremely helpful."

"Well, that's a turn-up for the books," Butler declared as they returned to the car.

"I was right! I can feel it in my gut!" Wallace said triumphantly. "There must be a link between Jessica Parker, Ella Chapman and the mystery woman."

"All we have to do now, boss, is find out how and why they are linked," Butler said gloomily.

63

Wallace stepped into his office when the telephone rang. It was Chief Superintendent Payne. He groaned audibly and hastily covered the mouthpiece.

"Well, Wallace, I hope you haven't wasted time and money on your little trip?"

"Quite the contrary, sir, it was very fruitful. We've now established a firm link between David Johnson's wife and our mystery woman."

"And…"

"That's the problem, sir." Wallace winced, waiting for the onslaught. "We know there's a link between the woman and Ella Chapman. We already know that David Johnson worked in the school where Jessica Parker was murdered. We had a long chat with the elderly verger, who identified David Johnson as a member of the church drama group. It was rather fuzzy, but a woman in the background looked very much like our mystery woman. Old Harry, the verger, thought it may have been Johnson's wife. It may or may not be the same woman who has been wandering around Shrewsbury."

Wallace could hear Payne sighing on the other end of the line.

"Well, you had better find out, pronto! I need more than supposition to give to the Chief Constable."

"Payne in the arse!" Wallace snarled, using a deliberate pun as he slammed the receiver back into its cradle. "Butler! Everybody in the incident room in ten minutes."

Butler pinned the photographs plus two blow-ups on the evidence board. They were more blurred than the smaller prints.

Baker grinned. "Holiday snaps, boss?"

Butler shot him a warning look as Wallace came further into the room. He glared at Baker and waited for the merriment to die down.

"Right, I want all of you to study the photos carefully. Is there anything that stands out for you?"

The team sat back and shook their heads. Wallace ran his hand over his jaw in frustration. If they couldn't see it, then he could be wrong. Hembrow stood up and walked up to the board. "It's her!" she exclaimed. "It's our mystery woman, or somebody exactly like her."

"Thank you, DC Hembrow. You're very observant."

Baker scowled and shot her a dirty look. "Trying to get into lover boy's good books again," he sniggered.

"I don't understand, sir. Where did you get it? "

"It's a photograph of the cast of *'An Inspector Calls'* from around 2003. The burly bloke in the front with the iron-grey hair is David Johnson. *She*," he said, pointing to the woman, "we think is David Johnson's wife."

A corporate gasp echoed around the room. Williams threw up his hands in puzzlement. "How is that possible, sir? She's dead."

"Is she? Her body was never found. We know that Johnson was having an affair with Emily Bryant. The mystery woman could have surfaced years later and now she's out for revenge."

"That doesn't make sense. Mrs Bryant's attacker was a man."

"Correct, but what if she had an accomplice? Someone close to her. What if she was washed up somewhere with her children? They could be in their thirties by now. Emily Bryant's attacker always wore a balaclava. He never spoke. All we know is that he was slim and fast on his feet. He could easily be a young man."

"It's a possibility," Williams said reluctantly, "but how does that tie in with Ella Chapman?"

Wallace picked up a marker pen and drew a line between the mystery woman from Shrewsbury, Ella Chapman, Emily Bryant, David Johnson, Jessica Parker and back to Johnson's wife in the photo Harry Bessemer had given them.

"That's how!" he declared.

"Makes sense," Baker said, "but we're still back where we started, aren't we? Until we track her down we've got nothing."

"Correct, Baker, which is why I want the whole team scouring Shrewsbury and the surrounding areas to find the woman. It's unlikely she travels into Shrewsbury from any great distance. She's definitely not a tourist.

She's been spotted too many times over the past few months. Sooner or later she'll get careless."

"Only if she knows we're on the lookout for her, and I don't think she does. Her movements are too mundane," Baker interjected. "Hairdressers, buying wine in Tanner's and chocolates. If she was worried about being seen surely she would avoid those places."

"Could be reverse psychology," Hembrow said.

"We don't know either way, so our only option is to keep on searching for her. I'll try and get some extra police out on the beat in the centre of Shrewsbury. It's Christmas week, so the town will be crowded with shoppers and tourists having a seasonal break. Let's hope she pops her head over the parapet."

Wallace marched back into his office, with Butler close on his heels.

"It's stretching things a bit, boss."

"I agree, but it's all we've got. Get a rota going from tomorrow. I want every available officer out in town. Any sighting must be reported to me as a matter of urgency. We're on borrowed time. *Crewcut Charlie* will take us off the case at the drop of a hat."

As soon as Butler left, Wallace quickly dialled a number. There was one person who could verify the identity of the woman in the photograph.

"Hello, Mrs Jackson? Chief Inspector Wallace. I'm sorry to call you at home, but this is very important."

"How may I help you?" she said wearily. It had been a long, arduous day.

"I'm going to email a photograph of members of

the church drama group you mentioned. I'd like you to identify any of the cast members of '*An Inspector Calls*' that you recognise. Don't tell me now, just study the picture, including people in the background. It could be of vital importance to the case."

"I'll get back to you within fifteen minutes," Mrs Jackson promised.

Wallace sifted through the papers on his desk, but he couldn't concentrate. He almost jumped out of his skin when his desk phone shrilled. It was Mrs Jackson. His stomach and chest felt tight with apprehension.

"I recognise most of them," she said. David Johnson is in the front and… "

"Go on!" Wallace said impatiently. Silence on the other end of the line. "Please, forgive me. I didn't mean to be rude. It's just that there's so much depending on this."

Mrs Jackson reeled through a number of names. "What about the woman at the back, in the hat?"

"That's David Johnson's wife."

"Are you absolutely certain?"

"Absolutely! That's definitely Mary Johnson."

"I can't thank you enough, Mrs Jackson. You've been extremely helpful."

"Butler, get in here!" he called into the incident room.

"What's up, boss?"

"I've just spoken to Mrs Jackson in Plymouth. I emailed her the photo we had from Harry Bessemer. She confirmed, without any doubt, that it's Johnson's wife, Mary."

"I'll be damned!" Butler exclaimed.

"I want to dig a bit more into Mary Johnson's family background. Let's see if she has any close relatives."

*

Mick Gilchrist settled back on the sofa and watched Isobel as she poured two cups of steaming tea. She was looking quite radiant in a red roll-neck sweater and smart black trousers.

"I wish you would reconsider and come to Italy with me in the New Year. Edward will be preparing for the new school term, so there's no danger of him turning up."

"I admit, I'm very tempted, but I need to have everything in place for next term. I don't want Edward to have any excuse to criticise me."

"He won't! He knows he has to toe the line as far as you're concerned."

"Let's arrange a Twelfth Night dinner instead."

"Super! What a lovely idea!" Isobel beamed. Mick always made her feel so special. "I'm afraid Christmas will be spent doing the usual round of cocktail parties. The Pryce-Jones's have invited us for Christmas dinner. Giles Ponting and Amanda Squires will also be there."

Mick wrinkled his nose. "Rather you than me."

"Amanda is a bit acerbic, but she's quite good fun. Edward will be in his element, scheming with Giles about the by-election. I'm very proud of him, you know."

Mick didn't respond. He hated Edward Booth with a

vengeance. One day he would get his own back for the way he had been treated, but he would always protect Isobel.

*

Wallace sat in the car for a few minutes when he arrived at the police station. He needed to collect his thoughts before going into the incident room. Something was bugging him about Mary Johnson, but he couldn't work out why.

The team looked up as he walked through the incident room. After acknowledging the chorus of 'morning boss' he went straight to his office and signalled Butler to follow him.

"There's more to Mary Johnson than meets the eye. I can feel it in my guts," Wallace said.

"It's a bit of a stretch. So, she wears a hat similar to our mystery woman. What are you trying to prove?"

"Honestly? I don't know." "Well, what have you got?" Wallace asked, walking back into the incident room. Silence. "Anything at all? Williams?"

"No, sir. There hasn't been a sight of the mystery woman in town or the surrounding areas. She may have left the area for the Christmas holidays."

"Anybody else?"

"I did some digging on the internet, boss," Baker chimed in. "Mary Johnson was born, Mary Macintyre. She had an older sister, Jennifer. Their father was Irish American and the mother Italian. He was in the United

States Air Force, stationed in England when the sisters were born. That meant the daughters had dual American/British nationality. After his tour of duty ended he and his wife went back to the States for about eighteen months, but the girls stayed in England in a boarding school. The parents eventually returned and settled in Lincolnshire. Their father was employed in a civilian capacity at the air base. He passed away in 1998."

"What about the mother?"

"Records dried up after 1998. She could have gone back to the States, but there should be a record of it if she went back home with the US Airforce."

"She may have remarried and changed her name, or reverted to her maiden name," Butler interjected.

Baker shrugged. "It's a possibility. Jennifer emigrated to Australia about a year after the tsunami. She came back to the United Kingdom three years later. Soon afterwards, she went to the United States and eventually dropped off the radar."

"Good work, Baker. That will give us something to go on. Cross match all her records with Mary Macintyre. Everybody leaves a trail, wherever they are in the world."

"*She* may also have remarried and changed her name," Hembrow commented.

"UK records state a woman's maiden name on the marriage certificate," Butler said. "If she married in the United Kingdom, we'll find her records."

"Right, let's start there," Wallace said.

"I've been tracing my family history," Hembrow said. There are billions of records on these family history sites.

The Mormons have caves full of records on everybody in the world stored in Salt Lake City in Utah."

"Right, Hembrow, you start researching the Mormon site. Baker, keep up the search on the internet. The rest of you split it up between the various sites and pray we come up with something. She's out there somewhere."

64

Wallace heard his mobile shrill from somewhere deep in his unconscious state. Startled, he shot upright. For a few seconds he felt completely disorientated. "What the hell?" Cursing, he felt around for the phone. "Where the hell is it?" It had slipped down between the leather cushions.

"Wallace!" he barked.

"Sir, we've got a lead," Butler said urgently. "We managed to trace Jennifer Macintyre. She moved around a lot, through five different states in the US. There hasn't been a sight of her since 2009. No records, absolutely nothing."

"Were there any work details? She had to have money from somewhere to live on."

"Your guess is as good as mine, boss."

"Thanks, Phil, I'll be with you in about forty-five minutes."

"It's your day off. I can take care of this until tomorrow."

"No, I need to be there."

He felt like hell. Groggy and a little unsteady on his

feet. He had fallen asleep on the sofa as soon as he sat down. He desperately needed a good night's sleep in his own bed, but he had to follow this up. He splashed some cold water on his face, hurriedly put on a clean shirt and headed for the car. So much for his day off.

Wearily, he perched on the edge of Butler's desk and gazed around the incident room. His team looked as weary as he felt.

"I know some of you should be going off duty now, but it's vital we discuss this latest lead."

"I think she was travelling around deliberately, covering her tracks for whatever reason," Baker said. "Her behaviour seems odd. There's absolutely nothing on social media. Most people post photos or comments on Facebook so friends and relatives can keep track of them. Jennifer had a Facebook page, but there's nothing on it. The last entry was December 2009 when she posted that she was flying to Paris. We've looked at marriage, divorce and death records. Zilch!"

Wallace rubbed his chin thoughtfully. Where the hell was she? Jennifer Macintyre had ceased to exit.

"Well, she couldn't have just disappeared from the face of the earth. Even if she went back to Australia there would be some kind of trail. Hembrow, Williams, any ideas?"

"My gut instinct is that she may have adopted a whole new identity," Hembrow said. "We know she flew to Paris in late December 2009. Was that a ruse to conceal her real plans? She could have gone anywhere in Europe afterwards."

"I agree," Wallace said. "I'll call in a few favours from my contacts in Paris. Just a thought. Did anyone check the sea routes?"

"We checked the ferry services. Nothing there," Hembrow replied.

"What about the ocean liners?"

Hembrow shrugged. "No, but I'll get on it straight away, boss." She scuttled off to her computer.

"Right, everybody back here tomorrow morning by seven thirty sharp! Those of you going off shift, get some real rest today and a good night's sleep. You're going to need it. The rest of you, get some strong coffee. You'll need to be on your toes. I don't want you falling asleep over your computers... and get some muffins, on me."

Wallace walked into his office to a chorus of "Thanks boss."

He gave Butler a weary grin. "They're a good bunch. Couldn't have a better team and that includes Baker, even though he's a pain in the arse."

*

When Wallace walked into the incident room the next morning he was relieved to see that his team looked perky and refreshed. He perched on the edge of a desk while they swung their chairs around and faced him.

"Well, what have we got?" he asked. "Anything, anything at all?"

"Yes and no," Hembrow said. "Nothing on her

whereabouts recently. Baker and I trawled all the records, but drew a blank."

Wallace raised an eyebrow. "And?"

"She booked passage on the QM2 leaving Hamburg in January 2010. The ship had sailed across the Atlantic from New York to pick up passengers. From there it was going on a world cruise."

"There were just over a thousand women on board. Only about twenty women had booked passage from Hamburg. Most of them German, as you would expect. A British woman also embarked."

"Why Hamburg?" Baker interjected. "She could have sailed from New York or Southampton."

Wallace nodded. "Probably covering her tracks, if she didn't want to be traced."

"We contacted a few hotels near the cruise terminal," Hembrow interjected. "Some people book an overnight hotel in case of travel holdups en route. Jennifer Macintyre had booked a room. It was a stroke of luck that the same concierge still works there. He only remembered her, because of the world cruise, and she gave him a huge tip for organising her enormous amount of luggage."

"So, how can we confirm she actually boarded the QM2?" Baker asked.

"The ship's manifest has a record of all passengers," Hembrow added. "Those records are archived. Everybody gets an ID card with a photograph that's taken at the departure desk. It must be produced when embarking and disembarking at every port of call."

"What about the photographs?" Baker asked. "Are they kept by Cunard?"

Hembrow shrugged her shoulders. "The ID card is for security purposes. Obviously passengers take theirs home. Personal information is kept by Cunard, but not ID photos. It's a way for the security services to check passengers' criminal activity, individuals suspected of terrorism, money laundering, etcetera."

"First of all, we need to know what Jennifer Macintyre looks like," Wallace said. "For example, does she resemble her sister Mary?"

"I'll have a trawl through the internet, boss. Somebody on the USAF base may be able to tell us which school the girls attended. There's sure to be school pics. I'll get on to it straight away."

Butler followed Wallace into his office, carrying two styrofoam cups of steaming coffee. He slumped into a chair while Wallace swung to and fro, tapping his top lip.

Butler grimaced. "This coffee is disgusting. It tastes like soup."

Wallace sipped his coffee. "You're right. It is disgusting! Hembrow and Baker have carried out some good work. This could be a real breakthrough."

"If it *is* Jennifer Macintyre, why all the subterfuge? What was she running away from, and why?" Butler asked.

Ten minutes later Baker knocked on the door. "I've found it, boss. The girls initially attended a local school near the USAF base before attending a private boarding school in Lincolnshire. They stayed at school when their parents returned to the States. In fact, all their education was in the United Kingdom."

"It seems pretty obvious that the parents knew they would be returning to England fairly soon, hence the boarding school," Butler suggested.

"I could look up universities. It may provide some more recent information."

"Good idea, Baker. She would be bound to be listed in their alumni records. Looking up the universities is a lot of work, so it requires more than Baker. Sort it out between yourselves. I want everybody back here by two o'clock this afternoon."

*

Wallace spent the morning contacting Mrs Jackson and old Harry in Plymouth. He drew a complete blank. They had never heard Mary ever mentioning a sister. He put his elbows on the desk, cradled his head in his hands, and closed his eyes for a few minutes. A knock on the glass door startled him. Butler came in armed with a pile of papers. Wallace glanced at his watch. He had been asleep for ten minutes!

Butler shuffled through the papers, pulled out a sheet and gave it to Wallace.

"I've got some more information on Mary Johnson. Apparently, she and David were already married when they settled in Plymouth. He had been married before, to Paul Bryant's sister."

"We already know that," Wallace said curtly.

Butler ignored the remark. "Yes, but we didn't know how he and Mary Macintyre met. They met at a big charity event in London to raise money for underprivileged children. What we also didn't know was that her mother was from a well-known American Italian banking family. Old money. Megabucks!"

"How did you verify this information?"

"I contacted a pal of mine in New York. He works on Wall Street. He knew all about the family. Everything was left to the two daughters by their maternal grandparents. They inherited huge sums of money and property."

"That explains how she afforded to travel around America."

"Exactly, money was no object."

"Was he able to give a description of Jennifer?"

"Only from a rare photograph he had seen in the newspaper when the girls were teenagers. It seems their parents kept them out of the limelight and shunned publicity."

"Another dead end!"

"Not entirely. Matt, that's my pal in New York, said there was coverage of Mary's wedding in the society columns. A lot of speculation about her marrying a penniless British school teacher."

"So David Johnson was well set up with a very wealthy wife when he started teaching in Plymouth. That's a bit odd, isn't it? He could have lived the life of Riley."

"Apparently, the girls didn't get access to their full inheritance until they reached the age of thirty-five."

"That explains Johnson's teaching post. He had to

wait to get what he wanted. Judging by what Paul Bryant told us, he was unscrupulous. He didn't see Johnson again until he moved to Plymouth for a job with a firm of architects. We know what happened between Johnson and his sister Karen. His behaviour forms a distinct pattern."

"Yes," Butler added. He became involved with various figures of authority to enhance his career. Maggie Clyne was a classic example."

"Mary Johnson was a bigger fish altogether," Wallace interjected. "That was the jackpot." He glanced at his watch. "Let's get back in there."

A flurry of activity greeted them as they walked into the incident room. Before Wallace had a chance to speak, Baker whirled around from his computer screen.

"Sir, she did go to university, but not in this country. She went to Harvard. "Look!" he said excitedly.

Wallace and Butler leaned over as Baker scrolled down the screen.

"This is the online version of Harvard's yearbook. It goes back decades. This is the one, 1991." He zoomed into the page of photographs. "There she is, that's Jennifer Macintyre!" Baker exclaimed.

"I'll be damned!" Wallace exclaimed. "Good work, Baker!" High cheekbones, blonde, blue eyes set in a heart-shaped face. "She's certainly a looker," he commented. "Beauty and brains." He scrutinised the image for a few moments. "It's difficult to compare with the photo of Mary we were given by old Harry. Still, the image was very blurred. Any other information?"

"Quite a bit," Baker replied. "Apparently, she was a brilliant student, majored in physics and chemistry. According to her mentor she was an ideal Ph.D. candidate. She got as far as submitting a formal proposal then changed her mind; said she wanted to travel for a couple of years. Since then, zilch!"

"Well, at least we know now what she looks like. She had dual nationality, so she could have been using an American or British passport. What puzzles me is why she didn't board in New York with her American passport, as you suggested earlier."

"She could have flown to London on her US passport and switched to the European passport when she got here, to cover her tracks," Butler intervened. "That would have made it a lot easier for her to travel across Europe with greater freedom."

"We need to find out if she completed all or part of the world cruise. Even if she signed up for the whole cruise, she could have disembarked at some European port," Hembrow said. "The ship won't wait for late passengers. They would have to travel under their own steam to the next port of call. That would be an easy way for her to disappear."

"You could be right, Hembrow. It could all have been planned in advance, but why? Get on to Carnival in Southampton. Send them a photo of Jennifer Macintyre. Even without the photo they would still know if she didn't get back on the ship at any point. That would at least pin her down to a specific country."

"It's going to be one hell of a job, sir. She could have

travelled on via car, plane, train or even a continental ferry."

"I'll call in every contact I've got. I've still got a few friends in Interpol. We know what Jennifer looks like, but we still need to know what Mary looks like. Phil, get onto your pal in New York. Ask him to send over any newspaper photos he can lay his hands on. Hembrow and Baker, scour the internet for any charity events in London involving underprivileged children. There has to be a photo somewhere of Mary Johnson."

65

The weather was atrocious. High winds and torrential rain had covered the whole of Shropshire for weeks. Icy rain covered the windscreen. It seemed never ending. Gutters and ditches were awash, spilling onto the road, making cars veer as they hit the water. The wipers couldn't deal with the volume of rain lashing against the windscreen. Wallace could barely see through the streaming rivulets. A dark, metallic sky hung ominously over the countryside like a malevolent demon intent on destruction.

He took a detour down towards Victoria Quay and drove on towards the Quarry. The River Severn was flowing fast and furious through the town. Another few feet and it would flood the low-lying houses that lined the river bank beyond the Quarry. A couple were piling sandbags up against their garden wall. There was little more they could do to prevent the misery of flooding. Now the Met Office had issued another snow warning.

His thoughts turned to Jo Barnett and his daughter. If the deluge didn't stop soon it would put the kibosh on his special plans for Christmas Day. He usually worked over the festive season, allowing some leeway for those with kids. He banished the thought as he parked up in the police station. He bounded up the stairs towards his office. The incident room was a buzz of activity and animated voices. Butler swung around in his chair as he passed and followed him into the office.

Wallace hung up his soaking overcoat, slicked back his wet hair and sat down. He looked enquiringly at Butler as he handed him a steaming coffee.

"What's up?" he asked.

"Quite a lot actually," Butler replied.

"Well, spill!"

"Matt sent over a photo of David Johnson and Mary's wedding photograph. It's not very clear." He handed the copy to Wallace. Mary Johnson's face was slightly obscured by her husband leaning towards her, lips puckered to kiss her on the cheek.

He squinted at the image. There's definitely a likeness between the sisters. I just wish the image was a bit clearer."

"Get this, boss… they're not just sisters. They're identical twins."

"Well, I'll be damned!" Wallace exclaimed.

"And there's more. Williams found this." He handed another sheet to Wallace." That's Mary Johnson. The image showed Mary in front of a rostrum, obviously delivering a speech. The same blonde hair, high cheekbones and luminous eyes.

Wallace marched into the incident room and pinned

the images on the evidence board. "Well done, Williams! Now we've got a real breakthrough!"

"What I don't get is why Jennifer disappeared," Williams said.

"She must have had a compelling reason to just disappear, leaving no trace behind her," Baker interjected.

"There's nothing suspicious about her time in America," Butler added, "but there has to be a motive for her behaviour. My gut instinct tells me it's connected with Mary Johnson."

"Identical twins sometimes suffer the same feelings as each other," Hembrow intervened. "They feel the same pain and emotions as their twin. "Perhaps," Hembrow ventured, "she was so traumatised by Mary being washed away in the Tsunami that she had to hide away somewhere on her own. Get away from everything familiar. Don't forget, it wasn't just Mary, but her children as well. All she had in way of family."

"Hmm. Whatever her motives, she's still out there somewhere and we have to find her. Until we do we're stuck between a rock and a hard place. In the meantime I'll ask my contact in Interpol to circulate this photograph as widely as possible."

66

Butler struggled to keep the car under control as he and Wallace drove north towards Oswestry. Every time they hit a pool of water the car swerved and wobbled dangerously. Butler cursed loudly.

"Bloody rain! Do you really want to drive up there in this stinking weather, boss?"

"It's imperative that we speak to Megan again. Now that she's out of hospital she may be able to give us more information about the attack. Having said that, I still feel she's hiding something. Something to do with that boy in her drawings."

It took them another hour to get to Pryce-Jones's house. Although it was mid-afternoon, it was dark and gloomy. Christmas lights blazed along the front of the house, alleviating the dark, gloomy day.

"What I'd give for a house like this," Butler remarked as he crunched to a halt. "I'd have to win the lottery."

Security lights blazed from the front and corners of the property, illuminating the driveway and the lawn. The front door opened as they approached the portico. Squadron Leader Pryce-Jones loomed in the doorway.

"Chief Inspector, what gives us the pleasure of your company? Have you had any more information on the attack?"

"No, but we're following up on our enquiries. We'd like to ask Megan some further questions about the night she was attacked. Her recollection of that night may be a little clearer now." Pryce-Jones's mouth clamped shut in a taut smile.

"Come in," he said curtly. "I'll call Megan. She's been through a terrible ordeal. I don't want her upset."

"Megan," he called up the wide, imposing staircase. The police are here. They want a word with you."

"Please sit down," Pryce-Jones said. "Would you like some tea, coffee? Maybe something stronger?"

"No, thank you."

Megan suddenly appeared at the top of the stairs, looking pale and frightened.

"It's all right, darling. No need to be afraid. I'll stay with you."

"Hello, Megan," Wallace said in a gentle tone. "There's nothing to be concerned about. Just a few questions. Could you tell if the man who attacked you was young or an older man?"

"He definitely wasn't a teenager. I told you I couldn't see his face. His voice was muffled by the balaclava, but it sounded like an older man."

"Was there anything at all that you found familiar about him?"

"No, nothing."

Wallace took her sketchbook out of his pocket. "I believe this is yours, Megan?"

Suddenly her face puckered up and she started to cry. "Where did you get it?"

"We found it when we searched your room in St Cadfael's."

"This is outrageous!" Pryce-Jones cut in.

"Who is the boy in the drawings, Megan?"

"What boy?" Pryce-Jones demanded. "You're going a bit too far, Wallace," he snarled.

"I don't know who he is!" Megan cried. "It's just something out of my head I drew after seeing a photograph in a magazine."

Wallace flicked through the sketchbook and showed Megan page after page of drawings depicting the same boy.

"That's enough!" Pryce-Jones exclaimed. "She's told you she doesn't know who he is. Now, please leave!"

"We have to follow up every lead if we are to solve Ella Chapman's murder, and that of Mark Hilliard."

Wallace nodded curtly and headed for the door. "We'll be in touch. If you have anything more to tell us, ring this number." He handed Megan his card. Pryce-Jones snatched it before she had a chance to take it.

"She's hiding something," Wallace said as he and Butler drove off. "Something she doesn't want her father to know about."

*

Baker looked up from his computer as Wallace walked into the incident room.

"I've found it, boss! Look, it's Mary Johnson!"

Wallace looked over Baker's shoulder. Jennifer Macintyre's double stared back at him from the computer screen. You couldn't put a pin between them. They all had raised glasses of what looked like champagne. She and another woman were holding a giant cheque.

"Can you zoom in on that cheque?" Wallace asked.

"No problem, boss. Phew! £250,000 payable to… " He squinted at the screen. "A homeless charity. *'Keep Kids Off the Streets'*."

"She seems to have done a lot of charity work, all of them connected with children. "

"When did this event take place?"

"2002."

"So, before the tsunami."

"Yes, there's nothing after 2004."

"That figures, but it doesn't help with regard to her twin sister. She's the one we have to concentrate on now."

"According to Carnival Cruise Lines, she disembarked in Barcelona and didn't return to the ship."

"We need to trace her movements after she left the cruise ship. She could be anywhere in Europe. She may even have doubled back and returned to the United States. Keep digging, Baker."

Turning on his heels, Wallace walked into his office and closed the door. A thrill of anticipation coursed through him at the prospect of talking to his old friend in Geneva. He quickly dialled a number.

"Ernst Dreher."

"It's Ben, Ben Wallace."

"What a pleasant surprise! It's so nice to hear from you. How is Jo?"

"We're getting married next February. I hope you and Sophia will be able to come to the wedding."

"Wonderful! I can't wait to tell Sophia."

"I also need your help with a murder case." Wallace gave him a brief outline on the disappearance of Jennifer Macintyre.

"We know she disembarked in Barcelona, but didn't return to the ship. There's no trace of her in the UK or in the USA, but we do have a photograph. Can you circulate it throughout Europe? It's our only chance of tracing her."

"I still have my contacts in Interpol. I'll call in a few favours. Give my congratulations to Jo. I'll be in touch."

"Thanks, Ernst."

He put the phone back in its cradle and sat back, rubbing his chin. If anybody could locate Jennifer Macintyre it was Ernst. Now he had to find out more about the boy in Megan Pryce-Jones's sketchbook.

67

It snowed heavily overnight, creating problems on the roads. Fat flakes cascaded in a frenzied dance, settling on the already overladen trees lining the driveway. Icicles hung from branches, glistening like silver swords ready to plunge to the ground. Fresh snow laced the Georgian windows, creating patterns of gold as light spilled onto the snow-covered grass outside. A few solitary footprints leading to the portico were swiftly covered, leaving no trace of the perpetrator. Everything was eerily quiet, still and totally deserted. St Cadfael's looked as if it had been lifted from a Jane Austen novel. Wallace half expected to see girls in Georgian dresses peering from the windows.

"Thank God they used a snow plough, otherwise we would never have got here."

"Couldn't this have waited, boss? It's bloody atrocious weather! What if we get stuck here?"

The drone of an engine pierced the air. A small snow plough emerged from the falling snow and drove towards them.

Wallace grinned. So that's how they cleared the road so quickly. A man muffled in scarf and fur hat waved at them as the plough came to a stop in front of the house. He waved back and got out of the car.

"You're taking a chance coming out in this weather, Chief Inspector," the caretaker said. He brushed snowflakes from his face and spat some out of his mouth. "Good thing I've got this contraption then, innit."

"We'd like to have another look at Megan Pryce-Jones's room."

"Oh, I dunno about that sir. Booth ain't here. You'll have to ask his secretary." He pointed a thumb at the house.

"Don't tell me she's still working," Butler said out of the side of his mouth."

"She's office staff, so she's probably expected to be here after school breaks up. Come on, let's get inside before my feet freeze solid."

A filigree of ice covered the steps where snow had been scraped away.

Gingerly, they walked up the steps and pushed open the heavy door. The foyer was deserted. There was no sign of Mrs James. Only the faint whirring of machinery coming from the office behind reception. Wallace pressed the bell on the desk with the palm of his hand.

"Just a minute," a voice answered in curt manner. "Oh, it's you," Mrs James said impatiently. "What is it this time, Chief Inspector?"

"I'd like you to take another look at the drawing we found in Megan's room."

"I've already told you…" Mrs James started to object then held her tongue.

"Just take another look and study it carefully. Don't you think it's odd that Megan had so many sketches of this boy?"

Mrs James examined the picture for a few moments and shook her head.

"No, I have no idea. She may have copied it from a magazine. The clothes look a bit dated. A bit James Dean. Tight jeans, leather jacket and T-shirt. Perhaps he was a biker. Still, it's a look that's stood the test of time."

"Thank you, Mrs James. You've been most helpful."

"Just a minute, let me take another look."

Wallace handed her the drawing. She studied it intently, then a strange expression came over her face. Hurriedly, she handed it back to him.

"We'd like to see Megan's room again, just in case we missed anything."

"Very well. This is my last day, although looking at the weather, I may have to stay here overnight. So will you, if you hang around much longer."

Wallace nodded and made for the stairs with Butler on his trail.

"Did you notice the look on Mrs James's face the second time she looked at the drawing?"

"Very odd. Perhaps she did recognise the boy and was covering up."

They made a fruitless search of Megan's room and started to walk out into the corridor.

"Nothing here, boss," Butler commented. "Wait a mo,

what's this?" He took a photograph off the back of the door. "Take a look, sir. He pointed at the picture. "It's a group of boys. Looks like a school photo." He poked at the picture. "That looks like the same boy in Megan's drawings."

"I'll be damned! This is a proper photo, not cut out of a magazine. Once this weather breaks I want her brought into the station."

"Pryce-Jones isn't going to like it, boss."

"Bugger Pryce-Jones. Apart from the attack on Megan, we're conducting a murder investigation. There's a dangerous killer on the loose. Let's get back before we get stuck in this snow."

They fought their way down the lanes, wheels slipping and sliding in the icy conditions. Once they got back onto the main road driving conditions were a bit easier. Snowploughs had been out and the roads were heavily gritted. There was a steady stream of traffic heading towards Shrewsbury, headlights blazing. The vehicle in front of them skidded and slewed dangerously towards the centre of the road before the driver managed to get it under control.

Wallace checked in with the station. Hembrow answered, sounding slightly frazzled.

"There are only a few of us left here on duty, sir. Everybody else has gone home early, because of the weather warnings. The roads are treacherous."

"Butler and I are off duty now, so we'll head off home while we can. You know where to reach me."

"Okay, sir. Take care."

68

Wallace peered out at the falling snow. Large, feathery flakes obliterated his view. He could barely see the house opposite. A bunch of snowflakes fell outside the window as though an invisible hand had gathered them up and flung them to the ground.

Conditions had barely changed since the day before. Sighing heavily, he donned his ancient duffle coat over a thick sweater and pulled a pea hat over his head. There was nothing for it, he would have to clear the driveway.

An army of neighbours had set about clearing the cul-de-sac that led to the main road. If the snow didn't stop soon they would be wasting their time. Grabbing a snow spade, he set about clearing a car's width towards his gate, then he went out onto the road to help.

A couple of the wives, bundled in warm coats, appeared carrying trays of drinks.

"We've got whisky, brandy and hot mulled wine, Ben," remarked Susy, his next door neighbour. She grinned. "Help yourself. Have one of each if it helps."

"Thanks, I will," Wallace replied.

"You'll have to drink it neat, I'm afraid."

"Suits me." A chorus of male voices echoed his sentiments. Eventually, the whole street was out puffing and blowing with the unaccustomed exercise. After a lot of exertion and banter everybody scurried indoors to luxuriate in the warmth of their homes.

Wallace spent the rest of the afternoon doing some paperwork and watching recorded rugby. Just before six o' clock he heated up a ready meal and settled down to watch the evening news. He had to get back to work tomorrow even if he had to ski in.

Frustrated, he thought about what they had discovered in Megan's room. What was it that Mrs James had seen in the drawing? Why was Megan making sketches of the mysterious boy in the photograph? Was it just a schoolgirl crush, someone she had seen in a magazine?

He remembered his daughter having crushes on pop stars, but she was quite open about it. Her bedroom walls were adorned with the crush of the month. That was normal teenage behaviour, so why is Megan so secretive? It didn't make any sense. His gut instinct told him that Mrs James had definitely recognised the boy. Would she ask Megan about him? He was still mulling over the questions when he fell into a deep sleep.

He awoke to sunshine piercing the drawn curtains. He had overslept. He looked at his watch. Nine o'clock. Sluggishly, he got out of bed and pulled them open, shading his eyes against the harsh brightness. A wintry, white sun hung overhead in a cornflower blue sky.

Miraculously, the heavy snowfall had stopped. Icicles glistened and dripped from the roof gutters. Melting snow plopped onto the grass. There was still a lot of the white stuff around, but it was quickly disappearing. For a brief moment he felt a twinge of sadness, remembering how his father had made him a big wooden sled: the hours of fun they had with it. He gave himself a mental shake. Now, he could get into the station.

69

The veins in Pryce-Jones's neck stood out like ropes. He could barely speak through his anger. Megan was visibly shaken. Her mother put a protective arm around her shoulders.

"What the hell do you think you're playing at, Chief Inspector?" he spluttered. "My daughter is *not* a criminal. You should be out looking for the perpetrator, not hounding an innocent young girl."

"It's important we try to establish the identity of the boy in her sketches."

"She's already told you, she saw his picture in a magazine!"

"We'd like to speak with her alone. This is an informal interview, sir," Wallace persisted. "Megan has agreed. DC Hembrow, please show Megan into the interview room."

"Not without her solicitor present!" Pryce-Jones barked.

Megan glanced at her father as Hembrow showed her into the other room.

"Now look here!" Pryce-Jones said.

"Megan has agreed to an informal interview, sir. I understand how you feel, but you know what teenagers are like. They won't always open up in front of their parents. There could be a serial killer on the loose. Megan has already been attacked once. Next time she may not be so lucky. We need to establish why Megan is being so evasive about the boy in the drawings. We found this on the back of the door in her room at St Cadfael's."

"We would know if she had a boyfriend." He glanced at his wife.

"The Chief Inspector may be right, dear," she said carefully. "I know I didn't tell my parents everything, for fear they would disapprove."

Pryce-Jones's shoulders dropped. "Very well," he said in a resigned tone, "but I don't want her upset. She's been through enough already."

"I can assure you we have Megan's interests and safety at heart. A female officer will be present when she's being questioned."

Before Pryce-Jones could say anymore Wallace and Butler went into the interview room and closed the door. Wallace sat down opposite Megan. Hembrow sat in a corner behind her while her solicitor sat next to her.

"Ten twenty-five a.m. Seventeenth of December, 2022. Interview with Megan Pryce-Jones. There's no need to be scared, Megan. You're very young and naïve, aren't you?"

She flinched. "Not that young. I'll be eighteen next week." Wallace looked surprised. She looked more like a fifteen year old. "Can you tell us any more about the boy in the drawings?"

"No, I told you it was just a picture I saw in a magazine."

Are you sure about that, Megan?"

"Of course I'm sure!"

"So how do you explain this?" He pushed the photograph across the desk. Megan stared at it, but said nothing.

"I've never seen it before," she replied defiantly.

"I think you have, Megan. We found it on the back of the door in your room at school." He pointed at the boy. "Who is he?"

Megan shrugged her shoulders and stared straight ahead. It was obvious she had no intention of answering. Wallace motioned to Hembrow. "Ask Squadron Leader Pryce-Jones and his wife to come in. Megan sat up, looking startled.

"I don't need my parents in here," she said sharply. "I can answer for myself."

"Well, perhaps you had better start with telling us about the identity of the boy in the photo."

"No, I told you. It's just a photo, that's all."

"It seems odd that you have so many pictures of him. Do you have a crush on him Megan?"

"No, why would I? It's just a picture. I enjoy drawing, that's all."

"I think you know who he is, Megan."

"I've told you over and over again. I don't know who he is!"

"Are you sure about that, Megan?"

"Yes, of course I'm sure," she snapped. "How many times do I have to say it?"

"Very well, you may go for now."

Megan left the interview room to join her parents. When Wallace emerged, Pryce-Jones snapped. "I hope this is the end of the matter, Chief Inspector!" Megan didn't wait to hear his response. She disappeared down the corridor.

"Calm down, dear," Mrs Pryce-Jones urged, noting his raspberry red face. "Think about your blood pressure." Pryce-Jones stormed off, leaving his wife with Wallace.

"I'm sorry, Chief Inspector. He's very protective of Megan. You know what fathers are like with their daughters."

Wallace knew very well. His own daughter had gone through a rebellious stage. He decided to take a chance on Megan's mother.

"I'd like to be frank with you, Mrs Pryce-Jones. I'm concerned about Megan's safety. She's holding something back about the boy in the photograph. Is there anything, anything at all you can tell me?"

For a brief moment a flicker of anxiety filled her eyes. Her shoulders sagged.

"I believe you're right about her not being entirely truthful about the boy. She admitted to me that she knows him, but made me promise not to tell her father. That's half the trouble. Don't blame him. He can't accept that she's all grown up. She'll be eighteen next week and he still treats her like a small child. He forgets that I was only nineteen when we got married. He's got her future all planned out, but it's not what she wants. I'm terrified that once she's of age she'll leave home to be with this boy."

Mrs Pryce-Jones stifled a sob. "What can I do to help?"

"I know it's a bit underhanded, but if you could just get her to confide in you, it would be helpful. Believe me when I say I have her best interests at heart."

She nodded. Wallace could hear her sobs as she walked away. *Kids,* he thought. *They tear your heart out.*

"Well, that was a non-starter," Butler commented.

Wallace sighed. "I still think Megan is lying, but why?"

"Obviously, she's scared of her father."

"He's over-protective, not abusive," Wallace replied. "I think we can depend on her mother to inform us if Megan spills the beans. During the interim we'll have to intensify our search."

70

Wallace had a restless night. He was exhausted. His dreams were full of screaming girls and masked killers lurking on the banks of the Severn. Every time he tried to pull off the balaclava the killer broke loose and ran down the towpath. His bed looked as though kids had been jumping on it, having a pillow fight.

He groaned and stretched. Hot needles of pain shot through his neck, the result of falling asleep on the sofa most nights after a long shift. He hadn't had a good night's sleep for months. Ella's murder weighed heavily on him. Shrugging off his night terrors, he hauled himself out of bed.

A hot shower and two cups of strong coffee bolstered his energy. He hastily swallowed a piece of toast and headed for his car. Gunmetal grey clouds hung ominously overhead. The recent snow had been washed away by more heavy rain. Gutters overflowed onto the road. Trees hung their sodden heads and dripped continuously, turning the ground into a mulch of mud and grass. The wipers could barely cope with the deluge as rain cascaded like a miniature waterfall down the windscreen. He sighed. At least the snow had looked pretty.

Pride Hill was full of early morning shoppers braving the weather. Huddled under umbrellas, they scurried like ants up and down the hill, in and out of shops, searching for last-minute Christmas bargains. Wallace sighed. He hadn't had a chance to buy gifts for Jo and Olivia. *I'd better get my skates on*, he thought, *or I'll have egg on my face*. He made a mental note to get to the shops later in the day.

A buzz of activity filled the incident room. Everybody was hard at it on their computers. Not for the first time Wallace realised the quality of his team. Even Baker had lost his arrogance and settled down.

He heard his phone ringing from the office. Giving a quick acknowledgement to his team, he quickly went in and picked up the phone.

"Ben, how are you?" the familiar voice said. It was Dreher.

"Ernst, how are things with you?"

"Very good. I have some news for you. We've located Jennifer Macintyre."

Wallace sat down heavily and held his breath. "Where?"

"She was living in Switzerland, but moved to Tuscany about nine years ago. She lives alone in Vinci, not far from Florence, and doesn't appear to have any family. We made some very discreet local enquiries. It seems she keeps herself very much to herself."

"That's fantastic news Ernst! I can't thank you enough."

"My pleasure, old friend. Sophia and I can't wait to come over for your wedding. Goodbye for now."

I knew I could rely on Ernst, he thought. Now all he had to do was convince *'Crewcut Charlie'* to finance a trip to Tuscany. He poked his head into the incident room and motioned to Butler to join him.

"I've just heard from Ernst Dreher. He's found Jennifer Macintyre living in Tuscany."

"Wow! Good old Dreher!"

"Get ready to pack your bags, Phil. If Chief Superintendent Payne agrees, we'll be paying her a visit."

71

The Tuscan hills spread out before them as the British Airways flight descended towards Florence Airport. As the plane dropped lower Wallace could pick out Italian cypress trees standing like sentinels, guarding cemeteries and driveways of large hotels. Somewhere down there Jennifer Macintyre was hugging a secret close to her heart. He was convinced that she was the key to solving the case.

"Fasten your seatbelts, please."

The steward walked up and down the aisle ensuring that each passenger had secured their belts before their descent into Florence Amerigo Vespucci Airport. An airport infamous for its dangerously short landing strip. Definitely not for the faint-hearted. A grizzled man, wearing a T-shirt that displayed his colourful tattoos, loudly protested as the steward leaned over to secure his safety belt. He had been drinking heavily throughout the flight. A grey-haired, matronly woman pursed her lips and glared across at him over the top of her half glasses.

Below him Wallace took in the red roofs of Florence

and the Duoma. Even from the air it looked magnificent. He determined to squeeze in a little sightseeing after he had finished his investigation.

The ground was coming up at an alarming rate. He felt the wheels hit the tarmac, then they were racing down the runway. It was too short! They would never make it! Butler's knuckles were white as he gripped the armrest: eyes closed, breath coming in sharp gasps. Gradually, the plane started to slow down and finally stopped. A corporate sigh of relief passed through the cabin. Only the tattooed man was oblivious to the danger. He was fast asleep.

Butler mouthed a silent expletive as the 'Unfasten Seat belts' light came on. Hurriedly, he unfastened his and reached overhead for his cabin luggage. He couldn't get off quickly enough.

After picking up a hire car they drove straight to Vinci via the SS741. It took them about an hour to get there, where they had booked a hotel for £75 a night, less than half the cost of a room in Florence. Payne had restricted them to around £80 a night maximum. Surprisingly, they managed to get a good room with breakfast thrown in.

The few items of clothing they had brought remained in the travel bags. They found a great little pizzeria, ordered a large margherita to share and a couple of bottles of Peroni to wash it down.

Wallace patted his stomach as he eased out of this chair. "Right," he said, "let's go find Jennifer Macintyre."

Butler gave a large burp and reluctantly followed him outside.

"Dreher gave us an address. He said it was tucked away in the hills overlooking the valley. I doubt it will be easy to find. "Come on, let's get going. We need to find the house before it gets dark. It's called 'Casa Serena.'"

They drove a short distance up a rough road until it turned into little more than a stony track. Through the twilight they could see the shape of a large building looming above them. It was shrouded in darkness, without a glimmer of light. They walked the last two hundred yards, cursing as they stumbled over protruding stones. They traversed the property, but it was still and silent.

"Just our bloody luck!" Wallace exclaimed.

"Hang on, sir, I'm sure I saw a flicker of light upstairs."

They walked back around the house and pulled the ancient doorbell. The sound echoed loudly, but there was no sign of any movement.

"Maybe it's just a night light, for security purposes," Wallace said. "We'll have to come back tomorrow morning."

*

Looking back towards the house as they descended the hilly terrain, Wallace thought he saw a faint shadow pass a window upstairs.

There was no point in going up to Casa Serena in the dark, so they had a late breakfast before setting off around ten o' clock. After parking the car at the end of the rough road, they trekked upwards towards the villa.

It didn't seem so far in daylight. It was a large building in three sections, constructed from rough stone, with a terracotta roof. It was very imposing. They skirted the front of the property and found themselves on a spacious lawn surrounded by cypress trees and shrubs. It was quiet and still, with just the odd bird flying from tree to tree. A large swimming pool covered with a tarpaulin was set on a separate grassy area.

Suddenly, the faint bark of a dog came from near the trees. Seconds later a woman emerged, calling, "Gina! Fabio!" A pair of golden labradors plunged out of the shrubbery and bounded towards the house. The woman stopped in her tracks when she spotted Wallace and Butler. She marched up to them with a surly look on her face.

"Who are you? What are you doing here? You're trespassing on private property!"

"Jennifer Macintyre? I'm Chief Inspector Ben Wallace and this is my colleague, Inspector Philip Butler."

"I'm not that person. What makes you think I'm this woman, Jennifer Macintyre? I don't know anyone of that name."

"There's no point in pretending. We know who you are."

Momentarily, her confrontational attitude declined. "What do you want?"

"We'd like to ask you a few questions about your sister, Mary."

She was visibly shaken. "Why? Mary has been dead for years."

"We are aware of that fact."

"Why come all the way to Italy?"

"You've been extremely difficult to trace. You seemed intent on covering your tracks when you left the Queen Mary. Fortunately, Interpol was able to trace your whereabouts. May we come in?"

After convincing her of their identity, she grudgingly lead them inside a spacious foyer. It was stunning! The floors were all marble. Antiques were arranged on occasional tables, beautiful paintings adorned the walls. When she showed them into the sitting room he was taken aback with the opulence of the furnishings. Then he remembered that she and Mary had inherited a vast fortune between them. Perhaps she had been the beneficiary of Mary's Will when the whole family died in the tsunami. It begged the question. With such obvious wealth, what was she doing living alone in such a place?

Good manners and courtesy compelled her to offer them refreshment. She rang a bell and a plump, middle-aged Italian woman dressed in black appeared. The tantalising smell of freshly ground coffee permeated the air.

"Coffee for my guests pleas, Rosanna."

The maid disappeared as silently as she had appeared. Ten minutes later she reappeared, bearing a silver tray holding bone china crockery and biscotti. She placed it on a highly polished table.

"Thank you, we'll take it in here."

"Will there be anything else, Signora Contarini?",

"No, thank you."

Wallace glanced at Butler and raised an eyebrow. "Contarini?"

"Contarini was my grandmother's maiden name. I chose to adopt it when I moved to Italy. Since when has that been a crime? Now, Chief Inspector, how may I help you?"

"We're trying to trace a woman living in or near Shrewsbury. We wanted to speak to her in connection with a case we're investigating."

"A case important enough to drag you all the way to Italy?"

"We traced your sister through our investigations in Plymouth. It's a complicated story. Suffice to say we discovered that your sister used to live in Plymouth. Her husband, David, was a teacher in the area. A member of the drama club she belonged to showed us some photographs of the cast of *An Inspector Calls*. A woman sitting in the back of the photograph was wearing a wide-brimmed hat like our mystery woman in Shrewsbury. He confirmed that it was Mary Johnson."

"Am I missing the point? So what if it was a photo of my sister? That was before she and her family perished in the tsunami."

"We know Mary was your identical twin. She, or *you*, have been seen on numerous occasions in Shrewsbury town and in Wellington. Logically, if Mary is dead, then our mystery woman must be you."

"That's ridiculous!"

"Is it? Why did you disappear after leaving the ship? Why did you use a false name? Why are you intent on hiding away up here, still using a false name?"

"I'm not hiding away. I wanted to be alone after

my sister and her family died. I couldn't cope with my grief."

"That's understandable, but people don't disappear and change their names. Are you the woman seen in Shrewsbury? What were you doing there?"

She shook her head. "I haven't left Italy for years."

Wallace was impressed by her composure, but he knew in his bones she was lying.

He motioned to Butler and stood up. "I suggest you give this interview some serious thought. We'll want to speak to you again."

They set out down the mountain, slipping and sliding on loose stones. Ominous rain clouds pressed down on cypress trees, looming like dark sentinels above the house. Only locals would be aware of Casa Serena and Signora Contarini.

"Bugger it!" Butler exclaimed as he caught his foot in the exposed root of a tree. "What do we do now, boss?"

"She's definitely lying, but why? What is she hiding? Who is she protecting?"

"Perhaps she's got a man in tow. An Italian gigolo, maybe a married gigolo."

Wallace grimaced. "Your imagination is taking over again, Phil. We'll pay her another visit tomorrow."

*

The following morning Wallace and Butler retraced their steps. The air was hazy, with a cold drizzle that soaked through their clothes. Little rivulets of water trickled down the uneven path. A curtain of rain and mist hung over the silent house. There was no response to Wallace's urgent knocking.

"Maybe she's done a runner, boss," Butler said. "We've come all this way for nothing."

Wallace stroked his chin. "She's here somewhere. I know it. We'll hang around for a bit." As if by magic, a dim figure emerged out of the murk. Breathing heavily, Rosanna struggled up the path.

"Signor, you startled me! Signora Contarini is not at home."

"Surprise, surprise," Butler murmured.

"She went to Florence yesterday, but she should be back this morning."

"Have you any idea why she went to Florence?"

Rosanna shrugged her shoulders and moved to open the huge door. Wallace and Butler followed her inside. "We'll wait."

Rosanna looked distressed. "Signor, I cannot allow that without permission from Signora Contarini. My job… "

"Don't worry, we're police officers from England. She's expecting us. How long have you been working in Casa Serena?"

"Nearly nine years. It is a good job. The money is good and Signora Contarini treats me well."

"Does she ever have any visitors? Family, friends?"

"She lives quite alone except for the summer; sometimes Christmastime. She does not need me during those times, but she pays me anyway. It is a good job," she repeated. Her face was a mask of anxiety.

"So, you have never seen her guests?"

Rosanna shook her head. "I stay away until she asks me to return. Go now," she pleaded.

"We'll wait down the hill until we see her return."

"She will not come that way. The helicopter… " Rosanna froze, realising that she had said too much. "Go! Go!" she urged, flapping her hands at them.

As they left they could hear the massive bolts being secured. The place was like a fortress.

"Interesting," Wallace said. "I think a little wander around may prove fruitful."

They searched about three hundred yards to the left and right of the house, then climbed higher up until they were in a dense thicket of trees.

"Nothing here," Butler said. "Just trees and more trees."

"Keep going," Wallace barked. "There must be a landing pad somewhere."

Suddenly, they heard the roar of a helicopter, then the whop-whopping sound of the blades as it landed. They climbed higher, beating their way through undergrowth and tree branches. Wallace put out an arm to stop Butler. "Wait!" he rasped breathlessly. Slowly, they pushed forward until they were at the edge of a large clearing, obviously man-made. There it was, a small helicopter, its blades still rotating.

"Well, well," Wallace said as a door opened and a woman stepped out. "If it isn't Jennifer Macintyre aka Signora Contarini."

As soon as she stepped away from the chopper the

pilot fired the engine and took off, giving a final wave. Jennifer walked over to a wooden shed and unlocked the door. Inside was a quad bike. She walked it out, padlocked the door and jumped on. As she revved the engine Wallace and Butler walked into the clearing.

The blood drained from her face, her shoulders slumped in resignation. There was no escaping, but she still tried to brazen it out.

"What are you doing here? You're trespassing on private property."

"I told you. We're investigating your sister, Mary."

"How many times must I tell you?"

"We need to speak with you, at length, at the villa. Rosanna wouldn't let us in to wait so we decided to look around the area."

The villa was luxuriously warm and comfortable. Rosanna served them coffee and delicious ciambella, an Italian breakfast cake. When she disappeared into the kitchen Jennifer sat up, back straight, and looked directly at Wallace. She sighed.

"What's this all about?"

"About nineteen years ago a young girl was strangled in Plymouth with her own school tie. I was the investigating officer. Her name was Jessica Parker."

"Yes, I heard about that from my sister. She was a sixth form pupil in her husband's school. What has that got to do with me?"

"That's what we're trying to establish. A few months ago another sixth former, Ella Chapman, was murdered in exactly the same way in Shrewsbury. She was also pregnant."

Jennifer shrugged her shoulders impatiently. *She's a real cool character,* Wallace thought.

"The similarities between the murder in Plymouth and the one in Shrewsbury were too obvious to ignore, hence our recent investigation. Did you know a girl called Ella Chapman? She was a pupil in St Cadfael's."

Jennifer's eyes darted around the room like a trapped animal. "I have nothing more to say. Now, please leave!"

"This isn't going to go away. Mark Hilliard, another sixth former in St Cadfael's, was also murdered. He was besotted with Ella. There are others involved who were wrongly accused of Ella's murder.

"I am an Italian citizen by descent 'jure sanguinis'. My grandmother was Italian. I have dual citizenship."

"That won't stop you from being arrested for murder. We have photographs of you, *or Mary,* with Ella Chapman in Shrewsbury. In addition, you, *or Mary,* were seen in a sports' centre in Wellington, deep in conversation. Not long afterwards Ella was murdered." "Since you insist that Mary is dead, then it must be you."

Jennifer was visibly shaken. "What made you think there was a connection with Jessica Parker?" asked Jennifer

A chance telephone call from a teacher who used to work in her school. Emily Lambert, who now lives a few miles from Shrewsbury in Acton Burnell. She has been stalked by a man in Shrewsbury and a number of attempts have been made on her life. We assume that this man was working with you."

"No! No! Please God, not again! Not again!" She

stood up and looked around wildly, as though looking for an escape route.

"I think you had better start telling us the truth."

She slumped back onto the sofa, covering her face with her hands. Loud sobs wracked her body. Wallace walked over to an occasional table laden with spirits. He poured her a large brandy and waited while she drank it.

"He was going to leave my sister. He promised me that he would stay with her if I helped him. She was besotted with David Johnson. He was her whole life. It's true they were caught up in the tsunami, but they survived. Their boys, their beautiful boys, drowned. How could I not help?"

"How did you help?"

"I claimed the life insurance for them so they could start a new life. It was the only way she could survive what had happened. David was a pig! One woman after another, including Emily Lambert. *She* had a nervous breakdown when she found out about his 'death.'"

"What else was he covering up?"

"Nothing, as far as I know. He was questioned about the murder of Jessica Chapman, but nothing came of it. Afterwards Mary seemed to shut herself off from the world. I always had the feeling there was something else she wasn't telling me about. We were very close, you see. I felt her pain and she felt mine. It's common with identical twins."

"Jessica's killer was never found. The case has never been closed. We believe that Jessica's murderer also killed Ella Chapman. Besides Emily Lambert, Bryant since her marriage, we also believe he is responsible for the death of the boy I mentioned earlier."

"So, they are still alive?" Jennifer asked.

"Where were they living the last time you heard from them?" Wallace queried.

"I'm not sure. Mary rang me once or twice. They moved around a lot. We lost touch. I think they went to live abroad. I don't know!" she cried.

"Is there anything else you want to tell me?" Wallace asked.

"No! No! Now please leave!"

Butler glanced at Wallace. He rose and followed him out.

"She's lying!" Wallace snarled. They followed the path down to the car. "She's lying through her teeth! She's still protecting her sister."

"What do we do now, boss? We've got an early flight to Birmingham tomorrow morning."

Wallace sighed. "This latest development opens a whole new bag of worms. Post-Brexit there are new rules in place. The legal eagles will have to look at this. *Crewcut Charlie* won't be best pleased."

"Do you think she'll do a runner?"

"It's a possibility. I'll contact Ernst Dreher and outline the situation. She won't go far without him knowing."

72

Superintendent Payne sat rigidly in his chair, tapping a pencil on his desk. His face was a practised mask of authority.

"Are you telling me you've come back from your little joyride to Italy with nothing?"

"Not exactly, sir. I believe she told us a pack of lies when she said she hasn't been back to the United Kingdom. She *must* be our mystery woman."

"So what do you think she was doing in Shrewsbury?"

"I don't know, sir."

"Well, you can forget an arrest warrant. There's not enough evidence to support it."

"But, sir… "

"That's enough, Wallace! We can't afford to waste any more funds on this '*mystery woman*'. Is that understood?"

"Yes, sir," Wallace said through clenched teeth.

As usual, '*Crewcut Charlie*' had cut him down without considering the obvious facts. Furiously, he descended the stairs to his floor. His face was blood red.

"Oh! Oh!" Baker said. "The boss must have had a rollicking from Payne."

Without acknowledging the team, Wallace strode into his office and closed the door. With studied calm he sat down, taking deep breaths until he regained his composure. Butler poked his head around the door.

"What's up, boss?"

"Bloody Payne, he's a pain in the arse! I didn't get anywhere with him. We can forget any extra funding. Come on, let's brief the team."

The team looked up expectantly when he entered the incident room.

"We tracked down Jennifer Macintyre in a small town in Vinci, Italy. She's been living there for years under the name of Contarini. She has triple British/Italian/US citizenship. This is a photograph of her." He attached a picture to the evidence board. "As you are aware, her identical twin, Mary, and her family, were reported lost in the 2004 tsunami. This is where it gets interesting. It was a pack of lies. Their children died, but Mary and her husband survived. Jennifer disappeared off the radar, after she helped them claim from an insurance policy so they could start a new life."

"They may have moved abroad," Hembrow said.

"She suggested that; claims she hasn't been in touch with them for years, but I think she's lying. She also claims she's never been to Shrewsbury."

"Every officer, including PCSOs, have a photograph of the *'mystery woman'*. No luck so far, sir," DC Williams said.

Wallace held up his hands, palms up. "Well, that's it. If we don't obtain any more evidence in the next couple of weeks Payne will probably put the case on the shelf."

The team looked dejected. They had put in so much effort, but there was nothing he could do to convince Payne to let him pursue Jennifer Macintyre.

*

Wallace spent a sleepless night turning over the case in his mind, desperate to find a clue he had missed. Even Jo had gone out of his mind over the last few days. Christmas Eve tomorrow. He would have to get his skates on if he was going to give her and Olivia the wonderful Christmas he had planned. He was running late; Shrewsbury town centre was heaving with shoppers scurrying from store to store. At least he had managed to get both his girls a present.

As he passed Marks & Spencer's a few people were coming out of the shop. His heart skipped a beat. One woman caught his attention. It was her, the *'mystery woman'* dressed in the same Barbour gear as in the photograph, her wide-brimmed hat pulled down over her eyes.

"Sod it!" She passed him and walked briskly down the hill towards the library. He double parked, flicked on his hazard lights and ran after her. She was nowhere in sight. Where the hell had she gone? "

His drive to the police station was hampered by heavy traffic. He blew his horn at a motorist trying to edge his way into the lane. The man showed him two fingers. When he finally reached the police station he bounded up the stairs to his office, breathing heavily: face red, heart thumping painfully.

"Sir!"

"Not now, Baker!"

Alarmed, Butler followed him into the office and closed the door before dropping into a chair. "Are you okay?"

"I'm more than okay, Phil. I've just seen our '*mystery woman*.' Hang on." He dialled a number and the familiar voice came over the line. "Ernst," Wallace said urgently. "I've spotted the '*mystery woman*' in Shrewsbury." He briefly outlined his visit to Italy. "Can you get in touch with the local police in Vinci and find out if Jennifer Macintyre has left her villa?"

"Of course," Dreher interjected. "I'll ring you back as soon as possible."

"Close the blinds, Phil. I don't want any speculation from out there."

Wallace sat back and swung from side to side, alternately devil-drumming on his desk. He couldn't sit still for long. He got up and paced around the office, his anxiety levels rising with every passing minute.

Suddenly, the phone jangled. Wallace grabbed the receiver. He could barely wait for Dreher to speak.

"Ben, Jennifer Macintyre hasn't left her villa. Her maid said she was unavailable, that Signora Contarini had Covid and was isolating "After telling her it was a police matter, she eventually transferred the call.

Jennifer sounded dreadful. She could barely speak. I am convinced the maid was telling the truth."

"Thank you, Ernst. I owe you one. Give my love to Sophia and the children and have a great Christmas."

Butler raised an eyebrow. "Well?"

"Jennifer is down with Covid. She hasn't left the villa."

"So who the hell did you see?"

"Mary Macintyre."

"But wouldn't she have holed up out of sight? Surely, Jennifer would have contacted her straight away."

"Perhaps she's been too ill. Covid can be really serious for some people."

"What now?"

"Unfortunately, after tomorrow people will be mostly indoors enjoying Christmas Day. They'll be back out for the Boxing Day sales. I want as many officers as possible in town. If she comes in tomorrow we'll be waiting for her. Every shop, every restaurant will be under surveillance. Mary Macintyre must be living in or around Shrewsbury. She must feel secure under her new identity, otherwise she wouldn't circulate so confidently where there are lots of people."

Butler nodded. "She could come into town for last-minute shopping. I'm off Christmas Eve and Christmas Day, but I'll turn up for a couple of hours."

"No, you stay home and enjoy time with your wife and kids. I'll be doing the same. Olivia hasn't been with me for Christmas since my divorce. I'm really looking forward to it, especially as Jo is coming as well."

Wallace wished his team a Happy Christmas as he

left, knowing that some of them would be on duty all over the festive period.

73

JANUARY 5TH 2023

Christmas Eve was a damp squib as far as the elusive mystery woman was concerned. There wasn't a single sighting of her between Boxing Day and the New Year. Wallace was on edge. It gave too much time for Jennifer Macintyre to contact her sister. There was only one course of action now. He would telephone her himself and to hell with the consequences. Ernst Dreher had managed to get her landline number.

The phone shrilled loudly, as though it was relaying from the next office. It was a very clear line.

"Casa Serena." It was Rosanna.

"Hello, you'll remember me; Chief Inspector Wallace. I'd like to speak to Signora Contarini."

"I'm afraid she is unavailable."

"It's a police matter, Rosanna, very urgent."

"I'm sorry. Signora Contarini is in hospital. She is very ill."

"Where? In Vinci?"

"No, in Florence. She was taken by helicopter. She has pneumonia and complications after Covid." Rosanna started to cry. "Such a lovely lady."

"What's the name of the hospital?"

"They took her to the Careggi University Hospital late last night," Rosanna explained. "I don't know what to do. I know she has a sister, but I don't know where she lives."

"Leave that to us, Rosanna. We may be able to help."

"Please, Signor, let me know how she is."

"Yes, we will." Wallace replaced the receiver. He quickly searched the internet on his iPhone and found the number for Careggi University Hospital.

"Buongiorno. Careggi Ospedale."

"Do you speak English?"

"Si, how can I help you?"

"I am trying to trace a patient, Signora Contarini. Can you confirm you have a patient by that name?"

"I cannot give out confidential information, signor."

"It is extremely urgent. Please let me speak to a doctor."

"I do not think that is possible. The doctors are very busy."

"It is a matter of international importance."

Wallace heard the exasperated sigh as the receptionist covered the mouth-piece. Moments later a male voice asked, "Why are you enquiring after Signora Contarini?"

"I am Chief Inspector Ben Wallace of the British police. Signora Contarini has been questioned regarding her twin sister. I need to know if her sister has been informed that SIgnora Contarini has been hospitalised."

"But surely, the Italian police can deal with the situation."

"She is also a British citizen. She has dual nationality. You can verify my identity by calling this number in Geneva." He hastily gave Dreher's number. "Chief Inspector Ernst Dreher is the person who tracked Signora Contarini to Vinci. I'll stay on the line." Wallace could barely contain himself. This was his last chance. He almost jumped when the doctor came on the line.

"Dr Matteo de Luca. I have confirmed your identity. Yes, Signora Contarini is our patient."

"Have her relatives in England been informed?"

"She was able to make a brief phone call to her sister. She wouldn't let us do it for her. She said she had no other relatives."

"What is her condition now?"

"She is very ill, but stable. That is as much as I can tell you. "

"Thank you, Dr De Luca. One last thing. Please do not inform Signora Contarini that I have made enquiries. Suffice to say my investigations are of a very serious nature."

"Very well. Arrivederci." Wallace walked into the incident room. "Listen up! Jennifer Macintyre is very ill with Covid. She's in hospital in Florence. She has contacted her sister."

"How did you find that out?" Butler asked.

Wallace glared at him. "Later! It's highly likely she

will travel to Italy to be with Jennifer. Flying is the quickest option. Inform border security to look out for a Mary Macintyre. I doubt she would travel under the name Johnson. Unfortunately, all we've got to go on is the blurred photo of her wearing a Barbour coat and hat. It's not much."

After forty-eight hours there had been no sign of her at the airports or in Shrewsbury. Wallace was convinced she had given them the slip. But how? "Bloody woman!" he fumed.

"Maybe she didn't go to Casa Serena," Butler mused. "I suppose you could always ring the hospital and find out if she's visited Jennifer. It's our only option."

Wallace rose and paced the room. What if he had got it all wrong? What if Mary Macintyre wasn't the mystery woman? He gave himself a mental shake. No, it had to be her, given the secrecy surrounding her disappearance after the insurance scam.

"The only link we have other than her twin is with Ella Chapman. There's also something decidedly odd about this 'boyfriend' of Megan Pryce-Jones. I think we'll pay Mick Gilchrist a little visit."

"I thought he was out of the picture," Butler said.

"He is, but he's on the staff of St Cadfael's. He may have picked up bits of gossip about Megan. It's worth a try."

*

Neither Wallace nor Butler relished another conversation with the draconian Mrs James. She was nowhere to be seen. The inner office door was firmly closed. As he about to ring the desk bell he heard a clatter of footsteps on the landing above. The secretary stopped at the top of the stairs and glowered down at them.

"Old dragon," Butler murmured. "She'd crack her face if she smiled."

"Well!" she barked. "What is it this time? I haven't got time for chit-chat. Dr Booth is in a meeting and he urgently needs some papers. He's very busy."

Wallace felt his hackles rising. "May I remind you that we're conducting a murder investigation? Dr Booth's meeting is the least of my concerns."

Mrs James looked genuinely contrite. "I'm sorry, Chief Inspector. How can I help you?"

"We would like to speak to Michael Gilchrist."

"That's not possible, I'm afraid. He went off sick a couple of days ago. He's tested positive for Coronavirus. Is there anything else I can do to help?"

"Thank you, Mrs James. We'll be in touch. On second thoughts perhaps you can tell me a little more about this. He pulled out a piece of paper from his jacket pocket. Is there any more you can tell us about this drawing? You seemed slightly startled when I showed it to you previously."

She stared at the image of the young man drawn by Megan Pryce-Jones. Her lips pulled into a tight line, as though struggling with her emotions. Mrs James shrugged her shoulders dismissively.

"He does seem vaguely familiar. I'm not sure."

"Have you seen him in or anywhere near the school? It's very important. He could be Megan's attacker. "

"Surely not! He wouldn't!"

"Who wouldn't, Mrs James? Is there something you want to tell us about this boy?"

"No! No! It's just… he doesn't look the type. Such a pleasant-looking lad."

"Well, if you do think of anything, contact me straight away." He handed her his card and marched briskly to the entrance. "Let's get over to Gilchrist's place."

"But sir, he's got Covid," Butler interjected.

"Put a mask on," Wallace said curtly. "The dragon knows something, of that I'm certain."

*

Butler banged Gilchrist's front door with his fist. They had waited before walking around to the back of the house. There was no sign of life. Wallace peered through the windows. Everything looked normal. Cushions plumped up in the sitting room. Dishes cleared away. The kitchen was spick and span.

"Hmm! He's tidy. I'll give him that."

"A bit too tidy if you ask me, boss. He's supposed to be ill. No box of tissues in sight, no dirty cups or glasses. Not a box of Lemsip in sight. My house looks like a tip if any of us are just down with a cold."

"He's obviously not here," Wallace said. "Perhaps he's pulling a sickie to have some time off."

A head peered over the garden hedge. "He's not there, mate. He's gone away. I saw him go off with a travel bag two days ago."

"Do you know where he's gone? He's got a dog, hasn't he? Who's looking after it?"

The man shook his head again. "I don't know, but he wouldn't just leave the dog. Somebody must be taking care of it."

"Thank you Mr… "

"Coslett. Ivor Coslett."

Wallace handed him a card. "Please let us know if and when he returns."

Ivor glanced at the card. "Police! What's he done?"

"We just want to ask him a few questions."

Ivor scurried inside to his wife, who had been observing behind partly open venetian blinds.

"Very odd, Butler. Very odd indeed."

"You don't have to isolate now if you have Covid, boss, but the advice is you stay at home for five days. Either Gilchrist doesn't have Covid, or he's not heeding medical advice," Butler continued.

"All we can do is wait three more days and check if he has returned to St Cadfael's, Wallace said. "I can't see him taking advantage for too long after struggling to get a position in the school."

74

Three days later Wallace and Butler returned to St Cadfael's. The school was buzzing with activity. Children scurried between the annexe and main building, clutching books and talking animatedly. There was an excitement in the air; a sense of jubilation after lockdown and online lessons.

Mrs James assured them that Gilchrist had returned to work even though he had been very poorly. Wallace and Butler looked at each other. Gilchrist definitely had questions to answer.

"He'll be in his classroom waiting for you," she said after calling him. "Over in the annexe, first floor, second classroom on the left. "

They took their time walking over. *Let him sweat*, Wallace thought. It will be to our advantage.

Gilchrist rose from behind his desk and put out his hand. "Chief Inspector, what can I do for you? " His eyes darted nervously between the two men.

"We're following up on a few leads regarding the Ella Chapman murder."

Gilchrist sat down abruptly and toyed with some papers on his desk. His face had lost all its colour.

"I told you I had nothing to do with it!"

"Can you tell us where you've been for the last few days?"

"At home isolating with Covid. "

"That's not strictly true, is it, Mr Gilchrist?" You definitely weren't at home when we called three days ago."

"It must have been when I popped out for some milk."

"You were seen leaving home with a travel bag. Can you explain where you were going?" Gilchrist slumped in his chair. He raised his hands, palms up. "Okay! Okay! I pulled a sickie to go away with a friend for a few days. It's not a criminal offence, is it?"

"Does Dr Booth know you lied about Covid?"

"No, he would be furious. Please don't tell him. I'll lose my job."

"Who was looking after your dog?"

"A friend did me a favour."

"Who is this friend?"

"I can't tell you. She would be very upset."

"She?"

Gilchrist rose and walked around nervously, realising he had inadvertently revealed something.

"We can do this here or down the station."

"Isobel, Isobel Booth. "There's an old stable in one of the fields. The farmer next door to her property looked after my dog on the farm until I returned home."

"Did Dr Booth know about this? After all, he is your employer."

"No, I told you Dr Booth knows nothing about it."

"How could Mrs Booth explain to him that she was looking after your dog?"

"She fed and walked him every day. We often walked our dogs together."

"I'll ask you again: where did you go?"

"Abroad."

Wallace was losing patience with Gilchrist. It was obvious he was manipulating the truth.

"So, you took time away from your job to go off on a joyride."

Gilchrist shrugged his shoulders. His eyes darted around the room as though looking for an escape route.

"Did you travel alone?" Wallace asked. Gilchrist shook his head. "Who accompanied you? A girlfriend?"

"No, it wasn't like that! Isobel…"

"Isobel? Isobel Booth?"

Gilchrist slumped forward and put his head on the desk. "Yes, Isobel Booth," he answered with resignation.

"Why did she ask you to go with her?"

"She was very upset. I went with her for emotional support. How could I refuse after the times she has supported me?"

"You say she was upset. Why?"

"Her sister is very ill." Wallace felt the hairs on the back of his neck stand up. "I've met her sister before. She lives in Italy. She is Isobel's identical twin."

"Would that be Vinci, near Florence?"

"Yes. How did you know?"

"We know where Jennifer Macintyre lives."

"I don't understand. Her sister's name is Louisa Contarini. She and Isobel have dual British/Italian citizenship. Apparently, their grandmother was Italian. That's all I know."

"We also know that Isobel Booth's real name is Mary Macintyre. Jennifer is living under an assumed name and, it seems, so is Mary Macintyre."

"Why would Isobel use another name?"

"That, Mr Gilchrist is what I intend to find out. Butler, take Williams with you and pick up Isobel Booth. She has questions to answer."

75

Isobel stared out of the window onto the rain-soaked fields surrounding the farmhouse. Trees weighed down by the driving rain dripped onto the lawn, creating large, black pools. Anxiously, her eyes scanned the meadow. Through the torrent of rain she could just make out the gate near the road. *Mick should have been here two hours ago. Where is he? It isn't like him to be late.*

Earlier that morning she had telephoned him to say she needed to speak with him urgently after their trip to Italy. Her eyes filled. *I don't know how I would have coped without him.* The sound of a car coming from the drive at the front of the house made her heart leap. *It was Mick!* She ran through the house, then stopped. The silhouette of a man filled the glass door. *It's not Mick!* Hastily, she opened the door to two men. She recognised Wallace immediately. Her heart thudded painfully in her chest. Taking a deep breath, she managed to regain her composure.

"Chief Inspector, please come inside out of this dreadful weather."

Both men entered the hall. "Mrs Booth, we would like you to come down to the police station."

"Oh my God, it's Mick, isn't it? What's happened?"

"He's perfectly fine. In fact, he's already in the station."

"But why? What's he done? He wouldn't do anything wrong!"

"I would appreciate it if you would agree to come with us, please."

Isobel reluctantly fetched her Barbour coat and hat and followed them to the unmarked police car. She looked frightened and disorientated.

When they arrived at the station Butler took her directly to an interview room where Wallace was waiting.

"Please sit down, Mrs Booth."

She slumped heavily into the chair opposite him. Wallace put his elbows on the table and leaned forward.

"We would like you to answer a few questions about your trip to Italy."

The colour drained from Isobel's face. Her hands trembled.

"Would you like a glass of water?" She nodded.

Butler placed the water on the table and she drank greedily. A little colour returned to her cheeks.

"We understand you travelled to Italy, accompanied by Mick Gilchrist, to visit your sick sister."

"Yes, Louisa has been very ill with Covid, but she's a lot better now."

Wallace sat back, his hands in a praying position under his chin. "Don't you mean Jennifer, Jennifer Macintyre?"

Isobel's lips trembled with emotion. She looked like a trapped animal caught in the glare of a car's headlights.

"Jennifer Louisa Macintyre. She's entitled to use the name Contarini. It was our grandmother's name."

"Let's stop beating about the bush. She changed her name for a reason. We know all about the tsunami and insurance scam. Jennifer told us. Now, let's hear your story."

Isobel's face contorted with grief. "I didn't want to live after my boys died. They were never found, you know." Her eyes filled with tears. "You never get over the loss of your children. We stayed in Thailand, hoping they would be found. Everyone had assumed we were washed away with the boys. I wish I had been. My life has never been the same since."

"Whose idea was it to claim the insurance money?"

"Edward's. Jennifer wasn't willing at first, but Edward persuaded her to help us. He arranged everything. I was so engulfed in grief I didn't care if I lived or died.

"My sister and I couldn't touch the bulk of our inheritance until we reached the age of thirty-five. The only way to fund a new life was the insurance money. Jennifer was my sole heir and executor of our Wills. She was also the children's guardian in the event of our deaths."

"So Jennifer agreed to all of it?"

"Eventually, but only after Edward kept putting pressure on her to help for my sake."

Wallace felt a twinge of sympathy for Isobel. In her state she wouldn't have had much energy to fight a controlling man like Edward Booth.

"The villa in Italy had been left to us by our grandparents. It's quite remote. Edward obtained new passports and all the relevant papers needed to live under our assumed names. He told us that friends helped him to contact the right people. Jennifer wasn't involved with any of it."

"Where did you go after you received the insurance money?"

"Various places. Bergamo, Castelluccio in the Apennines, Tropea in Calabria. Anywhere where there would be fewer tourists. We finally returned to Britain in 2009."

"What about St Cadfael's?"

"Jennifer inherited all our parents' estate and our grandparents, plus the insurance money."

"So, she inherited your wealth as well as hers."

"She divided everything equally. Edward opened a Swiss bank account under our new names. I don't know the technicalities of it, but trusts were opened in the Cayman Islands."

"That's how he acquired the money to open the school?"

"Yes. It had always been his dream to own his own school. He's worked so hard to make it successful. Please, Mick knows nothing about all this. All he knows is that I have a twin sister in Italy."

Wallace nodded. Isobel held up her hands in a futile gesture, then laid her head on the table with her eyes closed.

"Can I go now?"

"Not yet, I have a few more questions I would like to ask you. What was your relationship with Ella Chapman?"

"Relationship? I don't understand."

Wallace produced the photograph of Isobel and Ella outside the Bear Hotel and the one in the Quarry.

"Judging by these photographs you seemed very close. You were also seen together in Wellington Sports' Centre." Wallace paused for a few seconds. "Did you know she was pregnant?"

Isobel hung her head. "Yes, she came to me for help. I arranged the abortion."

"Why did she confide in you?"

"She was afraid to talk to Matron in case she informed her parents. The poor girl was beside herself with fear and anxiety. How could I not help?"

"Did you tell Dr Booth?"

"No, he would have been furious."

"Who was the father of the child?"

"I don't know, perhaps it was Mark. Ella wouldn't say."

"Ella regularly met someone called Prish. Do you know who that person is?"

Isobel sighed. "Yes, it's me. It was my nickname at school. I had braces. I couldn't say certain words, like pretty. It sounded like prishy. You know what kids are like. It stuck."Butler glanced at Wallace. *Where is he going with this?* Abruptly, Wallace stood up.

DS Butler, please have Mrs Booth shown to another interview room. Tell Mick Gilchrist he can go."

Isobel slumped back in her chair with a sigh of relief. *I don't care what happens to me as long as Mick is all right.* She rose slowly, desperately trying to maintain her usual elegance and poise, and followed Butler into the corridor.

"Right," Wallace said when Butler returned. "That's two of them. Now I want that supercilious creep, Edward Booth brought in. I can't wait to see his face when he finds out we know everything."

*

"Where's my wife?" Booth demanded as he walked into the interview room. "Did she drive through a red light or something?"

"It's a little more serious than a red light. Sit down, Dr Booth," Wallace said curtly.

Booth's face was blood red with rage. *Who does this Mr Plod think he is talking to me like this?* "You had better have a damn good reason for arresting my wife," he said in a superior tone.

"Nobody has been arrested… yet," Wallace replied through gritted teeth. "Our investigations revealed that Mrs Booth and her twin sister, Jennifer, have been living under assumed names." Booth visibly blanched. "And we know why."

"I don't know what you're talking about! What do you mean by this accusation?"

Booth squirmed in his seat, desperately searching for a way to wriggle out of it. He sat up, back straight, chin up, and stared contemptuously at the detectives. *Attack is the first line of defence.*

"You can't prove it!" he said coolly.

"DS Butler and I have visited Jennifer in Vinci, Italy. We know all about the insurance scam that you instigated. Jennifer told us herself, and your wife has confirmed it."

"My wife!" he spluttered. "She wouldn't do that!"

"Jennifer is still a British citizen. An application will be made for her extradition to the United Kingdom. For now you will remain here, so will your wife."

"I want my solicitor present before you question me again! The same goes for my wife. You have no right to keep us here!"

Wallace ignored him and nodded to the constable to take him down to the cells.

"Let him sweat for a couple of hours, then we'll question him again. I've got a niggling feeling there's more to this than meets the eye."

*

Two hours later Isobel was shown back into the interview room, followed by her solicitor. She sat down quietly, face ashen, eyes red and swollen from crying.

"Mrs Booth. I'll ask you again. Do you know the father of Ella's child?"

"No! I'd tell you if I knew!"

"Why did you agree to help her get an abortion?

Surely, you had a duty to inform her parents? Was Dr Booth aware of it?

"No!"

Wallace took a deep breath and leaned back casually in his chair, swinging from side to side.

"Didn't you notice the similarities between Ella's murder and Jessica Parker's in Plymouth?" Isobel's hand flew to her mouth, a stricken look on her face. "Their murders were identical. And there's Mark Hilliard. He didn't commit suicide. It was planned to look that way to put the police off the scent. He knew too much and had to be eliminated." Wallace knew he was on unsafe ground, but he ploughed on. "We also believe the same person was responsible for attacking Megan Pryce-Jones and Emily Bryant."

Isobel gave a low moan, like a wounded animal. Suddenly, she stood and paced the room in a frenzy, her eyes bulging. Her solicitor tried to calm her, but she continued moaning, wringing her hands and pulling at her hair. Wallace looked sideways at Butler. The woman was losing all control.

"This interview is concluded, Chief Inspector. My client is in considerable distress."

"No! No! Not again! Not again!"

"Chief Inspector, I must protest!" the solicitor interjected.

"What do you mean, Mrs Booth?"

Suddenly, she dropped to the floor in a dead faint.

"Get the custody nurse!" Wallace yelled to the constable outside the door. "Make it quick!"

After Isobel was taken to the medical room, Wallace and Butler sat staring at the walls of the interview room. Eventually, Wallace asked, "What did you make of that, Phil?"

"Was she talking about the insurance scam?" Butler asked.

"I don't know. Why did she say 'Not again?' Why did she start stressing at the mention of Jessica and Ella? Get Booth back up here!"

Booth entered the interview room looking poised and sure of himself. Without being invited, he sat down facing Wallace, back ramrod straight.

Wallace called Butler outside and waited a full five minutes before going back inside. "Right, let's see what the slimy prig has to say."

"Dr Booth, you were questioned about the murder of Jessica Parker in Plymouth back in 2003. The same applies to Ella Chapman."

"What are you implying, Chief Inspector?" he asked coolly. Wallace ignored the question.

"It's very strange that both murders were identical. There were also attempts on the life of Emily Lambert, a young teacher at your school. You had an affair with her."

"Hardly an affair. The silly girl was infatuated with me. She wouldn't leave me alone."

"Who would want to harm her?"

"Certainly not me! How could I? She was still living in Plymouth the last I heard."

"Was?"

"What I mean is, I haven't been near Plymouth since 2004. How should I know where she's living now?"

"Where were you on the night of Ella Chapman's murder?"

"I told you, in a hotel in Birmingham. I'd been to a conference at the university. I stayed overnight at the Edgbaston Park Hotel after the conference dinner rather than travel back late. It's on the campus."

"Can you verify it?"

"Of course, a few of the other delegates stayed there. We had a nightcap before retiring around eleven o' clock. It had been a long day."

"Names, please."

"Let me see. Les Turner, Bruce Standish and Will… Burns. I think it was Burns. All heads of private schools from different parts of the country. We didn't really know each other."

"How did you travel to the conference?"

"By train. Isobel ran me to the station in Shrewsbury."

Elbows on desk, hands cupping his chin, Wallace stared at him intently. Booth didn't flinch, just stared back.

"Play Mrs Booth's tape, Butler. Why did she say, '*Not again*,' Dr Booth?"

Booth sighed. "You must understand, my wife hasn't been the same since our children died. Until fairly recently she drank heavily. She was rarely sober. She imagined all sorts of things."

"What is her relationship with Mick Gilchrist?"

Booth's face hardened at the mention of Mick's name.

"There is no relationship other than friendship. She took Gilchrist under her wing, mothered him. It pains me to say it, but he was her salvation. She stopped drinking, smartened herself up, lost weight. She looked more like the old Isobel. She was happy. That made me happy."

Wallace leaned forward. "We know that your wife helped Ella Chapman to arrange an abortion. Why would she do that?"

"That's ridiculous! Why would she, unless Gilchrist was the father. She must have been protecting Gilchrist. She would do anything for him. Give her life, kill for him if she had to."

"You think she murdered Ella Chapman? What about Jessica Parker?"

"She didn't know Jessica, but she had heard a lot of gossip."

"Such as… ?"

"Jessica was a bit of a tease, liked to flirt with the male staff. Isobel was convinced she was trying it on with me. Nothing I could say would stop her accusations."

"So, let me get this right. You are saying that Isobel might have murdered Ella to protect Gilchrist, because he was the father of Ella's child. Are you also suggesting that she killed Jessica out of jealousy?"

Booth shrugged his shoulders. "I don't know."

Wallace shot him a contemptuous look. Booth stood up, still wearing the haughty air they were used to seeing. He stared at Wallace.

"I can't believe that Isobel would really be so brutal. It's incredible!"

"Thank you, Dr Booth. You may leave, but we'll need to talk to you again."

Booth leaned towards Wallace and offered his hand. Wallace ignored it. He wasn't going to shake the hand of this slimy snake.

"'Get on to Emily Bryant. I want her here by ten o' clock sharp tomorrow morning."

"Is there something you're not telling me, boss?" Butler queried.

"Just following up a hunch. I want to get Booth, Isobel and Emily here together."

76

It was a filthy night. Rain lashed at the windows. The Venetian blinds creaked as gusts of wind penetrated the vents, breaking into Wallace's fitful sleep. A cat wailed below his window. Suddenly, a bin crashed to the ground with a metallic clunk, setting off cats in nearby gardens. Groaning, he rolled onto his back and stared at the ceiling in the dim light. He'd lain awake most of the night, mulling over his strategy. He had told Butler very little, preferring to keep his thoughts to himself.

Finally, he looked at the time on his bedside clock, glowing red in the darkness. Four thirty-five a.m. Sighing, he dragged himself downstairs and made a cup of tea, thinking it might help him to sleep. It had the opposite effect. Wide awake, he dropped onto the sofa and sipped his tea. By six thirty he had showered, dressed and was ready to go. He had a double espresso and headed off into the darkness. Butterflies swirled in his stomach. His nerves felt like taut violin strings, ready to break.

Shrewsbury was gloomy and empty; not a soul to be seen on Pride Hill. He knew the homeless would be there, out of sight in shop doorways, surrounded by cardboard boxes. If they were lucky they would have a tattered sleeping bag to keep them warm. He drove around the town for a while, trying to relax, then headed for the police station.

His team was already at their desks, staring at their computer screens. Wallace looked at his watch. Eight 'o clock. Two hours before Emily Bryant arrived. Butler knocked on his office door.

"Phil, come in and close the door."

"Are you going to tell me what's going on?" he asked huffily.

"Not everything. I want you to bring Booth and Isobel up here just before ten o' clock. Observe their reactions when Emily Bryant arrives."

"Okay, boss, whatever you say."

Dr Booth swaggered in, followed by Isobel, who looked scared and miserable. Wallace motioned to the chairs while Butler took up his position next to Wallace.

"Well?" Booth barked. "I hope this little fiasco has been sorted out." Wallace ignored the question. "You can show her in now," he said.

Butler opened the door. Emily stood there for a few seconds. "I believe you all know each other," he said.

The Booths turned around at the same time. Isobel's hand went to her mouth as she tried to muffle a little cry. Edward Booth shot out of his chair and stared at Emily before regaining his composure.

"I don't believe we've met," he said in a measured voice.

"Stop it, Edward. You know very well who she is," Isobel said.

Emily was staring at Booth transfixed. "It's you, David. Your eyes. I remember your eyes when you attacked me. So cold and hard."

"You're being ridiculous!"

"I thought you were dead! That's why I couldn't fathom things out!"

"Edward, you attacked her?" Isobel cried in a strangled voice.

"Now, don't distress yourself, dear. You know what happens when you get upset."

"You promised me, after Jessica." She gave Wallace a pitiful look.

"She doesn't know what she's saying. She was mad with jealousy. She's not responsible for her actions." Booth said, reaching out to put his arm around her.

"Don't touch me!"

"Are you saying that Mrs Booth murdered Ella Chapman?"

Booth dropped his head into his hands. "I'll stand by you always, my darling."

"Are you sure this is the man who attacked you in hospital?"

"Yes, I'm absolutely certain," Emily Bryant replied in a firm voice.

"Mrs Booth, why did you kill Ella Chapman?"

"I didn't," she sobbed. "It was Edward. He was the father of her child. I tried to help Ella to get an abortion."

"What about Jessica?"

"He was the father of her child too. He vowed he didn't kill her, but I always had my suspicions. As soon as I heard the details of Ella's murder, I knew it was him. He must have killed Mark Hilliard too, because the poor boy found out about his affair with Ella."

"Why didn't you report it to the police?"

"I couldn't cope with it, so I drank instead, to banish the realisation of what he had done. Mick Gilchrist saved my sanity; helped me get back on my feet and stop drinking."

"Did he know about Dr Booth?"

"Absolutely not! Mick made me feel confident, of value. He was my saviour. I finally had the courage to stand up to Edward. What will happen to me now?"

"You'll be charged with fraud and withholding evidence of murder."

"Edward Booth, formerly known as David Johnson, you are under arrest for the murders of Jessica Parker, Ella Chapman, Mark Hilliard and the sexual assault of Megan Pryce-Jones."

"You do not have to say anything. But it may harm your defence if you do not mention when questioned something which you later rely on in court. Anything you do say may be given in evidence."

Isobel sobbed uncontrollably as a constable lead her away. She could barely stand up without his help. Wallace felt a pang of pity for the woman. She had been in a coercive relationship for years. Dr Booth stood silently, a supercilious smirk on his face.

"You'll be sorry for this, Chief Inspector. I have very important contacts in Parliament."

"Get him out of here!" Wallace snarled.

He dropped into his chair, breathing a huge sigh of relief. His strategy had worked. Booth would be behind bars for a very long time.

Unknown to Butler, Wallace had been having informal discussions with his old army pal, Vincent Conran, a psychiatrist. Wallace's suspicions about Booth were confirmed. Conran agreed that Booth displayed all the symptoms of narcissistic personality disorder, something they had both witnessed in an arrogant, overbearing fellow officer who treated his men like dirt. Just to be certain, Vince observed Booth from a one-way window when he was being questioned. Butler was deeply offended by Wallace's secrecy, but he had no choice if he was to nail Booth for the murders of three young people whose lives had been cut short.

Epilogue

VALENTINE'S DAY, 2023

The bells of St Chad's rang out over Shrewsbury as Ben and Jo exited the church. Phil Butler, beaming with delight, escorted Olivia down the steps. DC Hembrow looked elegant in a navy blue coat dress with matching hat. Even Baker had brushed up well. Ernst and Sophia Dreher, who had flown from Geneva the day before, hugged the bride and groom. Chief Superintendent Payne pushed through the group of guests and thanked them for his invitation. Wallace smirked inwardly. 'Crewcut Charlie' had invited himself.

A silvery sun pierced a bright, white sky, glittering on snow-topped shrubs. Soft, feathery flakes fell over the wedding party, sticking to their clothes like confetti. Overhead, ominous gunmetal grey clouds scudded across the town, threatening more snow. The air was crisp and pure, lending an air of pristine newness.

Everything was magical, picture postcard. It heralded a new beginning, a new life.

A fresh light snowfall covered the ground by the time they reached the Prince Rupert for the wedding reception. A welcome blast of warmth enveloped the guests as they entered the hotel. Waiters circulated amongst the chattering throng, handing out glasses of champagne and canapés. It gave Wallace a warm glow to see his team looking happy and enjoying themselves after a gruelling few months.

Suddenly, 'Crewcut Charlie' appeared at his elbow. "The Chief Constable wants you to be chief investigating officer on the theatre murders. Very high profile. Naturally, I agreed."

Wallace started to protest. A new life. A life with Jo and Olivia. He would make it work, but deep down he knew he could never ever resist a challenge.

*

In Long Lartin Prison a tall, imposing man with silver hair and Errol Flynn moustache walked around his cell, waiting for the bell to ring. He had asked the prison officers to get it from his school. *His* bell, *his* school. They couldn't possibly deny him. He smiled superciliously. After all, he was the Principal and head teacher of St Cadfael's. A very prestigious school. He was greatly respected. He was going to be a Member of Parliament. Suddenly, he lunged towards the cell door and started banging and screaming.

"Calm down, 'teach'" The prison officer turned to his colleague. "The nutter's at it again."

"How dare you! You can't keep me here! I am an important man! I am Dr Edward Booth." When the bell rings, I'll be free!" He laughed wildly, eyes popping, a manic grin on his face. "Where is it? The bell! Let the bell ring!"

This book is printed on paper from sustainable sources managed under the Forest Stewardship Council (FSC) scheme.

It has been printed in the UK to reduce transportation miles and their impact upon the environment.

For every new title that Troubador publishes, we plant a tree to offset CO_2, partnering with the More Trees scheme.

For more about how Troubador offsets its environmental impact, see www.troubador.co.uk/sustainability-and-community